PRAISE FOR WORDS

First-time novelist Yttrup writes a riveting, emotionally charged story about a 10-year-old sexual abuse victim, Kaylee Wren, who has literally lost her voice in the aftermath of ongoing trauma. Kaylee, living with her mom's abusive boyfriend after her mother abandons her, turns to the world of words for her comfort and sanity. Smart as a whip, Kaylee sounds out words in her mind and links words and phrases far beyond comprehension for her age as she puzzles out hour-by-hour survival. Enter the 30-ish Sierra Dawn, a grief-stricken artist whose own infant daughter died 12 years earlier. When these two meet, there is a supernatural connection. Rescuing Kaylee from her tormenter is only the first step to freedom for both of these characters, as they walk toward wholeness. Yttrup's story is particularly powerful as it in part mirrors her own painful past. Page by page, word by word, this talented author proves the adage "Write what you know.".

Publishers Weekly

"*Words* is a thought-provoking, tear-inducing, page-turning novel that will break open your heart and mend it back together with grace and love. This compelling story stays with you long after you've turned the final page. A true masterpiece by Ginny L. Yttrup." **Brenda Anderson**, Author of Inspirational Women's Fiction, Family Drama, and Romance http://brendaandersonbooks.com

"What an incredible book! I could not put it down! Ginny takes us on a path from pain and struggle to joy and wholeness as her characters discover that the author of truth is the way to freedom and healing. Sexual abuse may not be your story, but most certainly you have someone in your life for whom this is a reality. Read *Words* for them. Read it for yourself. And read it for those around the world who've yet to be set free." **Barbara Wilson, Ph.D.**, Author of *The Invisible Bond* and *Kiss Me Again* http://www.barbarawilson.org

ALSO BY GINNY L. YTTRUP

Lost and Found

Invisible

Flames

Home

Convergence, coming February 2019

WORDS

GINNY L. YTTRUP

SHELTERWOOD
PRESS

For Justin and Jared
It seems I've left so many important words unspoken through the years. I pray my written words will lead you to the Truth. You are my inspiration and joy.

"In the beginning was the Word."
JOHN 1:1

*"All those things for which we have no words
are lost. The mind—the culture—has two little
tools, grammar and lexicon: a decorated sand bucket and a matching
shovel. With these we bluster about
the continents and do all the world's work. With
these we try to save our very lives."*
ANNIE DILLARD

CHAPTER ONE

aylee

I COLLECT WORDS.

I keep them in a box in my mind. I'd like to keep them in a real box, something pretty, maybe a shoe box covered with flowered wrapping paper. I'd write my words on scraps of paper and then put them in the box. Whenever I wanted, I'd open the box and pick up the papers, reading and feeling the words all at once. Then I could hide the box.

But the words are safer in my mind. There, he can't take them.

The dictionary is heavy on my lap. I'm on page 1,908. I'm reading through the *S*s. When I finish the *Z*s, I'll start all over again.

Su · per · flu · ous.

I like that word. It means something extra, something special, something you don't need. It's super. But you don't need super. You just need good enough.

How does it sound when someone says it?

I didn't really think about how words sound until I stopped talking. I didn't mean to stop talking, it just sort of happened.

My mom left.

I got scared.

And the words got stuck.

Now I just read the words and then listen for them on the little radio in the kitchen, the only superfluous thing we have.

As I read, my hair falls across my eyes. I push it out of the way, but it falls back. I push it out of the way again, but this time my fingers catch in a tangle. I work for a minute trying to separate the hairs and smooth them down.

When my mom was here, she combed my hair most mornings. Our hair is the same. "Stick straight and dark as soot." That's what she used to say.

It hurt when she pulled the comb through my hair. "Kaylee, stop squirming," she'd tell me. "It'll pull more if you move."

Sometimes I'd cry when the comb caught in a knot and she'd get impatient and tell me to stop whining.

Maybe that's why she left. Maybe she got tired of my whining.

That's what he says. He tells me she didn't love me anymore—that she wanted out. But I don't believe him. I think something happened to her, an accident or something.

She probably has amnesia. I read that word in the dictionary.

That's when you hit your head so hard on something that you pass out and have to go to the hospital, and when you wake up, you don't remember anything. Not even your name.

Not even that you have a daughter.

I think that's what happened to my mom. When she remembers, she'll come back and get me.

So I just wait. I won't leave. If I leave, she won't know where to find me.

And when she comes back, I'll be good. I won't whine anymore.

I was nine when she left. Now, I'm ten. I'll be eleven the day after Christmas. I always know it's near my birthday when they start playing all the bell songs on the radio. I like "Silver Bells."

I like to think about the city sidewalks and all the people dressed in holiday style. But "Jingle Bells" is my favorite. Dashing through the snow in a one-horse open sleigh sounds fun.

It's not near my birthday yet. It's still warm outside.

As the sun sets, the cabin gets dark inside, too dark to read. He didn't pay the electric bill again. I hope he pays it before Christmas or I won't hear the songs on the radio.

Before I put the dictionary away, I turn to the front page and run my fingers across the writing scribbled there: *Lee and Katherine Wren. Congratulations.*

Lee and Katherine are my parents. Were my parents. Are my parents. I'm not sure.

My mom told me that the dictionary was a gift from her Aunt Adele. Mom thought it was kind of a funny wedding gift, but she liked it and kept it even after Lee left. We used it a lot. Sometimes when I'd ask her a question about what something was or what something meant, she'd say, "Go get the dictionary, Kaylee, we'll look it up." Then she'd show me how to find the word, and we'd read the definition. Most of the time she'd make me sound out the words and read them to her. Only sometimes did she read them to me. But most of the time when I asked her a question, she told me to be quiet. She liked it best when I was quiet.

I miss my mom. But the dictionary makes me feel like part of her is still here. While she's gone, the dictionary is mine. I have to take care of it. So just like I always do before I put the book away, I ask a silent favor: *Please don't let him notice it. Please don't let him take it.*

I put the dictionary back under the board that makes up a crooked shelf. The splintered wood pricks the tip of one finger as

I lift the board and shove the dictionary under. The shelf is supported on one end by two cinder blocks and by one cinder block and three books on the other end.

I remember the day she set up the shelf. I followed her out the front door and down the steps, and then watched her kneel in

the dirt and pull out three cinder blocks she'd found under the steps. She dusted dirt and cobwebs from the cracks and then carried each block inside. She stacked two blocks one on top of the other at one end of the room and then spaced the last block at the other end of the room, under the window.

"Kaylee, hand me a few books from that box. Get big ones."

I reached into the box and pulled out the biggest book—the dictionary. Then I handed her the other two books. She stacked them on top of the block and then laid a board across the books and blocks.

Even at seven, I knew what she was doing. We'd move in with a boyfriend and Mom would get us "settled," which meant she'd move in our things—our clothes, books, and a few toys for me. She'd rearrange the apartment, or house—or this time, the cabin —and make it "homey."

After she made the shelf, she lined up our books. Then she placed a vase of wildflowers we'd collected that morning on the end of the shelf. She stood back and looked at what she'd done. Her smile told me she liked it.

The cabin was small, but of all the places we'd lived, I could tell this was her favorite. And this boyfriend seemed nice enough at first, so I hoped maybe we'd stay this time.

We did stay. Or at least I stayed. So now I'm the one arranging the shelf and I'm careful to put it back just as it was. Our books are gone. In their place I return two beer bottles, one with a sharp edge of broken glass, to their dust-free circles on the shelf. I pick up the long-empty bag of Fritos corn chips and, before leaning the bag against the broken bottle, I hold it open close to my face and breathe in. The smell of corn and salt make my stomach growl.

Once I'm sure everything looks just as it was on the shelf,

I crawl to my mattress in the corner of the room and sit, Indian-style, with my back against the wall and watch the shadows. Light shines between the boards across the broken front window; shadows of leaves and branches move across the walls, ceiling, and door. Above my head I hear a rat or squirrel on the roof. Its movement scatters pine needles and something—a pinecone, I imagine—rolls from the top of the roof, over my head, and then drops into the bed of fallen needles around the front steps.

This is the longest part of the day—when it's too dark to read.

When I read . . .

I forget.

That's how it works.

∼

ONCE THE SUN GOES DOWN, I don't leave the cabin. I'm afraid he'll come back after work and find me gone. He's told me not to leave because he'd find me and I'd be sorry.

I believe him.

believe—verb 1. to take as true, real, etc. 2. to have confidence in a statement or promise of (another person).

My legs go numb under my body and my eyes feel heavy, but I don't sleep. Sleep isn't safe. Instead, I close my eyes for just a minute and see flames against the backs of my eyelids. They burn everything my mom and I brought to the cabin.

I remember the hissing and popping as the nighttime drizzle hit the bonfire. And I remember his laughter.

"She's gone for good, Kaylee. She ain't comin' back." He cackled like an old witch as he threw more gasoline on the flames. The smoke filled my nose and stung my lungs as I watched

Lamby, the stuffed animal I'd slept with since I was a baby, burn along with most of our clothes and books. The only exceptions were the three books he hadn't noticed holding up the shelf. My tears couldn't put out the fire, and I finally stopped crying. I wiped my nose on my sleeve and stepped away from the blaze. I squared my shoulders and stood as tall as I could. Something changed in me that night. I couldn't be little anymore. I had to be grown up.

I open my eyes and reach my hand under the corner of the mattress. My fingers dig into the hole in the canvas, feeling for the music box that had been inside Lamby. I'd found it in the ashes the morning after the fire. I tug it free, then wind the key and hold it up to my ear. As the music plays, I remember the words of the song that Grammy taught me just before she died. Jesus loves me, this I know . . .

The song makes me feel sad.

I don't think Jesus loves me anymore.

Eventually, I must fall asleep, because I wake up startled— mouth dry, palms damp, and my heart pounding.

I hear the noise that woke me, the crunching of leaves and pine needles. I listen. Are his steps steady, even? No. Two steps. Pause. A dragging sound. Pause. A thud as he stumbles. Pause. Will he get up? Or has he passed out? *Please let him be out.* A metal taste fills my mouth as I hear him struggle to get back on his feet.

"Kay—leeee?" He slurs the word. "You up? Lemme in."

He bangs his fist on the front door, which hasn't locked or even shut tight since the night he aimed his .22 at the doorknob and blew it to pieces, swearing that the nonexistent "whore" on the other side wasn't coming in. I assumed he meant my mom, since that's what he usually calls her.

The first time I heard him call her that, I didn't know what it meant, so I looked it up while he was gone. It was hard to find the word because I didn't think about there being a *w* in front of the *h*. I wasn't as familiar with words then as I am now. But finally, I figured it out. I read the definition but didn't really understand what it meant until I looked up some of the words from the definition.

Now, I wonder . . . am I one too?

The door gives way under the pressure of his fist. As it swings open, he pounds again but misses and falls into the cabin. He goes straight down and hits the floor, head first. A gurgling sound comes from his throat, and I smell the vomit before I see it pooled around his face.

I hope he'll drown in it.

But he won't die tonight.

Instead, he heaves himself onto his back and reaches for the split on his forehead where, even in the dark, I can see the blood trickling into his left eye. Then his hand slides down past his ear and drops to the floor. At the sound of his snoring, I exhale. I realize I've been holding my breath.

Waiting . . . waiting . . . waiting.

CHAPTER TWO

ierra

COCOONED IN CROCHETED WARMTH, I slip my hands from beneath the afghan and reach for my journal—a notebook filled with snippets of feelings and phrases. I jot a line: *Like shards of glass slivering my soul.* I set pen and journal aside and warm my hands around my ritual mug of Earl Grey, considering the phrase. I like the cadence of the alliteration. I see shining slivers piercing an ambiguous soul. I see a canvas layered in hues of red, russet, and black.

A memory calls my name, but I turn away. There will be time for memories later.

I close my eyes against the flame of color igniting the morning sky and allow my body the luxury of relaxing. I breathe deep intentional breaths, exhaling slowly, allowing mind and body to find a like rhythm. With each breath I let go, one by one, the anxieties of the past week.

Prints—signed and numbered. Five hundred in all.

Contract negotiations with two new galleries. Done.

Showing in Carmel last night. Successful.

Mortgage paid. On time for once.

Van Gogh neutered. What did the vet say? "He's lost his manhood—be gentle with him. He'll need a few days to recoup."

Good grief.

A whimper interrupts my reverie. The afghan unfurls as I get up and pad across the deck back into the bungalow. Van presses his nose through the cross-hatch door of his crate—his woeful expression speaking volumes. I open the cage and the spry mutt I met at the shelter a few days before staggers toward the deck, tail between his legs. I translate his body language as utter humiliation and feel guilty for my responsible choice.

"Sorry, pal, it's the only way I could spring you from the shelter. They made me do it." His ears perk and then droop. His salt and pepper coat bristles against my hand, while his ears are cashmere soft. He sighs and drifts back to sleep while I wonder at the wisdom of adopting an animal that's already getting under my skin. I consider packing him up and taking him back before it's too late. Instead I brace myself and concede, "Okay, I'll love you—but just a little." He twitches in response.

The distant throttle of fishing boats leaving the harbor and the bickering of gulls overhead break the morning silence followed by the ringing of the phone. I smile and reach for the phone lying under my journal.

"Hi, Margaret." No need to answer with a questioning "Hello?" There's only one person I know who dares call me at 7:00 a.m. on a Saturday.

Laughter sings through the phone line. "Shannon, when are you going to stop calling me Margaret?"

I dubbed her that after the indomitable Margaret Thatcher, former prime minister of her homeland. Her unwavering British accent, even after nearly half a century in the United States, and her strength under pressure inspired the nickname. It fits.

"Well, as I've told you, I'll stop calling you Margaret when you stop calling me Shannon. Need I remind you that I haven't been Shannon in more than a decade?"

"Oh, right. Let's see, what is your name now? Sahara Dust? Sequoia Dew?"

I play along. "Does Sierra Dawn ring a bell?"

"Right, Sierra Dawn, beautiful name. But you'll always be Shannon Diane to me."

The smile in her voice chases the shadows from my heart. "Okay, Mother. I mean *Margaret*." I pull my knees to my chest and reach for the afghan as I settle back in the weathered Adirondack for our conversation.

"Sierra, I didn't wake you, did I?"

"Of course not. What is it you say, 'You can take the girl out of the farm, but you can't take the farm out of the girl.'"

"That's my girl. Your daddy's been out in the fields since 6:00 but he let me sleep. I just got up and thought I'd share a cup of tea with you."

I do a quick Pacific/Central time conversion and realize with some alarm that it's 9:00 a.m. in Texas.

"You slept until 9:00? You never sleep that late. What's wrong?"

"Nothing's wrong, darling, I'm simply getting old. I had to get up three times during the night and by this morning I just wanted to sleep. So I indulged."

"Well, good for you. I'm glad you called. You know my favorite Saturday mornings are spent with you and Earl."

"I'm not drinking Earl."

A startling confession. "You're not? What are you drinking?"

"Sierra, I'm drinking Lemon Zinger!" Her declaration is followed by a giggle that sounds anything but old.

I stretch my long legs and cross them at the ankles and lean my head against the back of the chair. I feel as though my mother, with gentle skill, has distracted me while she's worked to remove a few of those slivers imbedded in my soul. But unless I stop brushing up against my splintered history, the slivers will return —or so she tells me.

Just before we hang up, she says, "Shannon"—there's such tenderness in her voice that I let the slip pass—"are you going to the cemetery today?"

Her question tears open the wound, exposing the underlying infection. I imagine her practicality won't allow her to leave the wound festering any longer. Instead she lances my heart.

I lean forward. "Yes, Mother. You know I will." My tone is tight, closed. But I can't seem to help it.

"Darling, it's time to let go—it's been twelve years. It's time to grasp grace and move on."

The fringe of the afghan I've played with as we've talked is now twisted tight around my index finger, cutting off the circulation. "What are you saying? That I should just forget—just let go and walk away—never think about it again? You know I can't do that."

"Not forget, Sierra—forgive. It's time."

"Mother, you know I don't want to talk about this."

"Yes, I know. But you need to at least think about it. Think about the truth. Ask yourself what's true."

I sigh at my mother's oft-repeated words and grunt my consent before I hang up—or "ring off" as she would say.

≈

I LEFT Texas at eighteen and headed to California, sure that was where I'd "find myself." On the day I left, my daddy stood at the driver's door of my overstuffed used station wagon gazing at the hundreds of acres of soil he'd readied for planting in the fall and gave me what I think of now as my own "Great Commission." In the vernacular of the Bible Belt, my daddy, a farmer with the soul of a poet, sent me out into the world with a purpose.

"Honey, do you know why I farm?"

At eighteen I'd never considered the why of what my parents did. "No, Daddy. Why?"

"Farming's not something that can be done alone. I till the ground, plant the seeds, and irrigate. But it's the rising and setting of the sun and the changing of the seasons that cause the grain to grow. Farming is a partnership with the Creator. Each year when I reap the harvest, I marvel at a Creator who allows me the honor of co-creating with Him."

He'd stopped staring at the fields and instead looked straight at me. "Look for what the Creator wants you to do, Shannon. He wants to share His creativity with you. He wants to partner with you. You find what He wants you to do."

With that, he planted a kiss on my forehead and shut the door of my car. With my daddy's commission tucked in my heart, I left in search of my life. My older brother, Jeff, was already in California completing his final year in the agricultural school at Cal-Poly in San Luis Obispo. Tired of dorm life, Jeff and two friends rented a house in town and told me I could rent a room from them for the year. I was thrilled.

Our neighbors and Mother and Daddy's friends couldn't understand why they'd let me run off to California. In their minds, California was a dark place where drugs and sex ruled. But Daddy assured them California was not the Sodom and Gomorrah they imagined. He should know. His roots were in California. He was born and raised there. Jeff and I grew up hearing about the Golden State and were determined we'd see it for ourselves one day. College in California seemed a logical choice to both of us.

As I headed west, I thought of my parents and what I'd learned from each of them through the years. Daddy taught me to see. Where others in our community saw grain, Daddy saw God. He always encouraged me in his quiet and simple way to look beyond the obvious.

"Look beyond a person's actions and see their heart. Look for what's causing them to act the way they act, then you'll understand them better."

When I was about twelve, Mother and Daddy took us with them down to Galveston for a week. Daddy was there for an American Farm Bureau meeting. After the meeting, we stayed for a few rare days of vacation. I remember standing on the beach and looking out at the flat sea. Daddy pulled me close and pointed at the surf.

"What do you see?"

"The ocean?" I asked more than stated.

"Yes, but there's more. You're seeing God's power."

I must have seemed unimpressed because Daddy laughed. "It's there, Shan. Someday you'll see it. But I'll admit it's easier to see it in the crashing surf and jagged cliffs of the California coastline."

I didn't understand what he meant then—and I'm still not sure I fully understand—but his description of the California coastline followed me as I was off to see it for myself.

My mother taught me to look for something else. "What's the truth, Shannon?" she'd ask over and over, challenging me to choose what was right. She taught me to analyze a situation and then make a decision that represented the truth foundational to our family.

Most often the truth she spoke of was found in the big family Bible she'd brought with her from England. She'd lay the book out on the kitchen table and open it to the book of John in the New Testament and she'd read from the King James version: "And ye shall know the truth, and the truth shall make you free."

"There's freedom in the truth, Shannon. You remember that," she'd say.

Again, I'm only now beginning to understand what she meant. But these were the lessons from home that I carried with me to California.

So why hadn't I applied those lessons? Why had I wandered so far from my parents' truth?

Those are questions I'd ask myself many times over. I'd yet to find the answers.

Restless after the phone conversation with my mother, I slip into the gardening clogs I keep under the deck and cross the postage stamp of grass to the flower beds that border the lawn. One lesson from home that I did learn and apply was how to grow things. Anything. As I deadhead the rose bushes, the bees in the lavender serenade me with their humming. I occupy my mind with a mental list of weekend chores: rake rose beds, turn compost pile, pull the trash can to the curb.

As I come to the Barbara Bush roses, I smile. I had to drive over the hill earlier this year into San Jose to find a nursery that carried the pale pink hybrid named after the conservative former first lady. There were none to be found in the nurseries of liberal Santa Cruz County. The bush is now heavy with large velvety blooms and, without thinking about what I'm doing, I cut an armful of stems and carry them into the kitchen where I wrap the bouquet in newspaper and place it in the fridge until I'm ready to leave.

As I shower, memories beckon again. My mother's plea to think about what she said nags at me. She is right—I have not, cannot, forgive. How do you forgive yourself for someone else's death? This is the burden she's asking me to let go—an encumbrance so intrinsic to who I've become that setting it aside would necessitate amputating a part of myself. I no longer know where I begin and the pain ends. We're inseparable, this burden and I.

A recent review from an art critic in the *San Francisco Times* comes to mind:

> *Sierra's work intrigues and torments all at once. The onlooker can't help but wonder at the story that makes each canvas bleed.*

The review felt—feels—invasive.

My work is the embodiment of my grief. Only on canvas do I

express the depth of anguish—there, without having to assign words to feelings, I writhe in agony. But for others to wonder at what drives my art disturbs me. This pain is private. The irony is never lost on me that my commercial success is the result of my most profound personal failure.

Standing in front of the mirror, I see an image that belies the aching soul within.

My mane of blonde hair is prematurely graying, but the effect enhances my natural highlights and gives me the appearance of an authentic sun-bleached California girl. And I realize that at thirty-four, I still appear more girl than woman. I wear the length of my years on the inside.

I dress in my standard uniform of khakis, T-shirt, and flip-flops, then throw socks, hiking boots, and a sweatshirt in my backpack. I will take the vet's advice and let Van rest—after all, I don't really deserve the solace his company might offer today. After giving him fresh water and food in the yard, I return and stand in front of the refrigerator contemplating the roses inside.

The first memory I allow to intrude stabs—

Her face, just moments before she died, is so clear. The blue veins so prominent beneath her papery skin as she fought for life have faded, leaving her pale—beautiful, with the blush of a rose—and to touch her skin was to touch the velvet of petals.

I open the fridge and cradle the paper-wrapped bouquet in my arms.

I lost her twelve years ago today. What would those years have held had she lived?

I take a deep breath and head out to my Jeep parked in the driveway.

CHAPTER THREE

aylee

THE MORNING SUN feels warm on my shoulders as I walk to the stream. But I still feel cold on the inside. I always feel cold afterward. After him. That's the only way I know how to describe it. For a little while, I don't feel anything at all except cold.

But I always know when I'm thawing out because that's when the scream starts.

I hear it in my head.

Sometimes, I can't make it stop.

When I reach the creek and see the blackberry bushes, my stomach growls. The berries are so fat they look ready to pop. I slide down a little hill to reach the bushes growing along the stream and begin picking the berries as fast as I can. The first warm berry explodes in my mouth and soon juice is dripping down the sides of my chin. I must eat a hundred berries before I stop.

I snuck out last night after I was sure he wasn't going to move from his place on the floor and checked his truck for groceries. Sometimes he'll stop at the store before he goes to the Stumble Inn, his "home away from home" as he calls it. But all I found in the truck was a twelve-pack of beer. There were five empty cans on the floor of the passenger side and seven left in the box that he'd probably opened on his way home from the bar.

I'm pretty sure he's an **al·co·hol·ic—noun** 1. a person addicted to intoxicating drinks.

It was a few hours later before I heard him move.

"Kaylee, help me up. Get me a towel or something." His voice was thick with beer and sleep.

I lay still, pretending I was asleep as he crawled toward my mattress.

He shook me, "Kaylee, wake up. Talk to me. What happened to my forehead?"

I didn't move.

He shook me again, hard this time. "You stupid mute, wake up!"

After a few minutes of silence, I felt his hand on my thigh and I knew I still had a long night ahead of me.

When I've had my fill of berries, I walk to the big rock that sticks out of the stream—the rock is low and flat. I lie on my back on the rock, face to the sun, and warm myself before getting into the water.

I wade in with my clothes on and shiver as the water reaches my waist. I pull my shirt up and struggle to get it over my head. Once it's off, I dunk it in the water. I ball it up, grind it together, and then let it loosen as I swish it around. I do this several times until I can hardly see the berry stains, then I lay it out on the rock to dry. With my shirt off, I look and feel for the sore spots on my belly just beneath my rib cage—sore from the weight of him.

I might not feel anything on the inside, but the bruises hurt.

Next I pull my wet jeans off. They're missing the top button, have holes at the knees, and are too short. But they still fit, sort of.

I've grown taller, but not much wider. I have some other clothes that he brought home from K-Mart last year. They fit better, but I like these. My mom bought these.

I wash my jeans and put them on the rock too, and then

I wash myself and feel the other bruises . . . I reach to the bottom of the creek and pull up handfuls of sand and scrub it over my body trying to wash away the smell of him.

When I finish, I take a deep breath and dive under the water into the deepest part of the stream. Water fills my ears until I can't hear anything but the pounding of my heart. I pretend I'm a mermaid. I cross my legs and kick, like I have one big fin. Then I twirl in the water and watch my hair swirl around me. I stay under until I see black and white spots in front of my eyes and my lungs hurt. I want to stay longer—I want to stay forever—but finally I have to come back up.

I get out of the water and climb back on the rock and lay out with my clothes to dry. I'm not afraid of anyone seeing me. I hardly ever see someone here—but I always hear them coming and I hide before they see me.

The rock is warm and my eyes get heavy. I want to sleep in the sun. But I can't—not here. What if I didn't wake up and get back in time? Instead, I get up, put on my clothes, and head across the meadow into the forest. It's a lot like the area right around the cabin with pine trees and redwoods. Only here the redwoods are like giants and the ground is covered with ferns, mushrooms, and heart-shaped clovers. The clovers are my favorite.

I'm careful as I walk, looking for banana slugs or anything that might squish under my toes. If anyone was paying attention, they'd see the trail I've made through the meadow into the forest. But he never comes out here, so it doesn't matter. The trail leads to my tree—a colossal redwood.

That's my favorite *C* word—**co · los · sal**. It means awesomely huge.

The bottom of the trunk was hollowed out by a fire a long

time ago, but the tree is still alive. The inside of the trunk is like a big room. When the light is right and shines through the opening, I can bend my head back and look way up and see where the fire stopped. I don't know how the tree can still be alive, but my mom said that redwoods are re—uh, resilmet, or something. I'll have to look it up. But anyway, I think it means they can take a lot. That would be a good word to put in my box.

When I go inside the tree, I see small tracks, probably from a squirrel. Then I see that a few of the pinecones I used to make my circle are missing. Definitely a squirrel then. They love pinecones.

I go out and pick up three pinecones and carry them back into the tree. I put each one down just right so the circle is whole again. Then I step over the line and sit in the middle. The circle is the safety zone, like in a game. No one can get you there. The only way to get into the circle is if you say, "Mother, may I?" I love that game. I like being the "Mother" who gets to say "Yes, you may" or "No, you may not." We used to play that at recess when I went to school. Sometimes I got to be the Mother, but usually Marcy Baker bossed her way into being it. But I was good at that game, I never forgot to ask, "Mother, may I?"

I lie back in the circle with my arms behind my head and watch dust float in the light shining through the opening in the trunk. It's so quiet and still here that the dust barely moves. It just sort of hangs in the air. I wonder how much dust I breathe into my nose every day. The thought makes my nose tickle. You can only see the dust if the light is right, most of the time you don't think about it being there.

This tree is my sanctuary.

sanc·tu·ary—noun 1. any place of refuge: asylum.

That means it's my safe place away from him.

It's about time to head back. He started another new job a couple of weeks ago and I'm still figuring out his schedule. He works at a gas station now. He's there on Saturday and Sunday and then again on Monday, Tuesday, and Friday. He has his schedule written on a scrap of paper in his truck, I checked it again last night. It's hard to know what his days off will be like. Sometimes he spends them at the bar playing pool. Other times he just hangs around the cabin. Those are the worst days. Either way, I stay in the cabin on his days off because I don't know when he'll come and go.

If I go back now, I can sleep until afternoon and then go over my words for a couple hours before he comes back. I want to find that *R* word I was thinking about. As I watch the dust and make my plan, I hear something. I sit up.

It's a car or a truck.

What if it's him? What if he came back early and couldn't find me?

The berries start churning in my stomach and I feel sick.

I stay in the circle and wait.

The engine stops. Turns off. Pretty soon I hear a door slam.

It sounds different than the slam of his truck door. My stomach settles a little when I realize, now that I think about it, the engine didn't sound like his truck either.

I crawl to the edge of the opening in the tree. Still mostly hidden, I sneak a peek outside and see a Jeep in the clearing by the point. I know the car is a Jeep, because Brent, my mom's last boyfriend, drove a Jeep. But this one looks a lot older than Brent's. What I don't see is the person who drove it. So I crawl back into the farthest corner of the tree trunk and sit in the dark spot where the sun doesn't shine.

I wait a few more minutes.

When I don't hear anything, I crawl back to the opening and look out again.

This time I see a woman at the edge of the point. She doesn't move. She just stands there looking out. On a sunny day like today, you can see the ocean from there. She stands there for a long time. Her back is to me, so I know she can't see me, so I just observe her. To observe means you pay special attention to something. I'm paying special attention to her.

I don't feel sleepy anymore.

The first thing I observe is her hair. It's so long that it almost touches her waist. She has it in a ponytail tied with something. Not ribbon, just a band or something, so it's probably even longer than it looks. It's blonde and curly and there's lots of it.

Then I see that she's tall, much taller than my mom. And right now she looks like a statue. She still hasn't moved. She must be thinking really hard about something. She just stands there looking out at the ocean. After awhile she turns away, reaches into the front pocket of her pants, and pulls out a piece of tissue. She wipes her eyes with the tissue and blows her nose. Then she balls it up and throws it on the ground. She throws it hard, like she's mad. Then she bends down and picks it up and shoves it back in her pocket.

She walks back to the Jeep but instead of getting in, she puts one foot on the front bumper and pulls herself up and turns to sit on the hood. She reaches over her head and pulls the band off her ponytail and shakes her hair loose. It shines like silver in the sun. She runs her hands through it and then twists it together into a large knot at the bottom of her neck. She puts the ponytail holder in her pocket, the one with the used tissue.

My legs are cramping under me because of the way I'm stooping to watch her. I ease back and stand up inside the tree and walk to my circle. If I sit back in the middle of the circle, I can still see her.

Once I'm settled, I look at her again and realize she's looking right at my tree. Did she see me? I sit very still. I don't even breathe.

She stares at the trunk of my tree. She looks surprised or something.

Finally she leans her head back and looks up. She shields her eyes with her hand. She's trying to see the top of the tree. She won't be able to see it though. She looks back down at the trunk and then she shakes her head and smiles a little.

She's pretty when she smiles.

After a few minutes, she lies back on the hood of her car with her feet still on the bumper. She puts one arm over her eyes, and rests there. She looks tired. I know how she feels, the sun can put you right to sleep on a day like this.

I decide I better go now while she's not looking. I don't know how long she plans to stay here, but if it's long, I might not have another chance to sneak away without her seeing me.

I start to get up, then sit back down. I don't want to leave.

I want to keep watching her. I wonder what it would be like to talk to her. I wonder if she's nice. She looks nice. Maybe I could tell her about my mom. Maybe she could help me find her. Just as I'm thinking this, the scream starts in my head.

I hear a long wailing *No* . . . I put my hands to my head and cover my ears, but it makes no difference. I shake my head trying to make it stop. But it's still there. I bang my fist on the ground until it hurts. The pain makes the scream stop. But I know it will start again.

I'm so stupid! I can't talk to her. I'd open my mouth and nothing would come out. How can I tell her or anyone else about my mom or about anything? This is my fault. If I could tell someone about my mom, then maybe they could find her and help her remember and then she could come back and get me. If I could tell someone about him, maybe they could make him go away.

The scream starts again.

I look at her one more time and make sure she's still asleep. Then I get up, hands still covering my ears, and I sneak out of the tree, and walk, real quiet, to the meadow. Then I run. I run through the meadow, past the stream, and back through the forest. I run as fast as I can. I run until my side aches. But I don't stop until I reach the cabin.

Once there, I can hardly breathe. I sit on the stoop and try to catch my breath. I don't hear the scream anymore, just my heart pounding and wheezing as I gulp for air.

I get up and walk back into the cabin. I look at my mattress and know I can't go to sleep now—not yet. Instead, I pull the dictionary out from under the board and turn to the *Rs* and begin my search.

re · sign · ee

re · sile

re · sil · ience

re · sil · ient

That's it, I think.
I read the definition:

—**adjective** 1. springing back; rebounding, returning to the original form, position, etc., after being bent, compressed, or stretched; elasticity. 2. ability to recover readily from illness, depression, adversity or the like; buoyancy.

That's just the long way of saying that some things can take a lot. Like that tree, it bounced back after adversity, the fire was its adversity. I turn to the *As* to make sure I know what adversity means, and I'm right, it's bad. It's the opposite of what you want to happen. I think again of his bonfire a few days after my mom left. That was just one adverse thing that happened to me that week.

A new thought comes to me. Maybe I'm like that redwood.

Maybe I'm resilient too. The thought makes me feel sort of hopeful.

For some reason I think again about the woman I saw in the forest. Then I wonder . . . why she was crying? What was wrong? Was she sad or just mad? Both can make you want to cry, I know that.

She looked resilient—tall and strong—like she'd bounce back —so she's probably okay.

After a few minutes, I try not to think about her, to think of something else instead. But the harder I try to think of something else, the more I think about her. I wonder again what it would be like to talk to her. I wonder what her voice sounds like and I wonder dumb things too, like if her hair smells good like my mom's did. The more I think about her, the more I want to know about her. Where does she live? What does she do? Why was she up here in the woods?

Before I even stop thinking about her, I know what I'll do. I'll go back to my tree tomorrow and see if she comes back. And if she doesn't come tomorrow, I'll go back the next day.

I'll just wait and see if she shows up again. If she does, I'll watch her for a while more.

CHAPTER FOUR

ierra

THE SUN in the clearing soothes me, lulls me to sleep. In sleep, I can forget the memories that haunt me today. Instead, with energy I barely possess, I pull myself from the fringes of sleep and sit back up on the hood of the Jeep.

Haunt. An appropriate word for this day. I've seen things here that I can't explain. Perhaps in my grief, my mind played tricks on me.

I put the thought aside. I have no desire to analyze my feelings or the deceits of my mind. I'm afraid to look too closely at what I feel or think. I know this about myself. The abyss is too deep, the grief too dark. The feelings are better kept at bay. I allow myself this one day each year to think about her, to honor her memory, and doing so always leads me to the edge of the abyss. But I won't succumb. I won't tumble over the edge.

Instead, I check my watch. It's later than I thought. I'm supposed to meet Ruby for lunch at the beach at 1:00. She insists we have lunch on this day each year. Today I'm thankful for the standing appointment and for her call yesterday to set the time. If anyone can pull me from this funk, it's Ruby.

I hop off the hood, but before getting back in the Jeep, I take a last look at the redwood across the clearing. Its grandeur awes me. It stands tall, oblivious to its wounds, a sentry guarding the forest below. I wonder what secrets it holds, this ancient keeper of the woods. I offer a silent salute to the old tree before climbing in the car and heading off to lunch.

Ruby. I think of her as I drive. We met at art school. I ended up there after a year of general education courses at the J.C. in San Luis Obispo. I took two art classes during that year—a drawing class and a painting class. My instructor encouraged what she called my "gift" and gave me information about the San Francisco Art Institute.

One visit to the campus and I was hooked. Creativity coursed like currents of energy through the students and faculty I met.

I left that week with a rising passion to leave my mark on the world through artistic expression. The idealism of youth, I suppose.

Ruby was my roommate while I was there. We connected through a SFAI list of potential housing situations and room-mates. Neither of us came from families who could afford much, but we found a studio apartment a few blocks up from the Presidio, owned by a local patron of the arts who rented the studio to students at rates unheard of in the city. We settled in together for the duration of our college careers.

Although Ruby and I came from different worlds, or maybe because we came from different worlds, we engaged right away. We were fascinated by our differences and spent many evenings that first year sharing our ideals, our beliefs, and the stories of our lives.

As I pull into the restaurant parking lot, I search for Ruby's car, a restored 1968 VW bug, an early fortieth birthday gift from her husband, Michael, a programmer who works over the hill in San Jose.

Looks like she's late as usual, but today I don't mind. I want the time to gather myself emotionally. Ruby knows the rules: we meet every year on this anniversary, but we don't speak of it. This is hard for her, she lives to talk, analyze, and figure things out. But she respects this rule, most of the time. However, if I arrive emotionally undone, she'll crack. I often tell her that she missed her true calling. She should have been a shrink. But she insists there's a lot of psychology in her art, sculpting. That's what I call a "Rubyism," a quirky belief all her own.

I enter the restaurant and ask the hostess for my usual table. Distracted, she hands me a menu and points to the stairs. I reach over the counter and grab a menu for Ruby and then make my way up to the outdoor balcony just off the bar where four of the best tables hide. Only here are the tables exposed to the elements —sun, wind, and surf. The other two outdoor balconies are enclosed to protect against such nuisances. Ruby will know to look for me here.

Crystalline sky, blue sea, and lapping surf fill my view. I try to clear my mind and soak in the healing elements of salt and sun. Instead, the images of the day replay. I see the small gravestone that marks my mourning: Annie Lynn Bickford. My mother chose her name—I was in no shape to do so. She told me that Anne was a strong English name meaning *grace.* Mother knew that a child born into such darkness would need grace.

Then the images from the forest come to mind, the giant redwood and . . .

"Hey, you."

I jump at Ruby's greeting.

"Whoa, you okay? I didn't mean to startle you."

"I'm fine."

Ruby squeezes my shoulder before going around the table and settling in the chair opposite me. And although I know her inside and out, see her frequently, had breakfast with her earlier this week in fact, I can find nothing to say to her. Today is different and we both know it.

She looks at me and I see the questions in her eyes, but she doesn't ask. Instead, she reaches for the linen napkin next to her place setting. "So, new outfit?" Her sarcasm breaks the tension.

"Very funny, Rube."

"Guess I don't remember seeing that particular T-shirt before. I like the streak of taupe across the shoulder. Looks like oil. Not your typical medium."

I rub my hand across the stain and smile. I often feel monochromatic against Ruby's color—fiery auburn hair springing in ten different directions, emerald eyes, and today, a burnt-orange peasant top with a patterned red, gold, orange, and green ankle-length skirt that looks like it's made of scarves. The heavy gold hoops at her ears complete her gypsy ensemble.

I finger the slim silver hoops that never leave my lobes and remind her that the taupe swatch is from my living room, "In fact, if I recall, it was you, Ruby, who was bored with painting walls and took your brush to my shirt."

"Ah yes, a moment of artistic expression, I remember."

We laugh and pick up our menus, though we know the offerings by heart.

She says nothing more for a moment. But the next time she looks at me, I see the questions in her eyes again and can tell she's weighing her words. "You really okay?"

Her question brushes the boundary I've set. I answer too quickly. "Of course, I'm fine."

"Really?" Her prodding, gentle as it is, angers me.

"Ruby, you know the rules."

"Your rules, Sierra, not mine. I'm tired of playing by your rules."

I turn my eyes from hers and look back at the ocean. I reach for my hair and unwind it from its knot and run my fingers through its length. I'm stalling, I know, searching for an answer that will appease her while wondering at the unaccustomed desire I feel to talk.

She takes my hesitation as an invitation. "Sierra, it's time to let go of the pain. It's time to let go of Annie."

Speaking her name breaks all the rules. It hangs in the air between us. The anger I felt just moments before dispels and grief, a dense gray fog, settles in its place.

"Ruby . . ." I stop, not knowing what to say.

"It's time, Sierra. It's time to talk, time to let go, time to accept forgiveness."

I recall my mother's words earlier this morning: *Darling, it's time to let go. It's been twelve years. It's time to grasp grace and move on.*

"Have you been talking to my mother?"

"Margaret? No. Formidable woman. Scares me to death. You know that."

I laugh in spite of myself. Only Ruby can navigate life's darkest caverns with a sense of humor.

Ruby loves my mother almost as much as I do, I know this. They share an unspoken bond born of shared love and shared pain. A bond that formed during my pregnancy, during Annie's birth and death, and during the hellish days and months that followed when I hit bottom. They became a team, my mom and Ruby. They nursed me back to the land of the living when I wanted nothing more than to climb into the grave with my daughter.

"Sierra?" She waits for a response from me.

I falter. "Margaret said the same things this morning—but I can't just let go. It's not that easy."

"I never said it would be easy. But if you share the burden, you lighten the load. The more you try to deny the pain, the more strength you give it. I see it, Sierra. It consumes you. It's in your eyes. It's in your art. It haunts you."

Maybe it's the familiarity of the thought—haunting—something I'd been thinking myself just before she arrived. Or maybe she's right, it's just time. Whatever the reason, I take a deep breath and follow her lead.

"I think the pain . . . the memories . . . they're making me . . . crazy."

"How so?"

"I don't know, it's just that today was odd, you know?"

I search for the words to explain, but they don't come easily.

She waits. Her silence spurs me on.

"I saw something today—"

"At the cemetery?" She whispers. She knows we're walking sacred ground.

"No. Afterward. I drove up near Bonny Doon. I hiked in that area a few weeks ago and wanted to return to study the light, the way it filters through the redwoods. After this morning . . . after . . . you know . . . I decided I'd go back. It seemed like a good day to be outside, to get away. There's a dirt road off the main road. You can hardly see it, but I'd noticed it when I was there and today, instead of hiking, I drove up there."

As I tell Ruby about my morning, I find myself back in the forest, standing at the point overlooking the ocean. Unlike the glimpses of the bay you catch when twisting over the mountains on Highway 17, from the western edge of the range, you see the open Pacific—an expanse whose width and depth seem to drop off the edges of the earth. At the horizon the sun reflects off the water casting a white sheen that blurs the line between sea and sky. Closer to shore, whitecaps slice the blue-gray palette.

I think again of my daddy's belief that the power of God is somehow displayed in the panorama before me. Intellectually I understand his meaning. The ocean is power itself: the pull of the tides, the crash of the surf, its ability to provide life and sustenance, and its ability to take life and drink it into its depths. It gives and it takes. Ebbs and flows. Providence and destruction are within its power.

But where this power reassures my daddy, it only reinforces my perception of God. He is arbitrary—giving and taking, ebbing and flowing, loving and judging at whim. I wonder if psychologists would question my background when analyzing my beliefs. They might run through a mental checklist of assumptions: *Father —authoritarian, stern, undemonstrative, uncaring.* But my earthly father is none of those things. He's a gentle and loving man who never hesitates to extend grace or give me his best. Yet, for reasons I don't understand, I can't translate that image to my heavenly Father.

Mother says it's my own sin that keeps me from doing so—she says that my own judgment is so harsh that I can't accept, as God's child, His lack of judgment in my life. I can't accept His forgiveness. "His forgiveness through the blood of His only Son," is how she'd say it. She says the natural consequences of my actions are God's allowance—His loving discipline in my life. But beyond that, my sin is as far as the east is from the west in His mind.

She doesn't understand though. She didn't make the choices I made. She wasn't responsible for her child's death. Murder is punishable and the sentence is stiff—an eye for an eye and all that. I chose drugs. No one forced them on me. And ultimately my choice stole my daughter's life.

I sought the hallucinations and enlightenment that other users touted. I wanted to open my mind to new possibilities and dimensions and then translate those images into my art. Looking back, it seems an odd choice for a Texas farm girl from a Christian family. But I think, to my parents' credit, I was confident.

I believed I could do anything I set my mind to. They'd always told me as much. But somewhere that confidence became confused with invincibility. I thought I could do anything, unscathed. And so I didn't think about the aftereffects of drugs. None of us did. We just did them. It was part of the culture—or at least, part of the culture I chose.

Ruby stayed away from all of it. She warned me. She begged me. Then she cleaned up after me.

It was Ruby who found me at parties and hauled me home via city bus or cable car. It was Ruby who, more than once, pulled me naked, in the middle of the night, from the bed of some guy I didn't even know. It was Ruby who first realized I was pregnant and had the sense to get me to a doctor. She never asked about the father, she knew better.

I have no idea who fathered Annie.

And finally, it was Ruby who called my parents—who spoke the truth that broke their hearts. I will never forget the morning they walked into our apartment—my mother, all British propriety and efficiency, and my daddy, tender but tough. They'd done their grieving in private, I suppose. By the time they reached me, they'd made a plan and intended to carry it through.

Those months, weeks, and days before and after my parents came, are just a blur to me. I do know that soon after they arrived, my daddy found the little bungalow in Santa Cruz and moved us there. They said they wanted to get me away from everything— the parties, the drugs, the people. And while part of that was true and wise, I know, I also think that my daddy needed to get away from the cacophony of the city, away from the San Francisco Bay bustling with sailboats, tour boats, and freighters. He needed the solace of the sea and the solitude of quiet beaches. He needed to do business with his God.

My mother told me later that Ruby insisted on coming with us. She argued that Santa Cruz was a community of artists and that she could work there. She could help them with their plan— to get the drugs out of my system, to watch me around the clock, and to keep me from what I wanted most.

So Mother and Daddy moved us into the bungalow, a summer vacation rental. They moved themselves into a little motel on Ocean Street. From there Daddy would walk to the beach that ran between the Boardwalk and the yacht harbor, a quiet stretch of sand hidden from the tourist-lined street by the cliffs that tower over it. I don't remember seeing him much during those months.

Mother and Daddy spent their savings that summer. All of it. I don't think it ever occurred to them to take me home where the members of our rural community would try and convict me in the court of legalism—the very court where I would later try and convict myself.

For me, those summer months were horrible. My body yearned, begged for the drugs that had become my addiction.

I spent countless hours either in bed or on the little sofa in the living room shaking, convulsing, and vomiting. I paced the floors at night unable to sleep, often Ruby paced with me. There was nothing that could be translated into "art" unless I wanted to paint the fiery landscapes of hell. I have vague recollections of my mother or Ruby or, occasionally, my daddy there at all times, whispering, comforting, and wiping my forehead with a damp cloth. They never left me alone.

During the days, one, or sometimes all three of them, would drag me to an NA meeting. They sat through those meetings with me and learned from others walking the road they hoped I'd choose. They mistook my passivity for acceptance—a choice even.

But I simply didn't have the strength or initiative to fight them.

THE MEMORIES, so carefully buried, so long hidden, taunt me, as does the shining Pacific in the distance. Why did I allow myself this jaunt into the past? I reach into my pocket for a Kleenex and wipe away tears I've waited twelve years to shed. They can wait a while longer. After I blow my nose, I ball up the Kleenex and throw it, as hard as I can, to the ground. The way in which I might throw myself to the ground if I had the courage. I hate what I did to my life—to *her* life—and I can't seem to get beyond it. I don't deserve to get beyond it.

Exhausted by the emotions of the morning, I bend to pick up the Kleenex and shove it back in my pocket and head back to my Jeep in the clearing. Chilled from standing so long in the shade, I climb on top of the hood of the car to warm myself in the sun. Intending to lie back and rest for a few minutes, I pull my hair from its ponytail and knot it at the nape of my neck where it's more comfortable.

Just then, something to my right catches my eye, a slight movement or shifting of light. It's then I notice the gigantic redwood with its hollowed trunk and what looks like a pale face gazing out at me from inside the burnt tree. I stare, unsure of what I'm seeing, although I'd swear it's the face of a child, a young girl. But how can that be?

I look away, up toward the top of the tree, and then return my gaze to the trunk. She's gone. Or it's gone.

My skin prickles as a chill runs through me. I smile at my crazy imagination and lie back on the hood of the Jeep to soak in its heat. As I lay there, I wonder what holding this pain so close has done to my psyche. I'm now seeing apparitions? Tiny faces gazing at me in the forest? Just then a sound, a rustling, nags me—a sound so slight, it's barely audible—yet it is distinguishable amidst the breeze in the branches and the birds overhead.

Finally I sit up. And there she is. A tiny thing. Long, dark hair. Small hands covering her ears. I watch as she tiptoes, then runs, from the clearing, hair flying behind her. She's there for just a moment. And then she's gone.

I recount all of this to Ruby.

"It was like seeing a ghost. She looked like she was about the age Annie would be, if . . ." I stop talking, realizing how crazy I must sound. I can't believe I've said all of this out loud.

I look at Ruby and really see her for the first time since I began talking. There are tears in her eyes.

"Ruby, I don't want your pity!" I spit the words at her. Then I apologize. "I'm sorry. I don't know what's wrong with me."

"Hey," the tenderness in her voice catches my heart, "it's okay. I don't pity you. I just realize how much I've missed you. When you lost Annie, I lost you. You curled into yourself. You shut me out. You shut everyone out."

"You didn't lose me, Ruby, I'm sitting right here." My tone is sarcastic, I know, but again, I can't seem to help it. "Just forget it. I don't even know why I told you. It's not a big deal. So, I'm seeing things. So what? Right? The light in the woods shifts in strange ways. I imagined it. Just forget it."

I see Ruby's countenance shift. The tenderness of a moment ago is gone. "I won't forget it, but since I know you don't want to talk about it anymore," she rolls her eyes as she says this, "then let's just deal with the facts for a minute.

"If you imagined this child, then why would you imagine her with her hands over her ears? Isn't that a little strange? Sierra, what if she is real? Consider that. Take yourself out of the picture for a minute and think about it. What would a child be doing up there all alone? Where did she come from? Something's wrong with that scenario, don't you think?"

I hate it when Ruby tells me to take myself out of the picture and reminds me, as she often does, that it's not all about me. I realize again the narcissism of the pain I carry. I struggle to see beyond it. Beyond myself. And in doing so, I make a snap decision.

"Fine. I'll go back. I'll see if she was real or just a *ghost*." I give Ruby my best haunting impression. "Boo!" If she thinks I'm fine, I'll be fine. If she'll let this drop, I'll be fine.

"Good. Go back. It seems worth checking out, right? If you see her again, then you'll know you're not crazy."

I ponder this a moment longer, "Right. I'm sure I just imagined it—her—but I'll look around and then I'll know for sure."

There is much left unspoken between us. We both know it. But

Ruby acquiesces to the rules again. The questions I saw in her eyes before have been replaced with a resolute control. Perhaps she got what she wanted from me this morning. Score one for Ruby.

I understand more than she thinks. Not only did she lose me when Annie died, but I lost her. My refusal to open up, to explore my pain, has distanced us. The intimacy we enjoyed early in our friendship is gone. One more thing to grieve, I guess. I know I could change things, I know I could find that depth with Ruby again. But it's too hard. Instead, we live, for the most part, at a surface level. We share our love of art and creation. We speak of family and mutual friends. But very rarely do I allow her to dip beneath that surface.

I wonder, as I often do, why Ruby sticks with me. What does she get out of our friendship? She says we're like family, we're bonded by our shared history. She says that she loves me. Sometimes I think I'm just another project for her, a lump of clay to sculpt and mold into something else, something worthwhile.

I suppose her reasons matter little. I need her. And I'm grateful for her presence in my life, for her commitment. Perhaps one day, I'll have the chance to repay the favor.

∼

As I PULL into my driveway, I see a beady eye glaring at me through a knothole in the side gate. Guilt tugs at my conscience. What was I thinking, getting a dog? "Hey, Van, sorry to leave you for so long."

A muffled whine greets me.

"Oh, you're good, boy. You've already got me figured out. Go ahead, drive the stake of guilt a little deeper."

I say this as I reach over the gate to undo the latch. As soon as I push the gate open, Van Gogh lunges at me. His speed and agility catch me off guard and as his front paws hit my shoulders, I fall, landing on my backside. Van lands on top of me and smothers me with what I can only interpret as doggy kisses.

I laugh so hard that tears run down my cheeks and into my ears.

Van, a lab and husky mix, lets out a low yapping howl. I'd swear he's talking to me in a language all his own.

I eventually get Van off me and get myself off the ground. Once standing, I look at the dog and realize he probably needs some exercise after being cooped up for a few days. I head to the garage and grab the leash that I bought yesterday. As soon as Van sees it, he jumps toward me again. This time I'm ready for him.

I recall the information I read in the dog training book that I checked out from the library and say, in a firm tone, "Off!"

At that, Van sits. He twitches with excitement as I attach the leash to his collar.

"Good boy, it looks like someone trained you well. Let's go."

With that, we head off toward the harbor, or at least that's where I assume he's leading me.

As I trot along behind Van, I wonder why I agreed so quickly to go back and look for the child I saw this morning. Was I just trying to get Ruby off my back? Trying to end our conversation? Or do I need to prove to myself that I'm not crazy? That I'm not seeing things? Now, in broad daylight, with several hours distance from my visits to the cemetery and the forest, the thought that I actually imagined the child, or worse, thought that I might have seen a ghost, seems absolutely ridiculous. I don't even believe in ghosts.

Then it hits me. Ruby will ask me about this again. She'll ask if I went back. I realize I've opened a door that I intended to keep shut. Maybe that's why she didn't push me further at lunch today. She saw the crack before I did.

Before I know it, we've reached the beach by the harbor. The sea breeze sends a chill through me and I turn and head back. "C'mon, boy. Let's go."

When we reach the bungalow, we go back through the side gate and the backyard. I unhook Van from the leash and he follows me inside. I fill the tea kettle with fresh water and set it to boil. While I wait, I grab my journal off the counter and head back to the deck where my morning began. I open the journal to

a blank page and sketch the pale face I saw staring at me this morning. The features are vague, except for the dark, doe-like eyes. I realize as I sketch that the eyes that stared at me this morning looked as haunted as I felt.

If she was real, she was scared.

This thought strikes me—propels me. Whatever the reason, I will go back. I know I need to find that little girl. There's more to this than appeasing Ruby.

The whistling kettle calls. I close my journal and my mind. My decision is made. I won't think of it again until tomorrow.

CHAPTER FIVE

aylee

IT'S STILL dark outside when I wake up. I slept a little during the
night after he came back and I was sure he was asleep in his room.
He left the door open, and I can still hear him snoring.

I lie back down, roll over on my side, and watch a sliver of
light crawl up the wall. As I lay there, I plan my day. I'm going on
a covert mission.

co · vert—adjective 1. concealed; secret; disguised.

After he leaves for work, I'll change my clothes. I decide I'll
wear my K-Mart jeans—they look better. Although, since I'm
going covert, it doesn't matter anyway. I reach up and run my
hand over my matted hair. If I borrow his comb, maybe I could
get some of the tangles out. As long as I get all the hair out of the
comb, he'll never know I touched it. Oh, but just the thought of
touching anything of his is so gross!

I flop over onto my back. I don't know why I think she'll come back. I've been telling myself since yesterday that it's silly to think I'll see her again. But I have this feeling that I can't get rid of—like I'm supposed to go back and look for her. It's probably dumb, but it's the first time since my mom left that I feel like I have something I'm supposed to do—something to look forward to. My tummy flutters. That fluttery feeling is called having butterflies in your tummy. Another word for it is **an · tic · i · pa · tion.**

The dictionary uses a bunch of big words to define it—expectation, foreknowledge, presentiment. But all it really means is that you're looking forward to something or you're excited about something.

After awhile, I turn and look at the wall again and notice that the whole bottom half of the wall is now covered in light. Usually, by the time the light reaches the middle of the wall, he's up and getting ready to leave for work. As I lay there and watch the light inch its way toward the ceiling, the butterflies in my tummy flutter away.

Maybe his schedule changed.

Maybe he got fired again.

Maybe he's too hungover to go to work.

Whatever the reason, it looks like he's staying here.

I feel like someone's taken one of the cinder blocks from the shelves and laid it on my chest, making breathing hard. A tear slides down my cheek. I remind myself that crying is for babies. What's wrong with me? She probably won't be there anyway.

It was a stupid plan.

The more I think about it, the worse I feel. Finally I decide that I need to think about something else—just like I do when thinking about my mom makes me feel too sad. I decide to play a game to keep my mind off my worries. I'll think of words I know that describe him. I'll pick one word for each letter of the alphabet.

The first *A* word that comes to mind is one I'm not allowed to say. I can't even think it, because for me that's like saying it. But it's another word for donkey. I smile.

For *B*, I choose Birdbrain. That's in the dictionary. It's slang for stupid. This is a good game.

Creep.

Dork.

E is harder. It takes me longer to come up with something, but finally I remember a word from the dictionary. Erroneous. That means he smells bad, I think.

Freak.

Gross.

Hateful.

Idiot.

Jerk.

K stumps me.

I roll over on my stomach and rest my head on my crossed arms while I think. I hear the springs squeak as he turns over in bed. After a minute, I hear him call me.

"Kaylee, come here."

I don't move.

"Kaylee, get in here!"

I get up and tiptoe to his room and stand in the doorway.

"Cat got your tongue?" He laughs like he always does when he asks me that. "Fix me some breakfast. I bought some eggs and bread last night. They're out in the truck. Scramble a few. You can have one too—just don't eat 'em all. And don't burn the toast."

I back out of the room, keeping an eye on him, then turn and run to the truck. Sure enough, there's a brown paper bag on the front seat. I find the eggs and bread in the bag along with two cans of tuna, a jar of mayonnaise, and some sweet pickles. I hate sweet pickles, but my mouth waters all the same. I might get breakfast and lunch today.

I carry the bag back to the kitchen and take the frying pan off the shelf under the counter. I put the pan on the stove, crack four eggs into it, and then beat them up with a fork, just like my mom showed me. I don't have any milk to add to them, but I sprinkle in some salt and a little pepper. Then I reach to turn on the front burner, but nothing happens. I turn it off and then on again. Still nothing. Then I remember—the power is off. We don't have any electricity. I can't cook the eggs or toast the bread.

I stand there not knowing what to do.

Pretty soon I hear him get out of bed and head for the kitchen. His bare feet slap the concrete floor with each step. He comes up behind me and stands so close that I can feel the hair on his arms tickling my arms. He bends down and whispers in my ear, "What's the holdup, sweetheart?"

His breath is putrid. That's my *P* word for him. Everything about him is putrid.

He reaches around me and tries to turn on the burner. He clicks it once, twice. I feel his body tense against mine. And then he slams his fist against the stove top, the electrical coils rattle and one of the knobs cracks in two. This so startles me that I jump and find myself pressed hard against him. I immediately try to move forward, but there's nowhere to go.

I'm trapped.

I feel like I might throw up. But instead of doing what I expect him to do, he shoves me aside and walks back to his room and slams the door.

After a few minutes, he comes back out. He's put on his jeans, a T-shirt, and boots. He grabs the Windbreaker that he threw over the kitchen chair last night and heads out the front door.

I hear the truck start and then gravel sprays the cabin as his tires spin in the driveway. The truck clunks into gear and he drives away.

He's gone.

I slump over the stove and concentrate on breathing.

Breathe in.

Breathe out.

Breathe in.

Hands shaking, I dump the egg mess into the sink and rinse the pan. Then I take two pieces of the bread and spread mayonnaise on them. I put them together like a sandwich and eat it.

I take small bites and chew really slow, hoping to make my breakfast last. The first bite is hard to swallow—hard to get past the lump in my throat. But each bite is easier and finally I feel normal again.

After I eat, I put on the K-Mart jeans and smooth down my hair. I open the drawer in the bathroom and find his toothpaste and then brush my teeth with my finger. I'm careful to put the toothpaste back just like it was.

Once all of that is done, I stand by the front window and look through the cracks in the boards. I wonder if she's there, in the clearing. I wonder what she's doing. Again, I feel like I'm supposed to go there, but I can't take that chance. I can't risk having him come back and find me gone.

I pace back and forth and finally decide I'll try to pass the time reading. I go to the bookshelf, kneel down, lift the board, and pull out the large blue book: *Etiquette—The Blue Book of Social Usage*—by Emily Post. It's a book that tells you how to do everything in just the right way. It was my Grammy's. It's really old. The date in the front of the book is 1955! I'm careful when I open it because I know there are two cards tucked inside the pages— Christmas cards from Grammy's friends, I guess. The postmarks on the cards are December 4, 1966 and December 7, 1966. I love reading the cards and looking at the Christmas scenes on the front, but today I want to read something I remember seeing in the book.

I flip to the contents and scan the page until I find what I want. It's in chapter two.

Introducing Oneself
  If there is good reason for knowing someone, it is quite proper to

introduce yourself. For instance, you would say, "Mrs. Worldly, aren't you a friend of my mother's?

I am Mrs. John Smith's daughter." Mrs. Worldly says, "Yes, indeed, I am. I am so glad you spoke to me."

But what if the person you want to introduce yourself to isn't a friend of your mother's? I keep reading.

Obviously it would be in very bad taste to introduce yourself to Mrs. Worldly if your mother knew her only slightly . . .

Oh. I skip down a couple of paragraphs.

Introduction by Letter
An introduction by letter is far more binding than any spoken introduction which does not commit you to anything. See chapter 42.

I take the book and crawl back over to my mattress and sit with my back against the wall. I turn to chapter 42 and begin reading. I read until my eyes get heavy. I set the book down and reach for the ceiling stretching and yawning. I stand up and walk to the front window and peer through the cracks in the boards again. The blue sky beckons me.

That means it lures me, which means I really want to go.

But I can't go.

He could come back any time.

I pace back and forth. I play an imaginary game of hopscotch. I read some more, but my eyes keep moving from the page to the door of the cabin. I spend most of the day just standing at the window wondering and waiting.

I waste the whole day just because I'm afraid he'll come back.

CHAPTER SIX

ierra

I STRUGGLE to get comfortable and end up wrestling with tangled sheets. My back aches from my fall with Van, and a dying fly buzzes frenetically in the nearby window frame. I get up, take a couple of aspirin, and put the fly out of its misery. I climb back into bed, wide awake. When I finally fall into a restless sleep, my dreams are filled with a series of chaotic mishaps.

In the final dream I'm frantic. I can't find Annie anywhere. I rush to look for her, but leaden legs slow me. One moment I'm in the hospital trying to get to her incubator, the next moment I'm in the clearing standing before an ominous redwood. It's the tree I saw earlier in the day—and yet it's not the same tree at all. I call out, "Annie, are you here?" Silence answers back. Again I try to yell her name, but no sound comes out of my mouth. I look around hoping to see Ruby or my parents but find no one. Then I see a dim light coming from the hollowed bottom of the tree.

I stoop down, crawl inside the cavernous interior, and there, with a single candle flickering in the dark, I see Annie in her tiny coffin.

And I know, all over again, that she is dead.

I awake drenched in sweat. It's been years since I've had a nightmare about her. Not wanting to risk another, I flip on the bedside lamp and climb out of bed. I shower, brew a strong pot of coffee, and dig through a stack of canvases in my studio, searching for one I've already primed. My studio, otherwise known as the spare bedroom, has an eastern exposure, which is why I chose it as my workspace over other areas in the house. I prefer working in the morning light. But tonight I drag my easel to the kitchen where the artificial light is the brightest. I punish myself with the bitter coffee and stare at the blank canvas. Soon an image begins to form in my mind. I traipse back to the studio and gather supplies: matte medium, a 4-inch brush, and oil pastels. Then I roll a set of plastic drawers, each drawer filled with torn bits of magazine pages, categorized by color, to the kitchen.

I open the top drawer and sift the bits of paper through my fingers. Varying shades of green float from my fingers back into the drawer. If there's anything that still connects me to God, it's color. I've yet to find a man-made color that wasn't first displayed in creation. From the deep fuchsia of a bougainvillea to the shocking chartreuse of the moss that clings to the rocks and trees in the damp coastal mountain range, all are unique to God's imagination. I've seen starfish donning brilliant neon orange and regal purple and wildflowers in every hue of the color wheel. We cannot out create Him.

I now fully understand my daddy's love of farming, of co-creating with the Creator. While I emote on canvas and create what

I dare not say, it's when I'm choosing colors, and maybe only then, that I'm at peace with God.

I open the second drawer and pull out a handful of the paper shreds in hues of russet and brown. Tiny typeface on the backs of some of the pieces tell partial stories. Every once in awhile, a word will catch my attention, and I'll set that bit of paper aside to possibly use later.

Often, on nights like tonight, when sleep eludes me, I pull a stack of magazines off the pile in my studio and tear pages.

I choose a page based on color, pictures, or words. For instance, I might choose a photo of a flower garden and tear out individual flowers, or I might haphazardly tear the photo because of the

colors represented. The tactile process of tearing and shredding has become an outlet for my emotions. When I'm angry, the process is less decisive—more visceral.

I open the gallon jug of matte medium, pour some into an old ceramic bowl, and set it on the kitchen table next to the small pile of papers. I choose the first bit of paper, a deep rust shade, and then dip the brush into the matte medium. I smear the goo over the shred of paper, thoroughly coating both sides. Then, using my fingers, I adhere the paper to the canvas. I do this over and over—choosing each bit of paper with care. The end result is a collage of color and words that form a scene of my choosing.

I step back to study the effect and wonder at the pall casting faint shadows in my kitchen. I've been so engrossed in my work that I didn't notice the sun rising behind a dense bank of coastal fog. I walk to the glass door that leads to the deck and observe my yard through a shroud of gray and notice for the first time this morning the distant wailing of a foghorn in the bay.

I dump the long-cold coffee and fill the tea kettle. While I wait for it to boil, I again study this first layer of work. I'm satisfied. After it dries, I'll add another layer—and then another and another and another. Each layer builds upon the previous adding dimension to the work. A finished piece often contains as many as fifty layers. After I've achieved the depth and texture I desire, I may add some of the words I've torn from pages—the words may be whimsical in nature or may "speak" a deeper meaning—all depending on the piece. Finally, I'll use the oil pastels to enhance the textures.

I began using this layering technique during my second year at SFAI, and it has become what I'm known for as an artist. Not long ago Ruby said the technique defines me—deep, impenetrable layers.

This particular piece, upon first glance, will look like nothing more than a grooved, rust-and-green abstract. But upon closer inspection, the astute will see redwood bark with all its intricate mapping and shading with sprigs of green foliage. It is the tree of my nightmare last night—or perhaps what you would see of the tree if you were standing with your nose against the trunk. My arrogance is that I believe only those who have "eyes that see" understand my work. But I don't do it so people will get it or interpret it. I do it to survive.

I set the canvas aside to dry. Then I shower again and scrub the matte medium from beneath my nails. I feed Van. Vacuum. Make a grocery list. Balance my checkbook. And clean out the refrigerator. When I can think of nothing else to fill the time, I concede, grab the keys to my Jeep, Van's leash, and we head out. Today I need Van. After my nightmare last night, I'm not looking forward to returning to the clearing and the redwood, and I'm certainly not going alone.

I take the back road that winds through the redwoods and then through Felton. By the time I reach Felton, the fog is dissipating. I head toward Bonny Doon where the sky is vibrant and the air heavy with the scent of mulching earth and pine. Van sits next to me in the passenger seat, tongue lolling and eyes squinting against the sun.

Again I drive to the area rather than hike. No need to waste time today. I'm here for only one reason, and it shouldn't take long. If this girl is real, what's the chance of me finding her in the exact same spot?

I park a hundred yards or so from the clearing just in case. If she is there, there's no need to alert her to my presence. I let Van out, attach the leash, and we make our way through a thicket of redwoods and pines. Van, rather than leading as he did last night, must sense my mood and walks quietly by my side as we enter the open space. I stop where I parked yesterday and survey the clearing. It's much the same as it was with the exception of the placement of sunlight and shadows. It's later in the afternoon and the sun is lower. While it was sunny in this spot yesterday, now it's shaded and the sunlight rests on the giant redwood across the way. I see now that it's one of five redwoods that make up a circle of trees.

I stare at the tree and see Annie in her coffin. I close my eyes, willing the image to disappear. I open my eyes and watch for a few minutes. A squirrel scampers up a nearby trunk and a blue jay swoops low beneath a redwood bough. Beyond that, all is still.

Van makes the first move and, nose to the ground, wanders toward the middle of the clearing—he goes as far as the leash allows then he turns back and looks at me.

"I'm coming." I follow his lead until we reach the group of trees.

Once there, I reach out and run my hand over the bark of the largest tree. I feel the charred edge of the opening. The words of a poem come to mind—something I had to memorize in high school no doubt.

One tree, by being deeply wounded, has been impressed as Witness Tree.

"So what have you witnessed?" I whisper.

I've tightened the leash so Van will stay by my side, but he's pressing forward, anxious to explore the cavern inside the tree.

I hold him firm and stoop, just as I did in my dream. I take a deep breath and begin to crawl inside. Then I stop and do something I haven't done in years. I pray: *Help me.*

I hesitate before admitting the truth to a God that I don't trust. *I'm scared.*

With that, I crawl in until I reach a point where I realize I can stand.

What strikes me first, before my eyes adjust to the dark space, is the smell. Like winter, like wood burning in a fireplace or like a campfire. I feel the beat of my heart slow.

And then I know . . . I just know. Before I see anything, I know she is real and that this is her place. Maybe it's intuition. Or maybe something more, something I don't understand. Whatever it is, I know I'm supposed to be here.

As my eyes adjust, I see that Van is sitting in what appears to be a circle. I bend down and touch the perimeter. Pinecones—in a perfect circle.

I step over the pinecones and join Van in the middle. I sit next to him. He nuzzles my shoulder and I lean into him. "Who is she, boy? Why does she come here? Why are we here?" He has no answers for me, but I'm glad he's with me all the same.

We sit for several minutes before Van spies a squirrel and darts out of the tree. I rise to follow him, but something catches my eye. In the farthest corner of this cavelike room, a shaft of sunlight coming through an opening higher up reflects off something. It appears to be some sort of glass. Careful not to disturb the pinecones, I step over them and reach for what looks like a mayonnaise jar.

I carry it out of the tree so I can see it in full light. The jar is filled with odds and ends. A smooth stone, a penny, a broken pencil, a few slips of paper, and what looks like a gold chain.

I unscrew the lid and empty the contents into my hand.

There's a paragraph printed in tiny letters on one of the scraps of paper:

Their names were Aunt Sponge and Aunt Spiker, and I am sorry to say that they were both really horrible people. They were selfish and lazy

and cruel, and right from the beginning they started beating poor James
for almost no reason at all.

James? How horrible. Who's James?

I pull the chain out of the clutter and see a small heart-shaped pendant hanging from it. Engraved in the middle of the heart are the initials K. W. I close my hand around the necklace and hold it tight.

Who are you? I remember her eyes. *And why are you afraid?*

I drop all of the items back into the jar, screw the lid on, and put it back just where I found it. I make sure all the pinecones are in place. And then I leave.

I find Van dozing in a patch of sunlight.

"Come on, boy. Let's go home."

He wags his tail and follows me to the Jeep.

As I drive home, my mind wanders back to Annie. I tell myself that thinking about her now is ridiculous. Yesterday was my day for memories. Yet, she feels closer than she has in years. Perhaps it was the clarity of the nightmare last night, seeing her small body nestled in the casket, or maybe the events of yesterday and today, seeing this unknown child, has taken me back.

I try to put the thoughts out of my mind. I flip on the radio set to a Bay Area news station and try to concentrate on a debate between two members of congress. Their arguing annoys rather than distracts.

I turn the radio off and think about the week ahead and realize I have little scheduled. I have one appointment with clients, but I left the rest of the week open so I can work. I have two commissioned pieces to complete for a couple from Sausalito. They saw my work in one of the galleries in Carmel and wanted something more specific to the decor of their waterfront home.

I don't enjoy working to someone else's specifications, but it pays the mortgage.

I think again about the piece I began last night. While I know it's the tree from my nightmare, I also know it's the tree in the clearing. They are not the same exactly, but my subconscious, in the depths of slumber, has somehow linked the two. One represents death. One represents survival. The two seem intrinsically entwined. Why?

Again, the haunted eyes of the child I saw yesterday come to mind. What has she survived that her young eyes reflect fear rather than the playful innocence one might expect to see from a child hiding in a tree? And why am I compelled to find out? Isn't it possible that I just startled her yesterday? But my instinct tells me there's something more.

Instinct? Intuition? These are senses I haven't considered in years—senses I've tried to shut down, I suppose. Because where they lead, I usually don't want to go. They are senses that require a knowledge and trust of oneself. I must trust myself in order to trust my instinct. And I don't trust myself. That's the crux of it.

I reach for the radio knob again and twist it on. I punch buttons until I hear a familiar beat. I turn up the volume until the pulsating music fills the Jeep . . . and my mind.

∽

IT WAS in the months following Annie's death that I began to realize what I'd lost. The magnitude of the loss crashed against me, drowning me in shame and sorrow.

A few weeks before her birth, I was finally coming out of my stupor. I began eating without having Mom or Ruby force-feed me, I showered daily of my own accord, a relief to them I'm sure. Most significant to me was that I began noticing the baby growing within me. I felt the nudges and kicks inside my womb and began to feel a sense of awe at what was transpiring inside my body. I put thoughts of how this child was conceived aside, and I claimed one of my mother's favorite promises: "God causes all things to work together for good . . ."

Mother had spent hours at my side the last two months talking and quoting Scripture. Even when she thought I was asleep or not listening, she talked. Mostly she imparted God's grace as she understood it and lived it. She assured me over and over that God had already forgiven me, loved me, and loved this baby. She reminded me that nothing could separate me from the love of God. She insisted that He had a plan for my life.

Some of that sank in—or at least I thought it did. I began to feel hope—hope for my own life and the life of my unborn child.

We hadn't talked about what I would do once the baby was born. Putting it up for adoption seemed like the logical choice. But each time I considered giving the baby away, the purpose I was trying to find in my pain slipped from my grasp. If I gave her up—I was sure the baby was a girl—then why would I have gone through all of this in the first place?

If I kept her, I could teach her everything I was learning.

I could give her the same love and stability my parents had given me plus the insight I'd gained through my own mistakes.

My mistakes . . .

There'd been so many. Guilt, that familiar intruder, hissed his accusations as each sin came to mind. *And now,* he reminded me, *you bear one of those consequences in your womb.*

But maybe, just maybe, I could turn this consequence around. It was this desire, along with the years of guilt I'd struggled with, that I finally shared with my mother two weeks before Annie was born. I remember the stunned look on her face and then her tears as she internalized my pain. After wiping away her tears, she held my face in her hands and looked me in the eyes, "You must always remember that guilt is not from God, Shannon. There is no condemnation for those in Jesus Christ. Don't ever let guilt make your choices for you. There's nothing God can't forgive. When you've sinned, the Holy Spirit will convict you, but His convictions are gentle. He doesn't accuse or condemn."

We cried together that afternoon. I told her that I wanted to keep my baby—that I'd love her and teach her and keep her from making the same mistakes I'd made. I think my mom wanted the same. She wanted this grandchild.

The next two weeks were better. Even good. My body still craved the drugs, but my mind and soul had found a new purpose. And drugs didn't fit with that purpose. My mother, daddy, and Ruby had made the first choice for me by forcing me to stay away from the drugs. The next choice was my own, which was the only choice that would ultimately make a real difference. I knew I was going to raise this baby and I would do it to the best of my ability. If that meant attending NA and working the twelve steps, then that's what I would do.

By August the doctor figured I was in the beginning of my last trimester and he warned me again of the risks to the baby because of my drug abuse. His litany included miscarriage, poor fetal growth, placental abruption, premature rupture of membranes, premature delivery, and stillbirth. All were just meaningless words to me. I wasn't worried. I knew God's plan and was willing to cooperate. I'd turn my life around and raise this baby, and He'd work all things together for good and ensure that she was healthy.

I began anticipating the baby's arrival. In the evenings I'd lie in bed with my hands over my mound of a belly and whisper my dreams to my daughter. I told her that I loved her, that I was sorry for putting her in danger. I told her about her grandma and grandpa, her uncle Jeff and Ruby. I even told her about Jesus and how much He loved us.

My first doubts about God's plan came the morning I awoke with a searing pain in my back. When I got out of bed, I felt fluid trickling down my leg followed by a gush that splattered the floor.

"Mother. *Mother!*" I didn't move. I bent over to ease the pain in my back and waited. She would know what to do.

She must have heard the fear in my voice because I could hear her quick steps from the kitchen to the bedroom. "Shannon, what's—"

She saw the puddle on the floor and the pain on my face and knew I was in trouble. She helped me back into bed and ran for the phone.

I heard her murmured conversation with the nurse from the doctor's office and then heard her dial another number. Within a few minutes she was back at my side.

"Darling, I've called for an ambulance. The nurse says we need to get you to the hospital immediately."

"Can't Dad take us?"

"There's no time, Shannon. Dad's gone to run a few errands and we can't wait for him to get back. We need to go now. Your water's broken. We need to go now—for the baby. It's too soon."

I felt the first shudder of fear. "She'll be fine though, right?"

"Shannon, where's your backpack? I'll pack a few things. Your toothbrush, a bathrobe, and . . ."

"Mother, what about the baby?"

"Let's not worry. Just pray. I'm sure everything will be fine."

I tried to believe her, but the next contraction shredded my waning certainty.

Within an hour of the first pain in my back that woke me, my baby was born. There was no stopping her. She was so tiny that she seemed to slip from my body of her own accord. As the doctor caught her in his hands, she let out a cry so small it sounded like the mew of a kitten.

The doctor brought her to me for just a moment. While he held her, I reached out and caressed her head. She was so small, so fragile. Then she was gone. The doctor handed her to a nurse who rushed her to the intensive care nursery.

For the next nine days I was at the hospital around the clock. When I wasn't sitting by Annie's incubator, I was in the hospital chapel. I begged God's forgiveness and I bargained with Him. If He'd save my daughter, I'd serve Him. I talked myself into believing that God had allowed Annie's premature birth as a test of my renewed commitment. And I planned on passing that test.

Never before or after did I pray like I did during those nine days. I was sure God would see that my commitment was real and then He'd restore Annie. She'd continue to develop and strengthen until the day I'd finally take her home.

Again, I'd figured out God's plan and was willing to work with it.

But then early on the ninth day, the doctor told us we were losing her. Her little lungs weren't developing and she was growing weaker each day. I sat with her in the predawn hours with the knowledge that God would betray me. I would lose her and all the dreams I'd dreamed for the two of us in the preceding weeks—all would be gone. I grieved Annie's loss, but perhaps more than that, I grieved losing what I'd hoped we'd share as mother and daughter.

I grieved my dreams.

My memories of the days, weeks, and months that followed are dark. I recall few details. Instead, I remember an impression— a hardening of sorts. I didn't relapse as my parents and Ruby feared. I wouldn't grant myself that sort of reprieve. Instead, I would suffer with the knowledge of what I'd done. I'd pay the price.

With steely determination, I set about putting my life in order. I put the past behind me. I disciplined myself. I took control of my life. I saw grief as weakness and strove to become a mountain of strength. It was then that I changed my name.

Sierra Dawn—strength for a new day.

aylee

"… a free belly dancing clinic on Capitola Beach this evening at 6:00 p.m. That's your community update. Monday, August 17…"

I jump when the radio and lights come on.

He paid the bill.

What does that mean? Yesterday was Sunday, so he must have paid the bill this morning sometime. He didn't come back after he left yesterday. He's not following the schedule I found in his truck, so now I don't know what to do except wait.

I hate waiting.

I tried reading this morning, but I couldn't concentrate on the words in the dictionary. Now I'm trying to read the third book that holds up the shelf—a book of poems by Robert Frost. I used to like poems. My teacher in third grade, Mrs. Stanford, taught me how to write haiku. That's a kind of poetry from Japan.

Mrs. Stanford said they don't teach that in school until the fifth grade. But she taught me because she said I was smart. I was the best reader in the class. Mrs. Stanford knew I wasn't good at math though so she made a deal with me. She'd teach me to write haiku if I'd practice adding and subtracting numbers with four digits, like 2,348 minus 1,262. So I stayed in at recess that day and worked on problems she wrote on the board for me. Then the next day, during lunch recess, she taught me how to write haiku poems. She taught me about syllables and how to count the beats. You have to know what syllables are to write haiku.

I put the Robert Frost book down and get up and go into his room and take a pen off his nightstand. Then I go to the kitchen and rip a piece off one of the grocery bags I've saved. I take them back to my mattress and lay down on my stomach. I put the paper on the floor in front of me and as I think about the first line, I tap out the syllables on the mattress.

I hide in the dark
The wind howls outside my door
He always finds me

Satisfied, I fold up the piece of paper as small as I can and then tuck it into the hole in the mattress.

By the time I got to the fifth grade I already knew all about poetry. But the Robert Frost book is hard to understand. I pick it up again and flip through the pages. Most of the poems don't make sense to me, even when I look all the words up in the dictionary. Mr. Frost writes a lot about trees and leaves and the weather, but it seems like the words he uses mean something else.

I can't concentrate on the poems either so I give up and just sit and stare at the walls and think about things.

Mrs. Stanford was tall, like the lady I saw. Maybe that lady's a teacher too. Or she could be a ranger. Maybe that's why she was up here. Rangers drive Jeeps, I think. But they wear uniforms. She wasn't wearing a uniform.

I get up and go to the kitchen to turn the radio off so I can hear him if he comes back. Then I make that scrambled egg he said I could eat yesterday. I'm so hungry that I want to eat the scrambled egg in one bite. Instead, I try to make it last, make it seem like more. I take tiny bites. I feel each bite on my tongue.

I chew slow so the flavor reaches my taste buds. I think of a word that I added to my box this week:

sa · vor—verb 1. to perceive by taste or smell, esp. with relish. 2. to give oneself to the enjoyment of: *to savor the best in life.*

I savor each bite of my eggs.

I bet Emily Post likes that word too.

When I'm finished—my stomach is still growling.

I go from the kitchen to the front window and peek through the crack between the boards. I know what I want to do, but what if he comes back and I'm not here? What would he do?

He says I'd be in trouble. But what kind of trouble?

I think of the worst possible thing he could do to me. It's the thing he started doing to me after we moved here. He only did it when my mom was gone or when she was asleep. He told me it was our special secret and that if I told my mom, she wouldn't love me anymore. He said she'd be jealous and then she'd leave.

Sometimes I think maybe that's the real reason she left. She must have known. If that's the reason, then she probably won't come back. She probably won't love me anymore. Ever.

I hate it when he does it.

The scream, a low howling, starts in my head.

I cover my ears and this time, it stops.

Then I wrap my arms around my middle and bend over trying to relieve the ache in my stomach. As I do that, a new thought comes to me: If that's the worst thing he can do, then I might as well do what I want, because he'll do it anyway. He always does. Almost every day now that he doesn't have to hide it from my mom anymore.

He could shoot me too, with his rifle. Maybe that's the worst thing.

No.

The other thing is worse.

I look down at my clothes. I'm still wearing the K-Mart jeans and T-shirt. These are my best clothes, even though they're not my favorites. Emily Post says:

Clothes do more than add to our appearance; they are our appearance. The first impression that we make upon others depends almost entirely upon what we wear and how we wear it.

I brush some dust off the knees of my jeans. This is the best impression I can make, not that I'm actually going to meet her.

I turn and look at the door.

I hesitate.

And then I go.

I walk away from the cabin fast. Then I run. I cross the stream where a fallen tree makes a bridge, arms stretched out to balance myself as I put one foot in front of the other. I jump off the log and sprint to the clearing, jumping over rocks and weaving through the trees. I run all the way to the edge of the clearing. By the time I get there, I'm breathing heavy and my stomach, instead of aching, is full of butterflies again.

CHAPTER EIGHT

ierra

I ROLL over and look at the clock radio: 6:45 a.m. I slept later than usual. I reach for the phone and dial Ruby's number.

"Hello?" and then a groggy, "Sierra, don't you ever sleep?" I can picture Ruby reaching for the eye mask she wears when she sleeps and squinting at the clock radio beside her bed.

"Of course I sleep. And I eat. Where's breakfast? Here or there?"

"Uh . . ." Ruby sighs. "Here, I guess."

"Okay, but no tofu scramble. Promise?"

"Right. I'll slaughter a pig before you get here."

"*Mmm* . . . bacon. Sounds good." Then I don my most casual, no-big-deal tone, "Hey, by the way, I'm bringing someone with me."

"What? Who?" She yawns. "Is Margaret in town?"

"No, he's a new friend." I pause. "His name's Van . . . I want you to meet him."

"What? A guy? Where'd you meet him?" Ruby is now fully awake. "Who is he? Sierra, this is great. Is this great? This seems great. Why didn't you tell me about him on Saturday?"

"Well, you know, I wasn't ready. This is a big step for me, Ruby." I twist the edge of the bed sheet around my finger as I listen for Ruby's predictable response.

"A big step? That's an understatement. Wait a minute—it's too big a step for you. What are you doing?"

"We'll see you in about an hour, Ruby. Better get up and get going."

I hang up, very pleased with myself. I can't wait to see Ruby's expression when I introduce her to the new love in my life.

Forty-five minutes later I pull into Ruby and Michael's driveway in Scotts Valley. The house is nestled at the end of a court in a new custom home development. The back of the home, and most important, the separate studio they had built for Ruby, look out on a small valley filled with ancient trees that stand taller than the highest roof peaks. They built the home after Michael's stock in the computer company he works for skyrocketed.

Ruby and I have met for breakfast at least once a week for a dozen years now. When we lived together, Saturday morning breakfasts became routine, the time we'd catch up with each other on the happenings of our week. Once Ruby and Michael married, we began meeting on a weekday morning after Michael left for work. We have no set schedule, but one or the other of us will call when we feel like it and we'll meet.

I let myself in the front door.

"Hey, Rube . . . we're here." I head for the large, contemporary kitchen.

When I see her, I can't help but smile. More often than not when we have breakfast at her place, she's still in her pajamas when I arrive. Today she's dressed, wearing makeup, and I notice that she's set the table for three. A twinge of guilt tugs at my conscience.

"Where is he?" She looks around me to see if he's coming.

"I left him outside. I wanted to make sure you were ready for us."

"Well, go get him. Don't leave him standing out there." She pushes me back toward the door.

I turn and head back to the front porch with Ruby at my heels shooting whispered questions.

"Where'd you meet him? What's he do? Is he good looking?" Just before we reach the door, she puts a hand on my shoulder and stops me. "Sierra, is this serious?"

I see her concern and answer her honestly. "Yeah, Ruby, I think it is . . . in fact, I think I'm falling for him."

With that, I open the front door.

Ruby looks out but sees no one. Then she looks down and sees Van sitting on her doormat. She looks at me, then back at Van, then back at me. "This is him, isn't it? This is Van?"

"Ruby, I'd like you to meet Van. Actually, his full name is Van Gogh."

"Of course it is . . . Sierra, why do I put up with you? Tell me. Why?"

By now I'm laughing so hard that I can barely answer her question. "You put up with me"—I gasp for air—"because you love me. Remember?"

"No. I don't remember. I seem to have forgotten that for the moment." Irritation etches her face.

Van, who's been a perfect gentleman thus far, paws at Ruby's leg. I see her irritation vanish as she bends to scratch behind his ears. "Well, you are a cute boy, I'll give her that. She has good taste. Come on in, Van. I have a piece of bacon for you."

With that, Ruby and Van head for the kitchen, leaving me alone on the porch.

"Hey, what about me? Where's my bacon?" I follow the sound of Van's nails clicking on hardwood.

Ruby glances over her shoulder at me. "You don't get any."

Once back in the kitchen I set Ruby's teapot to boil and then take the extra place setting from the table and put the dishes and silverware away. I pour juice for both of us as Ruby beats eggs and cuts vegetables for an omelet. Van rests at her feet hoping for more bacon.

"So, why a dog? Why now?"

Ah, the inquisition begins. "Wait a minute, Ruby, before you get going . . . am I forgiven?" Of course, I know her answer, but rather than coming right out and apologizing, it seems easier to hint at it by asking for forgiveness.

Ruby turns and looks at me. She attempts a firm expression, but I see the smile she's trying to hide.

"I'll let you know after breakfast." She turns back to the omelet she's working on and, undeterred, returns to her line of questioning. "So, why a dog? Why now?"

"Do I need a reason?" Admittedly, I didn't think through the "why" of Van before getting him.

Ruby slides the omelet from the pan onto a plate and then cuts it in half.

"I don't know—it just seems out of character—you being the Lone Ranger and all." I roll my eyes and then consider her question. I wrestle with the answer because I don't like admitting the truth it draws to the surface. "I guess . . . I guess I get lonely sometimes. I want company." Ruby softens. "Oh, well, that makes sense. We all get lonely sometimes. Does he sleep on the bed with you?"

"Good grief, Ruby. No. He has a crate. I said I'm lonely, not desperate. I don't want dog hair everywhere."

"Right. Well, I'm proud of you. I think he'll be good for you. It's a good step—it's progress."

"Progress? He's a dog, Ruby, not progress. Don't make such a big deal over nothing. He's just good company. So"—I change the subject before she delves into all the psychological reasons that getting a dog shows "progress" in my life—"what are you working on this week?"

Our time over breakfast includes a hilarious discourse from Ruby about her latest subject—or "victim," as we like to call them. Ruby sculpts the human form in all its varying states—men, women, children, the elderly. But somehow she captures more than form—she sees her subject's soul and translates that in her work. Hers is a rare gift. It just so happens that the soul of her latest subject is a bit warped, or so she says.

After breakfast I decide to take the lead and tell Ruby about my return to the clearing above Bonny Doon. I decide I'll save her the struggle of pulling it out of me. I figure I owe her that after my little stunt this morning. Anyway, I find myself wanting to talk—wanting to process what I found.

While Ruby pours me another cup of tea and herself another cup of coffee, I mention my discovery yesterday. "Hey, I went back up to Bonny Doon. Looks like I'm not crazy after all."

"You saw her again?" Ruby sits back down across the table from me.

"No. But I saw evidence of her." I fiddle with my spoon as I think about what I'd found.

Ruby leans forward, "What do you mean?"

"It looks like that tree I told you about is her place—like a fort, or something."

"Nobody lives up there, do they? Why would she play there?"

"She might live up there. Who knows? You hear about people like that. They find a deserted logging cabin and claim it as their own. Rent is free. Climate is mild. They make the best of it. Every now and then *The Sentinel* reports a special interest story about a family like that."

"That's true. Do you feel better? Less crazy?"

"Yeah."

"Good."

Ruby gets up and begins clearing the table like that's the end of it. Where's her persistence when I want it?

"Um . . . Ruby, wait. So . . . so you think that's it? I mean . . . you think she just lives up there, right?"

Ruby stops, tilts her head, and looks at me like she's considering more than I've asked. After a moment she sets the plates she's holding back on the table and sits down again.

"What do you think, Sierra?"

"Hold on, don't go into shrink mode on me. Don't start answering questions with questions. It's not a big deal, I'm just wondering if you think that's really all there is to it?"

Ruby ignores my sarcasm. "Well, I have no way of knowing. I didn't see her. I didn't see the tree. What's your instinct tell you?"

"I'm not sure . . ." I hesitate as I remember my sense of knowing in the tree the day before. I'd known the child was real and that she was afraid. "My instinct tells me something's wrong. But how do I know? My instinct's pretty rusty."

Ruby looks down at Van who's asleep at our feet then she looks back at me. "Sierra, I think you can trust your instinct—trust yourself. Look, your instinct didn't lead you astray with Van."

"What do you mean?"

"Think about it. How'd you choose Van? What made you pick him out of all the other dogs at the shelter?"

"Ruby, look at him, how could I not choose him? That had nothing to do with instinct."

"Sure it did, all dogs are cute in one way or another. But something drew you to this dog. Something made you choose him. You knew he was the one for you, right?"

"Maybe. I did just sort of know, I guess. He seemed like the right one." I reach down and bury my hand in the warmth of Van's fur.

"Sierra?"

For the second time in less than a week, I hear a tender tone in Ruby's voice, and when I look back up, I see tears in her eyes.

"What's wrong?"

She sniffs. "Nothing's wrong. In fact, I think everything is right. I'm glad you introduced me to Van this morning. He's a good dog. He's right for you. And he *is* progress." Ruby reaches across the table and places her hand on top of mine. "Now, trust your instinct again. If you think something's wrong, if you think this child's in trouble, then you need to find out for sure."

"But . . ." I hesitate to admit the truth. "I'm . . . scared." I whisper my confession.

Ruby teases, "Come on, *you*? You're a mountain of strength, Sierra Dawn, remember?"

"Oh, yeah."

"Sierra, God has a plan. Why not just go with it this time and see what happens?"

I get up from the table and gather the remaining dishes. "I'll think about it." I can't commit to more.

~

By the time I leave Ruby's, it's almost 11:00 and the sun is high overhead. I unzip the canvas top from my Jeep, and Van and I take off with the wind in our hair—or fur. I head out Mt. Hermon Road toward Hwy 17 with the intent of returning home to work for the remainder of the day. But as I tick off the miles toward home, something nags at me—a distinct feeling that I'm going the wrong way.

The closer I get to home, the more agitated I become. By the time Hwy 17 turns into Ocean Street, my agitation has turned to anger. I pull off the street and into an empty parking lot.

"*What?* What do You want from me?"

Van cocks an ear and then sinks down in the passenger seat.

I reach over and pat his neck, "Sorry, boy, I'm not yelling at you." I sigh, "I just . . . I just don't know what to do."

I rest my head on the steering wheel and try to figure out what to do. Should I go back and try to find the little girl again? No. That's ridiculous. This has nothing to do with me . . .

What if it were Annie?

The question pricks my conscience and then stabs my heart.

"But it's not Annie!" I scream. "She's gone. She's"—the word catches in my throat and I feel hot tears brimming—"dead."

I wipe away my tears with my fist and then bang my fist on the steering wheel.

"She's dead and this has nothing to do with her or with me!" With that, I put the Jeep back in gear and pull back onto Ocean Street. Within minutes, I'm in my driveway and out of the Jeep.

I hold the driver's side door open for Van. "Come on, get out." Van doesn't move.

"Van, come on!" He still doesn't move. I reach behind the front seat for Van's leash and attach it to his collar.

"Van Gogh, come!" I speak the command in my firmest tone and tug on the leash. He resists and remains in the passenger seat.

I throw down my end of the leash and walk around the car and open the passenger door. "Van," I say through clenched teeth, "get out now."

Van jumps from his seat to the ground, runs around the front of the Jeep with his leash dragging behind him, and jumps back in the driver's side door. He maneuvers over the gearshift and sits back in the passenger seat.

"Fine. Stay there!" I slam the passenger door and head for the bungalow. Again I feel hot tears slide down my cheeks. This time I don't even bother wiping them away. I reach the front door, turn the knob, and remember my house key is in my backpack, which, of course, is still in the car.

I turn back toward the car and see through a blur of tears that Van is still holding his vigil in the front seat.

"And she thinks you're 'progress'? You're just a pain in the neck!"

As I again reach behind the front seat, this time for my backpack, Van leans in and begins licking the tears from my face. "Stop it." I push him away. But he moves closer and rests his wet muzzle on my shoulder.

It's too much.

Twelve years' worth of pain rumbles to the surface. There's no stopping it. Like a train roaring through a tunnel, the sobs come with a force I can't stop—great heaving sobs. I hold Van tight and soak his fur. I don't care what I look like standing in my driveway, clinging to the dog in my car. I don't care about anything except this pain I've held for so long.

And can hold no longer.

I don't know how long I stand there—minutes? Hours? Finally the sobs wane. I climb into the passenger seat with Van and pull a few crumpled napkins from the glove compartment. I blow my nose and lean into Van again, resting my head on him and closing my eyes. Spent. Exhausted. But oddly at peace.

The question comes again: *What if it were Annie?*

I think of my daughter so long gone from me. I think of the dreams I had for us. I wonder, as I have a thousand times before, what she'd look like now if she were still alive. And then I remember the fear I saw in the eyes of the child in the clearing.

Yes. What if it was Annie and no one came to help her?

I get out of the Jeep and walk back to the driver's side and get in.

"Okay, you win. We're going back." I'm not sure if I'm speaking to God or Van—they're seemingly working together. But Van's tail wags in response.

As I turn the key in the ignition, I realize I'm taking my first step of faith in over a dozen years. I'm not in control here.

And I'm scared to death.

CHAPTER NINE

ierra

BY THE TIME I reach Bonny Doon I feel less scared and more resolute. I will find the child, figure out the situation, and then put this behind me.

I park a short distance from the clearing so I don't startle her if she is there. I get out, walk around the Jeep, open the passenger side door, pick up the end of Van's leash, and tell him, "Come."

This time he's out of the Jeep as soon as the word is out of my mouth.

"*Now* you're obedient . . ."

Standing by the Jeep, I close my eyes and inhale deeply. The scent is warm, organic—a blend of composting leaves and needles and the sharp tang of pine. The familiar smells of the forest soothe me and the intentional breathing relaxes me. Some of the tension I've felt the last few days eases from my neck and shoulders.

I like to think that since Annie's death, I've taken control of my life. I make decisions based on facts rather than emotions. For instance, I decided to get a dog because I spend a lot of time outdoors alone. A dog is protection. I should have thought to tell Ruby that this morning rather than going off about feeling lonely. Really, it was a simple solution to deter a potential problem.

Likewise, it now seems logical to seek out this child, make sure she's not in danger, call in the authorities if necessary, and then be done with this. The fact that this situation has tugged at my emotions for some reason is simply a result of fatigue, or hormones, or perhaps just the coincidental timing of the anniversary of Annie's death. There's nothing more to it than that.

I actually find myself amused at my earlier fit of tears. "I'm just tired," I tell myself. I smile and my shoulders relax. I've figured out the plan and now feel a measure of control. Van looks up at me, muscles twitching. Obviously he's eager to get going.

As we walk toward the clearing, Ruby's words come back to me. *Sierra, God has a plan. Why not just go with it this time and see what happens?*

God's plan. A fragment of a verse my mother often quotes plays at the edges of my mind: *I know the plans I have for you, says the Lord.*

For the first time it occurs to me that the verse implies that God knows His plans . . . and maybe I don't. A shadow of fear eclipses my resolve. The last time I thought I knew God's plan, Annie died.

My steps slow and Van looks back at me. I stop and he sits, seemingly giving me time to unscramble my thoughts.

Can I let go of my plan and trust God's instead? A plan that I have no control over? I don't think so. I turn back and head toward the Jeep. Van remains seated until the leash between us is taut.

I stop again.

Why not just go with it this time and see what happens? Ruby's words ring in my mind as if she were standing next to me speaking them again.

Why should I go with it? So far, I haven't liked God's plans. His plans included Annie's death. I know my mother would say that Annie's death was a natural consequence of my drug abuse. "A consequence God allowed for reasons we may not understand this side of eternity."

That's an understatement. I don't understand. I will never understand. God could have prevented Annie's death but He chose not to. As angry as I am with myself for causing her death, I realize I'm equally angry with God. I've never allowed this thought to fully form in my mind before now. I've never put words to the feelings I've worked so hard to deny.

This isn't a step of faith He's asking me to take. It's a lunge over a canyon of unknowns. Am I willing to risk falling into despair again? Am I willing to lose control?

Van turns to look at me again—this time with a tilt of his head and one ear cocked.

"Just a minute, boy . . ."

But instead of waiting any longer, Van is off. He springs forward pulling me with him. I stumble along until I find my pace behind him. He's headed for the clearing and intent on his purpose.

"Okay, okay, I'm coming!"

I realize my earlier caution and attempt at quiet were senseless. Anyone who's listening will hear us coming. Twigs, pebbles, and pine needles crunch under my feet and the links between Van's collar and leash clank, announcing our arrival.

When we reach the clearing—all is just as quiet as it was the last time I was here. Yet, I sense a difference. I look around, but see no one. Without getting too close, I look toward the opening in the tree, but see no movement. I hesitate before moving toward the tree—I have the distinct feeling that I'm being watched. The tiny hairs on the back of my neck stand at attention and my heart begins to race.

She's here.

It's been so long since I've prayed or dialogued with God that I stumble over the words that form in my mind. *What . . . What should I do now?*

So much for regaining a sense of control, I have no idea what I'm doing. But a moment later an idea comes to me.

I bend down and unlatch Van's leash. I'll let him approach her.

Nose to the ground, Van begins a slow, zigzagged advance toward the giant tree. Once he reaches the opening, he peers inside and his tail, his whole back end, begins a frenetic jig, a dance of jubilation.

She's in there.

Van moves into the opening and out of my sight.

I wait for a moment, hoping my big dog doesn't scare that little girl to death. Maybe this wasn't my brightest idea. What was I thinking? I take the last few steps to the tree and bend down and peek inside.

There, sitting in a patch of sunlight shining down from the opening burned higher in the trunk is the child I saw that first day. Knees to her chest, arms crossed over her knees, and her head buried in her arms. Van is licking one tiny ear that pokes through her hair. She lifts her head for just a moment to look at Van—just long enough for me to see the smile on her face and know that she's not afraid of my dog.

She doesn't see me, so I just watch—fascinated. Then a wave of fear washes over me again. What am I doing here? I can get up now, before she sees me, and leave. I don't have to do this. But the fear retreats as quickly as it arrived, and I feel something new, something familiar, but long forgotten. It's the feeling I had on Saturday mornings as a child, when the day stretched before me with endless possibilities.

I close my eyes, take a deep breath, and without any assurance,

I step out over the canyon. All I have is the hope that someone or something will catch me as I fall.

I open my eyes and whisper, "Hi."

Van hears me and turns to show me his find. He paces back and forth between me and the child, who keeps her head buried in her arms.

"Hi," I say a little louder. "That's my dog, Van. I hope he didn't scare you."

Slowly she raises her head and looks at me. The smile remains in her eyes. There's something else there too—curiosity, maybe?

I see none of the fear I sensed the first time I saw her.

She doesn't move. She just stares at me.

"I'm Sierra, what's your name?" I wait for a response, but she says nothing.

"Will you tell me your name?"

She still says nothing but instead moves to stand up. Once standing, she smiles, bows her head slightly, and then holds out her hand. For a moment I'm not sure what she wants. Then it occurs to me, and I reach and shake her hand. Her formal gesture makes me smile.

She sits back down next to Van who places his head on her knees. She reaches for him. Her movement is tentative—she never takes her eyes off me. Her eyes seem to convey a question.

"It's okay. You can pet him."

I watch as her fingers play across one of Van's silky ears.

For just a moment she glances away from me and back to Van. I see her smile widen.

I'm taken by her eyes—deep pools, fringed by a thicket of sable lashes. They stare at me from behind long, uneven bangs. Beautiful eyes, certainly. But it's not the beauty that captivates me—it's the story I read behind her eyes. A story she holds in the depths of her soul. I know it as certainly as I knew this tree was her special place.

Questions form in my mind and I long to toss each of them in her direction. I realize how much I want to know her story. How much I need to know her story.

"What's your name?"

Her silence spurs me on.

"How old are you?"

I realize as I look at her that I can't really gauge her age. Her frame is so tiny, but there's a maturity to her face and eyes.

She looks about seven or eight until you look at her face. Then she seems much older. Maybe she's near the age Annie would be now, if . . .

But I don't really know.

"Will you talk to me?"

I see her head turn—a slight shifting from left to right to left again—a barely noticeable movement.

"No? Oh . . ." My shoulders slump and I sigh. "Well, that's okay. I bet your parents told you not to talk to strangers. That's smart."

I wait, wondering what to do or say next. Maybe I should leave rather than keep up this one-sided conversation. Then I see her reach from Van toward me. I don't move. I wait to see what she wants. She sits back and puts her hand back on Van's head.

"It's okay," I whisper.

She stares at my face and then I see her gaze shift to my hair. She looks back at me with another question reflected in her eyes.

"It's okay."

I lean toward her just a little and she reaches for me again, this time her hand brushes against my hair—her touch light as a butterfly.

"I have a lot of hair." There's nothing like stating the obvious. But the lump in my throat won't allow for more. I stare at her for a moment until I can speak again.

"You have a lot of hair too. Your hair is almost as long as mine." At this she averts her eyes from mine and looks at the ground. She reaches for her hair and runs her fingers through it. I notice spots where her hair is matted and tangled and I wonder when it was last brushed . . . or washed.

I notice other things too. Her jeans and T-shirt look almost new, but her feet are bare and dirty. And she's thin. So thin. I can see the outline of her ribs under her shirt and her elbows come to sharp points as they rest on her knees. And while there's still a smile in her eyes, her face is gaunt—cheekbones prominent, eyes sunken.

I reach for my backpack and pull out two granola bars. I set the backpack aside and sit on the ground in front of her. I open one of the bars and take a bite and hold the other one out to her.

"Here. Have a snack with me."

She reaches for the granola bar, takes it, and peels back the wrapper. She takes a small nibble and then a bite. And another. And another. Before I've had my second bite, her bar is almost gone.

Her obvious hunger enrages me. Who would allow a child to go without? Even if there isn't enough money for food, there are shelters, churches, places where a parent can get a meal for a child. There's no excuse for what I'm seeing.

I reach into my backpack again and pull out an apple—the last of the food I have with me. I offer it to her.

"Would you like this too?"

Her eyes meet the ground again and she suddenly seems shy. "Go ahead. Really. I don't want it."

She looks back at me and reaches for the apple. She offers what I interpret as a smile of thanks before taking a bite.

We sit in companionable silence as she eats. I have so many questions for her, but I don't think I'll get answers. At least not today.

Now that I've found her, I realize I'm not sure what to do. Obviously she's undernourished, which counts as neglect in my mind. But I can't pack her up and take her with me, that's kidnapping. And unless the sheriff or someone from Child Welfare Services wants to hang around this tree and wait for her to show up, I have no address or information to give them as to where she lives or who her parents are. I don't even know her name.

I need a plan. And God has one—supposedly. Now might be a good time to fill me in on the details.

After she finishes the apple, I hold out my hand, and she places the core on my palm. This reminds me so much of something my mother would have done when I was a child—taking a gnawed apple, or a chewed piece of gum, or an olive pit from me, without a second thought. This is an act of motherhood. Moments like these are what I've missed. I look at this child and wonder . . . Does her mother appreciate the joy of such moments?

I lean back and set the core on the ground just outside the opening of the tree. "We'll leave it there for the birds and squirrels."

I reach again for my backpack and dig for the comb I keep there. I don't let myself think about what I'm doing. When I find the comb, I reach back and take the ponytail holder out of my hair. I shake my head and my hair falls loose around my shoulders and back. I run the comb through my hair a few times as I watch her watch me.

Then I stop and hold the comb out to her. "Would you like to comb it for me?"

She doesn't move. Instead, she seems to search my face, looking for . . . what? I don't know. Then she looks down again. After a moment she looks back at me. This time I see a slight blush color her checks—and something else—I see myself reflected in her eyes. I see fear, sadness, loneliness, and longing. My emotions—and hers.

I may not know who this child is, but I do know something about her. We share an understanding of grief. Again, I just know . . .

But what, at her age, does she grieve?

My wandering imagination pulls me from the moment.

She takes the comb from my hand and pulls me back.

She scoots closer to me, and I turn so that my back is to her. I know that sitting on the ground the way I am my hair is likely hanging in the dirt, but I don't care.

Her first strokes are slow—gentle. After a few minutes she stops. I wait and wonder what she's thinking. Then I feel the comb graze my back again and her strokes become more purposeful.

After she's combed my hair, the entire length of it, she gathers it together, holds it up, and combs through just the ends.

I imagine that she's combing out the particles of dust and dirt that gathered as it rested on the forest floor.

She reaches around me, while still holding my hair, and places the comb on my knee. Then I feel her separate my hair into sections and I smile when I realize she's braiding it. I haven't braided my hair since high school.

When she's finished, without saying a word, she puts her hand over my shoulder, palm up. What does she want? When it occurs to me, I place the ponytail holder in her hand. With that, she ties off the heavy braid and swings it over my shoulder. She gets up, comes around to face me, and smiles at her creation.

"Okay, my turn." I pick up the comb and motion for her to sit in front of me.

She hesitates and I see her hand go again to a spot matted with tangles. She shakes her head. No.

"It's okay, I'll be gentle. Let's see if we can get those tangles out."

She stares at me for a minute, finally nods her consent, and sits down in front of me. I'm faced with a mass of knots. Before I begin combing, I lean over and whisper in her ear, "Are you sure you don't want to tell me your name?"

She doesn't respond except with another slight shake of her head.

"Okay, little one, we'll do it your way." In silence, I begin the process of untangling her hair—and my emotions.

CHAPTER TEN

aylee

I WON'T CRY.

No matter what, I won't cry.

Or whine.

She starts with the hair just behind my left ear—there aren't any tangles there. First, she runs her fingers through my hair and the feel of her hand in my hair gives me goose bumps. I wrap my arms around myself.

"Did that tickle?"

I shrug my shoulders. She begins combing—taking long strokes from the top of my head to the bottom of my hair. After she combs that section a few times she runs her fingers through the other side. Almost immediately, her fingers catch in a knot and pull.

"Oh, I'm sorry. I'm going to try and work the knot out with the comb. Is that okay? I'll be gentle."

I nod. It is okay. I'll be good and sit still. I won't cry even if it hurts. But she is gentle—she holds the piece of hair just above the knot so it won't pull as she tries to untangle it with the comb.

While she works on the tangle, I remember the last time my mom combed my hair. It was the morning before she left for the store and didn't come back. Her hands shook as she pulled the comb through my wet hair. I asked her what was wrong, but she didn't say anything.

When she dropped the comb on the floor, she said a bad word.

On days when she was jittery and impatient like that, I knew she wasn't feeling good. She'd say, "It's a bad day, Kaylee. I just need a little something to make me feel better."

I didn't know how to make her feel better.

My throat aches and my eyes fill with tears. *I won't cry!* It's just that sometimes it feels like I'll never see my mom again—like she'll never come back. A tear slides down my check. I try to wipe it away without moving too much. Then I decide I have to think about something else.

I look straight ahead at the inside wall of the tree trunk.

The burnt pattern on the inside looks like thousands of tiny puzzle pieces all connected. It looks like if you pushed on it, all the pieces would crumble and the trunk would fall apart and the whole tree would fall.

That's how I feel—like I'm fragmentizing—like all the pieces of me are coming apart.

"That was an awfully big sigh."

I jump and then feel my face get hot.

"Oops, are you okay? I didn't mean to startle you."

I shrug my shoulders. I don't know if I'm okay. She's so nice that it hurts. But how can someone being nice hurt? She's patient too. She's been working on just one knot for a long time. She combs it a little, then stops, then pulls it apart with her fingers, then combs it again.

"Am I hurting you? You'll let me know if I'm hurting you, right?"

I just keep nodding my head up and down or side to side when she asks her questions.

Sierra. I like her name. I wonder if she's named after the mountains called the Sierras? I learned about those in school.

Sierra . . . I see her name in my mind written in cursive. A large sweeping *S*, a small *i* with a tiny circle for a dot, then a loopy *e*, and a hump for the *r*, then another one, and a round *a* with a little tail at the end.

I'll remember her name for a long time. Maybe forever.

I feel dumb not telling her my name or answering her questions. For a minute I thought she was going to leave when I wouldn't talk to her. I didn't want her to leave, but then I remembered what Emily Post wrote about the "personality of a handshake" and the "bow of a woman of charm." I guess those are considered nonverbal greetings. They must have worked because she stayed.

I think of what he calls me: "You stupid mute!" I looked up *mute* in the dictionary once. It said someone who's mute is "dumb, silent, not speaking, unable to speak; dumb." It used the word *dumb* twice in the definition. So I guess he's at least right about something.

As she combs, I consider—*consider* is just another way of saying *think*—all the things I'd tell her if I could. First, I'd say *thank you*. Grammy always said that you have to be polite to people—it's respectful. She probably learned that from reading *Etiquette*. So I'd say *Thank you for the granola bar and the apple*. I'd also tell her that I like her dog. *He's funny, and soft, and he didn't scare me.*

I've always wanted a dog.

After I was polite, I'd ask her questions. That's how you get to know people, you ask them things. Just like she was asking me— what's your name, where do you live—those kinds of things.

What I really want to ask her is why she was crying the other day. But if I asked her that, maybe she'd think I was spying on her. I guess I was, but I didn't mean to. Anyway, I just want to know why. Maybe I could help her feel better about whatever made her cry.

I know how it feels to cry when you're all by yourself and there's no one to give you a hug.

I feel the comb slide through my hair—down one side, down the back, and then down the other side. It slips through easily.

I reach my hand to my hair—it's smooth.

"Here." Sierra hands me the comb. "Want to comb it yourself?"

I take the comb and run it through my hair. No tangles. None. I look over my shoulder at Sierra and smile. If only I could thank her. As I hand the comb back to her, I realize it's a little darker inside the tree now. I look up to the opening and see that the sun is no longer shining in through the hole. I feel my stomach knot. What time is it? How long have I been here?

I stand, turn, and look down at Sierra. I have to go. I have to go now.

I look at the opening of the tree and back at Sierra. I start to step around her but she reaches out and puts her hand on my leg.

"Do you . . . Do you need to go?"

She can tell. She knows. I nod and look again at the opening in the tree.

Sierra stands, brushes dirt off the back of her pants, and bends to pick up her backpack. We both bend and crawl out of the tree.

I start to walk away, to head back to the cabin. My heart is beating so hard in my chest it hurts. My palms are all sweaty.

I have to get back.

"Hey, wait."

I turn back and look at Sierra. The lump in my throat feels like it will choke me. I wish . . . I wish . . . But no, I have to go.

"Can . . . I . . . Can I walk you home? Or . . ."

I shake my head hard. *No!*

"Oh, okay . . ." She looks around likes she's not sure what to do.

Her forehead creases and her eyes squint when she looks back at me. "Will you be okay?"

I nod.

"Will I see you again?"

Oh, I hope so. *Oh, please let me see her again.* I nod and point to the tree.

"We can meet here?"

I nod. *Yes, please come back here.*

"Okay."

I turn and start walking away. But then I stop and look back at Sierra and Van . . . and I can't help it. I turn around and run back to them. I bend down and put my arms around Van's neck and give him a tight hug. I stand straight and look at Sierra. I take a step toward her, then stop. Should I . . . ? Then, I just do it.

I just wrap my arms around her waist and hug her tight. Even tighter than I hugged Van.

Then I turn and run. I run until I know she can't see me anymore.

By the time I get back to the cabin, it's late. As I walked the rest of the way back, all I could think about was her. But when I crossed the stream and got closer to the cabin, my stomach cramped and I wondered if he was there. But by the time I could see the cabin, I saw his truck was still gone and I relaxed.

Sierra told me when she left that she'd come again, but not tomorrow because she has to work. I hope she doesn't change her mind or forget.

I sit on my mattress and think about all the things she told me. She said she named her dog after a famous painter, Van Go, I think. Kind of a funny name. She told me about her favorite painting—it's called *Starry Night Over the Rind.* She said she loves the way the lights reflect on the river. It sounds nice. Anyway, she just calls her dog Van for short.

I wish I could talk to her.

I could write to her! I scramble off my mattress and run to his room. I go to the table by his bed and look through the things piled there—some magazines, papers, a book of matches, a candy bar wrapper, a few pennies. Where's the pen? I look on the floor, but nothing. Finally I see it on the floor behind the table. It must have rolled off after I used it earlier. As far as I know, it's the only pen in the cabin. I grab it and go to the kitchen and tear another piece off the bag—a piece a little smaller than a piece of binder paper. Then I refold the bag and put it back.

I stand at the counter for a long time thinking of what to say: Dear Sierra . . . But then I remember that it's not polite to call adults by their first name.

In my best handwriting, I begin my note:

Dear Miss Sierra . . .

CHAPTER ELEVEN

ierra

"Stop . . ."

Getting the word from my mind to my mouth takes Herculean effort. I swat aimlessly at whatever's tickling my face. "Stop. I mean it." Still, something tickles just to the left of my nose. There's something else too—something warm and damp—like someone breathing in my face. "Stop it! Go away!" I finally open one leaden eyelid and—

"Van! Off! What are you doing?!" I shove him from the bed to the floor and then crash back against my pillow.

Then I remember. Ugh. I roll to the side of the bed and hang over the edge. Nose to muzzle with my dog, I apologize. "Sorry, guy, I'm used to sleeping alone. Come on, don't look so hurt. You're right, I invited you. Come on, come back up." I pat the bed and, with that, ninety pounds of fur leaps from the floor, over me, and settles—dare I say it?—onto *his* side of the bed. I scratch his neck. "You can sleep up here as long as you don't tell Ruby. Deal?" His tail wags against my leg.

The weight and warmth of him last night chased the chill from my body and heart—a chill that set in after I left . . . what's her name? Good grief, I don't even know her name, but I can't get her off my mind. After restless hours trying to push thoughts of her aside, I finally got out of bed, shuffled to the kitchen, opened Van's crate, and told him he could sleep with me.

In less than a week, I've completely lost my mind. I was content with my life. It worked. No surprises. I had everything under control. Now I have a dog on my bed and a child in my head—my life—whatever. How did this happen?

I throw the covers back, swing my feet to the floor, and set myself straight: "It's time to get a grip, Sierra!"

"Van, down. Outside." As though we have all the time in the world, Van stretches, eases himself off the bed, and saunters toward the kitchen. I let him out and set the teapot to boil. While I wait, I go to my studio and grab my calendar off my "desk"—two sawhorses and a piece of plywood.

At 11:00 a.m. I'm scheduled to meet with the couple from Sausalito to discuss their color palette. We agreed to meet at a gallery in Half Moon Bay, a half-way point. The couple—Robert and his young wife, Lindy—wanted to meet at my "studio." Instead, I called the gallery owner, who has a few of my pieces on display, and asked if we could use his office for an hour. He was happy to oblige "his favorite artist." Right.

I usually love the jaunt along Highway 1 to Half Moon Bay. The coastal route, if it isn't socked in with fog, is postcard perfect. But this morning I find myself dreading the time alone—time to think.

I pick up the phone and dial Ruby.

"Morning, Sunshine, want to have lunch in Half Moon Bay today? Maybe do a little shopping? Ruby? Are you there?"

"Sierra? It's . . . It's 5:45 a.m."

"Oh, uh, yeah—I forgot to look at the clock. Sorry. Well anyway, do you?"

"Do I what?"

"Want to have lunch in Half Moon Bay today?"

"No."

"No? Why not?"

"Hugo's coming."

"Hugo? Who's Hugo?"

"Hugo of the warped soul. Remember? He's sitting for me today. I'm working. It's a work day, you know?"

"Oh," I sigh. "Yeah, I know. I'm working too. I'm meeting clients—I thought maybe you'd like to join me."

"Sorry."

"You don't sound sorry."

"I'm asleep!"

"Right. I'll talk to you later."

"Sierra . . ."

"What?"

"Your water's boiling."

With that, the line goes dead. And Ruby goes back to sleep, I assume. I go to the kitchen, turn off the screeching teapot, reach for a mug, fill a diffuser with loose leaves, and . . . the phone rings.

"Hello—"

"Let me get this straight. Spur of the moment, on a whim, you want me to go with you to Half Moon Bay and have lunch? Spontaneously, drop of the hat . . . just do lunch?"

With the phone wedged between my ear and shoulder, I reach for the teapot and fill my cup. "Yeah, what's wrong with that?"

"You're not spontaneous. You don't have a spontaneous bone in your body. What's wrong?"

"Nothing's wrong. Did you change your mind? Do you want to come?"

"No."

"Fine. But I am spontaneous. What about breakfast? Our

breakfasts are always spontaneous."

"That's different. It's planned spontaneity. We do it every week. We never just pick up and do lunch . . . and shopping . . . or anything different. You always have to plan it."

"So, let's try it. C'mon."

"No."

For the second time in five minutes, Ruby hangs up on me.

~

HEADING north on Highway 1 out of Santa Cruz, much of the coastline is made up of agricultural land. Verdant rows roll toward the sea and an occasional farmer can be seen sitting atop a tractor surveying his crop. I think of my daddy and how much he'd love to farm land that dropped off into the Pacific—even on a gray and colorless day like today.

My daddy. What would he have done if he'd found . . . What *is* her name? If he'd found a little girl alone in the forest? I know exactly what he'd have done. He'd have picked her up, lifted her up onto his shoulders, and scoured the area for miles around until he figured out where she belonged. He certainly wouldn't have left her alone, without food, or shoes, or . . .

Guilt slices my conscience again. I shouldn't have just let her leave.

Before I left, I did ask if I could walk her home. Her eyes seemed to darken and she backed away from me. She shook her head so hard.

And then it was back. The fear I'd seen that first day. Those were the eyes I'd seen staring at me from inside the tree.

I moved toward her, careful not to startle her. "Will you be okay?"

A slower nod—up and down.

But honestly I knew better. She wasn't, isn't, and won't be okay. Something is terribly wrong.

These are the thoughts I wanted to avoid today.

"You're getting a grip, Sierra, remember?" The words ring hollow inside the Jeep. I turn on the radio and turn up the volume. Perfect.

I arrive at the gallery with the beat of the music reverberating through my mind. "Hey, Alec. How's business?"

Alec, donning his signature black silk tee, feigns delight, and kisses each of my cheeks. "Sierra, enchanting as always. Because of you, business is lovely. I just sold *Scattered*—that fall montage of yours. Buyers came in last night. Tried to talk me down, of course, but I wouldn't budge. I told them it will be worth three times that amount by spring. So I have a juicy check for you this morning."

"Great! And Alec, I trust you'll enjoy your juicy commission?"

"You know I will."

Alec drapes his arm across my shoulders as we walk to the back of the gallery. "Listen, cupcake, now that you'll have all that lovely money in your bank account, don't you think it's time for a little shopping trip?" He steps back and gives me the once-over. "Really, Sierra. Is this the best you could do?"

"Ah . . . saved by the clients," I whisper over my shoulder as I make my way back to the front of the gallery. "Robert, Lindy, nice to see you."

As I reach to shake Robert's hand, I notice a child tagging along behind Lindy—she can't be more than five or six.

"Sierra, good to see you again. Hope you don't mind but we brought Annie with us—the nanny's home with the flu. You know how that goes." Robert shrugs his shoulders.

"Annie?" *Annie!*

"Yes, our daughter. Haven't you met? Oh, of course not, she wasn't with us the night of the showing. Annie, come here, say hello to Sierra. Sierra's an artist."

The child leans into Lindy and gives me a shy smile. "I'm an artist too. See . . ." Pudgy fingers fumble with a coloring book she's brought with her. She finds what she's looking for and then holds it up for me to see—a unicorn colored in every shade of the rainbow.

I just stare.

After an awkward moment, Lindy waves a perfectly manicured hand in front of my face. "Hello, Sierra, is there a problem?"

"Uh . . . no. No." I bend slightly and smile. "Nice unicorn."

The meeting is a blur. I leave with paint samples and fabric swatches and pictures of an ultra-contemporary home overlooking the bay that I decline an invitation to see in person. Beyond that, I have no idea what was discussed or agreed to. Instead, I feel as though someone's knocked the wind out of me.

Of course, I've encountered children over the years. I see them on the beach, in the grocery store. I'm aware that there are other little girls out there named Annie. But I've protected myself. They have nothing to do with me. Even as recently as last week, my heart might have skipped a beat at the introduction of Robert and Lindy's Annie, but the discomfort would have passed since my memories were safely tucked away, only to be taken out once each year.

But now . . . Everything is different.

Why?

"Why?" I shout my question into the wind. "*Why?* What do You want from me?"

The crashing surf and the cry of gulls overhead are the only response.

I left the gallery determined I'd drive straight home. But my resolve—and any remaining sense of control—shattered when I saw the turnoff marked *Bonny Doon.* I veered to the shoulder of the road, parked, and made my way to the beach.

Now I turn and look at the mountains behind me. There, just a few miles above the beach where I stand, is a child who . . .

Questions swirl in the wind around me, *What if it were Annie? What's the truth, Shannon? What's true?*

The truth is that she's a child who . . . needs me. Me.

All my fears—all the pain of the last twelve years—bubble to the surface. I can't do this. Then comes another truth: I can't do this alone.

I need You.

At first it's just a thought, then a realization, then a plea—a cry of desperation from the depths of my soul.

I raise my head heavenward. "I need You." I drop to my knees in the sand. For twelve years I've stood on my own, depending on my own strength. I can do it no longer. The wind carries my wailing sobs out to sea. "I need You." The words come between sobs.

I cry for all I've lost—my daughter and my dreams.

When I think I can cry no more, when I think my tears are spent, another question breezes through my soul: *Who enclosed the sea with doors when bursting forth, it went out from the womb?*

I recognize the question—it comes from chapter 38 of Job—my daddy's favorite account of creation. "Straight from the mouth of God," he would say. Often, after dinner, when we were all lingering around the table, Daddy would pick up his Bible and read that chapter aloud.

The question silences me.

I lift my head and through swollen eyes I see the gray, tossing, expanse before me. So great is the power I see that I lower my head. Bowed before God, my own questions waft away like ash on the wind. My demands wither and wane. Humbled by the magnitude of His power and love, I finally do it.

I let go.

Then I cry again. This time the tears are for those I've caused such pain—Mother, Daddy, Ruby. And I cry for the pain my rebellion has caused God. I cry because I know that regardless of that pain, He stands with open arms ready to welcome me home.

My sorrows float away on a river of tears.

I've sat so long that the waves clamoring for the dunes are now lapping at my ankles. I get to my feet, bend to roll up the legs of my jeans, and wade into the surf. The water swirls around my feet as the sand shifts beneath me.

The water beckons and I inch my way in until my pants are soaked. When the water reaches my waist, I cry out one last time.

"Forgive me."

I look toward the horizon and see a break in the gray canopy above. Shafts of sunlight stretch from the sky and dance on the water surrounding me. As far as I can see, the world is gray. But where I stand—there is light—and it glistens on the water all around me. At that moment I know what I want to do. I take a deep breath and plunge beneath the icy water.

When I was thirteen, I was baptized. Mother and Daddy said it was time to make a public declaration of my belief in Jesus Christ. So I did.

Today, twenty-one years later, I make that declaration myself because I want to, because I need to. Because it's more than time. Alone before God, I declare that I will trust Him. I accept the forgiveness that He's offered all along, and symbolically, I leave myself—the old Sierra—on the ocean floor.

Why had I wandered so far from my parents' truth? Because I hadn't made it my own truth. Until today.

I come to the surface a new creation—cleansed, free, and for the first time in years filled with hope. As I swim for shore, I see the mountains ahead blanketed by thickets of redwoods. Somewhere on that mountain, there is a child. A little girl who hides in a tree.

And she needs me.

I emerge from the water and run to my Jeep. I grab an old blanket that I keep in the back, dry my hair, and wrap the blanket around my soaked clothes. I look one last time toward the mountains. "I'm ready to follow You, Your plan. Show me the way . . ."

I get in the Jeep, crank the heater, and head up the road to Bonny Doon.

I can't get there fast enough.

CHAPTER TWELVE

aylee

IF I READ SOMETHING, I usually remember it.

Brent, the last boyfriend, called me *Elephant.* My mom said I have a photographic memory. "Should be good for something, Kaylee."

I can read a book, and if I like part of it, then I'll read that part two or three times and remember it. Forever. It's not like I memorize the whole book or anything, I just remember the parts I like. That's how I remember the words from the dictionary—well, lots of them anyway.

My mom was right, it is good for something. Now when I'm bored, I can sort through the words in my head or remember something from a book. Sometimes I'll write down what I remember.

This morning a paragraph from one of my favorite books is running wild in my brain. It's all I can think about. It's from a book called *Mandy*. The author's name is Julie Edwards. Her other name is Julie Andrews. Maria, from *The Sound of Music*.

I go back to his bedroom, take the pen, go to the kitchen and tear another piece off the bag, and then grab the dictionary from under the shelf. I use the dictionary to write on. I can see the words in my mind . . .

> *At times she felt a soft, cool hand on her brow, and saw a woman's face, sweet and concerned. And often an arm was about her shoulders and a cup of liquid held to her lips. Mandy was aware of tender loving care, but sometimes it threatened to become the nightmare again and she cried out in fear.*

I remember the first time I read that paragraph. It was like a little hole opened up inside of me.

Void—noun 1. an empty space; emptiness. 2. something experienced as a loss or privation. 3. a gap or opening, as in a wall. 4. a vacancy; vacuum.

It feels like an empty spot that someone forgot to fill.

This morning the paragraph makes me think of Sierra—of her cool hand on my forehead or her arm around my shoulders. I remember the feel of her hand running through my hair yesterday and her breath on my neck when she whispered in my ear. *Sure you don't want to tell me your name?*

My mom loves me a lot, I think. But she's not really the cool hand on the forehead type. She's . . . well, she's just different than that.

The first time I saw *The Sound of Music*, I watched it on television one night when my mom and Brent were gone. I remember thinking how sad it was that all those children lost their mother. Now, I'm just like them.

Maybe Sierra could be my Maria.

I look down at my lap and wonder what my mom would do if she found out what I was thinking. Maybe she'd never come back.

Guilt pokes at my heart.

And the hole inside feels like it might swallow me up.

I look at what I've written, add a period to the end, then fold it up and put it in the pocket of my pants. I reach under my mattress and feel for the note I wrote last night. I fold that and put it in my other pocket, then get up and head for the door. Just before I walk out, I turn, look at the mattress, and my heart just about stops dead! I left the pen and the dictionary just lying there!

I run back, grab both, and put them away. I take a deep breath and then let it out. My neck and shoulders feel tight and my stomach hurts again.

Then, even though I know she's not coming today, I head for my tree. I want to leave her my note just in case I can't be there tomorrow.

There's no way of knowing what will happen tomorrow.

CHAPTER THIRTEEN

ierra

I REACH for the doorbell and my body shudders. Heavy footsteps echo from the inside hallway, the porch light clicks on, and Michael opens the door.

"Hey . . . Sierra? I didn't know . . . You look horrible."

"Tha-tha-thanks. May I come in?"

"Oh, of course." Michael opens the door wider and steps aside. "Holy cow, you're shaking." He places a hand on my shoulder and guides me toward the kitchen. "You're wet. Sierra, where've you been? Did Ruby know you were coming? Here, sit. Hang on a minute . . ."

Michael reaches for a pot, fills it with water, sets it to boil, then walks through the family room to the glass doors that lead from the house to Ruby's studio out back.

Within forty-five seconds, maybe less, Ruby's standing at my side. She takes one look at me then stoops next to the chair where

I'm sitting and places a hand on my knee, "Sierra?" Concern furrows her brow.

I'm so relieved to see her—so grateful for her—want so much to tell her everything. How sorry I am . . . how selfish I've been . . . how I understand everything now. But tears blur my vision and the ache in my throat keeps the words from my mouth. Instead, trembling, I reach into the pocket of my jeans and pull out a crumpled piece of brown paper. I hand it to her.

She looks at me then at the note she holds.

Dear Miss Sierra,

It was nice to meet you and Van. Thank you for the apple and the granola bar. They were scrumptious.

Please come back soon.

From, Kaylee

P.S. That's my name.

Ruby looks back at me. "Scrumptious?"

Teeth chattering, I nod my head. "Y-yes. Scrump-tious."

"Here, Sierra, drink this, it'll help warm you up." Michael hands me a cup of tea and then reaches and takes the note from Ruby. "Who's Kaylee?"

Ignoring Michael's question, Ruby takes my hand, pulls me from the chair. "Sierra, we need to get you out of these wet clothes. Come on."

She drags me to their bedroom, where she opens a large black lacquered armoire, and pulls out a pair of green velvet pajamas.

"Here, put these on. They'll keep you warm."

"Wait a minute, who's Kaylee?" Michael, perplexed, has followed us into the bedroom. "Why are you wet? And what, I beg, is so scrumptious about a granola bar?"

I take the pajamas from Ruby. "K-Kaylee is . . . a little girl. I baptized myself this afternoon. And when you're star-starving, anything is scrumptious."

Both Michael and Ruby look at me like I've lost my mind. And maybe I have.

I turn and head for the bathroom to change. As soon as I shut the bathroom door, Ruby's knocking on it. "What do you mean you baptized yourself? Is she really starving? What are you going to do? Do you know what you're doing? Sierra?"

I slip into the luxurious emerald green pajamas and feel like I'm playing dress-up. This is the most color I've worn. Ever. I open the door and tell Ruby exactly what I'm going to do. "I'm going to follow God's plan. I just don't know exactly what that is. Yet."

Ruby appears stunned. "Sierra, that color is gorgeous on you."

"Ruby! Did you hear what I said?"

"Sorry. It's just that you look so . . . alive."

With Ruby and Michael staring at me, it hits me. I am. I'm truly alive.

"I am alive, Rube. For the first time in twelve years, I feel alive." I reach for Ruby and embrace her. "I love you, Rube. I'm so sorry for the pain I've caused you. Thank you for hanging in there with me all these years."

Ruby steps back, looks at me, and her eyes well with tears. "You let go." It was a statement rather than a question.

"I let go."

"Will someone please tell me who Kaylee is?"

Ruby and I look at each other and smile. "Let's go back to the kitchen and I'll tell you both the whole story."

Michael pushes his glasses up on his nose. "It's about time."

∾

Sierra, you need to call the county—Child Welfare Services. Obviously, no one's taking care of this child."

"Michael, I know. But didn't you hear me? I don't know who she is or where she lives. I must have walked for miles this afternoon, searching for her—for a house, a cabin, a tent. Anything. All I found was a note in a tree. What do I do, send the authorities to a tree?"

Michael leans forward, elbows on the kitchen table. "No. But you report what you do know. Make the call first thing in the morning. Give them her first name, the general area where you've seen her, what you've observed—then let them tell you the next step. That way at least there's a report on record. It's a beginning."

"You're right."

Ruby comes back to the table with fresh coffee for her and Michael and a grilled turkey and cheese sandwich and another cup of tea for me. "You know, she can't just disappear into thin air. There have to be signs of her up there somewhere. Are you sure you covered the whole area?"

"I don't know. First I followed what looked like a trail through the meadow—the direction I saw her head that first day. It leads to a stream. It didn't occur to me that she'd cross the stream. But when I didn't find anything in the other directions, I looped back and was looking for a place to cross when the rain started. By then it was already dusk. I guess I'll go back tomorrow."

"Want me to come with you?"

Taking Ruby with me is tempting, but . . . "No, I think I better go alone. I told her I'd come back so, hopefully, I'll find her at the tree. I don't want to overwhelm her. Maybe she'll talk to me tomorrow and I can find out more.

"Okay. Call me when you get back and let me know if you find anything."

"Yeah, I will. It's getting late, I better head home and let you guys get to bed."

"Why don't you spend the night?"

"Thanks, Michael, but I need to get home to Van. He's been alone in the yard all day."

"Van." Ruby shakes her head and smiles. "I told you he was progress."

"He's a dog. He's not progress." I swat at Ruby, then give her a hug. "I'll talk to you tomorrow. And thanks, you guys—I won't make a habit of barging in unannounced. I just needed to . . . you know."

"Hey, you're always welcome." Michael puts an arm around me and gives me a slight squeeze. He knows I'd dodge a hug.

"Thanks. I'll talk to you tomorrow. Oh, and thanks for the jammies. I'll get them back to you."

"Keep them. They look great on you."

I look down at the beautiful jewel tone of the pajamas and am reminded that as of today, I am a new creation. The old has passed away. "Maybe I will keep them, if you mean it. They'll remind me of today, of starting anew."

Ruby nods. "They're all yours. And Sierra"—her voice catches —"I love you and I'm so proud of you."

"Thank you." I whisper the words and wipe the tears now streaming down my cheeks. I reach for Ruby and we hug each other tight—crying, laughing, and free.

~

ONCE HOME I walk into the kitchen and see Van outside, asleep against the kitchen door—fur pressed to glass. From inside, I tap on the door, wake him, and then open it. Van stretches, walks past me into the kitchen, stops, sniffs his crate, and heads straight for the bedroom.

"Hey, what's this, the cold shoulder?" I follow him into my room and watch as he, without hesitation, jumps up on the bed. He sighs and settles in.

"What have I done? Hey, you're not wet, are you?" I walk over and run my hand across Van's dry back. "Good. You stayed out of the rain. Sorry I was gone so long, boy."

I cup my hands around his furry face, and he opens his eyes.

"Tomorrow you go with me, Van."

I'm sure his expression says, loud and clear, "Of course I do."

With a smile, I scratch his head, then get ready for bed. We'll both need a good night's sleep to be ready for tomorrow.

To find Kaylee.

CHAPTER FOURTEEN

aylee

IT'S A DARK NIGHT—NO moon. Earlier the wind was blowing and then it started to rain. It felt more like winter than summer. It's times like these, when the cabin creaks and branches scrape against the roof and windows, that I hate being all by myself.

a·lone—adjective 1. apart from anything or anyone else. 2. without any other person.

That word's not in my box. It just describes me, so I remembered the exact definition. When he's here, I feel the most alone, which doesn't really make sense, I guess.

I turned the lights off right after it got dark just in case he comes back tonight. If everything is dark and quiet, maybe he'll forget I'm here. I lie on my mattress and stare at nothing.

Just as my eyes are feeling heavy and like I can't keep them open any longer, I see lights flash through the window, across the ceiling, and onto the other wall. Then I hear his truck.

I pull the scratchy wool blanket up over my face and hope that he either won't see me or that he'll ignore me. I wait as I hear his steps on the gravel, then on the stoop. The front door squeaks as it opens and the light comes on. It shines through the thin blanket covering my face and startles me. I jump. Then I lie perfectly still hoping he didn't notice. I take shallow breaths hoping not to rustle the blanket at all.

He stands for a long time. Then I hear him walk right past me —like he's going into the kitchen. I hear a cupboard door open and bang shut, then the refrigerator door opens and shuts. Then I hear his steps coming back my way—he stops right by me. He lifts the blanket with his foot and kicks it off me.

"What you doin'? Try'n to hide?" He laughs at me. "C'mon, Kaylee, ain't you happy to see me? I came home just for you."

I can tell by the look in his eyes that he did come home for me. And I know why. I pull my knees to my chest and curl into a tight ball. I want to hide. I want him to go away. I can't do this.

I can't.

"C'mon. Get up. You look like a baby all curled up like that. Get up." He pushes me with his foot. "Get up!"

I know how this goes. If I don't get up, he'll make me get up. I'm better off just doing it myself. But I don't know if I can. I feel like I'm frozen. I finally let go of my legs and slowly straighten them out, then I sit up. I pull my knees to my chest and lean my back against the wall.

"That's more like it. Now I can see your pretty little face." He walks back to the kitchen and grabs one of the wood chairs from in there and carries it out and sits it backwards in front of me. Then he straddles it and sits facing me. "What'd you do today?"

I don't react.

"I asked you a question. What'd you do today?"

I feel myself starting to shake—it starts deep inside—like in the bottom of my stomach, then works its way out.

"You too good to talk to me? That it? You ain't as good as you think. Stand up."

My legs feel wobbly as I get up. I keep my back against the wall —as far away from him as I can get.

"That's it. You just stand there and let me have a look at you."

I know what's coming.

I close my eyes and see letters in my mind—faint yellow words against the dark background of my closed eyes. They aren't in any order. Just a bunch of words.

Lackadaisical.

Cosmology.

Bazooka.

Platypus.

I feel him standing in front of me—then leaning against me— pressing me into the wall. I sidestep and it causes him to get off-balance. I run to the other wall, near the bookshelf.

The words come faster.

Marsupial, quaver, jacquard.

Then he pushes me, hard, against the shelf and the top shelf and my books go flying.

Oh no! Please don't let him take my books . . .

Then my head snaps to one side. I feel heat first, then pain. A sharp pain shoots from my jaw up to my eye. He slapped me. Hard.

He laughs again. "Open your eyes. This is too good to miss. You pay me some attention." Then he leans into me again and I feel his lips on my face where he just slapped me. "Feel better?"

I close my eyes again and see one word. Just one.

Flee.

flee—verb 1. to run away or escape from danger, pursuit, unpleasantness, etc. 2. to pass away suddenly; disappear; vanish.

Then, like he knows what I'm thinking, he whispers in my ear. "Your mamma might decide she wants you back—she might come lookin' for you someday. You gotta stay right here and wait for her. You can't go runnin' off. We'll just keep each other company 'til then."

With him still leaning against me, I feel him reach for his belt and take it off.

I hear the scream—no, I *feel* the scream—first in my chest, then my throat. But instead of coming out my mouth, it moves to my head where I hear it.

And hear it.

And hear it.

The last thing I remember is the scream.

CHAPTER FIFTEEN

ierra

3:28 A.M.

5:28 a.m. in Texas. I reach for the lamp by my bed and pull the chain, then squint against the light shining in my eyes. If I call now, I might catch Daddy before he heads out for the day.

I pick up the phone and dial.

"Good morning, Bickford Ranch, Ben here."

"Hi, Daddy."

"Pumpkin, you're up before the sun. Everything all right?"

"Yeah. I'm fine. I just wanted to talk to you. I . . . there's this . . . I'm . . ." I don't know where to begin.

"What's on your mind, Sierra?"

"Do you have a few minutes?"

I hear a scraping noise through the phone line and picture my daddy pulling a chair out from the kitchen table and taking a seat. "I have all the time in the world. What's up?"

"Well, it's kind of a long story. Did Mother tell you we talked last week?"

"Yes, she said you weren't too receptive to her suggestions. That you were still planning on going to the cemetery. Did you go?"

"Yeah, I did. But . . . Daddy, Mother was right. It's time for me to let go of this . . . this anger and guilt I've had since Annie died. I . . . I just didn't know how. I couldn't figure it all out, you know?"

"I know, pumpkin."

"Anyway, after I went to the cemetery that day, the strangest thing happened. I went for a hike and I thought I saw a little girl. She was all by herself. At first I didn't think she was real . . . I thought I was just seeing things. But then, I went back and . . ."

I tell my daddy the whole story. I tell him about Kaylee. I tell him how I feel like I'm supposed to do something. I tell him about the beach and finally accepting God's forgiveness and knowing that if I am supposed to do something, I can't do it alone. I tell him everything—I talk more than I've talked in years.

"What do you think I should do?"

My daddy is quiet—thoughtful—then, his voice thick with emotion, says, "Honey, you're on the right track. You've taken a step of faith. Now take another. Then another. You pray your way through each step and let God lead. But Sierra, you'll have moments of doubt. Anytime one of God's children turns back to Him, the enemy puts up a fight. You're going to second-guess your choices and you're going to want to turn back to what feels familiar. But don't you do that. You stay in close touch—you call us—you call Ruby. You keep close, you hear?"

"I hear you. I will."

"And about this child, Michael's right. You make a call this morning. You report what you've found. Then go back and try to find her again. Mother said you got a dog?"

I laugh and reach for Van. "Yes, sir, I got myself a dog. He's quite the guy."

"Well good. Take him with you when you go looking for her. Dogs have a sense about these things. He'll help you find her. And you be careful. If you figure out where she lives, report it to the authorities. Don't confront anyone by yourself."

"Okay. You're right—I'll just get an address that I can report. And I will take Van today. He was with me the day I met her and she seemed to like him."

"Good. Sierra, I love you. You know we're here if you need anything."

"I know, Daddy. Thanks. Will you tell Mother what's going on?"

"You know I will. And we'll be praying for you—and for this little girl."

"I'll keep in touch."

"You do that." He clears his throat. "Bye, pumpkin."

After I hang up, I lie in bed for awhile and consider our conversation and feel the warmth of my daddy's love . . . and God's love for me too. I glance at the clock again. It's almost 5:00.

I think about getting up, but there's a chill in the air and I realize I'm exhausted—the emotions of yesterday have taken a toll. I roll toward the middle of the bed and snuggle my back against Van who's still asleep on top of the comforter. I pull the soft down around my shoulders and languish in the warmth radiating from my dog.

As I lay there, I think about my daddy's words: *You've taken a step of faith. Now take another. Then another. You'll have moments of doubt. Keep close. Find her . . .*

Then a quiet voice in my head, or heart, or soul—somewhere inside me, says: *Trust me.*

"Okay." I mumble before succumbing to a deep sleep.

∾

I WAKE, sit straight up, and put one hand over my pounding chest.

Where am I? I look around and realize I'm at home, but light fills my room. What time is it? The digital numbers on my clock don't register. 11:17? 11:17 a.m.? Then I hear barking and recognize it as the sound that pulled me from sleep. I take a deep breath and remember that I laid back down after talking to my daddy.

I stretch, drag myself out of bed, and stagger toward the sound of Van's barks.

Van sits at the kitchen door, nose to glass. When he hears me, he turns and gives me a look of . . . desperation, I think. "Oh my goodness, I bet you do need to go out. Good boy." Before the door is fully open, Van squeezes through and makes a dash for the lawn.

I look at the teapot on the stove and decide I need something stronger. I set a pot of coffee to brew and head for the shower.

~

As VAN and I make the now familiar trek to Bonny Doon, questions fill my mind. Will she talk to me today? What if she's not at the tree? What if she came this morning while I was sleeping? Sleeping? Good grief. How will I find where she lives? Who would neglect a child like that? What do I do with her if I find her? Take her home with me? What? That's not part of the plan, right? Right?!

I called the county just before I left. I spoke with Bonnie— convenient. "Like Bonny of Bonny Doon?"

"No, like B-o-n-n-i-e. You called to report a case of possible child neglect?"

Bonnie sounded like she'd heard it all and wasn't too inter- ested in hearing more. But by the time I finished telling her what I knew, I realized I'd read her wrong.

"Poor little thing. It just irritates me to no end to think of a child going hungry. I'll file an initial report under the name Kaylee, last initial *W*, you think?"

"I think so."

"Fine. If you find out more, call again and ask for me. If you come up with an address or a more specific location, then we'll send a case worker to investigate."

"What happens then?"

"If there's evidence of neglect or abuse, then the child will be taken into the custody of the county and placed either in a children's home or in foster care, depending on the circumstances."

"Could I—could she be placed with me? In my home?" My question catches me off guard—one of those moments when my mouth seems to jump ahead of my brain. "I mean . . . I'm not saying . . . I'm just wondering if that's an option?"

"Maybe. Are you licensed?"

"Uh, licensed?"

"For foster care. A license. You need a license. If you're interested, you need to fill out an application, go through a background check, have your home inspected, do some training. It's a process. Again, it will depend on the needs of the child. She may need more intensive care—medical, psychological. Just depends."

"Okay, thanks. I'll get back to you when I find out more."

I hang up and glance at the ceiling, "Taking her home with me isn't part of Your plan, right?"

I look down at Van, but he offers nothing. "You're a big help."

The questions continue as I drive to Bonny Doon. My heart rate accelerates . . . as does the Jeep. "Okay, so I said I'd follow Your plan, but that's a little extreme, don't You think? I mean, a child? I just got a dog. I'm not ready for a child. So . . . if that's the plan, I'd like to know now so I can get ready."

My questions, both spoken and silent, go unanswered.

I receive no sense, no feeling, no words running through my mind. Nothing. The questions just hang in the air.

"Gee, thanks. Following Your plan might be easier if You let me in on a little of it."

Great. I'm already telling God what to do. Can you say Control

Freak? But then I remember something I've heard my daddy say more than once through the years: "God wants us just as we are—no pretense. He can handle our emotions and our doubts. He wants a real relationship."

Is it really that simple? My hands loosen a bit on the steering wheel and I relax against the seat. It's been so long since I've had a *real* relationship with anyone. "Do you really want me . . . just . . . just like this? I mean"—I clear my throat and wipe at my damp cheeks—"really?"

I round one of the many curves in the road and am awed by what I see. I've climbed out of the fog into dense forest. Regal redwoods stand guard, their branches a canopy of protection.

A shadowed coverlet of intricate lacework blankets the road ahead as sunlight dances and dapples through the trees. Yesterday's rain left the air clean, crisp—and the colors—they're nothing I could ever imagine—nothing I could ever mix on my palette. Vivid hues of blue peek through the branches overhead and every variation of green grows around me.

I catch my breath and whisper, "Thank You for this. For . . . everything."

Then unexpected words are spoken straight to my heart.

I love you.

I pull into my usual spot near the clearing and turn to Van, "Okay, boy, let's find her." He wiggles in his seat, anxious for me to open the door.

I grab my backpack and we head straight for the clearing.

I poke my head into the opening of the tree and am disappointed to see that it's empty. She's not here. I bend, walk inside, then stand to my full height inside the ring of pinecones. Van sits next to me, tail bumping pinecones in all directions. I take a deep breath and am again comforted by the warm scent of burnt wood.

I turn and look for the glass jar I saw that first day. There in the darkest spot, I see the shape of it. I reach for it and unscrew the lid. I notice she's added something. There's another piece of paper—brown like the one she wrote my note on. I pull it from the jar and read an obscure paragraph. At the bottom of the paper, in small print, she's written: *Mandy—by Julie Edwards.* Something she copied from a book maybe? I read the paragraph again and am struck by the sadness of it. I pull out the paper I read the first day and reread it. Sad. Must be from another book. I'll have to ask Ruby if she remembers an Aunt Sponge.

Why these paragraphs?

I dump the rest of the contents into my hand and pull out the locket to make sure I've reported the right last initial. *K. W.* That's it.

I replace the items in the jar and then reach into my backpack for my sketchbook. I jot a quick note, tear it from the notebook, and place it under the jar. I set two granola bars next to the jar. Then, just as I'm ready to shoo Van out of the tree, I notice something else hiding in the shadows. It looks like a paper bag. I look inside. Huh. She's definitely been here recently. I shoo Van out and put the pinecones back in place.

That done. Van and I head in the direction of the stream.

CHAPTER SIXTEEN

 aylee

I STAND on my tiptoes so I can see myself in the small mirror above the sink. The mirror is hung high so I can only see the top half of my face. I strain a little, standing as tall as I'm able and finally see what I feel. A red, purple, and yellow bruise surrounds my eye and the top of my cheek. And there are streaks of blood in my eye. From my angle, staring up at the mirror, my reflection ripples across the glass and looks nothing like me. I wonder who the monster is staring back at me?

When I walk back from the bathroom to the kitchen—every bruise on my body screams its presence.

Last night was different.

Worse.

Afterward I threw up.

"I better not get a flu bug from you. Get this cleaned up."

I wiped it up the best I could. There wasn't much.

This morning he left early. So I took a shower. There was only a sliver of soap and I used it up. I don't even care if he gets mad. The water in the shower never gets warm and there are cobwebs and spiders in the top corners of the stall. But I had to wash, to get clean, to get rid of him.

After my shower, I laid down on my mattress. I tried to think about my words, but I could only focus on one. It's an *R* word. I found it when I was reading through the dictionary for the first time. It's one of those times when reading one word, led to another word, which led to another. It seems to work that way, like all the words are related. First, I came to the word *abuse*. The fourth meaning in the list of definitions said, "to commit sexual assault upon." So then I looked up *assault*.

as · sault—noun 1. a sudden, violent attack; onslaught. 2. an unlawful physical attack upon another. 3. the stage of close combat in an attack. 4. rape.

Then I looked up the word *rape*.

Even though I've tried to forget the definition of *rape*, it's one I'll always remember. It's hard to forget the words you've lived.

I pull my knees to my chest and curl up tight. I lie on my side and put my thumb in my mouth, just like I used to when I was little. And then I listen to the scream. It plays like a loud rock song in my head. Over and over. This time I don't even try to make it stop. I just let it go on and on and on.

Eventually I must fall asleep. When I wake up, I try to stretch out, but my whole body aches. I move slow and finally get to my feet. I hobble over to the window and look out through the cracks in the boards. I squint my eyes against the glare of the sun and then decide to go out and sit in a patch of sunlight on the stoop and try to figure out what to do. I step out onto the porch and bend to brush pine needles off the top step. Then I sit, carefully, letting just one side of my back end rest against the wood of the deck while trying to keep pressure off the worst bruises. With elbows on my knees and my chin resting in my hands, I think about Sierra.

I need to go to my tree and see if she's there.

But it feels like such a long way today.

And what if she sees my face, the bruise, then what?

Maybe I can hide and just watch for her—just to see if she comes back. Today, more than ever, I want to see her, to be with her, to tell her . . .

What would I tell her?

My sigh breaks the silence.

I can't tell her anything.

I sit for a while longer listening to squirrels chattering overhead and two blue jays bickering over something nearby. I feel my body begin to relax in the warmth of the sun.

Finally I make my decision. I'll just go and look for her. If she's there, I'll hide and watch, just like I did that first day. That's good enough. And good enough is all a person needs. I stand up, go back into the cabin, and look at my books still scattered on the floor. He must have seen them last night. I can't leave them here anymore—now that he knows they're here, he'll take them for sure. I go to the kitchen and take the last brown paper bag. I put the books in the bag and walk back out the door and head for the stream, putting one foot in front of the other, lugging the heavy bag with me. Today it's a slow walk.

Every aching step is a reminder of him.

CHAPTER SEVENTEEN

ierra

I LET Van lead the way. Nose to the ground, he approaches the stream. Just like last night, I see nowhere to cross easily. "C'mon, let's head upstream a ways." I tug at the leash and Van follows. Just a few hundred feet from where I stopped last night, the stream makes a sharp S turn. I follow the first bend and see what I've been looking for—a log fallen across the stream.

Just as I'm ready to brave crawling across the slender log, something draws my attention to the woods on the opposite side of the stream. I see a flash of color—yellow—then nothing.

I stand perfectly still and watch. What did I see?

After a moment, between the trees, I see it again—yellow.

A yellow T-shirt. It's her. I reach to cup my mouth with my hands and call her name. But something stops me and I watch for a moment more.

Her gait is slow—careful. Her head is hung low. Her back is to me, she's walking away from me and I can see that her shoulders are slumped. She reminds me of one of Ruby's sculptures—an old homeless woman Ruby encountered in downtown Santa Cruz. Ruby was drawn to her because she said the language of her body spoke her plight. Ruby paid her to sit for her for several weeks.

Now I watch what I know is a little girl, but I see a hopeless old woman.

"Kaylee . . ."

She doesn't hear me over the babble of the stream.

"Kaylee!"

She looks my way and stops. She turns back the way she was going then stops again. She turns back toward me. I see her hesitation—her indecision. Finally she turns away and begins walking faster to wherever she's going.

I reach down and unfasten Van's leash. "Go get her, boy."

Van dashes across the log and catches her before I even reach the other side of the stream. Van dances circles around her, keeping her in one place. I run the distance between us. I'm breathless by the time I reach her. "Hey . . . wait. Don't leave. I have something for you."

She doesn't look at me or acknowledge me. Instead, she keeps her head down, hair hanging in her face. The only move she makes is for Van. She buries her hand in the fur around his neck.

"Kaylee?"

I notice a slight nod of her head—an acknowledgment of sorts, I guess.

"Thanks for the note. I found it yesterday afternoon. I came by after . . . after work. I was hoping I'd see you."

She still doesn't look at me.

I move closer, within reach of her. "Hey, I made lunch—peanut butter and jelly sandwiches. I thought maybe we could have a picnic. You know, if I saw you, I thought maybe . . ."

At the mention of peanut butter and jelly, she turns toward me.

"Would you like a sandwich?"

Still looking at the ground, she nods her head up and down.

"Hey, Kaylee . . ." I reach for her. I put my hand under her chin and gently lift her face up. She still refuses to look at me. And now I know why.

"Oh, little one, who did this to you?" I lift my fingers to her cheek and barely brush them against the bruise. I push her hair off her face and see what damage has been done. "Kaylee, look at me. Let me look at your eye." I try to keep the emotion I'm feeling out of my voice. I will myself to remain calm—to feel what I'm seeing later.

She raises her eyes from the spot on the ground she's been staring at. Her gaze meets mine for just a moment—then she looks past me. But in that moment, I see myself. I see what I've felt for so many years. I see a shroud of shame—that's what Ruby calls it—covering her little face.

"It's okay. You're okay. You haven't done anything wrong. I just want to take a look and make sure you're—you know—I just need to look." The lump in my throat burns—anger and tears push their way to the surface. But I swallow them back. I take a deep breath and collect myself. *I will feel this later. Not now.*

I sigh and take a step away from her. I take off my sweatshirt and place it on the ground. "Here, have a seat. Want a sandwich?" Without waiting for a response, I reach into my backpack and pull out the plastic baggies I packed at home.

"Here you go . . . two peanut butter and jelly sandwiches for you. Hope you like peanut butter. Some chips. A banana. And chocolate chip cookies—they're just store bought. I don't bake much. Hope you don't mind. Oh, and here's a soda."

I lay everything on the sweatshirt in front of her—then I sit down across from her. I reach into my backpack for my sandwich and watch as she devours the first of hers.

We eat in silence. After I've finished half of my sandwich, I decide I can't wait any longer to find out what I need to know.

"So, Kaylee, do you live around here?" I reach for a chip trying to appear casual, like I'm just making small talk.

She nods. Yes.

"Where?" I put the chip in my mouth although I'm not sure I can swallow it.

She shrugs her shoulders.

"Is it very far?"

She shakes her head. No.

"Do you live with your parents?"

At this, she looks at me. I see a wave of emotions cross her face but I don't know why.

"Hey, little one, will you talk to me? Tell me a few things—you know, where you live, what you like to do, your last name maybe? Whatever. Whatever you'd like to talk about is fine. I'd just like to get to know you."

Again, emotions flutter across her face. I think I see desire, shame, embarrassment, but, I'm not sure. Then she shakes her head. No. She won't talk to me.

"Why?" As I ask, it occurs to me. "Kaylee, *can* you talk?"

Tears swim to the surface and she swallows hard. Her face flushes. She lowers her head again and stares at her bag of chips. Then comes her answer—a slow shake of her head—first to the right, then the left, then back to the right.

No? She can't talk? Oh. I feel another fissure form in my heart. "Hey, that's okay. Don't worry about it."

We sit in silence another minute until an idea comes to me. I reach for my backpack again and pull out my sketchbook and a pencil.

"I know you can write, so let's start over. Kaylee, I'm Sierra Dawn Bickford." I write my name at the top of a page. "And you're Kaylee . . . ?" I hand her the notebook and pen.

She smiles—her first since I've been here—and begins to write. She hands the notebook back to me.

Kaylee May Wren.

"Wren? Like the bird?"

She smiles again and nods.

Now we're getting somewhere. "Okay. I live in Santa Cruz, about three blocks from the beach. Where do you live?"

I hand the notebook back and then scoot next to her so I can read as she writes.

I live

She stops, thinks a minute, then writes.

Up here.

"Where up here?"

She turns and gestures behind her.

"Do you live with your parents?"

She looks at me for several seconds—like she's weighing something, trying to figure something out. Then she looks back at the page and begins writing. I wait. I reach for a patch of clover growing next to me and pull several stems out of the ground. I pull the leaves off each stem as I wait.

Finally she hands the notebook back to me—her expression serious.

My mom has amnesia.

"Kaylee, you don't live alone, do you?"

She shakes her head.

"Who takes care of you?"

She looks back at the ground, and when I hand her the notebook, she makes no move to take it.

"Did the person you live with do this to you?" I reach for her cheek, but instead cup her chin in my hand and nod toward the bruise. I take her silence as my answer.

Anger churns beneath the surface. I want to find whoever did this to her and make them pay. But I have to hold on. I can't let her see my anger. I take a deep breath and exhale slowly. "Kaylee, I want to help you. Maybe I can help your mom too. Does your mom live with you?"

She looks at me, eyes wide, and shakes her head. She reaches for the notebook again.

I don't know where my mom is.

I read her note and a memory beckons: I'm five or six years old, standing in a crowd of people at a shopping center, looking for my mother. I remember my heart hammering like a woodpecker on a tree. Panic gripped me. But before the first tear slid down my cheek, I felt a hand on my shoulder.

"Shannon, I'm right here." Mother bent down and held my face in her hands. "It's okay. I'm right here, darling."

What must Kaylee feel? What panic has she lived with?

"Kaylee, maybe I can help you find your mom. But first, you're going to have to tell me where you live. I know some people who can help, but they'll need to know where you live."

She reaches for the notebook and I slump with relief. She's going to tell me where she lives. I watch as she writes:

I live

Then she stops. She looks at me, a question in her eyes. Her pen moves across the page.

I won't have to leave, will I? I have to stay.

She pauses again and then writes one more sentence.

Staying is imperative.

Imperative? The word makes me smile even as a knot forms in my stomach. "Wouldn't it be good to have someone take care of you? Someone who doesn't do this?"

Her head tilts down again and she stares at her lap then nods her head up and down. She looks at me, then back at the notebook. She takes a deep breath and underlines her last sentence.

<u>*Staying is imperative.*</u>

"Okay." Obviously, I need to change my tactic. Of one thing I'm certain: I can't leave her to go back to . . . whoever. I won't do that.

Now would be a good time to give me an idea of the next step of the plan. Please. Please show me what to do. "What if you come with me? Just for a little while. Just for the afternoon, and we can look for your mom. We can go back to my house and call the hospitals or the police. We can see if they know anything."

She seems to think through the idea. It's obvious she's hesitant. "I want to help you find your mom. I just want to help."

I need to be back before it gets dark.

I look at my watch. "Okay, that gives us a few hours." I have no idea what I'm doing. I'm not leaving her here, and if I can convince her to come with me, I'm certainly not bringing her back. *Oh, Lord, what am I doing?* "Do you need to get anything at home first, or leave a note maybe? We could go there first."

I see what I think is a flash of fear cross her face, then she shakes her head—an adamant *no*.

"Okay. Let's go." I pick up the remains of our lunch, stuff them in my backpack, and then stand up. She does the same.

I grab my sweatshirt and we head back to the stream. As we walk, questions assault me. Where is her mom? Does she really have amnesia? Who does Kaylee live with? And the most pressing question: what do I do next?

I have no answers.

CHAPTER EIGHTEEN

aylee

I STEP on the log that makes a bridge across the stream and put one foot in front of the other—like on a balance beam. I've gotten good at this. I go straight across. Sierra takes Van's leash off and lets him cross by himself. He's fast too. Then she starts across. She goes slow and sort of wobbles. She looks scared. Finally she sits down and scoots the rest of the way across.

While I wait for her, I think about what she said about helping me find my mom—about calling the hospitals and the police. I finally have someone who can help me find her. But . . .

I rub my palms on my pants and take a deep breath. My heart feels like it's going to pound out of my chest.

But, what if . . .

What if . . .

. . . my mom doesn't have amnesia?

This is the first time I've let that question fully form in my mind. It's come to me before, but I don't ever let it stay long enough to really think about it, because . . .

It can't be true.

She has to have amnesia or she'd have come back. That's the only explanation. She would have come back for me.

She would have.

Unless . . .

Unless she died.

This thought makes me feel small—like one of those little bugs that curl up into a ball when you touch it.

She can't be dead.

She's not old enough to die.

But then I remember Rochelle. She was in my class in third grade. She got sick and missed a lot of school. When she came back, she wore a pink beanie all the time, but there was no hair sticking out from under it. Then she got sick again, and she never came back.

My mom said Rochelle died.

She was my age.

"Kaylee, you coming?"

Sierra has Van back on the leash, and they're several steps ahead of me now. I nod my head. Yes, I'm coming.

But I'm not sure.

By the time we're halfway across the meadow, my head hurts. There are too many what-ifs pushing me to think about them.

What if today is the day she comes back and I'm gone?

What if he gets back before me?

What if she doesn't have amnesia?

What if he's right and she just doesn't love me anymore?

My legs get heavier with each step and I feel like I can't breathe. Maybe it's better if I just go back and wait because she's going to come back. She will. She has to. She'll get better. She'll remember. She'll come back.

What if Sierra doesn't understand?

What if Sierra never comes back to see me again?

My heart feels like paper, like one of those valentine hearts you cut out of a piece of folded construction paper. When you open it, you have a perfect heart with a fold down the middle and if you're not careful, the heart will tear on the fold. My heart is tearing. One half wants to believe my mom still loves me and will come back. The other half wants to follow Sierra.

It's like my mom isn't real anymore.

Sierra is real.

She's here.

But my mom *is* real too.

I stop walking. *She is real and she will be back.* I make up my mind. I know what I have to do.

"Kaylee?"

I nod and catch up to Sierra again. We walk side by side on the trail through the rest of the meadow and then on through the forest toward the clearing until we reach her Jeep.

"Here we are." Sierra walks around the Jeep and opens the passenger door. "Van, you get in the back so Kaylee can sit up front."

Van jumps into the Jeep and sits in the front seat.

"No, Van . . ." Sierra leans in and points to the back. "In the back, Van—go." But Van just looks at her. So she leans in farther and tries to push Van to the back. She's leaning way into the Jeep —her back is to me—she can't see me and neither can Van.

That's when I run.

I run away from the Jeep—away from Sierra. I run in the opposite direction that we came so that if she follows me she won't find where I live. She can't know where I live. I don't know what he'd do if she ever came there, but what I imagine isn't good. I think of his rifle and the way he likes to carry it around with him —the way he points it at me and laughs. I think of the "secret" and all the things he's told me he'll do if I ever tell anyone.

I weave my way through the trees, jumping over brush and

rocks and pushing my way through manzanita bushes that block my way. My shirt catches on a bush and jerks me backward and I feel the thorny branches digging into my skin, but I pull away and keep going.

The bruise on my face throbs and my vision begins to blur. Every bruise on my body seems to throb with the rapid beating of my heart. With each step I take, the pain reminds me what I'm running back to.

I'm running back to him.

That's when the scream starts.

And the tears.

I have to go back. I have to. I have to go back for my mom. If I don't go back, she'll never find me. She'll come back. She will. She will! She has to . . .

The more I cry, the harder it is to breathe. Tears blur everything and I can barely see where I'm going. Then my foot catches on something—a fallen branch or root or something—and I go down, hard. I lay there, face down in the dirt gasping for air, but I can't catch my breath. My lungs ache and I can't breathe.

I pound my fists in the dirt and gulp for air.

The scream rages in my head.

I finally roll to my side and then to my back. I wrap my arms around my waist and gasp for air again. This time I feel air fill my lungs. I breathe in and out through my mouth until I can almost breathe normally. Then I roll back over on my side, pull my knees to my chest, and curl into a ball. And I begin crying again.

I cry so long that is seems like I'd run out of tears.

But I don't.

It's all too much—my mom, him, Sierra.

It's all just too much.

I try to think of a word that describes how I feel. But as hard as I think and as many words as I know, nothing fits.

There isn't a word for what I feel.

CHAPTER NINETEEN

ierra

AFTER COAXING Van into the backseat with a leftover crust from my sandwich, I turn to let Kaylee get in the Jeep and . . . she's gone.

"Kaylee?" I walk around to the other side of the Jeep to see if she's there.

Nothing. Maybe she went to get something out of the tree.

I head across the clearing calling her name. "Kaylee? Kaylee!" As I approach the tree, my chest tightens and my breathing becomes shallow. I bend, look inside, and see nothing. She's not here.

Blood courses through my veins like galloping horses that trample my heart.

She can't be gone!

"Kaylee!"

I run back to the Jeep, "Van. Come!" Van, who's now dozing in the backseat, perks his ears and sits at attention. I pat the front seat, "Come!" He lunges forward and out the door. He circles me while I reach for his leash. He knows something is wrong. "Sit." He does and I clip his leash in place. With my dog at my side, my breathing and heart rate slow just a bit. "Good boy." I bend and rub Van's neck and behind his ears. "You're a good boy—I'm glad you're here. Now, let's find her!"

I slam the Jeep door and take off running in the direction of the meadow and the stream. Why would she have left? Why? Whatever her reason, I assume she's going back the way we came. She must be heading home. We'll catch her. We'll catch her and figure out once and for all where she lives. And if I can't get her to come with me, then I'll bring the authorities to her.

While I've never understood it, I've heard there are reasons people stay with those who abuse them—whether it's a battered wife or a child—they stay with what's familiar because as horrible as it is, it feels secure in some way. The fear of the unknown is greater than the fear of the known. Maybe that's what Kaylee's doing, going back to what she knows. Maybe asking her to go with me was too much to expect. I don't know.

And that's the problem. I just don't know. I don't know what I'm doing. I don't know what God's doing. The whole thing is a shot in the dark. I took that step of faith and now I'm plummeting to the bottom of the cavern. This is exactly what I expected. I'm flailing all on my own and there's no one to break my fall. What was I thinking?

I feel my newly softened heart hardening all over again.

Struggling for breath, I stop in the middle of the meadow. Van tries to pull me forward but I refuse to go any further. Like a petulant child, I stomp my foot. "Do You even care? Do You care about her? Do You care about me? *Do* You?"

Van tilts his head to one side and looks at me. Then he turns toward the stream again and walks the length his leash allows and sits with his back to me.

"What am I doing here?"

I wait. I want God to answer me. I want an audible voice from above. I want answers and I want them now.

Instead, my daddy's words spoken this morning come back to me. *Sierra, you'll have moments of doubt. Anytime one of God's children turns back to Him, the enemy puts up a fight. You're going to second guess your choices and you're going to want to turn back to what feels familiar. But don't you do that.*

It hits me then: I'm doing exactly what I think Kaylee is doing. I'm turning back to what's familiar—exactly what my daddy said I'd feel tempted to do. I'm second-guessing myself and hardening my heart. I'm going back to what I know.

One of us has to brave the unknown.

This is the answer God gives me. There are no instructions, no how-to's, no guidance, just the encouragement to brave the unknown. And it's enough for the moment.

"C'mon, buddy." We jog to the edge of the stream and make our way across the fallen log again. Once on the other side, I know I've reached the unknown. From here, I have no idea where to go. So I do what my daddy told me to do. I pray my way through each step and I let God lead.

What this means exactly, I don't know. But I pray, and I walk, and I pray, and I trust that He's leading the way.

CHAPTER TWENTY

aylee

I WAKE STARTLED, heart pounding, stomach churning.

Is he home?

I lift my face and brush something off my cheek and chin—it feels like pine needles and dirt. I sit up and look around but can see little in the dark. Where am I? I'm outside, but how did I get here? Finally the memories fall into place like pieces of a puzzle. Sierra was going to help me . . . I ran away . . . and then I fell.

My eyes feel puffy and my nose is stuffed-up. I look around again but don't recognize anything in the dark. When I stand up, I feel like the tin man from the *Wizard of Oz*—all my joints ache. I turn around and around, but all I see are the shadows of trees.

I don't know where I am or which way I came from.

He told me I'd be sorry if I ever left.

I'm alone.

I'm lost.

And I'm pretty sorry right now.

I think about what he'll do when he finds out I'm gone. I don't know which is scarier—being lost in the dark or thinking about what he'll do to me. I don't want to think about it right now.

I start walking in the direction I'm facing because I don't know what else to do. Twigs, leaves, pine needles, and rocks crunch under my feet with each step I take. For some reason sounds are amplified, that means they're louder, in the dark.

I stop for a minute and listen. I hear something rustling in a bush nearby and crickets chirp all around me. Just above me, an owl hoots and it's so loud that I jump like a scared rabbit and run. When I finally stop, my pulse is pounding in my ears.

I just want to go . . . Where? Home? No. I don't want to go back to the cabin. But I have to. I want to go . . . I wish I'd gone . . . with Sierra.

Leaving the cabin this morning was stupid.

Telling Sierra was stupid.

"Don't you tell nobody . . . it's our secret." I wanted to tell my mom the first time it happened. But he told me not to. Anyway, I was afraid I'd get in trouble if I told her. But then the more I didn't tell, the more I couldn't tell. It was like the secret was a huge snowball rolling after me—like in a cartoon. The longer I didn't tell, the bigger the snowball got. It was always there, just behind me, ready to flatten me.

After my mom left, things got even worse. "She only wanted one thing. Just wanted what I could get her. That whore just wanted one thing!" He grabbed my shoulders and shook me. "You get that, girl? She didn't care 'bout me. Didn't care 'bout you. Just wanted what she wanted!"

His face looked like a boiled tomato, and it was so close to mine that his spit sprayed my face as he yelled.

Then he slapped me.

And he pushed me down.

I landed on the corner of my mattress—my head and shoulders hit the mattress, but my back and tailbone hit the floor. Hard.

He held me down. I tried to get away from him, but he was on top of me and as hard as I tried, I couldn't get away. Then he . . . he hurt me.

"Cat got your tongue?"

After that, I couldn't talk. But it didn't matter by then because there was no one to tell anyway.

"You gonna let the cat outta the bag?" He used to ask me that. "Huh, Kaylee, you gonna let the cat outta the bag? Not now. Cat's got your tongue now." Then he'd laugh at me.

What do cats have to do with anything anyway?

But today, when I saw Sierra and she saw the bruise on my face, I knew that's just what I was doing. I was letting the cat out of the bag. I was telling her my secret—or at least part of it. I should have run earlier. I shouldn't have let her see me. I could never tell her the whole secret. I can never tell anyone.

Letting her see me today was stupid.

I'm such a moron.

mor·on—noun 1. a person who is notably stupid or lacking good judgment.

Then she wanted me to leave—to go with her.

Now I'll probably never see her again either. This thought makes my throat feel tight and tears blur my eyes again. It shouldn't matter anyway. It's not like I need . . . I mean . . . she's not important to me or anything. I don't even really know her. So it doesn't matter. She's inconsequential. Which means she's irrelevant. Which means she's not important anyway. Really. She's not.

Anyway, I couldn't go with her. I have to be there when my mom comes back.

What if today was the day?

What if she came today and I wasn't there? And she waited for me and I didn't come back? How long would she wait? If it was a good day, she'd probably wait a long time. But if it was one of her bad days, she wouldn't wait. On those days she doesn't have any patience.

I try not to think about her bad days—she couldn't help it if she didn't feel good. Instead, I think about how she liked to laugh and dance. She'd come home sometimes and turn on the radio. She'd find a station that was playing something she liked and then she'd turn it up real loud.

"Let's dance, Kaylee." She'd grab both my hands and we'd twirl around and around until she was so dizzy that she'd fall down. Then she'd laugh. Sometimes she'd fall asleep right on the floor while she was laughing. Before I went to bed, I'd go get a blanket and cover her up so she'd stay warm.

My favorite days with my mom were her medium days—not the bad days and not the good days—just the regular days. There were more regular days when we lived with Grammy. We moved in after my mom and Brent broke up. Grammy said she wanted to help my mom—help take care of her. At first my mom was sick. There were lots of bad days. But then she got better. She'd come out of her room and sit on the sofa and talk to me. Sometimes we'd watch TV together or play Parcheesi. Those were the best days.

But then one night my mom and Grammy got into an argument. My mom wanted to go out and Grammy wanted her to stay home. I begged her to stay home too. But she left anyway. Pretty soon after that, we moved to the cabin.

Then Grammy got sick.

I don't want to think about that either.

I convince myself that I didn't miss my mom today. This wasn't the day she came back—it couldn't have been.

My legs feel heavy like there are weights tied to them and my throat is dry and scratchy. I stop and listen. I keep hoping I'll hear running water—the stream. Once I find the stream, I can get back from there.

I walk and I walk. I walk until I can't lift my feet one more step. When I've taken my last step, I drop to the ground and just sit with my head in my hands. I look around and see the faint outline of a tree behind me; I scoot until my back is against the trunk and I lean on it. Pine needles and little rocks poke into my back end, but I'm too tired to care. I pull my knees to my chest and rest my arms and head on my knees.

I take a deep breath, bite my lip, and tell myself I won't cry again. But as hard as I try, I can't keep the tears from sliding down my cheeks.

It feels like all the hope is draining out of me.

CHAPTER TWENTY-ONE

ierra

AS THE SUN lowers on the horizon, shadows cast deceptive illusions. I think I see a deer up ahead, but instead, as I draw near, I see a gnarled tree stump. A branch appears as a winged creature. With the onset of dusk an eerie silence falls on the forest.

I've wandered for hours—in circles, in squares, in rectangles— each time covering a larger parameter. I've seen nothing except creatures. I flushed a gaggle of wild turkeys and several rabbits have scampered past. But there's no sign of Kaylee and no sign of anything that resembles a house or trailer. Nowhere someone would live.

I decide to make one last attempt before dark descends. Van is lagging behind, tongue hanging. I stop, open my backpack, and pull out a bottle of water. I pour some into my cupped left hand and let Van lap it up. I fill my palm again and let him drink. I take stock of where we are and where we've come from. I've left a trail for myself. Remnants from our lunch—a banana peel, cookie wrappers, plastic baggies placed under rocks. Once I've passed each piece in my loop, I pick them up and begin again.

This time I decide to work in a triangle—making the top of the triangle my farthest point in one direction yet. I ignore the shadowed illusions and press forward. This is my last chance today and I'm determined I will find something.

Let's go, Lord. This is it. I have to find something. Please show me the way.

My calves burn and my back aches. Although I'm used to hiking, I've never hiked with such purpose or under such tense circumstances. The knots in my calves and legs are likely as much from tension as overuse.

I trudge forward walking as far as I can while gauging how much light I have left—I need to figure it right or I'll never find my way back to my car. I figure I can go just a hundred more yards—the length of a football field. But I see nothing ahead.

As I approach what I've set as my stopping point, I see a light dim against the dusk. It's just to the left of where I'm headed.

I stop and stare. Is it a house? I pull Van's leash tight and keep him close as we approach.

There in a thicket of redwoods is a small house or cabin. It's made of logs—likely fallen by loggers half a century ago. The shingles on the roof are in disrepair with bald spots dotting the sloped rooftop. The front window is cracked and appears to have boards across it and the front door is ajar. But there are lights on inside.

I notice a truck in the gravel drive so I assume someone is home. I find the largest redwood and tuck myself behind it and observe the cabin. I see movement between the boards on the window and within a few minutes a man comes out the front door. He stumbles down the steps of the stoop and keeps himself from falling by grabbing the railing of the deck. He pulls himself back to his full height—which isn't much—and weaves his way to the truck. He opens the driver side door, reaches inside, and pulls out what looks like a six-pack of soda—or beer. I'll bet on the beer based on his performance so far.

He pulls one can from the pack and pops open the top. He stands at the truck and guzzles the entire can, then he throws the empty back in the truck, slams the door shut, and retraces his weaving steps back inside.

Is this it? Is this where Kaylee lives? Could this be the person who blackened her eye and bruised her cheek? A knot forms in my stomach—this one a sickening weight warning of impending doom.

Is Kaylee in there? I don't know what I'll do if she is, but I have to know. I can't leave her. I won't.

I wait, hoping this guy is settling in for the evening. When I see no movement for twenty minutes or so, I walk a few feet to a sapling and tie Van's leash to the slender trunk. "Stay." I whisper my command and then tiptoe toward the front window.

Once there I realize the window is too high for me to see inside. I look around and notice a boulder, just to my right, almost hidden beneath the stoop but still within the range of the window. I climb on top of it. The vantage point is just right.

I peer through the space between the boards across the window. I see a bare room—makeshift shelves against one wall and a mattress on the floor in one corner. And there on the mattress is the man I'd seen. His legs are kicked out and crossed in front of him and he has a beer in one hand and—I take a deep breath—a rifle lying across his lap.

It looks like he's waiting for someone.

My jaw clenches and my pulse throbs in my temples. My shoulders ache, my neck is stiff. Tense, I stand at attention. And I pray . . .

Oh God, now what? What if he's waiting for Kaylee?

I beg God, I implore Him, I cry out as never before. *Help me, please help me! I have to save her from this. Show me the way . . .*

No longer concerned about the darkness draping the forest, I determine to wait. I'll wait as long as he waits. I will stay here all night if I have to.

I step with caution, quietly making my way back to where I've tied Van. I untie his leash and we make camp at the base of the redwood I'd hidden behind. I sink down into the soft bed of mulch around the tree, Van at my side, and determine the darkness is advantageous. If he comes out again—I'll see him before he sees me. Here, I have a view of the door and can see anyone who comes and goes—including Kaylee. I'm close enough that I think I could stop her before she enters.

Yes, I've lunged over the canyon. But I'm no longer flailing and alone. I sense a presence waiting and watching with me.

Strong arms hold me.

~

As the first hint of dawn paints the morning sky, the front door of the cabin bangs open and the man steps outside. He stands there a minute, looks around, then reaches back and slams the door shut. He heads to the truck, rifle in hand, opens the driver side door, tosses the rifle inside, and then gets in and drives off.

I nudge Van who's asleep with his head in my lap and then move to stand up, which proves easier said than done. I stretch, do a few knee bends, and then shake my stiff limbs. My movements are reminiscent of doing the hokey pokey as a kid—but this morning I feel every one of my years. The limberness of youth is lost, especially after a night spent on the ground.

I walk toward the cabin, again keeping Van close. As I approach, I see the front door is still ajar. Although he slammed it, it doesn't appear to have latched.

I hesitate only a moment . . . then walk into the cabin. I have to know if this is the right place. Since I haven't seen any sign of Kaylee all night, I'm beginning to wonder.

As I step inside, my senses are assaulted. The air is damp,

musty. The main room is dark. I search for a light switch, find it near the front door, and flick it on. A bare bulb hanging from the ceiling glares at me. Cobwebs droop from the rafters, and fungus, mushrooms, and moss grow from the logs that make up the interior walls. The floor is nothing more than the concrete of the foundation—gray, hard, cold. A chill runs through me. This place is uninhabitable. Or should be.

I see the mattress in the corner covered with what looks like an old army green blanket. Empty beer cans litter the area. There's a small kitchen, and one bedroom and a bathroom. All can be seen from the main room. I walk into the kitchen and open the refrigerator—a few eggs, mayonnaise, pickles, and a loaf of bread —nothing more. The cupboards, with the exception of a few mismatched dishes, pots and pans, and a can of tuna, are empty. There's a portable radio on the counter next to the sink.

In the bedroom there's a rumpled bed, a dresser, and a night-stand piled with stuff—loose change, matches, a comb, a pen, miscellaneous papers, and a couple of magazines. One looks like a hunting magazine.

My pulse races as I look at the other magazine.

Oh, Lord, no . . .

I pick it up and flip through the first few pages.

Oh no. No. Not this. Please . . .

Anger, like bile, rises in my throat. The magazine is filled with lewd, sexually explicit pictures of men . . . with children.

Lord, please . . . no.

But then hope stirs. I realize I've seen nothing that indicates a child lives here. I walk back to the kitchen. The main room. Nothing. The only place I haven't looked is the bathroom. I turn quickly and take the few steps back to the bathroom. A toilet. A shower stall. A sink. Nothing.

Just as I turn to go, I see the edge of something—a piece of fabric maybe—poking out beneath the door. I step back into the bathroom, push the door closed, and there, behind the door on the floor is a small pile of clothes. Jeans and a T-shirt. I bend and pick up the T-shirt—it's the same one Kaylee was wearing the day I brushed her hair.

I hold the shirt close to my chest. *Oh, Kaylee, where are you? What have you suffered?* Thoughts and images crowd my mind and I want to yell . . . scream . . . rage. Urges I thought I was incapable of feeling course through me. I want to find him and turn his own rifle on him. I want to hurt him. Kill him, even.

I want to make certain he never touches Kaylee or another child. I want justice.

Vengeance.

I walk back to the bedroom, shuffle through the papers on the nightstand, take one, tuck it into the pocket of my jeans, and dash for the front door.

I untie Van's leash from the railing of the stoop where I left him. "C'mon, boy, run. We have to run!" I stop at the tree where we spent the night just long enough to grab my backpack and then take off again.

I have to get help. Now!

~

BY THE TIME I reach home it's just after 7:00 a.m. The county offices don't open until 9:00. So I call the sheriff's department.

"Yes, I'd like to report a missing child. An abused child. She's being abused physically and . . . sexually, I think." The sound of my heart hammers in my ears as I speak.

"Yes, that's fine. Thank you." I'm told an officer will come to take a report sometime in the next hour. I figure I have a little time to pull myself together.

Still feeling stiff and cold from my night outdoors, I go to my bathroom and fill the tub with steaming water. I sprinkle lavender bath salts in the water and light a candle that sits on the ledge of the tub. I may only have a few minutes, but I will make myself relax. Or at least try.

I peel off my dirty jeans and the rest of my clothes, reach for a band and pull up my hair, and then step into the scorching water; my cold feet and legs prickle. I sink into the tub and almost immediately feel my pulse return to a more normal rhythm.

I breathe deep and the lavender aroma calms my senses—but it doesn't clear my mind.

The images I saw in the magazine fill my head and questions fill my soul. *Why? Why would anyone do that? What has he done to her? Why.. . why would You allow that to happen to a child? Why didn't You protect her?*

The last questions are the ones I've tried to keep from asking since I saw the magazine. There aren't any answers, I know that.

I want to trust You, but this makes it seem impossible. I don't under-stand. I want to believe, but I need You to help my unbelief—it's bigger than my belief. Help me trust that You are the loving God You say You are. Help me believe.

I find myself wanting to linger in the tub for hours, letting hot water wash over me, cleansing me of these cares. Instead I emerge, wrap myself in a towel, and then dress in fresh khaki shorts and a long-sleeved, navy blue T-shirt.

A knock on my front door just as I'm slipping into my flip-flops tells me I got out of the tub just in time.

Two officers stand on my front porch. I notice their squad car parked along the curb in front of my house. "Ma'am, I'm Officer Mackenzie, and this is my partner, Officer Jameson." Both men take off their hats and reach to shake my hand.

"Hi, I'm Sierra Bickford. Please, come in." I step aside and they walk into my living room. Both are tall, imposing men who seem to fill the space. I motion to the sofa. "Have a seat." As I take the chair across from the sofa, I realize my palms are damp and my hands are shaking. So much for relaxing.

"Ma'am, you reported a missing child? Is she your child?"

"No. I just . . . actually, I don't even really know her. I just came across her last week while hiking near Bonny Doon. I saw her in the forest up there. She was alone, which seemed strange to me. A friend encouraged me to go back and look for her again. When I did, I found her in the same area. It was evident she's not being cared for. She's very thin and she was hungry. I gave her an apple and a granola bar. Her hair was matted and . . . I don't know . . . it just didn't look like anyone was taking care of her."

"What did you do?"

"I didn't know what to do. I'm ashamed to say that I left her there. I didn't think I could force her to come with me. Yesterday morning I filed an initial report with CWS, but I only had her first name and a last initial and no address. After I called CWS, I went back to look for her again."

"Excuse me, ma'am"—this from Officer Jameson, who's just taken notes thus far—"Why are you reporting her missing? How do you know she's missing?"

"When I went back yesterday, I found her. I tried to talk to her again, but discovered that she can't talk. She's not physically able to talk, I guess. So we wrote notes back and forth. She had a large bruise on her cheek and her eye was blackened and bloodshot. I asked who'd hurt her. I finally deducted that it was whoever she lives with. She wouldn't tell me where she lives. But after seeing the bruise, I didn't want to leave her again. I thought I had her talked into coming with me. She told me she doesn't know where her mother is—she thinks she might have amnesia or something. I don't know the situation, but I offered to help her find her mom. I told her we'd come here and call the hospitals or the police. But then she ran off. Maybe she got scared, I don't know."

I pause, take a breath, and look at both officers. Do they think I'm crazy? Will they write me off? No. They are listening.

Intently.

Assured, I continue. "After she ran, I decided I had to figure out where she lived so I could give a physical address to CWS. So

I searched all afternoon. Finally about dusk, I found a small cabin. Looks like one of those old logging cabins up there. I saw a man—he was obviously drunk. He had a rifle. It was the only place I'd found, so I decided to wait and watch for Kaylee. I didn't think she was in the cabin, so I spent the night outside waiting for her. I was afraid for her—if she came back . . . you know?"

"Yeah, sounds like a bad scene." Officer Mackenzie taps his pen on his clipboard. "So what happened?"

"Early this morning the guy left. Oh! I jotted down his license plate number." I get up, go to the kitchen, and pull a page out of my sketchbook. "Here it is. After he left, I . . . um . . . I went into the cabin. It wasn't locked. I know that's probably not legal . . . but . . . well . . . anyway, I went in."

"And?" He taps his pen again.

"I found her clothes—a T-shirt she was wearing the first day I saw her. And"—I hesitate—the memory still sickens me—

"I found some pornography. Pictures of children . . ."

Officer Jameson mutters an expletive. Though I wouldn't have said it myself, it expresses my feelings exactly.

"Ma'am—Ms. Bickford—I assume the child didn't come back?" The pen tapping stops as he copies down the license plate number I gave him.

"No, she didn't. Not while I was there. Do you think . . .

I mean . . . does the porn mean anything? I'm just worried that—"

"You're right to be concerned. The porn and the abuse usually go hand in hand." Officer Mackenzie shakes his head. "Hard to believe what people will do to a child."

I notice a gold band on his left hand and wonder if he has children of his own.

"Makes you want to take the law into your own hands sometimes. If anyone did that to my little girl"—Officer Jameson rubs his forehead and then shakes his head—"I don't know what I'd do. But I'll tell you what, he'd be sorry he ever messed with her."

"Keep your cool, man. Ms. Bickford, I assume there wasn't an address?"

"No. Nothing. In fact, I don't even know how to tell you to get there, but I could show you."

"Good. Sit tight. Let us run the plates and see what we come up with."

"Oh wait, I have one more thing for you." I get up and head to my bathroom. I grab my jeans off the floor and reach into the front left pocket and pull out the paper I took from the nightstand. "Here. Looks like a pay stub or something. It has his name on it—at least I assume it's his name." I glance at the slip of paper. "Jackson Tully."

"Thanks. That helps." Officer Mackenzie gets up. "I'll check the plates. You want to call in?"

"Ms. Bickford, may I use your phone?" Officer Jameson follows me to the kitchen as Officer Mackenzie heads for their car where, if television has taught me well, he'll radio in the license plate number.

I busy myself while they do their thing. I go back to the bathroom, pick my clothes up off the floor, and toss them in the laundry hamper. I go to the spare bedroom and move brushes and tubes of paint around to keep busy. The unfinished canvas—the abstract of Kaylee's tree—sits on an easel in the corner of the room.

I stand and look at it. I'm reminded of my dream the night I began painting it—Annie in her coffin inside the tree. The interior of the tree appeared as death to me that night, its burnt, charcoal interior a tomb. Yet for Kaylee, I realize the tree probably represents life. Safety. A place of her own.

From death comes new life. I ponder the thought a moment. It strikes me as something my mother would say—or maybe something I've heard her say. I'll have to ask her about it.

"Ms. Bickford?"

I walk out of the bedroom and down the hall. Officers Jameson and Mackenzie are standing back in my living room.

"I ran the plates and the truck is registered to a Jackson Emerson Tully, which matches the name on the stub you found. He lists a San Jose address, but that doesn't mean much. He has several unpaid tickets so there's a warrant out for him. We don't typically pursue unpaid tickets by tracking someone down and arresting them, but we can use them to bring him in if we need to." Officer Mackenzie glances at Jameson. "Are we cleared to go?"

"Yep. Another unit will meet us in Bonny Doon and we'll all go up from there."

"Once we meet up with the other officers, we'll have you give us a description of the girl. Ms. Bickford, you okay to follow us up there? If we make an arrest, we'll need the room in the squad car to take him in."

"Sure, that's fine."

"Okay, in case we get separated, we're meeting the other car at the elementary school. Know where it is?"

"I do. I'll see you there."

CHAPTER TWENTY-TWO

aylee

WITH MY HEAD resting on my knees, I scrunch my shoulders together so they cover my ears and block out the sound of something rustling leaves somewhere close by. If I don't hear it then I don't have to think about it. I swallow the lump in my throat and take deep breaths until my stomach stops clenching. With my ears covered, I focus on listening to my breathing and nothing else. This helps push away the thoughts scurrying through my mind like scenes from a scary movie. Though I can't seem to block them completely.

I open my eyes and see nothing but darkness surrounding me. I close my eyes and see him. I won't let myself think about him.

Instead, I open my imaginary box of words. There are yellow letters all jumbled inside—all the letters that make up my special words. Sometimes I take them out in alphabetical order. I have to do this with my eyes closed so I can see them in my head. I take them out and put them in a list. It takes lots of concentration. I can't think about anything else when I do this or I'll forget a word.

Allocate.

I like that word. I like words with double *L*s. I like the way they feel in my mouth when I say them. Even if no sound comes out, I like the feel of the tip of my tongue hitting the back of my front teeth.

I like some words just because of the way they feel in my mouth. I like other words because of what they mean. Sometimes I like a word for both reasons.

Zoology.

That's good for both reasons. *Z* words tickle my tongue. Maybe I'll be a zoologist when I grow up. I like animals.

I go back to alphabetizing my words.

Anteater.

That's my second word. Anteaters look funny. We saw a movie about them in school. I might like animals but I don't like skunks. And I smell one.

I lift my head off my arms and look around. Even in the dark, I can see the white stripe on the back of the skunk waddling straight toward me. I jump up and press my back against the tree I was leaning against. My heart flutters in my chest as I turn to run.

When I'm sure the skunk can't catch me, I find another tree to rest against and sit down. The bottoms of my feet sting, so I cross one leg over my other knee and turn my foot so I can see the bottom of it. It's too dark to see much, but when I run my hand over it, it feels sticky—like it's bleeding. I feel things sticking into my foot—pine needles, splinters, thorns, little rocks. I try to pull them out but it hurts so much. I do the same to the other foot. Then I lean my head back against the tree trunk, close my eyes, and take deep breaths again until the waves of nausea go away.

Azure.

Bazooka.

Colossal.

I get to the *Z* words and then start all over. When I'm back to my favorite *L* word for the second time—lackadaisical—I decide I can't be lackadaisical anymore. I have to get up and keep walking. I have to figure out where I am and how to get back to the cabin.

I stand and try walking on the outsides of my feet, but then my ankles hurt. I just have to walk normal. I take slow, careful steps and hope that I don't step on anything else that's sharp. Every step hurts.

I walk the rest of the night. I walk until I can't take another step. When I finally sit down, I hear birds chirping. I look up through the trees and see that the sky is starting to get light. Exhausted, I lie down.

I decide to just stay right where I am. I can't walk anymore and I still don't know where I am. I'll probably just lay here and die. That's the last thing I think. That I'll probably just die right here.

Maybe, just a little bit, I even want to.

I don't know how long I sleep, but when I wake up the sun is up and the birds have quieted some. I stretch and the muscles in my legs cramp and my feet ache—the pain makes my stomach clench again. I try to work the cramps out of my calves by rubbing them and then standing on each leg and taking small steps until my legs finally loosen up. As I stand there, I think I hear something. Something I didn't notice before.

Water?

Is it the stream?

The sound is faint; I can barely hear it. But it sounds like it's straight ahead.

Each step I take hurts, but I can't miss another day at the cabin. It's okay to be gone for an hour or two sometimes. But I can't be gone whole days. I have to get back in case today is the day. She might come back today.

With each step I take, that's what I tell myself.

Today might be the day.

Today might be the day.

My mom might come back today.

Finally I see the stream. I hobble to a part where the bank rolls into the water. I sit on the edge of the bank and dip my feet in. I flinch when the water touches my feet. I double over, my breathing heavy. But I keep my feet in the water, swishing them around, washing them off so I can see how bad they're hurt. They're bad. I put them back in the water and leave them there. The cool water begins to ease the pain.

I look around and try to decide which way the cabin is from here. I still don't recognize anything, but I know if I follow the stream I'll eventually find the log where I normally cross and then I'll know where I am.

I look up and down the stream and decide to go down. I don't know why but it just seems accurate.

acc·u·rate—adjective 1. free from error or defect; consistent with a standard, rule, or model; precise; exact.

For awhile the stream is shallow and sandy, so I walk right up the middle of it, which feels better on my feet than walking along the bank. But when the water reaches the tops of my knees and I see rocks on the bottom, I climb back up to the bank and sit for a minute.

For the first time since last night, I let myself think about what will happen if he's there when I get back. But then I remember that he doesn't come home every night.

Maybe last night was a night he stayed out.

Maybe I can sneak in and he'll never know I was gone.

I get up and start walking along the bank. I stay close to the stream so I'll see the log. Things are starting to look familiar maybe—like I'm getting close. Then, up ahead, I see the place where the stream bends like an S. That's it—that's where the log is! I run—well sort of run and sort of hobble until I reach the log. I sit down on my bottom and scoot across the log just like Sierra did. When I reach the other side, I know I'm almost there.

What if he's there?

I wish I had a dog like Van. He could protect me. I could train him to attack. This thought makes me smile. When I smile, my forehead feels like it straightens out, like it's been scrunched up all night. That's how my mom would look when she was worried about something—usually when she was looking into her wallet and it was empty—then she'd scrunch her forehead and squint her eyes.

The closer I get to the cabin, the harder I strain to see if his truck's there. But I can't see through all the trees. Finally I get a clear look at the cabin. His truck isn't in the driveway.

He's not there!

If everything didn't hurt so bad, I'd do a little dance.

I climb up the steps of the stoop and open the door to the cabin. When I walk in, my heart feels like it drops to my knees. I can't move. I just stare. Five empty beer cans lay on top of my mattress.

He knows.

He was here and he knows.

I bend, push the cans off my mattress, and lie down. I pull the blanket tight—the smell of beer surrounds me and reminds me what I've come back to.

I've come back to him.

He'll be back.

And he'll be mad.

CHAPTER TWENTY-THREE

 ierra

WE'VE MADE drug busts up here. There's a dirt road—an old logging road—that runs through this area." Officer Mackenzie points to the map that's spread atop the squad car. Officer Jameson and the other two officers nod. They know the road.

"Ms. Bickford—Sierra—you think the cabin is about here?" He points to the spot I indicated earlier—earlier when I'd had them dispense with the *Ms. Bickford.* "If that's the case, let's loop back and catch the dirt road and go in from here." He points to the squiggly line that marks the road. "If we don't find it, then we'll have you walk us in from the clearing you showed us."

"We'll find it. We were up here last month—there's millions of dollars' worth of marijuana growing in this coastal range. We arrested a pot farmer just last month. We've seen the old logging cabins. There are six or seven of them right in this area." Officer Newton points at the map. "Growers and dealers love it up here—

it's remote but close enough to a main road that there's electricity and other services."

"Let's hit it." Jameson reaches for the map and folds it up.

As I follow the squad cars back to where the dirt road cuts in, I wonder again about Kaylee. Have drugs played a part in what she's suffered? Maybe, like Annie, she's a victim of someone else's addiction. The thought saddens me, but the guilty verdict—the gavel pounding in my head—doesn't come as it usually does.

What happens if they find her today?

Officer Jameson told me they'd check with CWS for previous reports regarding her. But what if there isn't evidence of anything? What happens then? Maybe the jerk she lives with has a legal right to her—maybe he's her father or a guardian or something. What then?

And if there is evidence of abuse? What had Bonnie told me? CWS would place her in a children's home or foster care.

The thought pricks my heart. So that would be it then? Kaylee would become a ward of the county and my role in her life would be . . . what? Finished?

The satisfaction I thought I'd feel when I'm finished with all this doesn't happen. *Come on, Sierra, you've done your job. You found her, brought in the authorities. Once they find the cabin, you're free of this mess. That's what you want, right?*

The answer to the question I ask myself surprises me. No. No, that's not what I want at all.

Confusion swirls through my soul like a tornado, upending feelings long buried—love, hope, desire. I reach for the radio, turn it on, and crank the volume.

But my twisting soul won't still. It begs for attention.

I reach for the radio again and turn it off. I sit in silence. Feelings fly to the surface and I try to pin them down—examine each one. But I'm unpracticed. I pay attention to the emotions stirring and finally, I recognize the most prevalent feeling: Fear.

Fear incriminates: *This child is wounded—she needs more than you can give. You don't have what it takes. You'll end up hurting her like you've hurt everyone else.* I ponder the charges and then put them aside. Yes, there may be some truth there, but at the very least, I'm better than what Kaylee's had. I'd take care of her.

Fear changes tactics: *If you let yourself care for her—love her— you'll get hurt. You don't need to lose another child. You know that pain all too well. There's no happily ever after in this story. You'll end up alone again. Don't give her your heart.*

This argument traps me and there's no time to unravel the truth from the lies. The brake lights of the squad car ahead of me signal our arrival. I pull the Jeep to the side of the dirt road, take a deep breath—and get out.

I walk to the group of officers and listen for my instructions.

"Sierra, the first cabin in the cluster is about a hundred yards up the road. You walk in with us and point out the cabin you were in. Agreed?" Officer Newton looks at the others who nod their heads.

"Then, Mackenzie and Jameson, you drive in and make the arrest if the guy's there. We'll hold back and wait for your instruction. We know he's armed, so if you need backup—we're here."

"Good. Let's take a look." Officer Mackenzie motions for me to take the lead.

Walking the dirt road behind the cabins, I can't tell them apart. They all look the same. I don't remember cabins on either side of the place I saw last night, but maybe I just didn't notice—they are spread apart. Most of the places look vacant.

Jameson must sense my hesitation because he slows. "Sierra, whadya think?"

"I think it might be the last one. I was facing the cabin last night. When the truck pulled out this morning he backed out and then went around the right side of the cabin. I didn't notice another cabin on the right. I think his driveway curves around the side of the place out to the road."

"Jameson, why don't you and Sierra cut through there"—

Mackenzie points to a trail between two cabins—"and take a look from the front. Make sure we've got the right place."

Jameson follows me down the shadowed trail. We wind our way in between trees until we're standing in front of the row of cabins. I head to the right, off the trail, and trudge through ferns and undergrowth until I see a familiar sight—a truck parked in front of the last cabin.

"That's it. He's there. That's the truck." The fluttering in my chest feels like the beating wings of a trapped hummingbird. I take quick, short breaths, unable to find a natural rhythm. Is Kaylee there? Is she okay? What will happen? *Oh, Lord, are You here? Do You have a plan?*

My pulse slows again and peace, like a sheet of assurance, drapes my soul. I don't know what comes next, but I know it's completely out of my control. This is God's plan. It's in His hands.

Jameson clicks his radio. "Found it. We're on our way back. Looks like the guy's there."

We follow the trail back to the road and listen as Mackenzie gives instructions. "We know this guy is armed, so let's not take any chances—take both cars. I'd rather have you guys on site with us. Sierra, you stay put. Wait here at your car. I want you out of the way for your own safety."

"What if she's—what if Kaylee's there? I mean—she knows me. Maybe it would help if I'm there."

"We don't know what we're dealing with and we don't need you in the mix at this point. If the child's there, we'll bring her to you. Understood?" Officer Mackenzie puts his hand on my shoulder. "We appreciate your help, but it's our job to keep you safe. Got it?"

"Got it." I don't like it, but I get it. I watch the four men get into the squad cars and drive off. I walk back to my Jeep, open the driver side door, and climb in. I sit for several minutes—as long as I can stand. I hop back out and pace the length of the car—back and forth, back and forth. Finally I stop at the front of the car and look toward the trail I just walked with Jameson.

I need to know what's happening.

I'm content to let God have control, but I don't see how watching will hurt as long as I stay out of the way. I just need to know if Kaylee's there. I head for the trail and make my way to where Officer Jameson and I spotted the truck. Although I can see the truck—and now the squad cars in the driveway—I can't see the front door of the cabin from this vantage point.

I weave through the trees, making sure I keep my distance from the cabin. I want to find the tree where I spent last night. From there I can see, and hopefully hear, everything.

By the time I find the tree and can see the front porch, no one's visible except Officer Newton and his partner standing beside their car in the driveway. The cabin door is open and I don't see Officers Mackenzie or Jameson. They must be inside.

I press my face to the bark of the pine tree and breathe deep. The spicy scent speaks to me of strength, power. "Thank You." I whisper my gratitude to God for His peace. "And please protect Kaylee, wherever she is."

A loud crack shatters the silence and I jump. *Oh, no . . .*

Then the deafening sound comes again, flushing two quail from the dry grass behind me. They flutter so close that I can feel the breeze of their wings on my face. The sounds echo through the valley.

Who is shooting?

I lean into the tree and watch as Officer Newton and his partner draw their weapons and bound the stairs of the stoop in one seamless move.

"Oh, God, help them. Help them!"

I hear shouting from inside but can't make out the words. Then another shot reverberates through the cabin and into the forest, echoing in the distance.

I step away from the tree. Instinct tells me to run, but something stops me. Rooted, I wait. Then I see movement—a flash of yellow. Kaylee! She runs out the front door of the cabin. She's alone. Her movements frantic, erratic—like she doesn't know where to go. Her hands cover her ears. Her shoulders hunch, her chin presses to her chest. She's bending at the waist, leaning forward as she runs.

"Kaylee!" I shout and run toward her. "Kaylee!" I see her look up briefly—just long enough to see me. She weaves toward me, her steps uncertain.

I race to her and catch her in my arms. I press into her and hold her tight. Her heart pounds against my hip as she leans into me. Her body shakes and heaves, but no sound comes from her beyond the occasional sniffle and hiccup.

I gather her in my arms, lift her up, and carry her back to the safety of the tree. I'm struck by how light she is. "It's okay, Kaylee. It's okay. Oh, little one, you're going to be all right now. I'm here." Still holding her, I lean back and look at her. I push her hair out of her face and place my palm on her cheek. "Kaylee, look at me." Her eyes are squeezed shut. "Open your eyes. Look at me."

Slowly she opens her eyes and focuses on me. She drops her hands from her ears and throws her slender arms around my neck. She nestles into me and although she's light, because of her size, holding her is awkward.

"Kaylee?" I whisper into her ear. "I'm going to put you down. I'm not going anywhere. I'm right here. But I want to have a look at you—I want to make sure you're okay." I set her down—feet on the ground—and take a step back. I look her up and down.

I notice her jeans are unbuttoned and unzipped and I see what look like scratch marks on her abdomen.

I reach for her T-shirt, keeping my eyes on hers. "I'm just going to lift your shirt a little bit. I won't touch you. I just need to look." Her eyes never leave mine. I lift her shirt just above her waist and see five long, bleeding scratches on her lower abdomen —like someone tried to tear her pants off. I drop the shirt and look back at her face. Her eyes are focused on the ground and her face is flushed.

"Oh, sweetie . . . I'm sorry." Emotion chokes me and the words, I know, are barely audible.

Then I look down and notice her feet. She's standing on the outside edges of them and I see what looks like dirt and blood caked on the undersides.

"Kaylee, here—let's zip your pants and button them." I help her do this. "Now, sit a minute, get off your feet." As I help lower her to sit on the ground, I notice the scratches and bruises on her arms—two black and blue handprints encircle her upper arms.

I sit next to her and, with my arm draped across her shoulders, I notice the way her shoulder blades protrude at sharp angles beneath her shirt. There is no fat on her—not an ounce.

Every maternal instinct I've ever felt surfaces. I want to pull her close, pick her up, carry her to the Jeep, and take her home with me. I want to draw a hot bath and let her soak. I'd wash her hair and tend her feet and tuck her beneath clean sheets. I'd make her toast and macaroni and cheese and chocolate pudding and . . . anything and everything she'd want. I'd place it all on a tray and take it to her in bed. I'd sit with her—stay with her—all night if necessary.

My throat aches and I'm vaguely aware of tears on my cheeks, but I don't care. I pull her close and she rests her head on my shoulder. "Kaylee, I'm going to take care of you . . . I'll take care of everything."

"There you are!" Officer Mackenzie, out of breath, comes up behind us. "I . . . I told you to wait at your car!" Gasping for air, he reaches for his radio. "I . . . found them. We'll meet you at the road."

I see the pulse throbbing in the prominent veins on Officer Mackenzie's neck. I can almost see, I imagine, the adrenaline coursing through his system.

"I told you to stay put! You could have been hurt!" He runs his hands through his hair and then bends down. "Kaylee? Are you okay?"

Kaylee turns and gives Mackenzie a slight nod.

He stands and turns back to me. "Let's go. Medical personnel —ambulances—are on the way. We'll meet them at the road." He looks down at Kaylee and I see him eye her feet. "Kaylee, I'm going to carry you to the road."

Upon hearing this, Kaylee pulls her shoulders forward. Her head lowers and her eyes—those telling pools of emotion—widen. Fear, an insidious intruder, pulls her into herself. I watch, helpless.

"Hey, little one, I'll go with you. It'll be okay."

She pulls further away from me and shakes her head—the movement is slow . . . subtle . . . but it speaks both her fear and protest.

Officer Mackenzie squats next to Kaylee again and tries to reason with her. "Kaylee, we can't leave you here alone. You need to go to the hospital. There are nice people who will take good care of you."

I can see Officer Mackenzie's patience is waning. "And I'll stay with you at the hospital, you won't be alone." I look at Officer Mackenzie. "I can do that, right?"

"Yes."

I hope my presence will reassure her, but instead, she lowers her eyes, stares at the ground, and wraps her arms around herself. She's pulled deeper inward.

Pain wraps its tentacles around my heart and squeezes.

I don't know how to help her. I realize how little I know about this child. I don't understand her. Yet, I realize, I love her—something I can't explain. I wonder if she'll ever return my love.

But now isn't the time to ponder such thoughts.

I remember Kaylee's notes yesterday. Was it just yesterday? It feels like ages ago. *Staying is imperative.* The clutch on my heart tightens. "Kaylee told me yesterday that she has to stay here—for some reason, staying here is . . ." It doesn't make sense. I begin again. "Her mom has amnesia."

"Kaylee," Mackenzie bends so he's eye-level with her. "The Sheriff's Department and Social Services—the nice people who will help take care of you—can help look for your mom. We have ways of finding people. We'll start looking right away and we'll let you know if we find her."

Kaylee stares at Mackenzie's face like she's weighing whether or not she can trust him. I pull her close and feel her fear—it trembles beneath the surface.

"She's shaking."

"Shock, probably. She's been through a lot this morning."

Still holding her, I try one last tactic. "You know what, sweetie? Your mom would want you to go to the hospital. She'd want someone to take care of you. I think we need to do this for her."

She shakes her head again. But this time, the shake is almost imperceptible.

Mackenzie bends down in front of her. "Put your arms around my neck, and I'll carry you on my back to the road. Now. We need to go."

Kaylee hesitates a moment longer, then wraps her arms around his neck. He lifts her up and then turns and looks over his shoulder at me. "Let's go."

With that, we make our way through the trees and brush and head back to the road.

CHAPTER TWENTY-FOUR

aylee

EACH TIME HE TAKES A STEP, my body bounces on his back, and every bounce hurts. I try to hold on tight around his neck but my arms feel rubbery and I can't stop shaking. My head pounds, my legs and stomach cramp, and the bottoms of my feet burn. Sierra's walking next to us and keeps reaching up and putting her hand on my back. I like the feel of her hand on my back. It's the only thing that feels good.

I just want to rest my cheek on the policeman's shoulder and feel Sierra's hand on my back. I want her to keep it there. My eyes feel scratchy—like they need to close and stay closed for a long time. I want to go to sleep with Sierra's hand on my back. If I could talk I'd say, "Please don't move your hand—just leave it there until I wake up."

My face gets hot when I think about that. I'm not a baby.

I don't need someone to watch me sleep. But that's what I want.

I just want . . . I want . . . someone to stay with me. I don't want to be alone anymore.

What I really want, I tell myself, is my mom. Not Sierra.

I want my mom. I do.

But with each painful bounce the picture in my mind of my mom becomes less clear. It's like my brain is an Etch A Sketch—one of those red boxes with a screen and two white knobs that you turn to draw a picture. When you're done with the picture, you shake the box and the screen clears and it's ready for a new picture.

Bounce. The screen shakes and her dark hair becomes just a smudge.

Bounce. Her face erases.

Bounce. Her hands and feet slip away.

I try to hold onto the picture but I can't. Not anymore.

I tried, Mommy—I tried. Tears blur my sight. *I tried to wait.*

I waited as long as I could.

I can't wait anymore.

I'm sorry.

~

WHEREVER I AM, it's comfortable. I stretch my legs and then roll onto my side.

I feel something drape over me and tuck around me. I didn't know I was cold until the warmth sends a shiver through me. Now I feel snug—tight—like a caterpillar in a cocoon.

I hear voices but can't understand what they're saying. I lift my head up and look around, but the movement sends what feels like nails shooting through my forehead, so I lie back down and close my eyes again.

Then a soft, cool hand touches my forehead. The hand brushes the hair off my face and then gently rubs back and forth. A memory flickers, but it's too hard to pull it up and think about it.

"I'm here, Kaylee, you're doing great."

The voice whispering in my ear is familiar—kind . . . gentle— but I can't place it. I don't even know if it's real. I try to open my eyes, but it's too hard to bother.

"Okay, Kaylee, you'll feel a small prick. It's gonna sting, but just for a minute."

This voice is different. Someone I don't know.

I feel a tapping on my arm and then a sharp poke into my skin. I roll back flat and open my eyes against a bright light. I try to pull my arm away, but someone's holding it down.

"Whoa, girly, you need to hold still. We need to get some fluids in you. You're all dried up, dehydrated. This'll make you feel better. After this, we're taking care of those feet of yours. Gonna soak 'em in some nice warm water."

It takes a minute to come out of the fog of sleep and remember why I'm here. I squint against the light while pictures flash in my mind: The cabin. Him. The police. Shots. Sierra.

I remember the hand on my forehead and turn to see if it's her. Sierra. I squint my eyes against the light and try to focus on her face. Her eyes are different here, inside—more gray than blue. She's serious, concerned or worried maybe?

"Hey, you're waking up. How do you feel?" As she talks to me, her hand continues to smooth my forehead. Her hand is

still cool against my skin. Her voice is tender and caring. She still looks worried so I try to smile to reassure her, but my mouth is dry and my lips stick to my teeth. She asks someone if she can give me something to drink.

"Sure thing, honey. There's cups right there by the sink. Give her just a sip or two to start."

Sierra takes her hand off my head and I feel it's not being there almost more than it's being there—like when you take a Band-Aid off a sore before it's all the way healed up and it stings.

When she comes back with the cup of water, she helps me sit up. She stuffs a pillow behind my back then lifts the cup to my lips. A memory flickers to the surface again, but now I'm awake enough to remember it: The soft, cool hand on my forehead, the cup of liquid lifted to my lips. It's from *Mandy*. It's the part of the story I wrote on the scrap of paper and put in my jar.

I take a drink of the water and then lay back against the pillow. I stare at Sierra. Will my story end like Mandy's? Will Sierra love me and take me home with her . . . forever?

The thought makes me want to pull the blanket over my head and hide in the dark space under it where no one will know what I'm thinking.

I want to go home with Sierra, but . . . what about my mom?

Maybe the police will find my mom and we'll go home together.

I think about home. Is the cabin home? Will he come back too? Or is he dead? Maybe he's dead. Maybe they shot him.

I hope he's dead. I don't want to go back to the cabin. Ever.

So where's home?

The question makes me feel the way I felt in the forest last night: lost. But maybe home is more a feeling than a place. When they find my mom, or when she finds me, then I'll be home.

Sort of.

But what about Sierra? Would I ever see her again?

I look at her. She's standing at the foot of the bed talking to the nurse. When I look at her, something inside me hurts. I think of a word from the dictionary: **de·sid·er·ate.** It means you want something really bad. Or miss it really bad. *Desiderate* isn't in my box. It's a hurting word. But it's a word I remember because I know how it feels.

When she's done talking to the nurse, Sierra comes back to the side of the bed. She rests her hand on my shoulder. I think about the way her hand feels. The way it feels to have someone touch you and take care of you.

It feels like home.

CHAPTER TWENTY-FIVE

ierra

SURREALISM WAS a twentieth-century movement of artists and writers to capture, through the use of fantastic images and incongruous juxtapositions, a representation of unconscious thoughts and dreams.

If I were to capture this moment on canvas, it most certainly would fall into the category of surrealism. It's all incongruous juxtapositions. The first incongruity is me—a single, childless, independent woman, standing on the side of a dirt road, mentally wringing my hands, my heart, my soul, as a child is loaded into an ambulance.

The second incongruity is Kaylee—a motherless, independent "adult" in a child's body. She's taken care of herself until today when she, under duress, surrendered herself to the care of others —right now the paramedics, later the county, then . . . who knows.

Here we are the two of us, side by side. True surrealists would call this a chance effect, but they'd be wrong. Not by chance nor even by choice are we together, but by design. Of this, I am oddly certain.

And as much as I desire to look at this through the critical, detached eyes of an artist, instead I am the subject. These are my dreams, I realize. My yearnings and longings for motherhood are playing out before my eyes.

I try to etch these thoughts, these certainties, this moment of clarity, on the walls of my mind and heart for I sense I'll need them later.

I see Officer Mackenzie pat one of the paramedics on the back and then turn toward me. He motions for me to come over. Once the paramedics arrived, I stepped back to give them room to work.

"Sierra, they're ready to take Kaylee, do you want to ride with her?"

"Is she awake?"

"Nah . . . she's out. The paramedics say she's in shock, dehydrated, and exhausted. They gave her something for pain—her feet are pretty chewed up—so she'll sleep awhile."

"Okay, then I'll follow in my own car. I don't want to have to come back for it later."

Mackenzie nods. "We're done then. We'll be in touch. We'll likely have questions for you when we do our report."

"That's fine. Hey, I saw the other ambulance. What happened in there today? I mean—the shots—did you—did you have to . . ."

"He fired. He was erratic, but we had to protect Kaylee, and ourselves." Mackenzie's thoughtful for a moment. "I promised my wife and kids I'd be home for dinner tonight. I intend to keep that promise." He tilts his head and smiles. "He got two shots off before I shot him. That was two shots too many. I hit him below the right shoulder. So he's wounded, but he'll probably make it. His type usually does."

"What do you mean?"

"I mean he'll be back, free to do this to another child. He'll get off on a technicality or maybe he'll even serve a little time, then we'll get another call and go through the whole thing again."

I nod in understanding, although I know I don't truly understand. I can't imagine what it takes to do his job.

"Well, Sierra, as I said, we'll be in touch." He gestures to the ambulance that's turning around on the dirt road. I nod again.

~

WHEN I ARRIVE at the hospital, they're just unloading Kaylee from the ambulance. I follow the paramedics through the double doors and down a hallway to the nurses' station where the paramedics exchange information with a woman who looks as though she could wrap all of humanity in her ample arms and make us all feel better. She jots down the pertinent medical information then looks around the paramedics to me. "You her momma?"

"No. I'm just . . . No. I'm not."

Eyes the color of rich coffee stare back at me—wisdom swirls in their depths. "You have the worried look of a momma."

"I was . . ." The whispered words slip out of my mouth before they register in my mind. "I mean, I had . . . I . . ."

"Honey, you don't need to tell me nothin', but I'm tellin' you, once a momma, always a momma. That's just the way it is. There's no goin' back, no matter what happened. So if you're not her momma then who is? Do we have a parent here?"

"Oh—uh . . ."

One of the paramedics interrupts my stammering. "Charlene, Mackenzie notified CWS. They're sending a caseworker over for her."

"She part of that mess?" Charlene points down the hallway, and I turn and see one of the officers from earlier standing next to another gurney.

"Yep. They found her with him. Abuse. Neglect. You know . . ."

"I sure do know and wish I didn't." The nurse's soft features harden and fire ignites her eyes. She shakes her head. "Well then, we'll just give this one some extra lovin' while she's here." As she walks away to prep a room for Kaylee, I hear her muttering, "No excuse for that kind of thing. No siree, just no excuse."

Once a momma, always a momma. The truth of her words lingers. I became a mother the day Annie was born, and I assumed motherhood ended for me the day she died. Yet, the longings to love, nurture, and protect that her birth awakened in me didn't die with her. It's those longings, those desires, I've worked so hard to bury all these years.

But I dug a shallow grave. So here I am. Undone. Afraid. But hopeful. Hopeful that God will allow me a place in this child's life.

As the nurses get Kaylee into an examining room, I reach for my cell phone and dial Ruby.

Her simple "Hello"—the sound of her voice—dislodges a well of emotions. Everything I've held inside today comes pouring out.

"Rube . . ." I take a deep breath and try again, but instead of words, sobs emerge.

"Sierra? Oh sweetie, where are you? What's going on? Margaret's looking for you. She tried to reach you yesterday and again this morning and finally called me. Then I started calling you and couldn't reach you. Where are you? What's wrong? Sierra?"

I choke back another sob and, for lack of tissue, wipe my eyes and nose on my sleeve. "I'm . . . I'm okay. I'm at the hospital with Kaylee."

"Oh, Sierra, what happened?"

"Rube, can you come here? Can you . . . would you . . ." I take a deep breath. "I want you . . . here. Everything's okay . . . but I just want you here . . . you know?"

"I'm on my way."

I ask Ruby to stop by the bungalow and feed Van and let him inside for the evening and then I hang up. When I turn from the wall I've been facing, I see a man walk into the room where they've placed Kaylee. The doctor, maybe?

I wipe my eyes one more time and head for her room where I can see Charlene and another nurse lift Kaylee from the gurney onto a bed.

"She's light as a feather. She don't weight nothin' at all." Charlene shakes her head. "Oh, there you are. This gentleman is lookin' for you."

"Sierra Bickford?" He reaches to shake my hand and I'm struck by the size of him. He towers over my 5' 11" frame and his hand is twice the size of mine. He reminds me of a Viking. His glacier blue eyes are set in a tan, weathered face and his smile is warm and welcoming. I'm keenly aware of my disheveled appearance and wish I'd glanced in a mirror at some point today. But then, that's ridiculous.

"Yes, I'm Sierra."

"I'm Peter Langstrom, with Child Welfare Services." He hands me a card and I note the *PhD* after his name.

"Doctor of?"

"Psychology."

A shrink? Great.

"I've been assigned to . . ." He opens a file folder and glances at a sheet of paper. "Kaylee's case. I spoke briefly with Officer Mackenzie and he gave me your name and suggested I talk with you. Do you have a moment? I'd like to ask you a few questions."

"Sure."

"How well do you know the child?"

"We just met recently. I encountered her in a forested area near Bonny Doon. It seemed strange to me that she was alone. So I returned several times until I figured out where she lived. In the meantime, I filed an initial report with Child Welfare Services."

"Yes, I have that information on the report you filed. I understand she doesn't speak?"

"No, she doesn't. But she communicates—she writes." I think

of Kaylee's notes and smile. "She's smart too—quite the vocabulary." I pause a moment then risk the question nagging at me. "What will happen to her? Where will she go?"

"I'll need to speak with her doctor and determine how long she needs to be here. Probably won't be more than a day or two. But I want her checked thoroughly. We'll see if there's a medical reason for her lack of speech. Although, based on what it appears she's been through, it's likely an anxiety disorder. Then she'll be placed either in a residential treatment facility or in foster care—likely with a family licensed for emergency care. In the meantime I'll begin an investigation, search for her parents or extended family. If we don't find anything or if the parents aren't stable, then she'll be placed in another home. A more permanent situation. And, of course, we'll work with her and the foster family to provide for her needs."

"What about the abuse? How do you deal with that?"

"Counseling."

"Do you do that?"

"Not directly, although I'll assess her as I interview her and interact with her, and I'll work with the foster family to help them understand her needs." He consults his notes again. "I understand she's made reference to her mother?"

"She doesn't seem to know where she is. Kaylee said her mom has amnesia—or at least she thinks she does."

"Maybe Kaylee needed to make sense of it, to protect herself emotionally by devising a scenario that accounts for her mother's absence. Hard to say at this point . . ." He turns and looks at Kaylee and then back at me. His features soften and I see concern, and tenderness maybe, and something else, something that reminds me of my daddy.

Maybe it's that sense of familiarity that encourages me to delve deeper. "Is there . . . I mean . . . do you ever . . . could . . ."

I notice a slight crinkling of the skin around the outside corners of his eyes and realize he's trying not to smile at my stumbling. I feel the heat of a blush climbing from my neck to my face and feel disgusted with my inability to string together a simple sentence. I'm unaccustomed to pushing through choking emotions. I take a deep breath and begin again. "Dr. Langstrom, is it possible that Kaylee could be placed with me? We've developed a rapport. I believe she feels safe with me." I feign confidence I don't feel. "Wouldn't it be less traumatic for her to stay with someone she already knows?"

Before he has a chance to answer, I notice Kaylee stirring. She lifts her head and looks toward me. I see questions and confusion on her face.

"Excuse me . . ." I step around him to the side of Kaylee's bed. She's laid back down and her eyes are closed again. I place my hand on her forehead and brush her hair away from her face. "I'm here, Kaylee, you're doing great."

I see her eyes flutter, but they don't open until the nurse pokes her. I hold onto her as she tries to pull away from Charlene and then continue to soothe her by stroking her forehead.

She finally looks at me and focuses. I see recognition—and what I hope is relief—in her eyes. She tries to smile but her lips are dry and cracked. Oh, how I want to alleviate her pain, no matter how small. She's already suffered more than I can imagine, or want to imagine.

"May I give her something to drink?"

Charlene gives her permission and I step to the sink and fill a paper cup with water, and then offer Kaylee a few sips. I help lift her head and hold the cup to her mouth. She's fully awake now and her gaze as she watches me is intent. How I wish I knew what she's thinking and feeling.

I set the cup on a tray near the bed and then place my hand back on her forehead. I want, through my touch, to infuse her with strength, and peace, and love. I want to transfer all that's in my heart into hers. I want to gather her to myself and never let go

—never let anyone harm her again. The draw I feel toward her is strong, visceral, undeniable.

"Ms. Bickford?"

I startle at the sound of his voice—I'd forgotten he was here. I turn back to Dr. Langstrom. "Yes, I'm sorry. About my question . . ."

I see him look again at Kaylee and then back to me. He seems to weigh his words. "Placing her with you isn't outside the realm of possibilities, however, we'd need to do a background check, get approval, that type of thing. But at this point I don't have enough information to make such a recommendation. Let's take it one day at a time, all right? I've left instructions for the doctor to call me once Kaylee's been examined. We'll go from there."

He reaches for my hand again. His grip is strong, sure. "I'll check back in with Kaylee later this evening. Nice to meet you, Ms. Bickford."

"It's Sierra . . ."

"I'm Pete. I'll talk to you again soon." With that he turns and leaves the room, and it seems there's more air to breathe with him gone. I take another deep breath and note the rapid beating of my heart.

It's not outside the realm of possibilities . . .

I walk back to the bed and place my hand on Kaylee's shoulder. I realize again how little I know about her . . . how little I understand. I may want her, but there's no guarantee she'll want me.

 aylee

"SORRY, I forgot. If you do something—you do it all the way. There's never any middle ground with you!"

"Shh . . . you're going to wake her up. Good grief, Ruby! One minute you're bothered because I've shut down, the next minute you're upset because I've opened up—because I'm willing to try again—to love again."

"It's not that. You know it's not that. I just think you should take it slow. I don't want to see you hurt again. Oh, Sierra, this all happened so fast. You just got a dog. Give yourself some time. A child is a huge responsibility."

Sierra and someone named Ruby are sitting in the corner of the room. They're whispering, but they're not very quiet. I feel bad pretending to be asleep when I'm really not, but they're talking about me. About what's going to happen to me. I want to open my eyes and see what Ruby looks like, but I can't. Not yet.

Sierra's talking again. She's harder to hear than Ruby.

"I know it's fast. But remember what you told me, 'God has a plan. Why not just go with it this time and see what happens?' I think this is what happens. I can't explain it, Ruby, but I think He's given me glimpses today of what He's doing—how He's drawn Kaylee to me, drawn us together for . . . for . . . His purpose."

Sierra laughs a little and I hear her chair scoot back.

"Ruby, listen to me, I sound like my mother!"

"Your mother's a very wise woman, you know. And so are you."

I hear Ruby take a deep breath. She doesn't say anything for a minute. Then I hear her again.

"I'm sorry I got upset. It's just that I love you and want the best for you. I do trust your judgment. You've taken a risk following God again. You have. But He loves you so much . . . even more than I do. Sierra, this is *real* progress!"

I hear them both laugh.

"What? Better progress than Van? Hey, speaking of progress, did I mention the Viking?"

"The what?"

"Kaylee's social worker—he's a Viking."

A Viking? I picture a big man with blond hair and horns on the sides of his head. I don't know what a social worker does, but I don't think I want one with horns.

"Dare I ask how a Viking is progress?"

"He's a *cute* Viking."

They both giggle. The sound fills the room and makes me feel . . . happy.

"No, Sierra. No. That's too much in one day. Not a child *and* a man."

"I'm kidding. Anyway, there's probably a Mrs. Viking and little Vikings. And a man is the last thing I need." Sierra's voice gets serious again. "But he did seem . . . I don't know . . . like he'll be good for Kaylee. Like he really cares."

Good for me? How will he be good for me? What's he going to do to me? Why do I need a social worker?

I'm tired of listening.

I sit up and push the button on the side of the bed with a picture of a light bulb on it. The lights over the bed come on and both Sierra and the other lady look over at me.

"Hey, you, how do you feel?" Sierra gets up and comes over to the bed. She doesn't touch me this time. "You've had a good sleep and lots of fluids"—she points to the IV bag on the pole next to my bed—"Are you feeling better?"

I shrug my shoulders. I feel a little better. But right now I just want to know about the social worker. I pretend I'm holding a pencil in my hand and write something in the air. I need to ask a question.

"Oh . . . sure . . . hold on." Sierra reaches for the tray by the side of the bed and grabs a notebook and a pen. "I thought you might want these. I found them in the gift shop downstairs."

The notebook is bright pink and has sparkly silver stars on the front. The pen is pink too and the top is shaped like a star.

I open the notebook to the first blank page and run my hand across it—the paper feels clean and smooth. I hold it up to my nose and sniff. It smells like school and homework, like what normal smells like. I take the cap off the pen.

Are these for me?

"Yes, ma'am, I bought them for you. Ruby and I went down to the . . . oh wait, you haven't met Ruby. Kaylee, this is my friend, Ruby. My best friend. And Ruby, this is Kaylee—my . . . new friend."

Ruby's as sparkly as the notebook. It's hard not to stare at her . . . and I do for a minute. I've never met anyone with red hair, and her eyes are the color of a 7 Up bottle—clear green and shiny. Her earrings are long and dangly and have stones the same color as her eyes.

I look back at Sierra and write another note.

May I keep these? Are they really mine?

"Of course you can keep them. They're all yours. You can write whatever you want, but I was hoping you'd write me a few notes too."

I nod. I will. I need to know things.

What's a social worker?

I hand the notebook to Sierra and she and Ruby read my note. Then I see Ruby nudge Sierra with her elbow, nod her head toward the door, and whisper. "That, I'm guessing, is a social worker."

I look toward the door and see . . . a giant. Or a Viking, I guess. He is almost as tall as the door frame. Sierra stands and introduces us.

"Oh, Dr. . . . Pete. Kaylee was just asking about you. Kaylee, this is your social worker." Sierra looks up at the man. "She's wondering what a social worker is . . . or does."

"Hi, Kaylee. I'm Pete. And you're . . . ?" He turns to Ruby.

Ruby sticks out her hand and introduces herself. "I'm Ruby Morrissey—a friend of Sierra's."

"Ruby Morrissey? The artist?"

"Yes."

"I've seen your work. It's amazing. You capture the essence of humanity—the psyche of your subjects."

As the man talks to Ruby and smiles, I start to get it. He's social. That must be part of the work he does.

Ruby smiles and looks at Sierra. "Doctor of?"

"Psychology." Sierra rolls her eyes and gives Ruby a goofy look.

"Am I missing something?"

The social worker looks confused.

"Ruby's a frustrated psychologist at heart. You two should get along nicely."

Ruby swats Sierra's arm, then talks to the man again. "Thanks for the compliment. It's rewarding when someone sees beneath the clay."

The social worker turns back to me. "So, Miss Kaylee, you're looking lovely tonight. Much better than earlier. Do you feel better?"

I lean my head way back and look at his face. There are lots of lines and wrinkles, but they look like the kind you get from smiling lots—the kind my grammy had. He's probably near the same age as Sierra and Ruby. Maybe a little older than my mom.

I nod my head. Yes, I feel better.

He walks over and grabs one of the chairs and pulls it to the side of the bed and sits down. "Might be easier to talk if you can see me. Let me tell you what I do and why I'm here, and then if you have questions, maybe you can jot them down for me. Will that work?"

Maybe. I nod my head but shrug my shoulders too. I'm not sure.

I listen while he explains about his job and why he's here. He tells me he's already started looking for my mom. He's doing an "investigation." He asks if I know what that is. I know:

in·vest·i·ga·tion—noun 1. the act or process of investigating or the condition of being investigated. 2. a searching inquiry for ascertaining facts; detailed or careful examination.

Then he asks if I have any other family besides my mom—a father maybe, or grandparents, aunts, uncles . . . anyone?

There's no one.

Then he tells me about leaving the hospital when the doctor says I'm ready—that I'll go live with the Foster family . . .

The Fosters? Who are they?

What about Sierra?

I reach for my notebook. I have to ask. But when I try to pull the cap off the pen, my hands start to shake, and they're so clammy that my fingers slip off the cap.

I see him, Pete, watching me. He's patient. He just waits.

But the more he watches me, the harder it gets. I start gulping for air. I gasp. I need air. My hands begin shaking.

"Kaylee, look at me, look at my eyes. Now, take one deep breath. Try again. One breath." He turns and waves to Sierra, like he wants her to come over here. "Sierra, I think Kaylee's feeling some anxiety. Would you hold her hand?"

Sierra reaches for my hand. She holds it in both her hands.

"All righty, Miss Kaylee . . . try again. One deep breath. That's it. Now another. Keep looking at me. Good. Good girl. One more breath. Great."

I take another breath and then another. Pretty soon I'm breathing almost like normal and my hands stop shaking.

"Kaylee, does that happen sometimes? Do you have trouble breathing? And feel shaky? Maybe sick to your stomach?"

I think about what he's asked and wonder how he knows.

I nod my head.

"Okay. I know it feels scary, but it's okay. You've had a hard time—a lot to deal with. And sometimes when things are hard, we get anxious, and our bodies react. In fact, I think that's why talking is hard for you too. There's nothing wrong with you. Your body is just reacting to the stress you feel because of the difficulties you've faced. You're great, but your circumstances haven't been great. Does that make sense?"

What he says makes me want to cry. I take another deep breath and keep looking at his face. Nothing's wrong with me? I'm not sure I believe him . . . but I want to.

"Now, did you want to ask me a question?" Pete points to my notebook.

I swallow once, twice, then nod my head.

"Good. Questions are good. But first, may I ask you a question? Sierra will stay right here, right next to you, okay?"

Nod.

"Were you ever able to talk?"

I feel my face get hot and I can't look at him. I just stare at the sheet on the bed and think back to before . . .

Yes, I could talk.

I nod again.

"But then something happened and talking became difficult?"

Another nod.

"Kaylee, that happens sometimes and it's okay. You'll talk again, when you feel ready. But for right now, don't worry about it. And if even writing your question is hard, that's okay too. There's no rush."

But there is a rush. I have to know about Sierra . . . Will I still get to see Sierra when I have to go live with the Fosters?

She's still holding my hand so I pull my hand out of hers and reach for the pen again. My hands shake just a little but not so much that I can't pull the cap off this time. I open the notebook and write.

What about Sierra?

I start to hand the notebook to Pete, but then pull it back and hold it against my chest. He seems nice, but . . . Finally, I realize I don't have a choice. If I want to know, I have to ask, so I hand him the notebook. I watch him read. Then he holds out his hand. "May I borrow your pen?"

He writes something on the page and then looks at Sierra. Before he hands the notebook back to me, he asks if it's okay if Sierra goes and sits back down with Ruby.

I grab her hand again. But then I nod my head and let go.

When I get the notebook back, I don't see an answer, just another question. But now I understand why he wrote it instead of just asking me. He wants me to be honest. And if my answer to his question is no, then it might hurt Sierra's feelings.

But the answer's not no.

Yes, I like her. She's

I think for a minute . . .

phenomenal and she's very responsible.

I hand him my answer.

I watch a smile start at his eyes and then spread across his whole face and then he laughs—a deep, big laugh. "Really?" He puts his hand out for the pen again.

When I get the notebook back, I smile too. He says if she's that great, he'll have to get to know her better. He also told me I'd still get to see her—maybe even a lot.

"Miss Kaylee, thank you for this nice exchange. I do believe it's past my bedtime, so I'll be on my way." Then, he holds out his hand, just like he did when he met Ruby—just like I'm a grown-up.

I hold out my hand and let him take it. He shakes it. "Good night, missy. I'll be back in the morning . . . but not too early. I'll let you get your beauty sleep." Then, he puts his huge hand on top of my head and messes up my hair.

I like him.

And he doesn't have horns.

CHAPTER TWENTY-SEVEN

ierra

IT's past midnight by the time I leave the hospital. I want to stay, but Pete, before he left, advised me to let the night nurses do their job. He told me to get some sleep, to "give Kaylee some space."

Space . . . The word echoes in my mind like the trill of a lone hawk in a desolate canyon. *Space.* Did she ask for it? What did she write in her notes to him? Did she ask that I leave?

Doubt—a whirling vortex—sucks me into its depths.

Instead of turning toward home, I turn toward the ocean and head for the lighthouse on the point. I pull into the deserted parking lot, turn my headlights off, and stare into the inky night. I crack my window open and listen to the crash of surf meeting shore. Stars shimmy overhead and their dance allures. The beauty woos me, calls to me, and my fingers tingle.

The feeling is familiar—the need to work, to create. I long to splash emotions across a canvas. To daub, dabble, and dot my doubt in shapes and patterns. To release unspoken thoughts and feelings and see them take form.

Sleep? Sleep won't come this night. Instead I will work. I must work.

I think of the unfinished canvas in my studio. I back out of the parking lot and return the way I came. The streets between the lighthouse and home are empty, quiet—yet the short drive seems eternal.

~

MORNING FINDS me standing outside the Santa Cruz Public Library. I pace back and forth in front of the locked doors and check my watch again: 9:58 a.m. It opens at 10:00 a.m. *exactly*, evidently. My pacing is as much from impatience as from the caffeine coursing through me. A pot of coffee sustained me as I worked last night, but now my heart is racing and my patience waning. Finally I see a woman inside, keys dangling from one hand, heading toward the door.

"Good morning! Happy reading!"

Her greeting is much too chipper for me, a woman who hasn't slept for two nights running. "Morning. Is the reference desk open yet?"

"Of course! Follow me."

As I worked on the abstract of the redwood last night, questions nagged. How do redwoods survive after a fire like the one that hollowed Kaylee's tree? What gives it the ability to sustain such a wounding and continue to flourish? Why, in the forest, do they often grow in circles? What lessons do the redwoods hold? I intend to find out.

I also want to check out a few books for Kaylee—maybe a book or two will take her mind off her troubles. Once I reach the counter, I reach into my backpack and dig for my sketchbook. I jotted notes from the slips of paper I read in Kaylee's jar and I want to refer to those now.

"How may I assist you?"

I glance back at the librarian and almost chuckle out loud when I see that she's placed glasses on the end of her nose. Her inquisitive eyes peer at me over the rims.

I open the sketchbook and find what I'm looking for. "Um, I'm wondering . . . are you familiar with a book about a boy named James? I believe he has two aunts . . . Aunt Sponge and Aunt Spike."

"Spiker. It's Aunt Spiker. Of course I know it!" She claps her hands with glee, and I take a step back from the counter overwhelmed by her exuberance. "It's *James and the Giant Peach*, of course!"

"Ah . . . of course. What about a book called *Mandy*, by Julie Edwards?"

"Yes. Yes. Charming little story. Such talent! She sings, acts, and writes!"

I feel my eyes glazing over as I try to think who she might be talking about.

"Julie Edwards. You know, Julie Andrews! *The Sound of Music* . . . *Mary Poppins!* Edwards is her married name, and her pen name."

"I see. Well, yes, I'd like to find those books along with anything else you might suggest for a young girl."

"How old is she? What are her interests?"

"Um . . . well . . . she's . . . uh . . . maybe ten or so, but she's really smart. And she likes . . ." Of course, I have no idea what she likes. "Well, I think she likes the two books you've mentioned, so anything else you might have in similar genres would be fine."

"Oh, there are so many to choose from! But yes, of course, several come to mind right away. *The Secret Garden*, *The Anne of Green Gables* series. Oh and *Little Women!* Has she read *Little Women?*"

"*Little Women?* I don't know. But sure, *Little Women* sounds great. I'm also looking for information on redwoods . . . some research I'm doing."

"Redwoods? Oh, they're a fascinating species, aren't they?!"

Is there anything she doesn't know?

Fifteen minutes later I walk to my Jeep under the weight of six or seven books.

When I walk into Kaylee's room, I'm pleased to see more color in her cheeks and the dark crescents under her eyes seem to have faded some, but the bruise on her cheek is still visible, although it's more yellow than purple this morning.

She's sitting up with a tray in front of her laden with breakfast items: Cold cereal, hot oatmeal, bacon, pancakes, orange juice, and milk.

"Wow! That's quite a breakfast. You must be feeling better."

She smiles at me, a mustache of milk above her lip. For the first time, she looks like the child she is. For just a moment I see nothing in her face or eyes but contentment.

Then she points to the pile of books I'm holding.

"I stopped by the library. Do you like to read?"

I set the books on the table next to her bed and pull out the ones I chose for her. I hand her *James and the Giant Peach* and *Mandy* first.

She takes the books—her touch is gentle. She rubs one hand over each of the covers and then opens one of the books and holds it up to her nose and sniffs. She closes the books and touches each one again. She fingers the pages, and smiles at the pictures on the covers.

Finally, she looks from the books back to me. Her face is earnest, thoughtful, almost like she wants to say something. I wait . . . hopeful. But instead she just smiles. A wide, open smile. And she nods her head up and down.

"You're . . . welcome." I clear my throat and turn so she won't see the emotion her smile evoked. I busy myself with the other books, thumbing through them until I'm composed.

When I look back up from the pile of books, I see that she's holding *Mandy* close to her chest while eyeing the other books on her bedside table.

"Here, I got one more for you. *Little Women.* Have you read it?"

She shakes her head, no. She looks at me, eyebrows raised, and points to the other books.

"Oh, I'm doing some research on redwood trees. I'm an artist . . . I paint, sort of. It's hard to explain. I'll show you sometime." I shrug my shoulders and look at my feet. I've always found it difficult to explain that which is so personal to me. "Anyway, I'm working on a project now. Actually . . . it's your tree . . . in a way . . ."

Kaylee opens the drawer of the bedside table and grabs for her notebook and pen. I watch her scrawl something on a blank page and wait for her to hand it to me.

Once she's finished I take the note she holds out to me and read:

Redwoods are resilient.

I look at her, my mouth likely hanging open. "Exactly . . ."

She reaches for one of the books on redwoods and looks at me, eyebrows raised again. "You want to look at it? Sure, here, take it. Are you finished eating?" I take a napkin off the tray and dip it in a glass of water. I notice her watching my every move. "I'm going to wipe the milk off your face." I move toward her slow, cautious—as though she's a bird about to take flight. I've noticed she startles easily. I dab at her face just above her mouth and try to read her expression. But as soon as I touched her, she lowered her eyes and now they're veiled by her thick lashes. Once I'm finished, I move the tray away from her bed.

"May I look at that one?" I point to *James and the Giant Peach.* "I've never read it." I'd prefer to read *Mandy* . . . to find out why it's clutched close to her heart. But I don't want to take it from her. I sit in the chair next to her bed and we read in companionable silence. I yawn, once, then twice, and wonder what it is she likes about James and his evil aunts? Maybe she relates to James and the abuse he endures.

What a horrible thought.

CHAPTER TWENTY-EIGHT

 aylee

I LOVE the weight of the books on my lap. I like the way they feel and smell and I love all the words. So many words! I can't believe she brought me books—and my favorites! How did she know? I read a sentence and then, without moving my head, I look at her out of the corner of my eye to make sure she's still there. I don't want her to leave. I keep looking over to make sure she's there.

She keeps yawning and her head is bobbing up and down.

When I see her mouth drop open a little and her breathing becomes steady, I set down the book I'm holding and study her. I don't stare, exactly, because Emily Post would say that's rude. Instead, I just notice things about her. First, I notice her hands. They're resting on top of the book that's open on her lap. Her nails are short and it looks like there's something on a few of them—something shiny, but it doesn't look like polish. I see the same shine in patches on her hands and wrists too. It looks like glue that's dried on her skin. I remember that she's an artist—

maybe she uses glue. Her right hand twitches. The backs of her hands are dotted with freckles and I can see veins through her skin. They look like strong hands, hands that can take care of things.

There's a smattering of freckles on her face too, just across her nose. That means there's just a few here and there. She's pretty. Her lashes are long and darker than her hair. When her eyes are open, they're blue, sort of. Sometimes they're green. Sometimes gray. They change. And when she looks at me, I see things in her eyes, like maybe she's worried about me or maybe even like . . . like maybe she could even love me someday.

I want her to love me.

I look at her hair, the way it hangs over her shoulders and back. I remember how heavy it was when I braided it.

I decide I'll remember every little thing about her. Just in case . . .

Please don't go away. Please. I want you to love me. Please love me. I think these things while I look at her. I repeat the words in my mind over and over. Maybe, somehow, she'll understand. Maybe if I try hard enough, I can transfer my thoughts to her mind—like a Vulcan mind meld. I saw that on a rerun of *Star Trek* once when we lived with Brent.

But then I feel my face get warm and breathing gets hard again. I look from Sierra back to the book in my lap—the words, through my tears, seem to swim across the page.

Why would she love me? Or want me?

And what about my mom?

Thinking about my mom again makes me feel the same way I felt the time I snuck into Grammy's kitchen and took a cookie before dinner even though she'd told me I had to wait.

"Hey, missy, why the long face?"

I jump, even though he just whispers. I didn't know he was here. I wonder how long he's been leaning against the wall by the door.

"Looks like someone had a long night. I'll try not to wake her. You looked pretty deep in thought. Everything okay?" Pete walks around to the other side of my bed.

I shrug. Things are sort of okay.

Then he motions to the book I was looking at. "May I?"

I nod. "Redwoods? Doing some research, Miss Kaylee?" His whisper is raspy and makes me smile. I point to Sierra. "Ah . . . so she likes redwoods, huh?" I shrug again.

"And what are you reading?" I reach for the books Sierra brought for me and show them to him. "*Mmm* . . . good choices." He puts the books down and looks at me. "At least it looks like you slept well last night. More than we can say for our friend snoring in the chair."

Sierra's head jerks up and her eyes open for a second, but then they close again and her head bounces a couple of times and finally rests on her left shoulder. Pete and I look at each other and laugh. I feel my laugh in my chest, but I keep all the sound inside me.

"Wow. She'll have a kink in her neck when she wakes up, won't she? We better not leave her like that for too long."

Just then Sierra's head bobs again and she lets out a loud snorting sound. The sound must wake her up because her eyes open and stay open this time. She looks at us for a minute, and then I notice her cheeks turn a deep pink.

"Good morning." Pete stops and looks at his watch. "Actually it's almost afternoon. You look like you could use a cup of coffee."

Sierra runs her hands through her long hair. "Um . . . coffee . . . yes. How . . . how long have you been watching me sleep?"

"Oh . . ." Pete looks at his watch again. "Not more than an hour or so—"

"What?!"

Pete laughs again. "No. Just a few minutes. You looked like you needed the sleep. I didn't want to wake you. But now that you are awake, how about a cup of coffee? I'd like to discuss a few things with you. The cafeteria, maybe?"

"Sure. Kaylee, do you mind? Can we bring you anything?"

I shake my head.

I know they're going to talk about me, about what to do with me. My palms get sweaty when I think about it. What if they put me in an orphanage? I've read about orphanages. They're cold and dark and they only feed you runny oatmeal and stale bread. The people are mean too.

I guess it would still be better than living with him, but, what about my mom and what about Sierra?

I watch as Pete and Sierra turn to leave the room. I want to tell Pete something. One word drops from my mind to my throat. I can feel it there, pushing its way to my mouth. *Stop!* I have to tell him to stop. I have to tell him something! My tongue moves to the roof of my mouth as I form the "*S*" but then I stop. I swallow. And the word is gone.

And so are Pete and Sierra.

CHAPTER TWENTY-NINE

ierra

PETE MAKES small talk on our way down to the cafeteria, which is fine with me. I still feel groggy and more than a little embarrassed at waking and finding him staring at me. Once there, we find a table and he pulls out a chair for me and then promises to return with two cups of coffee. I fold my hands on top of the table and notice traces of matte medium under my nails and on my hands. I move my hands from the table to my lap and determine to leave them where he can't see them.

But then, who cares, really? Will a little glue keep the county from placing Kaylee in my care?

Because that, I've determined, is exactly what I want.

I want to take care of her. The thought is absurd even to me, or maybe especially to me. Ten days ago I didn't even know she existed. But I keep returning in my mind to those moments as I watched the paramedics loading her into the ambulance. The impression, the sense, was so strong. So sure. We're meant to be together—I'd bet on it.

Although, even as I make that bet, a ripple of fear quivers through me. I know loving Kaylee will cost me.

I pull a band from my pocket and gather my hair into a loose ponytail, then I rub my fingers under my eyes in case the little bit of mascara I bothered with this morning ended up beneath my eyes as I dozed. I watch Pete approach from across the cafeteria. He holds two steaming paper cups in his large hands. I'm taken again by the size of him.

He sets one of the cups in front of me along with packets of creamer, sugar, a stir stick, and a napkin.

"Thanks. Were you a waiter in a former life?"

He chuckles and pulls out the chair across from me and eases into it, stretching his long legs under the table. "Waiting tables got me through college." He takes a sip of his coffee. "So . . . I thought I'd let you know where things stand this morning. Kaylee's doctor will release her tomorrow. He reported evidence of both sexual and physical trauma—bruising, a bladder infection. She's undernourished. She'll leave with some nutritional needs and a prescription for antibiotics. Other than that, she'll be fine. Physically."

"What about her speech?" I stay focused, tucking the information I've heard away for later. I can't let myself think about what Kaylee's suffered.

"The doctor says, medically, there's no reason for her lack of speech. It's likely a psychological issue. As you heard me tell Kaylee yesterday, extreme anxiety can cause a child to stop speaking. Typically we see it in kids who struggle with anxiety in specific situations, say school for instance. The child will stop speaking at school but may seem fine at home. They communicate where they feel safe. Occasionally we see a case like Kaylee's where a child stops speaking all together. We likely can't imagine the anxiety and trauma she's faced. She needs a safe environment to heal."

"Where"—I take a deep breath—"will she be placed?" I pick at the glue on my hands.

"We have a foster family who's licensed for emergency care on standby."

"I see." I look down at my hands in my lap so he won't see the disappointment I feel.

"No, I don't think you do, actually."

His tone is kind, thoughtful, so I glance back at him and try to read his expression.

"They're on standby, but I'd like to place Kaylee with you."

"Oh." I want to say more but can think of nothing. Forgetting about the glue, I reach for the stir stick laying on the napkin next to my cup.

"Sierra, there's an obvious connection between the two of you. I'm encouraged that she's communicating with you. Kaylee thinks you're, in her words, 'phenomenal,' oh, and also 'responsible.'" He grins and raises his eyebrows. "Not bad."

I smile at her description.

"Sometimes, in my job, I have to go on what my gut tells me. And my gut says she's better off with someone she's already established a relationship with, no matter how brief your acquaintance. As I said, her willingness to communicate with you is a good sign."

"So what do I do? I mean, there must be procedures for this kind of thing."

"You bet. We need to have you checked out, and fast. I took the liberty of scheduling a background check and a home inspection this afternoon, if you agree. The county always wants to place a child with someone they know and are comfortable with, if we have that option."

"A background check?" I twist the stir stick around my index finger.

"You look hesitant . . ." He cocks his head to one side as if considering what I might be hiding. "Anything I should know about?"

I swallow. "Well . . . It's just . . ." I clear my throat and take a deep breath. "I . . . had a daughter . . ." While staring at the coffee stirrer, I struggle for words I've rarely spoken aloud. "She was born twelve years ago. Premature. I . . . I lost her after only nine days." I take another breath and make my confession: "I was in college . . . young . . . um, and I was . . . using when I got pregnant."

"How long have you been clean?"

I look up again to read his face. I expect judgment but see none. *He's a good actor,* I think.

"Twelve years."

"No relapses?"

"None. I'll never . . . I'm done with that kind of thing."

"Arrest record? Anything like that?"

"No."

He pauses and seems to search my face. I assume he's running me through some psychological filter so his next question surprises me.

"Sierra, do you believe in redemption?"

"Redemption?"

"Yes. It's when—"

"I know what it is."

"Good." He reaches toward me and I feel my shoulders stiffen. His hands, twice the size of mine, take my hand in his and I watch as he unwraps the red piece of plastic from around my finger. I feel the heat of a blush creeping up my neck as the blood rushes back into my finger. He takes the lid off his coffee cup and drops the stick inside, then stuffs the lid inside the cup. "Will 4:00 this afternoon work for you?"

"Sure."

~

WHEN WE WERE TEENAGERS, Jeff and I swore Mother had ESP. If I snuck in late after a date, Mother would remind me of my curfew the next morning. If our grades were slipping, Mother called us on it before we mentioned it. If Daddy came in from the fields unexpectedly, Mother had put on lipstick and a splash of cologne five minutes before he walked in the door. "I just had a feeling . . ." she'd say.

So when I drive into my driveway at 2:30 p.m. and see a car with rental plates parked along the curb and a woman sitting on my front step, I'm surprised, but not shocked.

"Margaret? Mother?" I call from the driveway.

She stands, brushes off her camel-colored slacks, and smiles. "Hello, darling."

Her graying hair is still streaked with gold and is pulled into a French twist. Small pearls dot her lobes and a navy cardigan is draped over her shoulders.

"Something told me it was a good time for a visit. I hope you don't mind. I tried to call but couldn't reach you." She's talking as she walks toward me, then stops and embraces me. Her hug, like her, is quick, strong, and efficient. For years I've shied away from such displays of affection, but today I hug her back. Actually, I cling to her.

When I let go, she steps back and with a practiced eye looks me up and down. "You haven't slept."

"No."

She reaches into the Jeep and grabs my backpack. "I think a cup of tea is in order."

I follow her to my front door, hand her the key, and follow her into my kitchen where she washes her hands and sets the teapot to boil.

"How long are you staying? Where are your bags?"

"They're in the boot. We'll get them shortly. I'm staying as long as you want or need me."

"How . . . how did you know? I mean, how did you know I needed you? I didn't even know until I saw you."

"Teacups?"

"Top shelf, behind the plates. I don't use them much. There are mugs on the bottom shelf."

She turns on her heel and searches my face. "A mug? Without a saucer?"

"Mother . . . ?"

"Oh yes, how did I know? I spoke to Ruby, of course."

So much for ESP or some mystical connection between mother and daughter.

"She told me about the child. That there was a possibility she'd come here to live." She falters. "Sierra, are you . . ."

She is so seldom unsure. Her squared shoulders relax, droop even. In that moment I realize the burden she's borne for me, her child, all these years.

"Am I ready for this?"

The whispered words fall between us.

Not since Annie's death have I delved beneath the surface with my mother. I take a breath and dive deep. "I don't know if I'm ready. But I know I'm not who I was two weeks ago." I take a step closer to my mother. "I'm . . . I'm changing. Something happened when I met her. Something in me . . . changed. She needs me. She needs someone to take care of her, someone to . . . love her. Mother . . . I can't imagine what . . . what she's been through. You and Daddy would never have let those things happen to me."

My mother closes the distance between us. She reaches up and holds my face in her hands and wipes the tears from my cheeks. Then she embraces me and I'm five years old all over again, crying in my mother's arms, only this time it isn't a skinned knee or bruised elbow that draws my tears.

Today I cry for Kaylee's wounds.

CHAPTER THIRTY

aylee

I STILL CAN'T BELIEVE it's true, but Pete nods his head.

"It's true," he says like he can read my mind. "The county has decided to place you with Sierra. That means you'll live with her for now. Is that okay with you?"

I reach for my pad of paper fast and scribble my answer.

Yes!

Pete laughs and shakes his head. "All righty, Sierra it is, then." He pulls a chair next to my bed and sits down. "Kaylee, we'll keep looking for your mom, but in the meantime it's important that you have someone who will take care of you, someone you're comfortable with. I know you haven't known Sierra long, but I see a connection between the two of you."

I scribble another word on my pad and hand it to Pete.

Rapport.

He looks at me and raises one eyebrow. "Yes, missy, you and Sierra share a close rapport." He smiles and shakes his head.

He seems to think about something for a minute and then he says. "I think Sierra will be a sagacious caregiver."

I reach for my notebook and he hands it back to me. I smile at him and then write:

She's perspicacious.

I hold it up and watch his face as he reads it. He throws his head back and laughs and laughs.

Just then, Charlene pokes her head in the door. "Hey you two, keep it down in here. We got people tryin' to sleep." She winks at me before she walks back down the hallway.

Pete wipes his eyes. "Oh, Miss Kaylee, you're something else. I can't wait to hear those big words come out of your mouth."

~

THIS IS where you'll stay. It's your room." Sierra pats me on the back. "You can go in, Kaylee. It's okay. It's yours."

I look back at Pete, who barely fits in the small hallway, and at Mrs. Bickford, Sierra's mom. Van's tail thumps against my leg.

Pete winks at me and smiles. "You better take a look, Miss Kaylee. Make sure it meets your standards."

My own room? I take a few steps in. I can't believe how pretty it is. Light shines in through the open window over the bed and white curtains sway in the breeze. The bed is covered with bright colored pillows shaped like flowers. Sitting on the bed, in the middle of all the pillows, is a big stuffed bear. The bedspread is white, like the curtains. Next to the bed is a round table with a flowered cloth and a lamp on it, and something else . . . My jar!

I walk to the table and pick up the jar and look back at Sierra, who's standing in the doorway.

"I thought you might want it. I went up and got it this morning after Mother and Ruby and I fixed up your room."

Glittering at the bottom of the jar is my mom's locket with her initials on it: K. W. I unscrew the lid and dump the contents into my hand, pulling the locket out of the little pile. Then I put everything else back in the jar. I run a finger over the initials engraved on the little heart.

"Would you like to wear it? I'll put it on for you." Sierra, who is standing next to me now, holds out her hand. I give her the necklace and she reaches around my neck and fastens the clasp.

"It has your initials on it."

They're not my initials. They're my mom's initials. Our initials are the same, but this was her necklace. I haven't thought of my mom since I walked into Sierra's house. The little heart hanging around my neck is cold against my skin and a chill runs through me.

What if she comes back now? Of course, I still want her to come back. I do. I just haven't thought about it as much lately with everything else that's going on.

I turn and look at the rest of the bedroom. On the wall next to the bed is a low bookshelf made out of wood that matches the bed. I look at the books and the shelf and can hardly believe my eyes! There on the shelf are my books—my dictionary and the other two books sit on the top shelf, held up by two bookends that look like fat, funny mice. The two lower shelves are filled with books—most of them look old. I turn and look at Sierra.

"I found those books in your tree too. I thought you'd want them. The other books were mine—I had a box of books in my garage from when I was a child." Sierra bends and pulls one of the books off the shelf. "Nancy Drew was my favorite."

There are about ten of the Nancy Drew books all lined up,

each book has a number on it. I can't believe my books are here—
and that I have new books to read too.

In one corner of the room is a rocking chair. On the chair is a
blue backpack—it's just like Sierra's. I walk to the chair and pick it
up and look at Sierra again.

"It's for you. I thought you could keep your notebook and pen
in it, and whatever else you want."

I wonder if I can keep it—forever. Or will I have to give it back
when my mom comes? Will I have to give everything back? I look
around again. The room is amazing. Beyond amazing. It's
marvelous. It's stupendous! I can't believe it's mine.

"You put this together in record time." Pete leans into the room
as he talks to Sierra. Then he says to me. "Pretty nice digs, missy.
What do you think?" Pete looks at me, eyebrows raised.

I nod and smile. I can't believe I get to live here, in my own
room, in Sierra's house. I bend down and put my arms around
Van's neck and bury my face in his fur.

I don't want them to see me cry. With my face still buried in
Van's fur, I feel a hand on my shoulder.

"Kaylee, how about some dinner? Do you like macaroni and
cheese?"

I look up at Sierra and my stomach rumbles in response.
Sierra, Pete, and Mrs. Bickford all laugh when they hear it.

"I think that's your answer, Sierra." Pete bends down and takes
my elbow in one of his hands and helps me to my feet. "You're in
good hands, missy. I'll check back in with you tomorrow."

CHAPTER THIRTY-ONE

ierra

PROFESSIONALLY I'M KNOWN as a layerist. Though Ruby, in her frustration, says my art defines me—"deep, impenetrable layers"— I hope that's not true. Or at least is less true today than it was a few months ago. But there is something self-defining in the layering process that intrigues me. The process speaks to the hidden nuances, quirks, and even darkness in each of us. Often, when searching for the perfect words to incorporate into the collage I'm working on, I'll find just the opposite of what I want. Say "hate" versus "love"—I'll cut the word from the page where I've found it and glue it onto the canvas. Then, I layer over it, hiding the paradoxical truth.

My soul, I know, is made up of such paradoxes.

But now, with Kaylee, I'm learning to reverse the process. Instead of building layer upon layer, I'm gently peeling away the layers and exposing the truth underneath. I see this process taking place in both myself and Kaylee.

Emotions I'd long kept hidden are now exposed and the exposure leaves me feeling raw, vulnerable. I tell myself that as I shed each self-protective layer, growth is taking place and it is good, even when it hurts. But to watch it in Kaylee is harder. She's already gone through so much. At a stage in her life when she should feel secure in her trust of loving parents, she finds herself in the home of a stranger. Self-protection seems appropriate, and yet it keeps her from speaking. Oh, how I long to know what she's thinking and feeling. And slowly, as the layers fall away, even without words, I'm learning.

Most of our "conversations" take place on a pad of paper. Everything I know about her, beyond what I observe, I'm learning through her written words. But conversations without intonation and inflection often become a puzzle—a puzzle I must work with because it holds the very essence of life. Kaylee's life. So I watch for intonation, inflection. I'm learning it's there in the slump of her shoulders as she writes or in the jab of the pen when she adds an angry period to an otherwise innocuous sentence. I see it in the veil that drops over her eyes and face when I ask a question that's too deep, too painful for her to consider. Those questions stop all conversation, and I watch as she walks away from her pad of paper—sometimes with her little hands covering her ears.

I'm learning what to ask and what not to ask.

Although I long to hear Kaylee's voice, to know she's healing under my care, I'm also growing accustomed to the companionable silence we share. To some extent the silence suits me. It gives me the space I need to ponder the thoughts and feelings growing within since Kaylee's come to live with me. Thoughts left dormant too long. Thoughts of motherhood. I think of Kaylee's first night with me—of having her stand on a chair in front of the kitchen sink while I washed her hair, unabashed tears streaking my face and dripping into the sink as I gently massaged shampoo through the dark mass. All the while my mother looked on and shed her own tears. Then later, the tears Kaylee shed as I combed her wet hair. Tears she tried to hide.

I think of the nights I've tucked her into bed, covered her with sheet and blanket and then bent to brush a kiss across her forehead. The warmth of her breath against my cheek as I lean in thaws my soul. Those first nights I stood in the hallway outside her room, arms crossed over my chest trying to hold my own trembling body, so shaken was I by the simple acts of nurturing, of loving a child. Fulfilling a role snatched from me so early—one I thought I'd never know again.

Those nights, standing in her doorway, watching the rhythmic rise and fall of her chest, the house as still as a breezeless afternoon, I wondered what knowledge she held. What pain silenced her? As I watched her sleep I thought of what was torn from her. Her innocence, certainly, and so much more. Never will she know the wonder of giving the gift of her virginity to her husband on her wedding night. Instead, will she be plagued by haunting memories? I pray not.

Of course, then it occurred to me, neither will I know that wonder. But I gave myself away by choice. Kaylee had no choices, except perhaps the choice she made to disappear by no longer speaking.

I long to get to know Kaylee, to hear the melody of her voice, to have her put words to the expressions I see flutter across her face. Will my presence, my care for her, be enough? Can I provide the stability, security, and safety she needs to dare speaking again? This is my hope, my prayer. But as each day passes, my doubt grows—an invading cancer eating away at my fledgling faith.

I respect her silence but desire so much more for her.

At the end of each day, I sit with my mother who's brewed a pot of tea while I've tucked Kaylee in, and I share my yearnings for Kaylee and my fears that I'll fail her. I ask for my mother's opinions and advice based on what she's observed during the day. I unwind the day's events and emotions with her.

Our first days with Kaylee began early as she woke with the sun. I'd feel her presence more than hear her as she stood at my open bedroom door watching me sleep. I'd stir and even before opening my eyes, I'd know she was there. I'd sit up, focus, and see her little frame in the doorway. The first morning she turned away as though by watching me she'd been caught doing something she shouldn't. "Kaylee . . ." I whispered. "It's okay. Come back." I sat up and patted the edge of my bed. "Come sit with me a minute."

She turned back and took a couple of steps toward me, then hesitated.

"It's okay. C'mon." I patted the bed again.

She came and leaned against the side of the bed, her eyes lowered, focused on the floor.

"Did you sleep okay, little one?"

Her nod affirmed that she'd slept.

I glanced at my clock radio: 5:15 a.m. Good thing I was raised on a farm. I can keep farmers' hours, which are evidently the hours Kaylee keeps. "Are you ready to get up now?"

Another nod.

"Hey, kiddo—look at me." I waited for her to respond. When she finally turned her face toward me, it felt as though my heart skipped a beat—so touched was I by the vulnerability I saw on her face. One layer stripped away. I reached for her and placed my hand on her back and gently rubbed up and down. I felt her shoulders and back relax as I chattered about whatever came to mind. After a few minutes, she moved, reaching for something on the nightstand. She handed me the comb I'd laid there the night before, and I sat up and took a clump of her long hair in my hand and began stroking it with the comb.

This is how we began that day in her tree.

This became our morning routine.

By the end of the first week when I wake to her presence, she no longer waits for an invitation, but instead makes her way to the other side of my bed and crawls in. She turns her back toward me and I reach over and rub my hand up and down her back, feeling each bony knob of her spine. As I touch her, I am aware that she is unaccustomed to being touched appropriately with love, and I pray my touch will be a healing balm. Then, when she's ready, she sits up and I comb her hair, section by section. This becomes an act of love—a giving and receiving—something we share. By the time we get up, my mother has breakfast going in the kitchen.

At dinner one evening Mother tells us she's leaving in the morning.

"What?! How will I . . ." I stop before Kaylee sees the panic I feel rising within. *How will I do this alone? Who will I ask my questions? Who will listen to my fears? Who will be there waiting with a cup of hot tea at the end of another long day?*

"Oh, darling, you'll both be just fine." She turns and winks at Kaylee and then gives me her most reassuring smile. She reaches over and puts her hand on top of mine and mouths the words, "You're doing great" so Kaylee can't hear. My mother sees the panic I'm trying to hide.

After I tuck Kaylee into bed for the night, I return to the kitchen and the cup of tea I know will be waiting on the counter. My mother nods toward the cup, then pours one for herself. I follow her outside where we sit to discuss the day.

"I'm not ready for you to leave. Can't you stay a few more days?"

"Darling, you're more than ready. It's time. You don't need me."

"But—"

"But nothing, Sierra. You are doing great. You don't need me. You never really did." She reaches over and pats me on the back. "You're good for her, you know."

My mother's tone, often brisk, is now tender. I turn to look at her and see her love for me scrawled across her face.

"Thank you . . . for everything. I did need you here. I couldn't have done this without you. I needed . . ." I stare out at the shadowed yard and think of all my mother's done in the last week—cooking, cleaning, listening, and advising. But only when asked,

I realize. She's stayed in the background, helped but not intruded. Encouraged. Cheered me on in her own reserved way. "I needed to know you were here. I needed your encouragement."

"Sierra, you're a good mother. I've always known that about you."

Tears come to my eyes and my throat constricts, making it difficult to say anything more. My mother's support through difficult years has sustained me, I know. She's never judged me—only loved me. Even when I was at my worst, when all evidence pointed to complete failure in my life, my mother expected the best of me.

I whisper a choked "Thank you," then take a deep breath.

"I had the best example."

My mother reaches for my hand and holds it tight. We sit, holding hands, in companionable silence. We stare out at the shadowed yard, each lost in our own thoughts. Slowly, gratitude replaces my sense of panic. "I'll miss you . . ."

"I'm just a phone call away."

"I know."

"Sierra . . ." She turns to face me and squeezes my hand. "I'll miss being here. But I know you're in good hands."

I shake my head. "I know."

And in the still of that moment, I really do know.

CHAPTER THIRTY-TWO

 aylee

Everything here is different.

Even though things were bad at the cabin, I knew what to do there. Here, I have to learn everything all over again. And I realize I've forgotten some things.

Like manners.

I know all about manners, of course, because I read Emily Post's book. But I've forgotten to actually use what I know. You don't have to worry about manners when you're alone all the time. Even when I wasn't alone, when he was there, I didn't need manners, because he didn't have any anyway.

When we sat down for dinner the first night here, I almost didn't know what to do. I hadn't sat at a table to eat a meal in a long time. And the food all looked so good! My mouth watered and my stomach growled, so I reached for my fork and started to eat before I even put my napkin on my lap. And even before we said grace! If I don't use good manners, Sierra might not let me stay. So I'm working on remembering. When I have time, I'm reading *Etiquette* again so it's fresh in my mind. The dictionary defines *etiquette* as the conventional requirements for social behavior. But basically, it just means good manners.

So far, only Mrs. Bickford has said grace at meals. Now when we sit down at the table, I don't even look at the food until I've put my napkin on my lap and Mrs. Bickford has said, "In Jesus' name, we pray. Amen."

Mrs. Bickford must know Jesus like Grammy did.

I wonder if Sierra knows Jesus too?

I still wonder about the "Jesus Loves Me" song that Grammy taught me. Now that I'm here with Sierra, I wonder if maybe Jesus does still love me a little bit.

The other thing I'm learning is our routine. Mrs. Bickford says we need a routine. I like routines. I like doing the same things every day. That way you know what to expect. Like right now, it's 12:00, which means it's time for lunch.

"Kaylee, it's time for lunch." Sierra calls from the kitchen.

You can count on a routine.

I mark my place in the etiquette book and put it back on the shelf; then I head for the kitchen.

"Hi, little one. How are you?"

Most of the time Sierra asks me yes or no questions, things I can answer by nodding one way or the other. Otherwise, she'll tell me to get my notebook. But sometimes she'll ask me something else and look at me like she hopes I'll answer. I don't want to disappoint her. I would talk to her if I could. Honest.

"Hey . . . Kaylee, it's okay. Are you hungry?"

I nod.

"Did you enjoy reading?"

Nod again.

"Good."

I sit down at the table and notice there are only two places set. Mrs. Bickford went to church with Ruby this morning; but, I thought she'd be back by lunch time. I look from the table back to Sierra.

"Oh, Mother called. She and Ruby decided to go to lunch together after church."

I begin to wonder about Ruby and Sierra's mom. I know Sierra's mom lives in Texas so I wonder how she and Ruby got to know each other. I haven't seen Ruby again since that night in the hospital. I liked her. I hope she'll come over sometime.

"Mother and Ruby are pretty close. They got to know each other while Ruby and I were at art school." Sierra carries a bowl of soup and a plate with half a sandwich to the table and puts it in front of me. "Well, actually it was after art school that they became close." She walks back to the counter and gets her soup then sits down across from me. "Ruby and I have breakfast together at least once a week. Did I tell you that?"

I shake my head.

"We started that when we were roommates. She'll come over one day next week for breakfast."

Can Sierra read my mind?

"Sometime soon we'll go over there too and you can meet her husband, Michael. Ruby's a better cook than I am so we eat there more often than we eat here."

I take a bite of my soup. How can Ruby be a better cook than Sierra? Sierra's a gourmet. That means she cooks fancy food. The best I've ever had!

Every day since I've been here, which is five days now, I take a nap after lunch. Sierra says my body is still healing and that until I gain some weight and stop taking the medicine the doctor gave me, I'll probably need some extra sleep. So we have lunch, then I take a nap. That's part of the routine. After that what we do is a surprise, but that's part of the routine too. Yesterday we took Van on a walk to the beach. The day before that Mrs. Bickford and Sierra taught me how to play spoons. That was fun!

Tomorrow afternoon Sierra says I have to go back to the

doctor for a "follow-up appointment." She said the doctor wants
to make sure I'm eating well and that the cuts on my feet are
healing and that the infection I have is going away.

I don't like doctors very much. When I was in the hospital, the
doctor poked at every part of my body—even my private parts. He
told me he needed to check down there, but that Charlene, my
favorite nurse, would hold my hand. He said he wouldn't hurt me.
Sure enough, Charlene did hold my hand and talked to me the
whole time he was checking, but I couldn't listen to what she was
saying. I had to close my eyes. And I felt my face get hot and tears
rolled down my cheeks. I wondered if the doctor could tell—
would he know what *he'd* done to me?

Would the doctor know what I was?

After Sierra told me about having to go to the doctor again, I
reached for my pad of paper.

I'd prefer not to go to the doctor.

When I put the period at the end of the sentence, I hit the
paper hard with the point of the pen. I really don't want to go.

"You have to go. But it'll be okay. I'll go in with you."

Will I have to take my clothes off?

Sierra looks at me and seems to think for a minute. "Not this
time. He'll probably just have you take your flip-flops off and look
at your feet to make sure they're healing." Then she reaches down
and tickles the top of one of my feet. "And they're healing nicely,
so no problem there, little one. But before that, the nurse will
weigh you to see if you've gained some weight, and she'll take
your temperature. They always do that. Then the doctor will ask
you some questions and might listen to your chest with his
stethoscope."

What about the infection?

I don't tell Sierra this, but I'm not going if he has to check my private parts again.

"The bladder infection?" Sierra looks at me, and again it seems like she knows what I'm thinking. "It'll be okay, kiddo, you won't have to get undressed and the doctor won't have to check you. They'll just take a urine sample. And after your appointment I'll take you for a special treat."

A special treat? That will be the surprise part of our routine.

I guess it will be okay.

My favorite part of our routine is bedtime. Every night, after I wash my face and brush my teeth, Sierra tucks me in. First, I sit on the side of the bed and let her comb my hair. She takes long, careful strokes. "Your hair is smooth as silk, little one." Then, before I go to sleep, she reads to me. She knows I can read by myself, but she says she likes to read to me—to share the story together. I climb into bed and get under the covers, and then Sierra lies next to me on top of the covers with a pillow behind her to prop her up. I like having her next to me. Last night I fell asleep listening to her voice as she read. I don't like it when I fall asleep when she's reading because then I miss the best part—the part of the routine where when she's done reading, she leans over and kisses my forehead and says. "Good night, little one. Sleep well." Or sometimes she says. "Sweet dreams, kiddo."

I like it when she calls me *little one* or *kiddo*. Those are her special names for me. No one's ever had a special name for me before.

I like it here.

I like learning our routine.

After lunch Mrs. Bickford comes back and finds us in the kitchen doing dishes. She sets her purse, a big book, and a paper on the kitchen table. "Tea anyone?"

Sierra says she doesn't want any, then Mrs. Bickford looks at me and I nod. I love her tea—she makes mine special with lots of milk and honey. She walks to the cabinet and gets two cups and saucers and two dessert plates and sets them on the table. Then she goes to one of the drawers and pulls out two cloth napkins; she folds them and puts them next to the plates. She gets out the milk and pours it into a small pitcher and places it, along with a jar of honey on the table. She sets another plate in the middle of the table with shortbread cookies and nut bread on it.

Emily Post would like Mrs. Bickford.

I help her arrange things on the table, adding two spoons next to the plates and a glass dish with jam in it; then I move her purse and things to the counter. I notice the book says *Holy Bible* on the front—it looks like one Grammy had. The paper is sort of like a brochure and has a picture of a church on the front of it. On the bottom there's today's date and a sentence: "In the beginning was the Word, and the Word was with God, and the Word was God." Then there's a man's name, John, and two numbers 1:1.

I read the sentence again and then reach for the pad of paper and pen that Sierra keeps on the kitchen counter for me. I write down the sentence along with the man's name and the numbers, then I tear the page off the pad and fold it up and put it in my pocket.

"There's our whistle, darling. Ready for your tea?"

CHAPTER THIRTY-THREE

ierra

KAYLEE?" I call down the hallway. She pokes her head out her bedroom door and looks at me. "It's Ruby's turn to come here for breakfast, would you like to help me?"

She nods and follows me back to the kitchen. I open a cabinet and pull out three plates. "How about if you set the table." I hand her the plates. "You know where everything is, right? If you need something just ask." I pat her pad of paper sitting on the kitchen counter.

She nods.

"The fork goes on the left and . . ."

She holds up her hand like a traffic cop. Her message is clear. *Stop. I know.*

"Okay, okay!"

I laugh to myself. In the month since she's been here her personality is coming through more and more. She is independent, but then, I suppose she's had no other choice. But sometimes, like now, her independence is spunky. There's verve to her that I'm beginning to see and love. And honestly, with that vocabulary of hers, and other things too, she's quirky. I love that about her too.

As I whisk eggs with half and half, grate cheese, and slice green onions for the quiche, and slice grapefruits in half, I hear drawers and cabinets opening and closing behind me. She pulls one of the kitchen chairs to an upper cabinet, stands on it, and reaches for something up high. Then I hear the clink of glasses and the clank of silverware. She goes out to the backyard for something and comes back in. She asks no questions, just busies herself with her job.

I think of the day ahead. Breakfast first, then Kaylee's appointment with Dr. Beth—Bethany Petrovoski, the child psychiatrist appointed by CWS. She has the "kids," as she refers to her patients, call her Dr. Beth rather than having them struggle with her last name. "They have enough to struggle with as it is," she explained when we first met just over two weeks ago.

That first meeting. That was . . . interesting.

With damp palms gripping the steering wheel, I'd pulled into Dr. Beth's office parking lot. A dozen questions raced through my mind. *What will she ask me? How much of my background will she want to cover? Will she approve of Kaylee living with me?* And on and on . . .

I took a deep breath, shook my head a bit hoping to clear my mind, and then put the Jeep into Park. "How bad can it be, Sierra?" I gave myself a little pep talk as I walked toward her office until it occurred to me that I'd look crazy talking to myself! I peered toward the suite with her name on the door and prayed she wasn't looking out the window.

But my concerns were unfounded. Dr. Beth was warm, welcoming, and accepting. When I left her office that afternoon, she stopped me at the door and put her hand on my arm. "Sierra, from everything you've told me and from Pete's reports, it's evident to me that Kaylee feels safe with you. It's that sense of safety that will promote her healing."

"Hey, girls . . . Good morning!"

Ruby's greeting interrupts my reverie. She lets herself in and calls to us as she breezes through the living room to the kitchen, her ankle-length gauze skirt flowing with her. She stops in front of the kitchen table and stares. "Wow! Who did this?" She looks from me to Kaylee and puts her arm around Kaylee's shoulders and gives her a quick squeeze. "Hey you, good to see you again."

I look at the table. "Wow . . . Kaylee . . ." The setting looks like something from a magazine or a fine restaurant. While I was lost in my thoughts and breakfast preparations, she dug out my only matching place mats and cloth napkins. The napkins are folded in triangles that look like sails from a boat and are set atop each plate. But that's not all. A stemmed water goblet is situated just above the knife on the right, along with a juice glass at each setting and teacups with saucers placed to the right above the fork. There are regular knives, forks and spoons, all appropriately placed, along with—

"What are these?" I pick up a spoon with a serrated tip. "Grapefruit spoons? Where'd you find these? I didn't know I had these." There's also a butter knife at each setting and a vase with cut roses in the middle of the table. "Little one, who taught you how to do this?" I look down at Kaylee, who smiles that sweet, shy smile of hers again.

"Let me guess, you used to work in a restaurant? Caterer? Servant to the rich and famous?" Ruby teases. "Too bad Margaret's not here to see this." Ruby turns to me and winks. "Your mother is a woman who appreciates a little culture."

I watch Kaylee. She takes a deep breath, stands a little straighter, and opens her mouth . . . but says nothing. Instead, she turns and scampers out of the kitchen and down the hallway. She's back in a matter of seconds holding a large blue book out to Ruby.

"*Emily Post's Etiquette?*" Ruby flips open the cover. "Copyright 1955." She laughs and wraps Kaylee in a hug. As she holds her, she looks over Kaylee's head at me. "Sierra hasn't read this book." I watch Ruby's face change—tears brim in her eyes, and then she says, as much to me as to Kaylee, "It's a good thing she has you!"

I nod at Ruby, my own emotions welling. "Yes. It sure is a good thing." I put my arms around both Ruby and Kaylee. "Group hug!" I give them both a squeeze and then, fearing we might squish Kaylee, I step back.

"*Etiquette* is one of the books Kaylee brought from . . . one she brought with her. Right?" I look at Kaylee and she nods.

Kaylee nods her way through breakfast.

Later, after I drop Kaylee off for her appointment with Dr. Beth, I think again of her encouragement the day we met. "Kaylee feels safe with you, Sierra . . ."

I think of Kaylee's tree—the warm scent of charred wood, the embrace of the small space. I'm drawn back there, to that place of safety for Kaylee. I need, for some reason, to see it again. I check my watch. Fifty-five minutes until the end of Kaylee's session. Can I make it?

I pull onto Ocean Street and head for Highway 17. The winding route through the redwoods will take too long. I speed up the highway to the Mt. Hermon Road exit, then crawl through the Scotts Valley traffic. I check my watch again. I won't have time to linger once there.

As I twist my way up Empire Grade, I roll down my window and the spicy scents of eucalyptus and pine fills the Jeep. The crisp air speaks of fall as do the oak leaves twirling to the ground. I turn onto the now-familiar dirt road that leads to the clearing.

The last time I was here, almost a month ago, was the morning of the day Kaylee came to live with me. I returned to get her jar. But now everything is different. A month feels like a lifetime, and Kaylee is no longer unknown to me. She is known, loved, and an inextricable part of my life. To place her here, hiding in a tree, seems unfathomable. Yet, she found shelter here—she created a safe place in her tumultuous world.

Kaylee's tree, the largest of the five in the circle, faces the clearing, which must account for the fire-ravaged trunk—the other trees appear unscathed. I hold out my arm, and run my hand across the trunk of each tree as I walk around the circle—*a family circle.* This, I realize, is why I've come today. To see with eyes of understanding what I didn't know before. Redwood "sprouts," or young trees, grow from the roots of a parent tree— they grow in a circular pattern around the parent tree.

The other fact I learned is that redwoods, being fire resistant, thrive after a fire has ravaged the forest around them. The burnt debris from other plants enriches the soil, thus supplying nutrients, which encourage the growth of both the trees and new seeds.

I remember Kaylee's written words: *Redwoods are resilient.*

Yes, little one, they are resilient, just like you. You, too, have survived the ravages of fire—yours came in the form of abuse. And you, too, will thrive. I know this as surely as these redwoods stand in front of me.

Kaylee is a survivor. But more than survive, she will thrive.

"Thank You . . ." I whisper my prayer of gratitude to a God, who, I'm learning, speaks. Today He speaks to me through the grandeur of His creation.

And I am learning to listen.

CHAPTER THIRTY-FOUR

athryn

SHE COUGHS AS SHE EXHALES. She waves her hand, fanning the cloud of smoke hanging in front of her face and blocking her view. She peers at the young girl, taking in her features.

It can't be . . .

But looking at the girl is like looking into a mirror—which she doesn't do anymore. She can't handle seeing her daughter's dark hair hanging on her shoulders or her eyes staring back at her from the mirror. So she just doesn't look. The girl is a little taller and thinner, but it's her. She'd know her anywhere. No matter how hard she's tried to forget her.

She convinced herself the girl was better off without her.

She is better off without me. She is. Better off without me. The thoughts race through her mind.

She watches the girl as she walks. She's with a woman who has her arm around her. She looks fine. *She's okay.* As the thought runs through her mind, she exhales years' worth of guilt. *She's okay.* She takes another deep drag from her cigarette, turns her head, and blows the smoke over her shoulder.

The woman and Kaylee—*her Kaylee*—walk into the ice cream shop next door. She leans against the wall behind her and slowly slides to the ground, crushes her cigarette into the sidewalk, and wraps her arms around her knees. She determines she'll sit and wait. She will see her as they walk out—see her one more time.

She is better off without me.

As she waits, she thinks back to that last day.

A quick trip . . .

That's what she told herself when she left. But it turned into one trip after another. As she drove away from the cabin that afternoon, she argued with herself. *Just go to the grocery store, Kat. Just go. Drive into the parking lot. Get out of the car. Walk the aisles. Get milk, cereal, pork chops, a pack of bubble gum for Kaylee. Give the cashier the money. Give it to the cashier, Kat. Don't be an idiot.*

But who was she kidding? She knew where she was going. Her need was stronger than her sense, as usual, and she never made it to the store. Instead, she ended up at an apartment—a friend of Jack's. She balled her fist and pounded on his door. "Randall, open up!" He had to be here—had to . . .

When the door finally opened, Randall stood there, wearing boxers and a T-shirt. He said nothing, just opened the door wider and motioned for her to come in. The apartment was stuffy and smelled of bacon grease. He watched her for a minute then put his hand out, palm up. "How much do you have?"

She opened her purse and took the bills from her wallet and gave him all of it.

He counted and then smirked. "That'll do. Have a seat."

She sat on his threadbare sofa and studied a poster of Kiss hanging on the wall across from her—the ghoulish faces of the band glared at her. Her hands shook and her skin crawled. She tried to ignore the pit of dread in the bottom of her stomach.

I need it. That's all. I just need it. I can't help it . . .

But then, she thought of her again—her little girl. The pit in her stomach lurched. Would Kaylee be okay? "Hey! I don't have all day!" she yelled over her shoulder.

Within a few minutes he was sitting next to her tying a rubber strap around her arm. The needle digging for a vein was pure relief. Soon the arguments and the justifications would stop. Everything would stop. And that's all that mattered. And maybe, maybe this time would be like the first time—that elusive first high that she'd been searching for ever since.

When Randall was done, she returned the favor. She searched his arm for just the right spot and inserted the needle, smooth as silk, into one of his veins.

As she did, she could feel the meth burning its way into her system. She coughed—a choking cough—then began to relax. *This is all I need—ever. This is it. With this, I can do anything.* Her mind began to race. *I'll leave here, go get Kaylee, and we'll start fresh. Of course! Why didn't I figure this out before?*

"Hey, you know what I'm going to do?" She paced back and forth in front of the sofa, sometimes taking laps around it. She looked at Randall, still on the sofa, lighting a joint. "You know what I'm going to do? I'm going back to school. Yeah. I'll get my degree. That's it! I'll go get Kaylee, get us set up in an apartment near the campus, and I'll go back. I'll have to work too. Right?"

She didn't wait for a response. Instead she followed the thread of energy and jabbered on. "Yeah, I'll work and I'll get my degree. Like, um, I don't know, maybe nursing or something. You know? I could be a nurse, right? I know how to give shots, right?" At this, she laughs—a deep, satisfying laugh straight from the gut. She laughs until tears roll down her cheeks. "Get it?" She gasps. "Get it? I can give shots—I'm good at that. It's perfect. It's the perfect plan!"

"Yeah, babe, sounds perfect. Want a hit?"

She sits back on the sofa and reaches for the joint. She inhales deeply and then swallows the smoke. "Yeah, it's perfect." She can see the plan in her head—the apartment she'll get . . . she sees every detail. The moss-green carpet lit by rays of sunlight coming in through the sliding glass door that leads to a little balcony. And plants—lots of plants everywhere. "Yeah, it's perfect." She leans her head back and lets the ideas swirl.

But when that trip ended—when the euphoria of escape began to wane—she was still there, with Randall. Euphoria was replaced by anxiety and the shame of what she'd done.

Again.

She had to have more—had to find that energy again. Just a little more. Randall consoled and assured her he had more. But the grocery money was gone.

"There are other ways to pay for what you want . . ."

His stale breath was hot against her ear and his suggestion was clear.

Why not? Huh? Why not . . .

She finally gave in to the nagging justification: *She's better off without me.* So she gave him what he wanted and he gave her what she needed.

When he finally tired of her—it was weeks, maybe months later, she didn't know for sure—he kicked her out. Her car was gone. He'd sold it. She had nothing and nowhere to go. She couldn't go back to the cabin, to her, not now. She couldn't even think about what might have become of her. Couldn't go there. Wouldn't go there. She walked the streets until nightfall, until she found someone else willing to make the same trade. It was easy as long as she didn't think. She thought only of her own need.

Besides . . . Kaylee was better off without her.

When she couldn't get what she needed, she took anything. Alcohol, pot, heroin, whatever. Because when she went without, when she couldn't find what she needed, she'd begin the agonizing withdrawal. Shaking, skin crawling, vomiting, and—worst of all . . . the very worst of all—the flashing pictures of before.

Of who she'd been before.

She'd see her father leaving when she was four—see his back walking out the door, leaving not only her and her mom but leaving a gaping hole in her heart. A hole she'd tried to fill over and over and over again.

Or she'd see Lee—the guy who, at nineteen, held all her dreams in the palm of his hand. She named Kaylee after herself and Lee, symbolic of their shared union. Of course, he was already gone by then, but she thought he'd come back. Kaylee was her claim on Lee, her assurance that he'd be back. So she'd thought. But she was wrong. Kaylee wasn't enough.

She wasn't enough.

But that's life, right? So what? She learned how to take care of herself.

Stupid. Stupid to think of the past. It was over.

She looks from the ice cream shop to the guy next to her, reaches over and takes the bag out of his hand. He's too wasted now to notice. She lifts it to her lips and gulps the sour wine. She drinks until the bottle is empty, but it isn't enough. She can still see Kaylee inside the ice cream shop. She can still feel her.

She scoots closer to her new friend and leans over to kiss him. As she does, she runs her hands up and down his arms and then down his waist. She reaches into his front pocket and feels for his last bill—a ten.

She pats his arm and then gets up and walks back into the liquor store.

CHAPTER THIRTY-FIVE

 ierra

WE ROUND the corner and walk into the parking lot of Marianne's, a Santa Cruz icon. I drape my arm around Kaylee's shoulders and walk toward the entrance to the ice cream shop. I come here often to indulge with a scoop of my favorite flavor: Highway 17, otherwise known as Rocky Road.

But today, having Kaylee with me, the hyper-vigilance I've felt since she's become my responsibility returns. I glance at the other business that shares the parking lot with Marianne's and see a couple loitering out front. The man drinks something hidden in a paper bag and the woman, slight and pale, stares at us. I pull Kaylee, who seems mesmerized by the activity of the ice cream shop, a little closer as we walk inside.

"Those are the flavors." I point to the board on the wall and watch as Kaylee's eyes widen. I've delighted in introducing her to a few of life's pleasures in the last couple of weeks. "You may have one or two scoops, either on a cone or in a cup. Whatever you'd like."

Kaylee slips the backpack that almost never leaves her back now off her shoulders and pulls out her notebook and pen.

Which one is your favorite?

"I like Highway 17—it's chocolate ice cream with marshmallows and cashews—and Peanut Butter Cup, which is chocolate ice cream with a peanut butter ribbon. I like having them on a sugar cone. Want to try one of those?"

She nods her head, a smile stretched across her face.

"One flavor or both?"

She nods again and I laugh. "Okay, both."

I place our order, grab napkins, and watch as Kaylee takes her top-heavy cone from the server and takes her first taste. With chocolate ice cream on the tip of her nose, she smiles at me again. Two smiles in two minutes.

It's a good day.

"Can you eat and walk at the same time, kiddo?"

She nods and we head back outside and around the corner and down the street toward home, each of us lost in our own thoughts.

As we reach the bungalow, I tuck my thoughts away. I notice Kaylee's gait has slowed and her shoulders droop. Fatigue seems her constant companion still.

"How about we wash that ice cream off your face, little one, and then you and Van can take your afternoon nap."

She nods her agreement.

This has become our routine as her body heals and she catches up on what seems like a lifetime of sleep. And Van, my traitorous dog, has taken to sleeping with her rather than me. I smile at the delight I see in her eyes each time Van leaps onto her bed.

She will likely sleep away the rest of this lazy Indian summer afternoon. As I tuck her in, I make sure the book she's reading is on her night table in case she wakes and wants to read. Rather *when* she wakes and wants to read. She's making quick work of the Nancy Drew novels. But as far as I can tell, with the exception of the etiquette book, she hasn't touched the books we brought from the cabin. The dictionary, I assume, is the source of her well-developed vocabulary. But the times I've asked if she'd like to read it, she averts her eyes and shakes her head. Maybe they are a reminder of what she left behind.

I also notice she removed the locket from around her neck and placed it back in the jar. Another reminder, maybe?

After I see that she's settled, I head to the kitchen where my easel and drawers of shredded papers now stand in one corner. I reach for the jug of matte media I now store in a kitchen cupboard. Standing back, I peruse the canvas and plan the next layer of my work. I've let my art go since Kaylee arrived, but today I feel compelled to finish the picture of the redwood.

Just as I begin slathering glue on the first bit of paper, I hear a knock at the front door. I'm not expecting anyone and am tempted to ignore it. But then it comes again, more insistent this time. I place the shred of paper on the canvas, then wipe the glue from my hands on an old towel and head for the door.

I open the door to a woman who seems familiar, though I'm not sure why.

"Hi . . ." As I wait for her response, the skin on the back of my neck prickles and the muscles in my jaw and shoulders tense. I'm looking into Kaylee's eyes—though the eyes of the woman in front of me seem glazed, tired. Then I remember where I've seen her. Just an hour ago, in the parking lot of Marianne's.

"You have her, don't you? You have my little girl."

The woman is small, birdlike. She shifts back and forth from one foot to the other and her hands quiver at her sides. Her complexion is sallow against her dull, dark hair. And her eyes, the deep green of Kaylee's, seem lifeless.

"Who are you?" The strength of my voice surprises me.

I exude a calm I don't feel.

"Kathryn. Her mother. You have my Kaylee."

"Excuse me . . ." I step out the door causing her to move back. The smell of cigarette smoke assaults my senses. I close the front door behind me—I don't want Kaylee hearing this exchange. As much as I'm sure Kaylee wants her mother back, something isn't right here. I know it. Intuition?

Mine is screaming.

"What makes you think I have her?" I'm stalling. Thinking. Pleading with God. *Help me!* I realize she must have seen Kaylee and followed us from Marianne's. How stupid of me! So caught up in my thoughts that I didn't notice her following us. I'm supposed to protect Kaylee. What happened to that hyper-vigilance I'd felt?

"I saw you. I saw you with her—your arm around her like she's yours."

I notice the frenetic tapping of her left foot, an involuntary movement, it seems. The sense of familiarity grabs me again. Standing in front of my house, looking at the woman who holds the power to wrench Kaylee from my life, I experience an epiphany—a sword that slices my soul in two.

Like me, the woman standing before me, Kaylee's mother, fell to drugs.

It's the drugs I see—the nervousness, the involuntary twitches and movements, the pockmarks and scabs on her face. I see her need, so like my own at one time. But I was not the sum of the drugs. She is not the sum of the drugs. For the first time I see myself, through someone else, separate from what the addiction created.

Acceptance . . . mercy . . . freedom—all are held within this revelation. But there's no time to consider that now.

The epiphany leads to the recognition of truth: She stands to lose her daughter. She is the victim of her choices. And I, more than anyone, know the agony of the road she walks. Compassion stirs and I want to reach out, to spare this stranger the pain I've known. But that's only half of what I feel.

The other part of me wants to use this knowledge against her. To take her daughter as my own.

"Are you just going to stand there staring at me, or do you have something to say?" Agitation marks her words.

"What do you want?"

"I want my baby back."

I speak from what I'm sure is true. "You can't take care of her. You need help."

"I don't need help. I just need my baby. She's *mine!*" Her eyes come to life.

"How will you take care of her? It doesn't look like you're even taking care of yourself." My voice remains calm, caring even. I watch her. She shifts from foot to foot and her eyes dart from me to the ground and back again.

"You don't know anything about me." She spits her words at me.

"I know more than you think." I can see I've disarmed her, frightened her.

"What do you know?"

Lord, help me. What am I thinking? She's right. I don't know.

I look her up and down again—her clothes are rumpled, dirty. Her tennis shoes are worn, a hole in the canvas top of one reveals her sockless feet. And again, I notice the telltale jitters. In the recesses of my mind, I hear my mother's voice: *What's the truth, Shannon?*

I speak what I'm sure is truth. "You're an addict. You can't even take care of yourself, let alone Kaylee. You need help." I take a deep breath and go on. "I know—I've been there."

She looks me in the eyes for the first time, but only briefly. "You don't know what you're talking about."

I take a step toward her, trying to close the gap between us both physically and emotionally. "I do know." *What am I doing?*

I flinch when I consider the consequences of what I'm about to say. I stand to lose Kaylee. But with a strength I know is not my own, I press on. "I know because I've been there. I was an addict and . . . and I had . . ." I take another breath. "I had a daughter once. Her name was Annie. But . . . I lost her. I was using during my pregnancy, and . . . she . . . she died shortly after she was born."

For just a moment, our eyes, maybe even our hearts, meet—mother to mother. The veil drops and I see understanding in her eyes.

"You don't have to lose your daughter. You can get help. Your story can end differently than mine."

She steps back, her expression veiled again. "I told you, you don't know what you're talking about! I'm . . . I'm fine—except that I did lose my daughter." She falters, fumbles for words.

"I . . . I lost her in the grocery store. She was kidnapped. And now you have her. Maybe you're the one who took her!"

Her accusation stuns me. Could Kaylee have been kidnapped? The story is plausible. It happens. A child is wooed away by a pedophile offering candy or some other enticement and then, the child is gone. Is that what happened to Kaylee?

No. She's lying. Covering herself. "I don't believe you." There is no accusation in my tone. It's just a statement of fact.

"I saw the way you held on to her, the way you looked at her. She means something to you and you don't want to give her up."

I open my mouth to respond, but nothing comes out. I have no response. This time she speaks truth. The division widens—

I see it in my mind—a gaping chasm plastered on canvas, jagged edges in dark hues depict the image.

"Are you taking good care of her?" Her voice softens with her question.

"Yes."

"Do you love her?"

I sense she's changing tactics—that she has a plan I haven't yet figured out. I leave the question unanswered.

"I'll tell you what. I've had some hard times lately. You can imagine, right? Losing my daughter made me a little crazy. I . . . um . . . I lost my job. And now I don't have a place to live. I'm getting one soon though. So maybe . . . maybe for a price . . . you can keep her a little longer."

"A price?" Indignation rises like bile in my throat.

"Yeah . . . you know . . ." Her "transaction" is interrupted by the opening of the front door. We both turn to see Kaylee standing in the doorway, her little body trembling like a fall leaf.

I move toward her, reach for her, "Oh, Kaylee . . ." But she pushes me away. Her gaze is locked on her mother. Her face a puzzle of hope, longing, confusion . . .

Pain.

I look at Kathryn and see she wears the same expression. Mother and daughter face to face. But then Kathryn's expression shifts—changes—hardens. She says nothing to Kaylee, instead she looks back at me.

"You think about what I said. I'll be back." With that, she turns and walks away. By the time she reaches the sidewalk, she's running.

And Kaylee is running after her! I reach out and grab her as she passes me. I hold her flailing body in my arms, her back pressed against my chest, her tears soaking my arms. She kicks and pulls away, but I hold on tight, every muscle straining against her.

I can't let her go.

CHAPTER THIRTY-SIX

athryn

SHE RUNS down the sidewalk in the direction she came. She doesn't look back, but she doesn't really look where she's going either. All is a blur. Kaylee's face and the hope she saw in her daughter's eyes is her only focus.

When she can't run anymore, when she's gasping for breath, she stops and looks back the way she came to make sure Kaylee didn't follow her. But no one's there. She grabs her side as a sharp pain causes her to double over. Nauseous, she drops to the ground on her hands and knees, sure she'll be sick. She gulps for air and waits until the feeling passes, then turns over and sits on the sidewalk. She rests her head on her knees and, for the first time since walking away from the cabin that day, she cries. Her body shudders as much from her sobs as from her unrelenting need.

"More. I always need more!" She pounds the cement with her fists. *It will never end . . . never.* Then she sees Kaylee's face again. Memories attack her. Holding Kaylee's tiny hand as she took her first steps. Her smile as she'd look up with a toothless grin and say, "Ma-ma!" Kaylee's first day of school and the tears she'd shed when left with her kindergarten teacher. She remembers the weight of Kaylee on her lap, the fresh scent of her hair, as she read to her, and how quickly Kaylee picked up the words and was soon the one doing the reading. Life was hard then, Lee was already gone, but she'd had her mom and, with her help, was making it. She was making it. Then she remembers when things began to change . . .

Oh baby, I'm so sorry.

The memories are too much.

She closes her eyes and covers her ears. She shakes her head, hoping to rattle the images. Another wave of nausea hits her and this time her stomach convulses and she's sick. There, sitting on the sidewalk, a block from Ocean Street where traffic whizzes by, she vomits. She knows she should feel shame and embarrassment. She is aware enough to know what she should feel. Instead, her body shudders and the crawling feeling on her legs and arms and neck and face begin again. She reaches for her neck and scratches and scratches. The sensation doesn't stop. She scratches until there's blood under her nails—until her neck is raw.

It will never end.

She thinks back to what she told the woman who has Kaylee— that for a price she could keep her daughter a little while longer. She's not selling her daughter. She's not.

I'm just going to get myself back on my feet. With a little extra money, I can wean myself off the meth. I just need a little—just enough to stop the crawling, the shaking. Then I can think. I can make a plan.

Just a little more . . . that's all I need.

CHAPTER THIRTY-SEVEN

aylee

THROUGH MY TEARS, the ceiling seems to float overhead. Tears drip into my ears, but I don't care. I roll over and rest my check against the damp pillow. It's cool against my cheek but offers little solace.

Solace.

I feel the word in my mouth and imagine the hissing sound of the *S* and *C*, but still I find no comfort. I mentally spit the word out. It's useless.

I search my mind for the right word—the perfect word. It doesn't take long to find it:

con·found·ed—adjective 1. bewildered; confused; perplexed. 2. damned.

Damned. That's a word I'm not supposed to say. They say it's a swear word, but all it really means is that I'm doomed, that bad things are just going to keep happening to me for no reason. That's why I'm confounded. Nothing makes sense.

She came back.

She found me.

I thought I was dreaming because I was almost asleep, but then I heard her. I heard her voice. I opened my eyes, looked around, and knew I wasn't asleep. The window above my bed was open and I heard them on the porch outside. I stayed very still and listened, although it was hard to hear over the beating of my heart thumping in my ears. But I heard enough.

I heard my mom.

I heard her tell Sierra I was kidnapped. Maybe she still has amnesia. Maybe she doesn't remember everything the right way. She had amnesia. That's why she didn't come back. I know it. Now she only remembers some things. That must be how it works.

I listened for a few minutes more, then I got up and ran to the door.

Mom! Mommy! I yelled the words in my head, but they wouldn't come out my mouth. I opened the door and . . . and there she was.

She found me.

I wanted to say things to her, to tell her I love her, to ask her where she'd been, to tell her everything's all right now. But I couldn't.

"Stupid *mute*."

He was right.

Now she probably thinks I don't care. What if she never comes back again? Or . . . what if she does?

Bewildered. Confused. Perplexed.

Damned.

I can hear Pete and Sierra whispering in the kitchen. After my mom left, after she walked away, I tried to follow her. But Sierra grabbed me and carried me into the house and held onto me while she called Pete. She wouldn't let go of me, no matter how hard I fought her. Finally I just gave up. I couldn't fight anymore. I'd cried so many tears I was exhausted. When she finally let go, I curled up on the kitchen floor like a big question mark.

I didn't understand. I don't understand.

Sierra sat next to me on the kitchen floor and rubbed my back and told me she was sorry—that I was her responsibility now—that she couldn't let me go with my mom because my mom is sick.

She must understand about the amnesia too.

Then Sierra said. "I love you, Kaylee."

But I don't care.

I don't.

It doesn't matter anymore.

When Pete came, he picked me up in his big arms and carried me to my room. Sierra followed him. Pete laid me on my bed and Sierra covered me with the blanket. Pete sat next to me on the bed, but because he's so big, it made the bed sink down and made me roll toward him. I sat up, scooted way over to the other side, and laid back down with my back to him.

"Missy, I want you to listen to me for a minute, okay?"

I didn't nod or anything. I just laid there.

"I'm not going to try and guess what you're feeling right now. But whatever you're feeling is okay. And it might take some time to make sense of it all. Whether you're sad, or angry, or relieved, or confused, or all of that, it's okay. We'll work it out together when you're ready."

Then I heard Pete whisper to Sierra. "Get her notebook and pen. I'll leave it here on her table."

I heard Sierra unzip my backpack, and I could picture her handing the notebook to Pete.

"Kaylee, I'm putting your notebook here on your table. If you want to write about what you're feeling, or if you have questions, it's right here. Sierra and I are going to sit in the kitchen for awhile and let you rest. But if you want to ask me anything, or if you want Sierra, you just come get us. We're just down the hall."

Then I felt Pete tuck the blanket in around me. He put his hand on my shoulder and gave it a little squeeze. "You rest, Kaylee."

Now they probably think I'm asleep, but I'm not.

I throw the blanket off, get out of bed, go to the bookshelf, and reach for the dictionary. I set it on my bed and climb back in. It's the first time I've read the dictionary since coming here.

I decide I'll read whatever page I open it to. Page 279—the Cs —they're my favorites.

co · ag · u · la · tive

co · ag · u · la · tor

co · ag · u · lin

I don't bother reading the definitions. The words are swimming on the page. I try not to think about the cabin and all the times I read the dictionary there. Instead, I try to remember
the times my mom had me look up words.

Go get the dictionary, Kaylee . . .

But I can only hear her mean voice in my head. The way she sounded when she was talking to Sierra on the porch, and the way she was at the cabin sometimes.

She wasn't always mean.

I skip down.

co · a · lesce

co · a · les · cence

I like the way those words feel in my mouth. I bet they sound pretty when someone says them out loud.

I hear Sierra's voice get louder in the kitchen. I can't hear what she's saying, but she sounds upset.

Sierra . . .

I can't think about Sierra.

co·a·les·cent

Does she really love me?

coal·field

It doesn't matter anyway, not now that my mom's back.

coal·fish

Coalfish? That's a funny word. What's a coalfish? I don't remember that word. I wipe my eyes and read the definition:

a dark-colored fish belonging to the cod family: also called black pollack.

Coal is black—that must be why the fish is called that. Soot comes from coal. *Stick straight and dark as soot.* That's what my mom used to say about our hair. I run my fingers through my hair. It's clean and feels like silk now. No tangles. I look over to the table by my bed and see the pink comb Sierra combs my hair with every night before I go to sleep. It's sticking out under my notebook. I reach for it and run my thumb over the teeth.

I remember what I heard my mom say . . .

She'd had a hard time, she'd lost her job. And for a price I could stay with Sierra for awhile. What did she mean?

I comb through a section of my hair and think of Sierra.

My eyes fill with tears again and the lump in my throat aches. My chest gets tight. Then I take the comb, pull my arm back, and throw it as hard as I can. It bangs against the closet door and then drops to the ground.

I don't need the stupid comb!

I wipe my eyes and nose on the sleeve of my shirt. Crying is for babies. I know what I have to do, and I'll do it. I get out of bed again and reach down to the lower bookshelf and pull out the last Nancy Drew novel—*The Clue of the Whistling Bagpipes.* It's the only one I haven't read. I'll start it today and as soon as I finish it, I'll leave.

That's what I have to do.

I have to leave.

I have to find my mom.

She needs me.

CHAPTER THIRTY-EIGHT

ierra

"I KNOW THE SIGNS. The nervousness. Twitching. Even her complexion. She's an addict."

I turn and stare out the kitchen slider but see nothing in the yard beyond. Instead, I see myself all those years ago—young, impressionable, ready to take on the art world.

The drinking and pot seemed harmless. As I told Ruby at the time, "Everybody's doing it." But heroin? Heroin was a different deal. I shudder as I recall the insidious need for more—always more.

"Hey, Sierra, you still with me?"

I turn my attention back to Pete, who is sitting at my kitchen table. "Um . . . yeah, I'm listening."

"Kaylee's mom said she'd be back?"

I nod. "She'll be back if she thinks there's any chance she can get some money out of me." I lean back in the kitchen chair and stretch my legs in front of me, trying to ease some of the tension

I've felt since answering the door a couple of hours ago. "Pete, is there any possibility Kaylee was kidnapped by that"—I shudder as I think of him—"by that monster she was with?" A stronger word comes to mind, but I refrain.

"It's possible. The police report indicated there wasn't any evidence of Kathryn having lived in the cabin with Kaylee. Kaylee is the only one who knows for sure. Her psychiatrist is making some progress with her. You'll appreciate this—she's using art therapy as a means of exploring Kaylee's background. A nonverbal means to work with a nonverbal child. But Kaylee seems reluctant when asked about her mother. She won't respond in writing, pictures, or otherwise. She may be protecting her, which isn't unusual. According to the police reports, the guy claimed to be the mother's boyfriend, but we don't know for sure. Pete shakes his head and his face softens. "His is a sad story . . ."

"*His* is a sad story? How can you say that?" I feel absolute revulsion even thinking about him. All I can think about is Kaylee and what he put her through. "You feel sorry for him?" Heat rises to my face.

"Sierra, he was a kid once too. Think about what his life must have been like for him to end up like he is. He told the police his old man used to beat him with a baseball bat. And that was the least of it . . ."

It's Pete sitting across from me, but I hear my daddy: *"Look beyond a person's actions and see their heart. Look for what's causing them to act the way they act, then you'll understand them."*

I nod. "I understand what you're saying, but I can't feel sorry for the guy. I'm too angry."

"Anger is the appropriate response, Sierra. 'Whoever causes one of these little ones who believe in Me to stumble, it would be better for him to have a heavy millstone hung around his neck, and to be drowned in the depth of the sea.'"

"Is that from the Bible? It sounds familiar."

"Matthew 18. Red letters. Straight from Jesus' mouth."

Again I'm reminded of my daddy. "Well, I'd like to hang a rock around his neck and drop him to the bottom of the ocean!" I seethe as I say the words.

"I'm not justifying his actions. He's responsible for his choices. I'm just saying there are factors behind his choices. Unfortunately, all too often, this is how these things turn out. A child is abused and because the child never talks about it, has nowhere to turn, can't get any help, that child ends up perpetuating the cycle. The abused becomes the abuser. It's what these children know. It makes me mad too. It's why I work with these kids. I want to help break the cycle. It doesn't have to be this way."

He studies my features. "Use your anger, Sierra. Use it to help Kaylee. When you're exhausted after another long day of talking to her and getting nothing in return, when you wonder why you got involved in the first place"—he softens again—"when loving her hurts too much, let that anger spur you on. Use it."

When loving her hurts too much . . .

His words invade my soul. How does this man already know me so well? Or is it just the PhD after his name, all that psychological training giving him license to assume he knows what I'm feeling?

I nod my agreement, hoping that will end the conversation.

I have no desire to discuss my feelings for Kaylee. *Hurt.* What does he know about hurting?

"When I was about Kaylee's age . . ."

I look back up—the timbre of his voice has changed—lowered. And now he's the one staring out the slider. But like me, he doesn't seem to see the yard beyond. He stops as though carefully choosing his words.

"I had a coach—Little League." Pete looks back at me. "He molested me. It happened over the course of several weeks, and I was too embarrassed—too ashamed—to tell my parents. But they noticed a change in me, in my behavior. I was lucky—blessed, actually, with great parents. They paid attention. They figured it out. They filed charges and followed the case through the court system. And they got help for me."

I didn't know what to say. But Pete didn't seem to expect me to say anything. His eyes meet mine again.

"I understand the shame and hurt Kaylee's experienced. I didn't go through what she's gone through. But I suffered enough to understand, to some degree, her pain. I also know there's hope for her." He stretches and looks at his watch. "Well, I've already stayed longer than necessary. I better go . . ."

"Pete, do you have children?" The question is out of my mouth before I consider whether or not it's any of my business.

"No. But I'd like to, someday. Guess I'll have to get married first." He raises one eyebrow and smiles. Then he seems thoughtful again. "I'd like to be the kind of parent my parents were."

"Yeah, me too."

Pete stands, picks his iced tea glass up from the table, and walks to the sink. He rinses the glass and sets it in the sink, then turns back to me. "You keep an eye on that little gal tonight. That was traumatic for her this afternoon. In the meantime we'll keep looking for her mom. We know she's close. It shouldn't take the police department long to pick her up. I'll call Dr. Beth in the morning and give her a heads-up and see if she can see Kaylee tomorrow afternoon. Will that work for you?"

"Sure. Whatever Kaylee needs."

"Call me if you need anything."

"I will. Thanks."

After he leaves, the bungalow feels empty. I head down the hallway and crack open Kaylee's door. She's asleep, her book open on her lap. I tiptoe in, take the book, and put it on her night table, and then bend to kiss her forehead. "I love you, little one." She stirs at my whispered words but doesn't wake. "Van, come on, you need a trip outside." Van jumps off the bed and follows me out of the room.

I open the slider and follow Van to the backyard. I ease into the Adirondack chair as Van wanders around the yard. The setting sun casts a luminous glow over the deck and yard. As I lean back in the chair, a sigh escapes from the depths of my soul. I close my eyes, hoping to turn off my mind, but thoughts of this afternoon continue to intrude.

I think again of the division I felt in myself—the desire to draw from my own experiences to help Kaylee's mom, and the stronger desire to exploit her struggle for my own gain, to keep Kaylee with me. Are my desires selfish?

Yes. And no. I care deeply what happens to her. I long to ease her pain—to give her the love she deserves—the love I experienced as a child. I want the best for Kaylee.

"So what is best for her?" I speak my question into the dusk. It's a question I asked Pete earlier, but I couldn't accept his response in the moment. Now I ponder his words. "Don't we serve Kalyee's best interests by helping her mom?"

"And how do we do that?" I'd asked.

"We let the system work. When we find her, we let her know our goal is to reunite her with her daughter, to help make her situation workable. Through CWS, she'll attend parenting classes, we offer job placement assistance, there will be supervised visits, and eventually, if all goes well, Kaylee is returned to her mother."

"What? That's it? A mother neglects, abandons, and allows her daughter to be abused and you help her get her daughter back?"

"Of course not, Sierra. If there is evidence of abuse of any kind, charges will be pressed. If drugs are involved, as you suspect, then we also hope for evidence of that—possession ensures court-mandated rehabilitation. In the meantime Kaylee remains a ward of the court, she receives the help she needs and a safe environment in which to heal. Either way, it's a long road ahead."

A long road . . .

Each day Kaylee is here the pain at the prospect of losing her becomes greater. Ruby would tell me I'm being too "all or nothing" again. How many times has Ruby said. "It's both/and Sierra, not either/or." Is that true in this situation? Is it possible Kaylee could love both her mother and me?

I think of what Pete shared about his childhood. He turned his pain around—found purpose in it. For the first time I see new purpose in what I've suffered. Maybe I can use the pain of my past to help shape the future of another—of Kaylee, and perhaps, even her mother.

Van stands there, his chin resting on my leg. I scratch behind his ears, grateful for his companionship. "Are you hungry, boy?" His tail wags in response. "C'mon, I'll feed you."

I get up from the chair, Van at my heels, and return to the kitchen where I fill Van's bowl with food. Then I open the junk drawer and dig until I find a pair of scissors. I walk back outside to the far corner of the yard and clip a small bough from the towering redwood likely planted there by the original owners in the thirties. The bough is deep green, with lighter green at the tips —the new growth of summer.

I take the bough back into the house and set it on the tray of my easel, then head down the hallway to check on Kaylee. She's still asleep. I walk to her bed and sit on the side, next to her.

I brush her bangs off her forehead and gently nudge her shoulder until her eyes open. It takes a minute for her to focus on my face.

"Hey, do you want some dinner? Homemade macaroni and cheese?" One of her favorites. She shakes her head and rolls on her side, away from me. As she does, I hear her stomach growl.

What is she feeling? I can only imagine . . .

"Kaylee, you need to eat, to keep up your strength. Is there something you'd rather have? Chicken maybe? Or there's leftover meatloaf from last night." I hear her stomach rumble again.

She sits up, edges her way to the other side of the bed, and gets out. Without looking at me, she makes her way to the door. I follow her down the hallway and into the kitchen where she opens a cupboard, takes out a bag of shell-shaped macaroni, and hands it to me.

"Okay, mac and cheese it is." I reach for a pot, fill it with water, and set it to boil. Kaylee takes a seat at the kitchen table and rests her head on her folded arms. She will ignore me.

Her anger, or anguish—I'm not sure which—fills the small kitchen.

CHAPTER THIRTY-NINE

aylee

Dr. Beth, my psychiatrist, is pulling out paper, pens, and paints while I wait at the little table in her office. Bethany is her first name. She told me I can call her Dr. Beth because her last name is too hard to pronounce. Like I'm going to pronounce it anyway.

She talks to me like she thinks I'll talk back.

Mute, remember?

1. dumb; silent. 2. unable to speak; dumb.

She asks me lots of questions, especially about my mom. But I don't want to tell her about my mom. She asks me questions about him too. On days when she asks me about him, I'm glad I can't talk. I don't know what I'd say. When she asks me too many questions, the scream starts and I have to cover my ears.

She doesn't ask as many questions now, instead she lets me draw or paint.

She's nice, but I know what a psychiatrist is. They're doctors for people with "mental disorders," that's what the dictionary says. I don't have a mental disorder. I just don't talk.

At first I liked it when I got to draw and paint. I'd pretend I was an artist like Sierra. But I won't draw or paint today, no matter how much Dr. Bethany wants me too.

I can't think about Sierra.

Instead I'll think about my plan. I'm going to find my mom. Which means . . .

I have to leave Sierra.

"Kaylee, you look sad today. I heard your mom paid a visit to Sierra yesterday."

I just look at her.

She's quiet for a minute then says. "I'd imagine seeing your mom stirred up lots of feelings in here." She points to my chest. "Would you like to draw, maybe work on something to help you work through some of those feelings?" She sets the paper and pens in front of me.

I fold my hands in my lap and stare at the paper. I don't mean to be stubborn, but I just can't draw today.

"Would you rather use the paints?"

I shake my head. No. No paint either.

"Okay. Let's do something different." Dr. Bethany gets up from the little chair she sat in next to me, takes the paper and pens and paints with her, and goes back to her art cupboard. She puts them away and pulls something else out and comes back to the table. "Let's make something with clay." She sets five bricks of clay in front of me—all different colors. "You can make a sculpture."

A sculpture? Like Ruby?

I pick up the brown brick of clay and look at Dr. Bethany.

"Go ahead, Kaylee. You can unwrap it. Open all the colors if you'd like."

I open the brown clay and begin smashing it in my hands, getting it warm and soft. While I do that, I think about what I'll need to take with me when I leave. I can only take as much as will fit in my backpack—just some clothes, my new sweatshirt and shorts. My toothbrush. My notebook and pen, in case I need to ask someone a question.

I smash the clay a little more, then shape it into a square, like a cube. Then I reach for the black clay and unwrap it. As I work with the clay, it feels like all the jumbled thoughts in my mind are working their way out through my fingers. Like all those feelings are coming out of me and going into the clay. Then I remember one of the definitions I read for the word *therapy*: any act, hobby, task, program, or whatever, that relieves tension. I've got a lot of tension right now, so maybe this therapy is good. I look up at Dr. Beth, who's sitting across from me, and I smile. Then I get back to my list.

I have to take my mom's three books with me, but I don't think they'll fit in my backpack. They're heavy too. Maybe I can just take the dictionary.

I also have to take my Bible.

The morning Mrs. Bickford left I found a present on my bed. It was a square package wrapped in blue paper with white fluffy clouds on it and there was a white bow on the top. Tucked under the bow was a white envelope with my name on it. I carried the present out to the kitchen where Sierra was working and I showed it to her.

"That's for you, little one. Mother left it for you. Open it."

A real present? For me?

I pulled the card out of the envelope and read Mrs. Bickford's note:

Dearest Kaylee, I noticed you copied a verse from the church bulletin the other day. The verse came from this book—the Bible. I thought you might enjoy reading the stories of Jesus and how much He loves you. I've placed a bookmark in the book of John so you can find the verse you copied.

Jesus loves you, Kaylee, and so do I.

Blessings, darling.

Love,

"Grandma" Bickford

I pulled the bow and paper off the package and then opened the box. Inside was a book with a white leather cover. On the front in gold letters it said: *Holy Bible.* On the bottom, in smaller gold letters, was my name: *Kaylee Wren.*

I turned to the kitchen counter and reached for the pad of paper and pen.

Is this really mine? Do I get to keep it?

"It's all yours, kiddo. It has your name on it. Mother thought you might like it. The Bible is . . . well, it's really important to her. It's an important part of her life. She wanted to share it with you. She thought it might help you."

Sierra reached for the Bible and picked it up. She opened it and flipped through a few of the pages. "I have one just like this. Mother and Daddy gave it to me the day I was baptized." She seemed like she was thinking back—like she was talking to me, but also to herself. "Maybe we could read this at bedtime, sometimes. Would you like that? It might be good for both of us."

I nodded. She handed the Bible back to me and I opened it to where Mrs. Bickford had placed the bookmark. I pulled the marker out—it was almost the same blue as the wrapping paper and it had little butterflies all over it. There was a blue and silver tassel hanging from the top. I looked at the open page. At the top it said: *The Gospel According to John.* The first sentence on the page was the verse I'd copied.

I ran my hand over the page—the paper was thin and felt delicate, which means it felt fragile, like it would crinkle easily. I closed the book and held it up to my nose and breathed in the scent of leather; then I ran one finger over my name. I couldn't believe it was really mine.

That's it. I'll take the dictionary and the Bible. I hope they'll both fit in my backpack.

I make two flat squares with the black clay and put them on top of the cube, like a roof on a house.

I hope my mom won't be mad if I leave the other two books.

I reach for the white clay and unwrap it. I make four little rectangles out of the white clay and put them on the front of the house—shutters. I make one big rectangle for the front door.

I don't want to steal anything from Sierra, but she can't use my clothes or toothbrush anyway. And she said the backpack and notebook and pen were mine to keep. The dictionary and Bible are definitely mine. I need some money too. I don't know what to do about that. Maybe if I leave my other two books, that will make up for anything I take. Ruby said Sierra hadn't read *Etiquette*, so maybe she'd like to have it.

Out of the red and yellow clay I make little flowers. I stick them on the bottom of the house all the way around.

Maybe I could ask Pete for some money. I could tell him I want to buy a present for Sierra. But that's a lie. I don't want to lie.

I look at the little house sitting in front of me and feel that familiar lump in my throat. I swallow, but it's still there. My vision blurs as tears fill my eyes.

I take my fist and smash the little house—I smash it hard.

I smash it until it's just a lump of colors that don't mean anything.

Making a sculpture was a stupid idea!

Dr. Bethany doesn't say anything. She just scoots a little closer and puts her hand on my back and pats me like I'm a dog or something. Probably to make me feel better.

But it doesn't.

Nothing will. Not ever again.

CHAPTER FORTY

ierra

After I drop Kaylee off at Dr. Beth's, I go to the bank. As I stand in line waiting for the next available teller, I ask myself what I'm doing. When I talked with Pete yesterday, it all seemed so clear. *Let the system work . . .*

But how can that be best for Kaylee? Hasn't she lived through enough upheaval in her life? Doesn't she deserve to move on—to enjoy the stability of a safe environment—someone to love her and care for her—someone she can depend on? Isn't that what I offer her?

"Next."

Enough analyzing, Sierra. Just do it. I approach the teller. "I'd like to withdraw $1,500 from my savings account, please."

"How would you like that?"

"Hundreds."

As the teller counts out fifteen one-hundred-dollar bills, I remind myself that I'm not responsible for what Kathryn does with the money. I'm simply helping her get back on her feet so she can provide a home for Kaylee, if that's what she wants. I'm taking what she said at face value. If she chooses to use the money for something else, well, that's her problem.

"Thank you." I take the cash, tuck it into an envelope, and put it in my backpack. I'm ready for her if she returns.

No . . . *when* she returns.

When I pick up Kaylee, she appears sullen and more withdrawn than usual.

Dr. Beth pulls me aside and whispers. "Lots of love today, Sierra, give her lots of love."

"Is she okay?"

"We had a small breakthrough—lots of interior churning going on inside her. Of course, I'd expect that after seeing her mother. It's hard to know how to help her, but I think she was able to express some of what she's feeling through her art. By the way, what color is your house?"

"Brown with white trim. Why?"

"Just wondering. Call me if you see signs of extreme angst."

I nod. "Thanks, I will." Then I wonder who I call when *I'm* feeling extreme angst? An apt descriptive for what's churning in me today. I put my arm around Kaylee's shoulders as I guide her out of the office but feel her stiffen as soon as I touch her. I take a step back and let her walk out on her own.

As we walk to the Jeep, I make suggestions on how we might spend our afternoon. "Would you like to go to the park?" She shakes her head. No. "How about the beach? We can take Van with us." No. "Ruby's back from her showing, we could call and meet her for lunch." This suggestion is met with an adamant no—a definite shake of her head. "I thought you liked Ruby?" She shrugs her shoulders. "Well, back home, I guess?" Yes.

As we drive home, I chatter at Kaylee about what I'll make for lunch, and how I need to pull some weeds and mow the lawn. I tell her we need to return our library books and go to the grocery store tomorrow. She responds to nothing—no smile, no recognition of my presence. She stares straight ahead and as soon as we pull into the driveway, she's out of the Jeep and standing on the front step before I've even unbuckled my seat belt.

I join her on the porch and unlock the front door. "What's the hurry, little one?"

She pushes past me, goes inside, walks straight to her bedroom, and closes the door.

I decide I'll give her a few minutes. I let Van in from the backyard and then walk to my bedroom and stash my backpack in the back corner of my closet. The cash inside nags at my conscience. "Out of sight, out of mind," I tell myself.

I go to Kaylee's room and tap on the door, then open it a crack and poke my head inside. She's lying on her bed, reading. "I'm going to make lunch—I'll call you when it's ready."

She ignores me.

I stop at the linen cabinet in the hallway and pull out an old quilt. I drape it over a chair in the kitchen. I open the fridge, pull out three hard-boiled eggs, mayonnaise, and mustard. As I chop the eggs and mix the ingredients, I wonder how long Kaylee will stay angry. Before Kathryn showed up yesterday, we'd developed an easy rapport. Kaylee trusted me, it seemed. And although silent, our relationship was marked by warmth and affection.

But now? This morning, when I went to the bathroom to comb her hair, she took the comb from my hand and began combing it herself. Her message was clear: I'll do it!

It seems I'll have to earn her trust again.

I stop stirring the egg salad and consider the dichotomy between the thought of regaining Kaylee's trust and my decision this morning to pay Kathryn off—to essentially aid her demise in order to keep Kaylee for myself. *Can* Kaylee trust me?

It's for her best, I remind myself. And I'm *not* aiding in Kathryn's demise. I'm helping her get back on her feet. End of story.

I make two sandwiches, slice two apples, put the sandwiches and fruit on plates, then grab a couple of the small individual bags of chips Kaylee likes so much and put it all on a tray. I pull a pitcher of lemonade out of the fridge and fill two tall glasses and add those to the tray as well. I also cut a slice of the angel food cake I made yesterday morning and put it on a plate for Kaylee.

I grab a fork for the cake, and add a couple of napkins. The perfect picnic.

I take the quilt out to the backyard and spread it on the lawn, then go back in the kitchen for the tray. I yell over my shoulder as I pick up the tray. "Kaylee, lunch." When I see her in the kitchen, nose still in her book, I call for her to come outside. "I thought we'd have a picnic."

She looks uninterested, plops down on the edge of the quilt, picks up half a sandwich, and eats while she reads.

There's so much I want to say to her. I want to talk to her about her mom, but then what would I say? Today her silence is contagious. I watch as she devours her lunch, with the exception of the chips, which she picks up and takes with her, back to her room, I presume.

And so the day goes. Kaylee reads, only coming out to get things from the kitchen. A banana once. A granola bar the next time. Then another bag of chips. She takes them all back to her room.

I let her. I'm glad she's eating.

After a long, silent day, I tell Kaylee it's time for bed. She washes her face and brushes her teeth, while I wait in her bedroom. She finally snuggles into bed and when I lean down to kiss her forehead, I'm met with the scents of soap and toothpaste.

"Would you like me to read to you for awhile?" I expect her to shake her head and turn away from me, just as she did when I offered to comb her hair, part of our nightly routine, but instead she looks at me and nods. My heart aches at the grief I see in her eyes.

"I'm sorry you're so sad. You are so lovable. Do you know that?" The shrug of her shoulders is barely noticeable—then she reaches for her book and hands it to me.

I look at the title, *The Clue of the Whistling Bagpipes*. "This is a good one." I sit on the edge of the bed next to her and she leans into me. *Okay, now we're getting somewhere.* "Last chapter?" She nods.

When I finish the chapter, I close the book, put it back on the shelf, turn on her night-light, and lean to kiss her good night one more time. As I bend over she reaches for me and clasps her little arms around my neck and clings to me. I hold her close, feeling each knob on her spine as I do, and I whisper in her ear, "I love you, Kaylee Wren." She squeezes hard, then lets go of me and lies back on her pillow.

"Tomorrow will be a better day, little one."

Later I climb into my own bed exhausted by the emotional strain of the day. I fall into a fitful sleep. I toss and turn, and when I sleep, my dreams seem straight from hell. The prick of a needle going into my arm wakes me from the last dream. I sit up in bed, heart pounding, palms sweating. I untangle myself from the sheets, and then turn and hang my legs over the side of the bed. I take deep breaths until I'm oriented.

I glance at the clock: 2:11 a.m. Great. I shake my head and shoulders, trying to loose the remnants of the dream from my mind. When I finally lie back down, all I can think of is the money in my backpack.

What was I thinking? In the hush of the night, without the murmured distractions of day, there is nowhere for my mind to go except to the truth: I'm not seeking Kaylee's best interest, I'm seeking my own. Protecting myself. Returning to the familiar rather than forging my way through the unknown. Relying on myself rather than God.

If I love Kaylee, and I do, then I have to love her mother.

I have to make the choice to love her. The choice my daddy

spoke of so often. "Real love is more than a feeling, it's a choice." He'd say.

I lean over and switch on the lamp on my nightstand, get out of bed, and rummage through the box on the floor that holds the things from the desk I'd had in Kaylee's room. I find what I'm looking for—a deposit slip—and fill it out in the amount of $1,500. I walk to my closet, reach for my backpack, and feel for the envelope of cash. I pull it out and put the deposit slip in with the cash. Tomorrow I'll return to the bank.

CHAPTER FORTY-ONE

aylee

AFTER SIERRA TUCKS ME IN, I lay awake for a long time. I can't let myself fall asleep tonight. I don't feel sleepy anyway. All day I've felt angry at Sierra, but tonight, when I knew it was the last time ever that she'd tuck me in, I couldn't be angry anymore. I wanted to be close to her, to feel her hair tickle my face as I hugged her, and to smell the flowery scent of her shampoo. I wanted to feel her warmth next to me and to have her kiss my forehead again.

More than anything, I wanted to say. "I love you too." But I couldn't.

I probably don't really love her anyway. Or maybe sometimes it's just easier to be mad at someone than it is to love them. I don't know.

con·found·ed—adjective 1. bewildered; confused; perplexed. That seems to be my permanent state of mind.

Sierra doesn't need me.

need—noun 1. to have need of; require: to need someone.

I don't need her either.

I did just fine without her before—sort of.

And she was just fine without me. Wasn't she? I think again of the things I heard her tell my mom—of her baby that died. When I think about that, it feels like someone is squeezing my heart. I roll over and lay my head on Van's back. I pet his forehead and scratch behind his ears.

I'll miss Van.

Sierra will come and get him and let him outside one last time before she goes to bed. She's really quiet when she lets him out, but I always feel Van jump up on my bed when he comes back in.

After Van comes back tonight, I'll wait for a long time until I'm sure Sierra's asleep. Then . . . I'll go. I have everything ready. My backpack is in the closet, all packed, except for the dictionary and Bible. I'll put those in last. I didn't want Sierra to notice them missing off the shelf. I'll have to be careful not to let them crush the bags of chips or squish the banana.

My plan is to walk to Marianne's, where my mom saw us. Maybe she lives around there somewhere. I can write people notes and ask if they know her and know where she lives. Nancy Drew always finds what she's looking for, so maybe I will too.

I don't have any money, but I have the chips and banana. That will last a couple of days; I've eaten less than that before.

When I'm sure Sierra is asleep, after the house has settled and everything's quiet, I tiptoe from my bed to the closet. I see Van lift his head to watch me, but he doesn't move. I grab my backpack and the granola bar I put next to it, then go to the bookshelf and get the dictionary and Bible. I shove them into my backpack. I pull the sides of the backpack together and struggle to zip it. It's a squeeze, but I finally get it zipped. Then I unwrap the granola bar and put it under Van's nose. He loves granola bars! This way he won't follow me to the front door.

I run to the bedroom door, crack it open just wide enough for me to fit through, then—I stop. I wait. I listen. I think again about all the things I heard Sierra tell my mom.

I poke my head out my bedroom door and look down the hallway.

Everything is dark.

I take a step into the hallway then stop. I swallow. The inside of my mouth feels like cotton and my tongue gets stuck on the roof of my mouth. I swallow again and it feels like I've swallowed a whole bag of cotton balls.

I wipe my palms on my shorts and readjust my backpack then tiptoe down the hallway. I keep one hand on the wall to help find my way in the dark. I stop at Sierra's bedroom door and listen.

Nothing.

I hesitate for just a minute, my feelings pulling me two different ways, but then I turn and go.

I don't need her.

I don't.

But before I reach the living room, my stomach lurches and

I feel like I'm going to be sick. I know this feeling. It's the feeling I used to get when I'd hear his truck coming into the driveway. It's the same feeling I had when I was lost in the forest.

I take a deep breath and stand up straighter.

Then . . .

I turn around and run back to my bedroom.

CHAPTER FORTY-TWO

ierra

I AWOKE this morning to the realization that I need to get back to work if I'm going to pay my bills without depleting my savings. Reality strikes. I have two commissioned pieces to complete and I'm anxious, as therapy for my own soul, to finish the painting of the redwood. That's not a piece I'll sell—I'll keep it for Kaylee. I'll work this morning and go to the bank this afternoon.

After breakfast I busy myself preparing a canvas in the kitchen. For awhile Kaylee sits at the kitchen table with a book, but I notice her eyes aren't moving—she stares at one page. She is a quick reader and I've grown accustomed to the slow, rhythmic sound of turning pages. This morning the pages don't turn. All is still.

Kaylee is out of rhythm. The difference is subtle but noticeable, because I've watched her so closely this last month—watching her is the way I've gotten to know her. Rather than listen to her words, I've watched her movements, her moods, her rhythms—and this morning she's out of sync. Perhaps it is the residual angst of yesterday.

"Hey . . ." My tone is soft—she still startles easily—but there's no response. She continues staring at her book—her face an unreadable mask.

"Kaylee . . . Are you okay?"

She nods her reply—that familiar up and down bobbing of her head. But I don't see affirmation of her well-being in her eyes. She reaches for her pad and pen.

Can I build a fort?

This is her first real communication of the day. "Sure. What do you need?"

The quilt.

Eyebrows raised, the look she gives me asks if that's okay. "That's fine."

She puts down her book and heads for the cabinet in the hallway. I hear the door bang shut and she comes back through the kitchen and goes out the sliding glass door to the backyard. She obviously has a plan. I watch as she uses chairs, the quilt, and rocks to build a fort. Then I see her coax Van inside and she, on her hands and knees, follows him. And I'm left wondering . . .

How do I know when to ask her deeper questions—to draw out what I sometimes see churning inside of her—or when to just let her be? What must she feel after seeing her mother—and then having her leave again? The familiar ache enters my heart when I consider, again, what she's been through. How does she deal with it all? Is her time with Dr. Beth helping? Will she finally open up and talk to her? Dr. Beth's words run through my mind again:

She feels safe with you, Sierra.

Oh, how I long to erase everything she's experienced and replace it with only love and tenderness. If only I had that power.

I turn my easel a bit so I can both work and watch the yard to keep an eye on Kaylee. She and Van seem settled for now. As I work, the familiar creative energy courses through me. For years creating was the only time I felt truly alive. But now, with Kaylee in my life, all that is changing. The ice that encased my soul for so long is melting. Underneath I'm finding a truer version of myself.

It's these thoughts and emotions I layer on the canvas in front of me. I used to lose myself in my work—it consumed my mind and all else fell away—including any sense of time. But now I know even the creative process can't block out the responsibility I feel for Kaylee. This, I realize, is another trait of motherhood.

I glance out at the yard again. Nothing has changed. Yet . . . something nags. I set my brush in the tray on my easel and wipe my hands on the old work shirt I wear when I work, and then

I head for the backyard.

Barefoot, my step is light across the deck as I avoid places where the wood is splintered. I step onto the grass and stand rooted, listening. I'm not sure what I expect to hear. Suddenly the middle section of the fort, the quilt, pushes into a pyramid shape and then pulls out from under the rocks and in a flurry it falls to the ground. Kaylee stands, eyes squinting against the sun, the quilt around her feet. Her hands cover her ears—just like they were the first day I saw her. She looks right at me but doesn't seem to see me. She stands like that for a moment and then, slowly, her hands drop from her ears to her side. Her little body trembles.

Van crawls out from under the quilt where he was buried. He stands, looks at Kaylee, and then walks across the crumpled quilt and sits next to her. Something is wrong, and Van senses it too.

The answer to my earlier question stands before me. I *will* know when it's time to try and draw her out when the time is right.

And the time is right now.

CHAPTER FORTY-THREE

aylee

THE FORT IS dark and warm inside. I sit, Indian style, in the middle of the small space, resting my elbows on my knees and my chin in my hands. Van lies down in front of me.

I breathe in through my nose, hoping for the smell of burnt wood, but instead smell fresh cut grass. It's not a bad smell, it's just not the same.

I need to ruminate. That means I need to think hard about some things—like why I didn't go last night. And other things too. Things I should probably think about before I leave to find my mom. That's probably why I didn't go. I just had a feeling I needed to think through a few more things.

That's all.

It's not like I was scared or anything. I'm not a baby. I can do whatever I need to do. And I need to find my mom. And I will. But first, I just need to think and plan a little more.

That's the smart thing to do.

First, I need to think about the things I heard Sierra say to my mom. Lots of things. Like for one, that my mom's an addict. I know what an addict is and not from the dictionary. I learned about it at school during Red Ribbon Week. That's when they teach you about drugs and how they can hurt you. I knew my mom used drugs because I heard Grammy talking to her about it —that's what they got in a fight about before we moved out of Grammy's house. But I couldn't think about it then. People who use drugs are bad. That's what the kids at school said.

Maybe . . .

Maybe my mom didn't have amnesia.

My breath seems to catch in my throat and I swallow hard.

I consider that thought. I lay down on the grass with my head next to Van's head.

Maybe the drugs just made her forget me.

Ruminating gives me that heavy feeling in my chest—a hurting kind of feeling.

But there's more . . . Sierra said she was an addict too. More than Sierra taking drugs, I need to think about Annie. Sierra had a daughter—a baby who died because Sierra took drugs. I feel like I'm wearing 3-D glasses, like the kind I got out of a box of Froot Loops once. When you put them on, you see things in a different way. You see more than one of whatever you're looking at. Now, when I look at Sierra, that's how I feel—like I'm seeing more than one of her—like she's two people. There's the Sierra I know now. And then there's the Sierra who used drugs and whose baby died. It's hard to make them seem like the same person.

I remember how I felt when Grammy died. Was that how Sierra felt when Annie died? My throat gets tight and the weight on my chest gets heavier.

I remember the first time I saw her standing in the clearing. She was crying. Was she thinking about Annie that day?

I roll over and put my cheek on Van's back—his fur tickles my nose. Does Sierra love me because I remind her of Annie, or does she just love me because I'm me?

Maybe she needs me too, just like my mom needs me.

Will my mom be okay? If I don't find her, who will help her? How will she get better? I have to go. I have to find her. But that means leaving Sierra . . . How can I leave Sierra, now that I know she needs me too?

I have other questions too, questions I don't want to think about—questions that make me feel sick to my stomach. Like did my mom take drugs because of me? Did I do something wrong? Was it because of what he did to me? I think back . . .

No, she took drugs before him. When we lived with Grammy, or they wouldn't have had that fight. We moved in with him after that. But still maybe what he did made it worse for her.

And why . . .

Why didn't she . . .

How come she didn't . . . make him stop?

That's not a question I can ask anyone. I can't tell anyone.

I close my eyes, but when I do, I see him. I remember the things he did. I open my eyes and sit up. I put my hands over my ears.

I shake my head and rock back and forth.

Please make it stop. Please make it stop!

But the scream keeps going, on and on in my head. The scream rages louder than ever. Finally, I stand up—fast. I forget about the quilt and when I stand it comes undone from under the rocks and falls off the chairs and I'm standing in the sunlight.

In the light the scream stops.

athryn

"I'M . . . Kathryn. Kathryn Wren. My . . . my daughter, Kaylee Wren, is in foster care. I need to talk to someone."

She stops, not knowing what else to say. *I abandoned my daughter but I'd like her back now.*

Like that's going to happen.

The receptionist writes down her name and, pointing to a row of blue plastic chairs against a wall, tells her to have a seat. Kathryn looks around the stark office and thinks of the last time she renewed her driver's license. Maybe all county agencies look the same. She takes a seat and tries to hold still. She clasps her palms together to keep them from shaking and wills her feet not to tap, but it doesn't work. She takes deep breaths hoping to at least keep the insistent nausea from taking over.

I want, I need, to get out of here. But the words that woman, the one who has Kaylee, said run through her mind for the thousandth time since standing on her doorstep a few days ago: *Your story can end differently* . . . She wants to believe her. She gets up and walks back to the reception desk. "I don't have a lot of time. I need to talk to someone now! She's my daughter. I have rights!"

"It will be just a few minutes, Ms. Wren. Please, take a seat."

She walks back to the chairs along the wall but knows she can't sit still. Instead she walks back and forth, keeping her eye on the receptionist. She sees her pick up the phone and call someone. The receptionist watches her as she talks to whoever's on the other end.

What is taking so long? She opens and closes her mouth trying to stretch the muscles in her jaw. She sits. She stands. She scratches the back of her neck. She sits again, this time crossing one leg over the other. Her foot bounces. Finally she sees a large man come out of an office behind the reception desk. He has a file folder in one hand. When he reaches the receptionist, he bends and says something she can't hear—then they both look at her. She stands again.

"Ms. Wren?" He comes around the reception desk toward her and reaches out his hand. She wipes her palm on her jeans and then shakes his hand.

"Yeah, I'm Kathryn Wren. I'd like to talk to someone about my daughter, Kaylee Wren."

"I'm glad you're here. We've been looking for you since Kaylee came our way. I'm Peter Langstrom."

She frowns. Wants to ask, "How did she 'come your way'?"

Did Jack bring her here? Was she okay? What happened? What did she tell you?

But each question, she realizes, incriminates her. She walked away from Kaylee. *You abandoned her.* The voice in her head, the one she wants to muzzle, begins its accusations.

Accusations? It's the truth—you abandoned her.

I thought she'd be better off without me.

Really, or was that just your excuse?

She is better off without me. She is. I should just leave her where she is—with . . . With who? I don't even know who she's with. Guilt chokes her.

Whoever she is, she's better for Kaylee than Jack. You didn't mind leaving her with him, why does it matter who she's with now?

She shakes her head and tries to focus—to ignore the argument going on in her mind. She looks up at the face of the man in front of her and realizes he's said something, but she doesn't know what. "What? What did you say?"

She hears his voice again. He must repeat what he's said, but still she only hears the voices in her head. *She's better off without you. She is. You're worthless. She doesn't need you.*

"I'm . . . I'm sorry. I . . . I made a mistake. I shouldn't have come . . ." She turns and begins to walk toward the door. She wants to run. Away—away from herself—as far away as she can go. She wants to run . . . But there's only one way to get away from herself, to turn off the voices in her head.

Yes, you know the way. Craving claws at her from the inside out. *You know what you need. You know . . .*

Somewhere behind her a voice shouts. "Wait. You can't leave. Wait!"

She can leave.

She knows.

She's done it before.

Your story can end differently . . . differently . . . It can end differently.

She hesitates for just a second, but in that second the voice behind her reaches her. The man—what did he say his name was? —puts his hand on her shoulder and she hears him speak again. "Ms. Wren. Please wait. Let us help you. We're here to help—to reunite you with your daughter."

Help? Help me? I'm beyond help . . .

She hesitates. "Reunite me with Kaylee?"

"Yes, eventually, if possible. That's always our goal. I need to ask you some questions." He puts one hand on her shoulder and motions behind the reception desk. "My office is this way. I'd like to go over Kaylee's file with you and . . ."

He steers her in the direction of his office, asking her questions along the way. "First, we need contact information. Your address, phone number . . ."

Your story can end differently . . .

No it can't, you know it can't. Who are you kidding?

Differently . . . It can end differently.

You're beyond help.

"Ms. Wren? Did you hear me? How can we reach you? We'd like to help you, but we'll need some information—"

"Help me?"

He can't help you. He doesn't have what you need.

She scratches the back of her neck again—this time, her fingers come away bloodied. She's scratched off one of many scabs. She looks at the blood on her fingers and then looks at the man to see if he's noticed. He has. He watches her for a moment, then turns around and reaches for a tissue from a box on a file cabinet behind his desk. He hands it to her.

"Thanks . . . mosquito bites."

He nods. "Ms. Wren, Kathryn, let us help you."

Your story can end differently . . .

CHAPTER FORTY-FIVE

aylee

I SHIVER as I feel the warmth of the sun on my shoulders. The quilt is on the ground around my feet. There's a lump in the middle—Van! Then I see Sierra standing in front of me. I don't know how long she's been there. When she sees that I see her, she walks toward me and puts her hands on my shoulders then she wraps me in a tight hug.

"Hey, little one, are you okay?"

I pull back from her and I nod—I'm fine. I'm not fine, but I don't want her to know—to ask me questions.

Sierra bends down and picks up the quilt. "Here, let's spread this out on the grass. She grabs an edge of the quilt and starts to drag it away from the chairs. "Want to help me?"

I know it's not really a question but more like a statement. So I grab the other side of the quilt and follow her. When she stops, we shake the quilt out together and it lands flat on the grass.

"Have a seat, kiddo. I want to talk to you." Sierra looks at me—

her face is serious. But then she smiles—it seems like kind of a sad smile though. "Stay put a minute—I'm going to get your pad and pen."

I watch her walk away and wonder what she wants to talk about. I have a bad feeling. When she comes back, she hands me the pad. I open it and write:

Am I in trouble?

"Oh, Kaylee, no, of course not, I just want to talk. You have lots going on in your life, and I thought it might help if we talked about some of it, okay? I'll talk, and you can write."

I nod. But I don't know if it's okay or not. Some things aren't okay to talk about or write about. Van comes over and lies next to me—he puts his head in my lap.

"That dog sure loves you." She watches us for a minute—then she comes and sits across from me. She takes a deep breath and then she reaches out and pets Van's back. She looks like she's trying to figure out what she wants to say. I wait. The scream is still ringing in my ears.

"Um . . . Kaylee, I've never . . . I'm not used to . . ."

It sounds like Sierra's words are a little stuck. I know how she feels. She's pulling at a thread in the quilt as she tries to talk. But then she stops and looks at my face. I can see she's having a hard time. She starts again. "Kaylee, do you know how much I love you?"

I start to nod, but then I shrug my shoulders instead. I'm not sure how much—or if she even does—even when she tells me she loves me—it's sort of hard to believe her.

"I love you so much, little one. And because I love you, I hurt when you hurt. Does that make sense?"

I think about what she's said for a minute. But she doesn't wait for me to respond, instead, she keeps talking.

"And when I see that you're hurting, I want to help if I can. But

I don't always know the right thing to do. I haven't been a parent before—I mean, not a parent to . . . I mean, I'm not your parent. You have a parent . . ."

I look down at my pad and think about what I want to ask. Will it hurt Sierra to talk about it? I don't know. But I need to know about Annie.

But, you had a daughter. Right?

I hand my notebook to Sierra and watch her face as she reads. She looks startled. Her gaze moves from the page of the notebook and focuses on the quilt.

I take the notebook out of her hand and scribble a quick note.

I'm sorry.

I put the notebook back on her lap and she looks at it then looks back at me.

"No, Kaylee, it's okay. I just didn't know that you knew.

I didn't know how much you heard the day I talked to your mom. Yes, I had Annie. I was Annie's parent—her mom." Sierra seems to think for a minute—she seems to make a decision. "Kaylee, there's nothing I won't talk to you about. I will tell you anything you want to know—anything. If you have questions about Annie, or about your mom, or about anything, I'll try to answer them. I will always be honest with you. Okay?"

I nod. I have lots of questions. But I've never really had anyone to ask. I know there are some things, like the questions that made the scream start, that I can't ever ask. But there are other things I want to know.

I take the notebook back again and think for a minute. Then I write what I've been wondering about.

The first day I saw you

I stop. I don't want to make her feel bad.

"The first day you saw me . . . It's okay, Kaylee. Go ahead. You can ask."

I realize she's watching me and reading as I write. I finish my question.

You were crying. Was that because of Annie?

Sierra looks from the pad of paper out to her rose garden. She sighs. I look down at the quilt and trace the pattern of a flower on one of the squares of fabric.

"I want to tell you, Kaylee. I'm just not used to talking about this so you'll have to be patient with me. Not everything is easy to talk about." She reaches over and puts her hand under my chin and lifts my face up so I'm looking at her again. "Okay?"

I nod.

"Yes. I was crying about Annie that day. It was the anniversary of the day she died and I'd just come from the cemetery. I go there once a year. I was . . . angry. Angry at myself. Angry because she died."

Because of drugs?

I can tell my question hurts her. I don't want to hurt her, but I need to know.

"Yes, because of drugs." Sierra starts pulling on the thread in the quilt again. She doesn't look at me when she talks. "Drugs can take over a person's mind, and then they do things they'd never do otherwise. It's like the drugs start making the choices—not the person. Or something like that. It doesn't mean I wasn't responsible for what happened—I was. But . . . It's hard to explain . . ."

Is that what

I stop.

Never mind.

"Is that what happened to your mom?" Sierra whispers the question. "Little one, is that what you were going to ask?" She reaches over and takes my hand in one of hers. She brushes her other hand across my forehead and then smooths down my hair. I swallow and my throat aches. Then I nod my head—yes, that's what I was going to ask.

"Kaylee, look at me." She tilts my head up again. "First, I want you to know that you didn't do anything wrong. You aren't responsible in any way for your mom's problems. Do you understand that?"

I try to wipe away the tears running down my cheeks, but they just keep coming. I shake my head—just a little.

"Kaylee? Do you understand that nothing you've gone through is your fault?" Sierra scoots over and sits right next to me. She puts her arm around my shoulders and pulls me close to her.

Tears drip onto my notepad. I lean into her and bury my face in her sweatshirt.

"It's okay. It's okay to cry. Just let it all out. You've been through so much." She hugs me tighter and whispers in my ear. "Oh, Kaylee, I love you."

I feel like something inside me breaks, like a water balloon pops and everything comes gushing out. My whole body shakes and it gets hard to breathe. I gulp for air. I see dark spots on Sierra's sweatshirt where my tears have fallen. Sierra holds me close and keeps whispering in my ear. "It's okay, little one, it's okay. Just let it all out. It's okay . . ."

I hiccup and finally pull away. I pick up my pen again.

She didn't have amnesia, did she?

Sierra is quiet. I look up to see her face—she's staring out at the grass. I can tell she's being careful about what she's going to say. "I don't think so, Kaylee. I think the drugs made her forget . . . everything. At least for awhile. I don't know for sure, but that's my best guess. I think she's taking drugs and it's made her do things she wouldn't have done otherwise." She looks down at me and then pulls her sweatshirt sleeve down over one hand and wipes my eyes and my nose with it. Then she shrugs and smiles. "We'll wash it later."

I nod, then I ask another question, just to make sure.

So using drugs is kind of like having amnesia?

"Drugs can make you forget what's important and forget who you are." Sierra gives me a squeeze and then wipes her own eyes with her sleeve.

Do you think she loves me?

"Of course she loves you. After all, you're soooo lovable!" She smiles and then leans down until the tip of her nose is touching the tip of mine. "How could she help but love you? She's just not herself right now. May I ask you a question now?"

I nod.

"When I saw you that first day, you had your hands covering your ears—like this." She puts her hands over her ears just like I do. "And then today, I saw you do the same thing. Can you tell me why you do that? Can you explain it to me?"

I feel my face get hot. I look down at the quilt and the squares blur in front of me. I wipe the tears and try to swallow the lump in my throat again.

"Kaylee?"

Aardvark.

Albino.

"Little one, does it . . . does it have something to do with . . . the man at the cabin. Something to do with him?" She puts her hand under my chin and lifts my face up so I'm looking at her, but I look away.

Babka.

Bombastic.

Cloister.

"Kaylee, I know what he did to you and I think it will help you if you can share it with someone. Either me or with Dr. Beth."

Cohort.

I put my hands over my ears and pull my knees to my chest. I wrap my arms around my legs and bury my face against my knees. The scream, louder than ever, rages through my mind and body. My legs and arms start to shake and I rock back and forth.

Colloquial.

Crescendo.

The scream won't stop.

Cretin.

I can't make it stop.

I feel Sierra lie down next to me. She puts her arms around me and holds onto me.

I can never tell her.

I can never tell anyone.

Never.

CHAPTER FORTY-SIX

ierra

I HOLD the phone in my hand and try to decide who to call. Dr. Beth is probably the right choice, she told me to call if I noticed "extreme angst" in Kaylee, but it's Pete's card I hold. I dial his number.

After identifying myself to the receptionist who answers the phone, I wait. And wait.

"Hey, Sierra?"

"I blew it. I think I really blew it. I don't know what I was thinking. I just thought if we could talk about it, if she could share it with me—maybe it would help. But I didn't know. I don't know. I shouldn't have asked. I don't know what I'm doing. I don't know!"

"Whoa, Sierra, slow down. Take a deep breath. Good. Take another. Okay. One more. Great. Now, tell me what you're talking about."

I feel my heart rate slow as I take Pete's prescribed breaths. The strength and warmth I sense in his voice reassure and my mind begins to clear. "Okay, I think I blew it with Kaylee. Something seemed to be bothering her this morning. She wasn't herself. She hasn't been since seeing her mom. So I thought if I could get her to talk about it, I mean write about it, maybe it would help. Dr. Beth says Kaylee feels safe with me, so I thought maybe she'd share it with me and it was going pretty well, until . . . until . . ."

"Until?"

"Well, earlier, I was watching her in the backyard and I saw her cover her ears—like she was trying to block out a loud noise, and then I could see her begin to tremble. Her whole body was shaking like a leaf. So I began questioning her. I finally asked her why she'd been covering her ears. I told her she'd done that the first day I saw her, and I wondered if she could tell me why . . ."

"Good. Did she respond?"

"Good?" I'm baffled by his response. "No, she didn't respond. So then, oh I can't believe I did this, but . . . I pressed a little more. I asked her if it had anything to do with Jack. I could see I'd embarrassed her or that she felt ashamed or something. Oh, Pete, I could see it on her face. She began to cry and then turned away from me. After a minute she covered her ears again. Then she laid down in a fetal position, with her hands over her ears. It was like she wasn't there anymore—like she was somewhere else. Oh, it was awful. I didn't know what to do."

"What did you do?"

Pete's voice remains calm, like he has complete confidence in me. His tone implies concern for Kaylee but holds no condemnation for me—which, honestly, baffles me. "Um. I laid down next to her and put my arms around her. I stroked her back and her hair. I knew she wouldn't hear anything I said, so I just held her until she calmed—until she finally took her hands away from her ears."

"Good. Good. So when did you blow it?"

"What?"

"You said you blew it. When did you blow it?"

I try to shake the confusion from my head before I respond. Didn't he hear me? "The whole thing. I blew the whole thing. I shouldn't have asked her those questions—shouldn't have referred to Jack . . . Obviously I handled it wrong."

"Tell me what happened next."

"Well, I kept stroking her back and when she took her hands off her ears and I thought she could hear me again, I told her that I loved her and that nothing she'd experienced was her fault. I'd told her that earlier too when we talked about her mom."

"Wait . . . Did she talk about her mom?"

"Yes, she wrote down a few questions for me. Questions about things she overheard when Kathryn was here. She asked about her mom using drugs. Oh, Pete, she has so much to deal with." I sigh. "I'm so sorry. I pressed her too hard. I should have left that conversation to Dr. Beth or you—someone who knows what they're doing."

"Huh. Sierra, from where I'm sitting, you handled everything just right. Your instinct is great. Kaylee communicates with you. She's open to you—at least more open than she is with anyone else. If she's going to open up, my guess is she'll open up to you. I really think you did just fine."

"What? Really? But . . ."

"Tell me what she's doing now. How is she now?"

"Now?" I peek out the kitchen window and look at her again. "She's sitting on a quilt in the backyard, eating a sandwich, and playing with Van."

"She's eating and playing?"

"Yes. After she calmed down, I asked her if she was hungry." I laugh when I remember her response. "Want to know what she wrote?"

GINNY L. YTTRUP

"Sure."

"Her note said she was ravenous. She even defined *ravenous* for me. Evidently she doubts my vocabulary skills."

"You did know what ravenous meant, didn't you?"

I can almost see the smile on his face as he teases. "Duh!"

With Pete's chuckle, I feel my neck and shoulders relax. The tension from the last hour eases. I listen as Pete fills me in on some recent developments with Kaylee's mom, but it's too much for me to think about now. I'm spent. I'll have to consider his news later.

"Sierra."

I strain to hear him. His voice has softened to a whisper.

"You're amazing." He clears his throat. "I mean, you did an amazing job with her. You really did. From a professional standpoint, you may have pushed her, but you also opened a door for her. Kaylee's in bondage—a prison of silence. Speaking, especially speaking the truth about what happened to her and allowing those around her to help her understand that it wasn't her fault, will help set her free. She needs to speak, and she needs, when she's ready, to speak the truth. Be cautious—don't push her too hard. You're walking a fine line. But today you gave her permission to tell you what she's been through. You invited her to share her story."

"Okay, thanks. I won't push her too hard. I just . . . I just want to help her."

"You are helping her. And you're doing a great job."

Okay, thanks. Thanks for your time and for . . . you know . . . your encouragement and everything."

"No problem."

Just as I'm ready to hang up, he stops me.

"Sierra?"

"Yes?"

"Hang in there. I meant what I said earlier, you are amazing. Good-bye."

I hold the phone in my hand, startled. I don't know what to do with his compliment . . . Soon, I realize, I'm grinning like a school girl with her first crush. "Oh good grief! Get a grip, Sierra!" I bang the receiver down and head outside to check on Kaylee.

aylee

"KIND OF A LONG DAY, wasn't it, kiddo?"

Sierra sits next to me on my bed. I see her reach for the comb and I shake my head. NO. I take the comb from her hand. Combing my hair isn't her job. I can do it myself. I run the comb through the sides and back a few times and then reach around her and put it back on the table. She just watches me.

"Would you like me to read to you tonight?"

I shrug.

Sierra gets up, bends down in front of the bookshelf, and pulls out my Bible. She opens it to *The Gospel According to Mark*. We started with *The Gospel According to Matthew*. She said the Gospels are the stories about Jesus. That's what Grandma Bickford thought I'd like. And she was right. Sierra told me that Matthew, Mark, Luke, and John were some of Jesus' disciples and that they each wrote about Jesus from their own perspective.

The first three definitions for **dis·ci·ple** all say that it's someone who follows Christ. Christ is Jesus' last name, I think. So I guess even the person who wrote the dictionary knew about Jesus.

Sierra's voice is soft as she reads and my eyes get heavy. I have a hard time keeping my mind on the story about someone who was deaf. Instead I keep thinking about Sierra's questions earlier today—her questions about him. But I don't want to think about him anymore. I yawn and pull the blanket up around my chin and close my eyes.

Sierra keeps reading. "'He has done everything well, they said. He even makes the deaf hear and the mute speak.'"

I sit up. What did she say? I grab Sierra's arm and pull the Bible toward me so I can read it myself.

"Kaylee, it said Jesus can make the mute speak." She points to the verse she just read.

I read it for myself. Jesus can make the mute speak? Can He make me speak? I lie back down and think about what I would say if I could talk. I think again of the questions Sierra asked me this afternoon. Would I have to answer her questions if I could talk?

"There's another verse somewhere in the Bible that says 'all things are possible with God.' Or something like that. Jesus can do anything."

I turn my head away from Sierra and face the other wall. I've heard enough for tonight. She seems to understand and leans over and kisses my forehead. "Good night, little one." She stands and reaches for the lamp and then stops. "Shhh . . . Do you hear that?"

I listen and look up at Sierra. She's smiling. The noise—what sounds like screaming—comes again. I can just barely hear it. Sierra's looking at the window that's open over my bed.

"It's the Giant Dipper. The ride at the Boardwalk. There it is again, hear it? You can hear the people screaming as they go down the biggest drop. Sometimes the sound carries on the breeze in the evenings. Do you like roller coasters?"

I shrug. I don't know. I've never been on one.

"Oh, the Giant Dipper is really fun! I'll have to take you soon, before the Boardwalk closes for the winter. Would you like that?"

I shrug again. Maybe. I'm not sure about the screaming part.

She leans over and kisses my forehead again and squeezes my shoulder. "Want me to close your window? Or does the breeze feel good?"

I just look at her. Does she expect me to answer?

"Sorry. Sometimes I forget. I'll close it when I come in later and let Van out." She gently tugs on a clump of my hair and bends down again and whispers in my ear. "I love you, Kaylee Wren. Sweet dreams."

Sierra turns to leave but I reach for her. I catch the hem of her shirt and pull on it. She stops, turns around, and looks down at me. I hesitate but then I open my mouth and even though I know nothing will come out, I mouth the words, *I love you, too.*

She bends down again and puts her arms around me and gives me a tight squeeze. When she looks at me her expression is serious, like she might cry. Finally she says, "Kaylee, you just gave me a precious gift. Thank you." She walks to the door and turns off the light. "Good night, little one."

I lie still for a long time. The questions from earlier keep me awake. When Sierra asked why I cover my ears, she knew, somehow, that it had something to do with him. How did she know? If she knows, what does she think? Does she think I'm bad?

She said today that nothing I've gone through is my fault, but she doesn't know everything. If she knew, she wouldn't say that. It had to be my fault.

I must have done something wrong or that wouldn't have happened.

I roll over and bury my face in my pillow. I reach behind me for Van, and sink my hand in the fur on his back. He turns and I feel his wet nose nuzzling my hand. I roll back over and scoot down next to him. I pull my pillow down and lay my head next to his.

I can't think about all that now. I need to think about my plan. I have to go. I have to find my mom, to help her. I knew I couldn't go tonight because—well, I just couldn't. But I'll have to go tomorrow. I feel that big boulder sitting on my chest again.

I turn my head so I'm nose to nose with Van; I put my arm around him and hug him tight.

I lie there with Van for a long time thinking about my plan—and listening to the screams of people who are supposedly having fun.

CHAPTER FORTY-EIGHT

ierra

I LOVE YOU, too . . .

Kaylee's words—the words she mouthed—hold so much for me. Too much, probably—comfort, hope, even healing.

Her love is God's grace to me.

Is it truly possible that what my mother and daddy have said all these years really applies to me too? All my sins are forgiven? Even what I did to Annie? What my choices caused? My mother's oft-quoted verse comes to mind again. "The truth will set you free . . ." And I hear the question she asked equally often, *What's the truth, Shannon?*

Finally I'm beginning to understand the freedom found in the truth. Christ died to forgive my sins and He has forgiven me. Even more amazing is that He loves me. *He* loves *me*. The accusations I've lived with for so long have quieted. My mind is still and I'm resting in truth. Freedom.

Tonight I also dare to hope. I hope for an enduring relationship with Kaylee. I pray for Kaylee, her healing—her freedom.

I don't know what I'm doing, I don't know how to help her. All I know how to do is love her. I give the rest to God; I try something new: I turn all my hopes and dreams over to Him . . . and I trust.

Then I think again of Kaylee. Pete is right, the truth *will* set her free. She must speak her truth so we can speak truth back to her. I will spend the rest of my life telling her that what she went through —her mother's drug use, the abuse, all of it—wasn't her fault. She paid the price for others' actions. The familiar anger I feel whenever I think of what Kaylee suffered wells within me again. Then a new thought hits me—and stuns me. Kaylee, an innocent child, paid the price for others' poor choices—just like Christ, who was also completely innocent, paid the price for my choices.

"I get it." I whisper into the dark, choking back tears. "I really . . . get it." I pull myself out of the Adirondack chair and step down to the lawn. There, standing barefoot on the grass, I lift my face to the sky. The Big Dipper hangs low over the bungalow against the black velvet sky and millions of stars dance overhead. Who am I to deny God's mercy? His forgiveness? Who am I to think I know more than the Creator?

Who am I? I know who I am. I am completely unworthy. But I am completely loved. I bow my head, humbled, and offer my gratitude . . . "Thank You for loving me and forgiving me. Thank You." I wrap my arms around myself and head back into the bungalow. It has been a long day.

I'm sure I fell asleep with a smile on my face, but I wake with a start, heart pounding, body tense, and fully alert. The sound that woke me comes again shattering the silence of the night. Screaming! Coming from Kaylee's room!

I bolt from my bed and down the hallway, reaching her in seconds, I'm sure, although it feels like it takes much longer. Too long. She is in her bed, thrashing back and forth, arms flinging overhead as though she's trying to hit something or someone.

I reach for her shoulders to shake her awake and notice that her sheets and pillow are soaked. Tears glisten on her cheeks. She screams again—a deep, primal, agonizing scream.

The first sound, I realize, I've ever heard come from her mouth.

"Kaylee!" I shake her. "Wake up! Little one, wake up! It's just a dream!" I shake her again—less gentle this time. I must wake her. I must pull her from whatever horror has her in its grip.

"Kaylee!"

She quiets, the thrashing stops, and her eyes open. But she isn't seeing me—she's still lost in the nightmare.

"Look at me. Look at my face. It's me. You're having a nightmare—everything's okay. You're okay." I sit on the side of the bed and reach for the lamp and turn it on. Then I put my arms around her, but she pushes me away. One of her fists flies toward my face. I dodge her blow and grab her arms. "Oh, Kaylee, it's okay. It's just me. You're okay."

As she tries to focus on me, I realize that she's not okay. Of course she's not okay. I put my hands on either side of her little face. "Shh . . . it was a nightmare. You're here now."

Her eyes, wild with fear, finally focus on my eyes, but her body trembles. Then she lifts her hands and covers her ears.

I drop my hands from her face and wrap my arms around her shoulders and hold her trembling body tight. For the second time in twelve hours, I stroke her back and her hair and hold her until finally her arms drop back down to her side and her breathing returns to normal. I finally let her go, but just long enough to move from sitting on the edge of her bed to lying down next to her. I put one arm under her shoulders and the other around the front of her, then pull her close. And there, with her head on my shoulder, she falls back to sleep.

I lie awake holding her all night. I hold her until the rays of a new day filter through the curtains above her bed. I begin the day with a whispered prayer. "This is the day the Lord has made . . ."

It is a verse I remember from Sunday school, and today it is a prayer of commitment. I commit Kaylee's day, and mine, to God. He is in control.

He has to be, because I have no idea what I'm doing.

CHAPTER FORTY-NINE

aylee

I HOLD my breath and count.

One thousand one, one thousand two, one thousand three . . .

When I reach one thousand forty, my lungs burn and I let out a *woosh* of air and then suck in a deep breath. Then I hiccup again.

"Okay, let's try something else." Sierra gets up from the table and goes to a cabinet and pulls out the sugar bowl. Then she gets a spoon and a glass. She fills the glass with water and brings it to the table. She dips the spoon in the sugar bowl and takes out a heaping spoonful.

"Open your mouth and swallow the sugar as fast as you can. Then drink the whole glass of water."

She puts the spoon of sugar in my mouth and I try to swallow the dry granules, but they get stuck in my throat. I swallow again but feel like I might choke. I reach for the glass of water.

"Drink the whole thing without stopping."

I gulp the water and drink the whole glass. I set it on the table and wait. Sierra watches me. We both wait.

"Hey, that did it!"

And then, I hiccup again.

"Oh no. Well you may just have to wait them out. Do you want to try to eat some breakfast or do you want to wait until the hiccups are gone?"

I grab my pen.

Wait.

I slump in my chair and scribble little circles in my notebook. The nightmare last night seemed so real, just like I was back at the cabin with him. But in the dream my mom was there too. She was sitting on a chair in the kitchen, which wasn't really like the kitchen in the cabin at all, but that's how dreams are. She was watching him and he was watching me. Then her head sort of rolled to one side and rested on her shoulder. Her eyes were still open but she wasn't really looking at anything. He looked at her; then he came and sat down next to me and put his hand on my thigh. I knew what was going to happen but instead of just waiting for it to happen, I pushed his hand away. But then he grabbed me. I started to scream and tried to fight him, but he was too big. I kept screaming for my mom, but she never came to help. She just sat in the chair, staring at nothing.

Now I can't get the nightmare out of my mind and the scream is in my head. I shake my head, I hiccup, and I shake my head again. But this morning I can't make the scream go away. I cover my ears and lay my head on the table.

Pretty soon Sierra sits in the chair next to me. She reaches over and takes my hands off my ears. "Little one? How can I help?"

I don't know. All I can think about is my mom and how she looked in my dream. And I think about him and I hear the scream.

Then I hiccup again. Sierra scoots her chair closer to me. Finally she asks me if I'd like to listen to some music. "Would that help?"

I nod. I don't know if it will help, but maybe . . .

She gets up and goes to her room. When she comes back, she has headphones connected to her MP3 player. She puts the headphones on my ears and turns up the volume. The music fills my head. Sierra sits by me again and starts rubbing my back.

With my head resting on the table, and Sierra's hand on my back, and the sound of the music filling my ears, my eyes get heavy and my breathing gets more normal. The hiccups go away. I sit like that for a long time.

Sierra always knows how to make me feel better.

That should make me feel good.

But it doesn't.

Sierra lifts a headphone off one of my ears. "Hey, kiddo, that was an awfully big sigh. I'm sorry you're having a hard morning. I wish I could make whatever's troubling you go away." She leans forward and whispers, "How about some breakfast now?"

I lift my head off the table just enough to nod. I better eat. This might be the last day I get to eat for a while.

"Another sigh? Do you want me to call Dr. Beth? Would it help for you to see her this morning?"

I sit up, pull the headphones off, and shake my head. No. No way. No. That won't help. She'll just ask me questions I can't answer and make me draw something. That won't help. I know what I have to do. I reach for my notebook.

May I have oatmeal and bananas?

Sierra reads my note. "Oatmeal and bananas it is." She gets up and starts to make my breakfast. While she's cooking, the picture of my mom from my nightmare last night stays in my mind. It isn't hard to remember, because I've seen her like that before: just staring, sometimes scratching at her neck and face, shaking.

When she was like that, I'd get a wet washcloth and hold it on her forehead or neck. Or I'd get a glass of water and hold it while she'd take sips. Sometimes I could get her to lie down in her bed and I'd lie next to her. When she'd get sick, when she'd throw up, I'd hold her hair back, like she used to do for me when I was little and I got sick. Then I'd put toothpaste on her toothbrush and help her brush her teeth.

When she was like that, I don't even think she knew I was there. Maybe she was like that because of the drugs—maybe I'm starting to understand. One thing I know for sure is that she needs someone to help her.

And it has to be me.

I'm the only one she has.

I look at Sierra who's standing at the stove stirring the oatmeal and I slump back down in my chair. She doesn't need me. She doesn't. She has Ruby and her parents and her job. She'll be fine. I tell myself this over and over. But then a little voice in my head interrupts and says, *But you need her . . .*

I lay my head back down on the table.

I don't need her.

I just like her and I like being here. But I don't really need her. I don't!

"Here you go. Go light on the brown sugar, okay?" Sierra sets the bowl down in front of me, but I push it away.

It's time for me to go.

And this time I'm resolved.

re · solved—1. firm in purpose or intent; determined.

Resolved means this time I won't change my mind.

I spend the day getting ready again—just like I did last time.

I spend most of the day in my room reading. Sierra comes in several times and asks me questions. "Would you like to go to the wharf this afternoon? We could watch the seals."

No.

"What about a drive over to Monterey? We could go to Dennis the Menace Park—I bet you'd love it."

No.

"The Boardwalk? We could ride the Giant Dipper this afternoon!"

To this suggestion I shake my head hard. No!

"Okay!" Sierra's voice gets quiet. I can tell she's worried. "Kaylee, are you . . . are you upset because of your mom? Or . . . does it have something to do with Jack? You know you can tell me anything. If you'll just tell me what you're feeling, I think it would help. If you could just tell me . . ."

No! I take the book I'm holding and throw it against the wall. No! No! *No!*

Sierra jumps. I see anger replace concern on her face. She walks over and picks up the book, sets it on the bookshelf, and then walks back to my bedroom door. "Kaylee, I only want to help you. Throwing things is inappropriate behavior, even if you are angry." Her words are steady, like she's working really hard to say the right thing. "I know you're tired. So am I. We didn't sleep much last night, did we? I guess we'll stay here and rest for the day. Maybe I'll work a little and you can read, or . . . whatever." She turns and walks out of my bedroom.

I follow her and shut my door. I shut it hard—almost a slam. I need her to leave me alone today and maybe that made it clear. I lean against my door and then slide down to the floor. I sit with my back against the door and my knees pulled to my chest. I hug my knees and rest my head on them. I feel a tear slide down my cheek and onto my knee. *I'm sorry, Sierra . . . I'm sorry.* I choke back a sob.

I can't cry now. I have too much to do.

I am resolved.

CHAPTER FIFTY

ierra

"YOU SAID to call if I noticed extreme angst in Kaylee . . ."

As I listen and respond to Dr. Beth's questions, I open the slider and walk to the Adirondack chair and sink into it. I should have called her earlier—for Kaylee's sake of course, but also because as I listen to Beth, I realize, as I did when speaking to Pete yesterday, that I'm not in this alone. God has provided tangible evidence of His care for me, for Kaylee, through others. It's been so long since I've let myself rely on anyone else.

"It seems like she's on an emotional roller coaster. Up one minute, down the next. I think I've seen every emotion cross her little face: fear, anger, sadness, happiness, joy, peace, and then back to fear and anger again."

"Sierra, we can't discount the trauma Kaylee's experienced— we don't even know the depth of that trauma. But what we do know is enough to expect that Kaylee will experience a wide range of emotions that she's not prepared to deal with. What you're seeing is, sadly, within the range of what I'd consider 'normal' under these circumstances. And seeing her mom likely unearthed feelings she's managed until now.

"Sierra, Kaylee aside for a moment, how are you doing? This is a lot for you to handle too."

I lean my head against the back of the chair and breathe deep, filling my lungs with warm sea air. "Honestly? I think I'm riding that roller coaster with Kaylee. I feel so much love and concern for her, but at the same time her silence and moods frustrate me. I'm having to walk away from her because I'm angry that she won't answer my questions and because I can't figure out why she seems angry with me." I close my eyes and sigh. "I don't know how to help her."

"Sounds like you're feeling as though you have no control . . ."

"Exactly."

"Those are emotions I'd expect you to feel. It's hard to work with someone when communication is so limited. Kaylee needs you to be steady—someone she can count on. You won't handle everything perfectly. None of us does. But your steady countenance provides Kaylee with a sense of safety, and that's what she needs now."

"And what about her emotions? She seems so angry today."

"I don't know, Sierra. I can't know what she's feeling. It's possible she is angry with you, or needs to feel angry with you. Maybe she's struggling with what she feels for you and what she feels for her mother. It's not unusual for a foster child to feel they're betraying their parents by caring for their caregiver. She may be pushing you away right now as she deals with whatever she's feeling for her mom. Again, these are only assumptions. Hold on a minute, let me check my schedule . . . Can you bring her in tomorrow morning? I'm not supposed to see her again until next week, but it sounds like sooner might be better than later."

I get up and walk back to the kitchen to hang up the phone, having agreed to bring Kaylee in to see Dr. Beth in the morning. I feel more settled knowing someone else will see and talk to Kaylee right now.

I'll check on her again and then decide what to do about dinner. If it were just me, I'd open the fridge and grab a piece of cheese or fruit and call it good.

But it's no longer just me.

I blink my eyes several times trying to clear what feels like a thin veil of sand.

I tap on Kaylee's door and then crack it open and peek in. She is lying on her bed reading, of course. But today she's reading her dictionary. "Hey, are you about ready for some dinner?"

She shrugs, never taking her eyes off the big book.

"I think we'll make it an early night."

Still no response. She keeps her gaze riveted on the dictionary.

I close her door and shake my head. Another long, silent evening lies ahead. I wander back to the kitchen and set the teapot to boil. As I wait for the whistle, I think back to my conversation with Pete yesterday and allow myself to consider what I haven't until now: Kathryn has entered a rehabilitation program.

I recall Pete's words: "Sierra, Kathryn's entered a residential rehabilitation program. She showed up at CWS this morning. She was in pretty bad shape, but I was able to talk to her, to convince her we would help her, if she'd accept our help. She finally agreed."

I haven't let my mind jump ahead to this possibility, not in all these weeks. I was so sure she'd come back here looking for money. "So, what does this mean? For Kaylee?"

For me?

Pete exhaled. "Well, it could mean Kaylee is returned to her mother's care if Kathryn successfully completes the program. She wasn't arrested for possession, so there are no legal ramifications—"

"*What?*" My pulse throbs in my temples. "No legal ramifications? What about abandoning your child? Is that legal these days? Neglect? Abuse? What about that?"

"Whoa, hold on. Of course there are legal ramifications for abandonment and abuse. But right now we don't know the whole story. Kathryn's sticking with the kidnapping story and so far, all we have is her word against Jack's. I don't believe either of them has told the truth, but we don't have proof either way. When the police arrested Jack, there was no evidence of Kathryn having lived in the cabin. For all we know, Kaylee *was* kidnapped by him. But Kaylee is the only one who knows the truth."

"She has to tell us, Pete. She has to talk."

"Yes. But she'll only talk when she's ready to talk, and right now I think pressuring her, telling her too much, will only increase her anxiety and inability to speak. Her emotional health, her well-being, are the priority. I do think it's important she know that her mom is all right, that she's getting the help she needs. She needs to understand that Kathryn is sick, that she's dealing with the disease of addiction, and that she's receiving the care she needs."

Pete pauses and I hear him sigh. "You know, that little gal gets to me." He chuckles. "I work with kids everyday and I'm supposed to maintain a professional distance, not become emotionally involved in their lives. Though, honestly, I've never understood how not to become emotionally involved. If you care, you're involved. And Kaylee, well, she's just something else. She's very easy to care about."

"I know. She's so quirky and so lovable."

"Of course you know. I want the best for her, Sierra. Never doubt that."

"I know, but, ultimately, isn't the truth the best for her?"

"Sure it is. But for now Kaylee's not ready to tell the truth. Or much of anything."

"So what do we do?"

"You keep on doing what you're doing. Provide a safe place for her, care for her, love her. And I'll keep doing my job. We have some time—rehabilitation doesn't happen overnight."

"Okay." A ragged sigh marks my resignation. "I know you're right. But . . . there's one more thing we need to do."

I picture Pete cocking his head to one side, much like Van does when I talk to him. "What's that?"

"We need to pray."

He is silent for a moment—thoughtful, I think. "Yes. We'll pray. Good to know we're not the ones in control, isn't it?"

"That's for sure. I have no idea what I'm doing."

"You know more than you think. Hey, don't mention any of this to Kaylee just yet. We don't know if Kathryn will stay in rehab. Let's not rock her boat for the moment. As I said, it's important she knows her mom is okay and being cared for, but let me consult Beth today and get her recommendation on how she'd like to handle this information with Kaylee."

"Okay." I think about the ups and downs Kaylee's already experienced this week and agree with Pete's assessment. "She's dealing with a lot right now. There's so much going on inside her already."

Tonight, as I consider that conversation, I realize prayer *is* the only answer. The emotions welling in me at the thought of Kaylee being returned to Kathryn are more than I can handle. And getting Kaylee to speak—that's definitely out of my control. As much as I long to help her—to encourage her—to provide the safety she needs to speak again, I know I can't do this on my own. I need help—I need divine intervention.

I take my cup of tea out to the deck and stare up at the sky, as has become my habit lately. Stars layer the blackened canvas overhead, and I think of the Creator who can name every star in the sky—surely He has the power to help a little girl speak.

"Please . . ." I speak into the night. "Please let her speak again."

aylee

I LOOK out my window and decide the dark seems omnibus tonight. Omnibus? I unzip my backpack and pull the dictionary out and look up *omnibus.*

> **omni·bus—noun** 1. a volume of reprinted works of a single author or of works related in interest or theme.

That's not it. I read through the Os until I find what I'm looking for.

> **om·i·nous—**1. portending evil or harm; foreboding; threatening; inauspicious; an ominous bank of dark clouds. 2. having the significance of an omen.

That's it. The dark seems ominous tonight, which is kind of weird because I got used to the dark at the cabin. *You're just being a baby,* I tell myself. What I'm really doing, I know, is stalling.

I reach for my backpack and zip it closed. I unwrap the granola bar and tiptoe to the door; Van follows me. When I get to the door, I open it slowly so it doesn't squeak, then I turn around and put the granola bar on the floor for Van—just like last time.

I close the door and begin to tiptoe down the hallway, but my feet feel like they have bricks tied to them and my heart feels the same way. But it doesn't matter. I have to go. I make myself remember the way my mom looked in my dream—and the way she looked so many times before.

She needs me.

She does.

I reach the front door and stop to listen. I hear the hum of the refrigerator in the kitchen, and the clock ticking on the wall, but nothing else. Nothing moves. I reach for the door knob, then hesitate. I turn back toward the living room and look down the hall at Sierra's bedroom door. *Good-bye, Sierra.* The lump in my throat aches.

I turn back and open the door and walk out, careful to close the door tight behind me. I go down the steps and stop at the lawn. I look in the direction of the ocean. The moon is shining on what looks like an ominous bank of dark clouds.

I start out across the lawn when I realize something doesn't feel right.

I stop. Something really doesn't feel right. My backpack is so light . . .

The dictionary! I left it on the bed!

I turn and run back to the front door and grab for the knob, but it doesn't turn. I try again, harder this time. But it won't budge. I jiggle it and then twist it as hard as I can. I push against the door, but nothing happens.

It's locked!

I shake the knob and push harder on the door. It has to open.

It *has* to! I look over my shoulder into the dark front yard and feel my heart pounding harder and harder. I have to get in. I have to! I gulp for air. I have to get the dictionary!

Then I hear something behind me—something rustling in the flower bed in front of the house. I lift my fist and begin banging on the door. I pound as hard as I can. I open my mouth to yell for Sierra, but nothing comes out.

I can't talk.

I can't breathe.

Tears choke me.

I have to get in! I keep banging on the door—pounding—until finally, the porch light comes on and the door opens. I look up and see Sierra standing there and then, before I can push past her into the house, she is holding me in her arms.

"Oh, Kaylee, what are you doing?" She holds me so tight, and I know I don't ever want her to let me go.

But . . .

I don't need her.

I don't.

She's talking, saying something, telling me to do something, but I can't. I can't do what she wants. I have to go. I have to.

I stand there until I can breathe again and then I step back—step away from her. I know what I have to do. I pull away and look past her to the living room. I have to go get the dictionary and then I have to leave.

I have to go.

I walk around her and head for my bedroom. When I open the door, Van darts around me and heads down the hallway toward Sierra, who, I think, is following me. I grab the dictionary off the bed, stuff it into my backpack, and struggle to zip it closed. It's so heavy now. Instead of lifting it to my shoulders, I drag it behind me as I head back down the hallway. Sure enough, Sierra's there, but I push past her.

"Kaylee, wait! Where are you going?"

I don't stop. But just as I reach the front door and try to open it, she's behind me and grabs my wrist. I twist hard and shake her hand off me. I reach again for the knob, but this time she grabs me from behind. Her arms are around my waist. I swing my arms and kick my legs, but she keeps hanging on. My feet aren't even touching the ground anymore. Then, just like she did the day my mom was here, she picks me up and carries me back into the living room. I'm kicking and crying, but I can't get loose.

When we reach the middle of the room, she puts me down but doesn't let me go. She spins me around so I'm facing her. She's still holding on tight.

"Kaylee . . ."

She says my name in a whisper, and even in the dark I can see tears glistening on her cheeks. But I can't let myself feel sorry for her. I can't!

I wrench one arm out of her grip and lean toward the door. I pull as hard as I can. But again she grabs me around the waist and picks me up. I kick and swing my arms, but she doesn't let go. All the time I'm fighting her, the words *I don't need you!* rage in my head.

I don't need you!

The words drop from my head to my mouth—I can feel them there like marbles rattling against my teeth.

The harder I kick, the more marbles fill my mouth. *I . . . don't . . . need . . . you!*

I swing behind me, trying to loosen Sierra's grip.

Anger pushes from my chest up into my throat, I feel the lump of it stuck there for a minute, but it keeps pushing, forcing its way to my mouth. I open my mouth and the anger comes out in a scream!

I feel Sierra jump at the sound.

Then I spit the marbles out one by one. "I . . . don't . . . need . . . you! I . . . don't . . ."

The sound of the words startle me so much that I stop fighting and I feel Sierra's grip loosen. She puts me down and spins me around again. She gets down on her knees so our faces are almost touching.

"Kaylee!"

I look at her, and spit the rest of the marbles out. ". . . need you. You're . . . super . . . You're super . . . fluous!"

"Kaylee, you're talking!" She puts her arms around me and hugs me tight. "Oh, little one, you're talking!" She pulls back from me, holding my arms again, and looks at my face. Our eyes meet and both are filled with tears.

"You're talking!"

I'm as surprised as she is.

"Wait . . . What did you say? You don't . . . I'm super . . . what? Super fluous? I'm superfluous? Is that what you mean? I'm superfluous?"

I nod my head. But in my heart, I know I don't mean it.

She's not just something super, something extra, something I don't need.

She's not superfluous.

She's Sierra.

CHAPTER FIFTY-TWO

ierra

HER VOICE COMES to me in colors. I see hues of umber and pumpkin and the vibrant gold of fall aspens—rich, warm colors. Her words hold both emotion and energy. I've waited so long to hear her voice and the sound enchants me. She sounds like someone who's just woken from a deep slumber.

Then the words themselves hit me.

I pull back from her so I can see her face again. "Wait . . . What did you say? You don't . . . I'm super . . . what? Super fluous? I'm superfluous? Is that what you mean? I'm superfluous?"

She looks at the floor and I see a slow nod. Yes. That's what she said.

Her words taunt me to believe the fears that have nagged me since she arrived here. She doesn't need me, doesn't want me. Then I look into her eyes, deep pools swirling in confusion. I see her tears brimming, overflowing. And for once, I know, this isn't about me.

"Superfluous? Wow. That's quite a word." I wrap her in an embrace. I'm gentle at first, but then my love for her takes over and I cling to her, crying, laughing. And she clings back, crying her own tears, and whispering, stammering, saying nothing that makes sense to me. But she is speaking!

I pull back and put my hands on her face. I hold her there, just inches from my own face. She quiets, and I tell her. "Kaylee, I love you. You are so precious to me." She wraps her arms around my neck again and holds on tight. After a few minutes I hear her sniffle again. I pull back from her.

"C'mon. Follow me." I get up off my knees and take her hand and lead her to the bathroom. The steps there give me a moment to stitch my emotions back together. When we reach the bathroom, I grab a few tissues and wipe her eyes and her nose. Then I take another tissue and hold it to her nose and tell her to blow. She does. I grab another tissue and wipe my own eyes. Then I remember what led up to this moment. "Kaylee, where were you going?"

She looks down at her feet and shrugs her shoulders.

"It's the middle of the night. You weren't leaving, were you?"

She looks up at me without lifting her head and peers at me through her dark lashes and bangs. Her face flushes. Then her expression changes, like she's just remembered something.

"Oh . . ." She turns and heads back down the hallway.

"Oh?" I smile again at the sound of her voice. Amazing! I follow to see where's she's going now. She opens the front door and bends down and grabs her backpack off the step. I reach to help her. I take it from her, set it on the chair in the living room, and unzip it. I pull out her Bible, a couple of bags of chips, apples, a pair of shorts . . .

"You were leaving, Kaylee?"

"I . . . I have . . ." Her voice is raspy. She clears her throat and begins again. "I have to find . . . I have to find my mom. I have to . . . help her."

"Oh, little one. Oh, no." I wrap her in another hug. "I love you."

"I . . . love . . . you too." She whispers and then pulls away from me. "But . . . but . . . what . . . what . . ." She leaves her question hanging.

"But what? It's okay, you can ask me."

With furrowed brow, she tries again. "What . . . what about . . . my mom? I'm . . . I'm supposed to love *her*." She hiccups and sniffs.

Ahh . . . Dr. Beth was right. I brush Kaylee's bangs off her forehead. "Kaylee, you can love both of us. I'm glad you love your mom, and I'm glad you love me. We both love you."

Doubt darkens her features and she looks at her feet. "I don't . . . I don't know . . . if she loves me." Her words are barely audible.

"Oh, she does. I'm sure. But . . ."

Kaylee's expression changes and I see the same emotion—what is it . . . determination? Resolve, maybe—that I saw before, and then she interrupts me. *She interrupts me!*

"It doesn't matter if she loves me. She needs me. I . . . I have to . . . take care of her."

"Take care of her?"

Her head bobs up and down.

And now I understand.

Kaylee carries a crushing weight of responsibility. I see it pressing on her. I consider Pete's instructions to keep the news of Kathryn's rehabilitation from Kaylee until he'd consulted with Beth. But now I must tell her. Perhaps if I'd told Kaylee of her mother's choice as soon as I knew, we could have avoided tonight's trauma. But then, maybe it was just this trauma that led Kaylee to speak.

Maybe this was God answering my prayer, God causing all things to work together for good.

"Kaylee, your mom is getting help. We were going to tell you— Pete or Dr. Beth—one of them was going to talk to you about it. I'm sorry. Maybe I should have told you. I just found out.

Yesterday your mom went to Child Welfare Services and talked to Pete. She agreed that she needs help and now she's in what they call a residential rehabilitation program. She'll live in a facility where there are doctors who will help her get off the drugs. They'll help her get healthy again."

I see hope blossom in Kaylee's expression. "Kiddo, as long as she agrees to be there, they'll take care of her. I promise."

"Cross your heart?"

I laugh, and draw an *X* over my heart with one finger. "Cross my heart and hope to die—"

Kaylee reaches for me again, holds me tight and whispers in my ear. "Don't die. Please . . . don't die."

I hold her tight. Die? No. Not now.

I'm finally alive!

CHAPTER FIFTY-THREE

aylee

I TOUCH my finger to my lip, when I pull it away there's blood on it. I guess I was chewing on my lip while I was thinking. I have to figure out some things. Like what to say when Sierra starts asking me questions again. Questions about him.

And questions about my mom.

I look at my hands and then start chewing on my nails. I know I'm supposed to tell the truth. But I heard my mom tell Sierra that I was kidnapped. Why did she say that? If I tell the truth, will my mom be in trouble?

Maybe not talking was easier.

I woke up late this morning, so late that I missed the appointment Sierra had scheduled with Dr. Beth. Sierra didn't wake me up.

She finally came in to check on me. "Hey, sleepy head, are you about ready to get up?"

I shook my head. No.

"Oh, little one, please use your words. I've waited all morning to hear your beautiful voice again."

I rolled over, turning my back to her, and spoke over my shoulder. "I'm ... not ready ... yet."

She leaned down and whispered, "Thanks, kiddo. Go back to sleep. You had a long night." Then she left my bedroom and shut my door.

She doesn't know how long my night was. After we went back to bed, I spent the rest of the night thinking about my mom. At first I thought I was dreaming because the thoughts didn't make sense. But I was awake. I was just remembering—remembering things I'd forgotten.

Now I can't make the memories stop. They keep coming.

I look at the ceiling for a long time and hear things in my head.

Use your words, Kaylee, use your words! I don't have time for your stammering!

I see things too. My mom grabbing me by the shoulders and shaking me so hard it feels like my brain is rattling in my head.

Stop your stammering!

I see her taking my can of Pick-Up Sticks off the shelf and throwing it at me—all the colored sticks flying in the air toward my face.

The memories fly at me, like the Pick-Up Sticks, each poking and stinging as they hit.

I close my eyes and cover my ears.

I want to shove the sticks back in the can. I want the memories to go back to wherever they were before. Before I talked out loud.

With my eyes closed, I see him. And I hear my mom. "I told you to keep your hands off her, you pervert. Don't touch her again."

"Or what? Whatcha gonna do to me, Kat? Turn me in? Ha! You need what I have too much to do that."

"I mean it, Jack. Don't touch her!" Then she looked at me. "And you stay away from him!" She turned and walked out of the cabin.

That was it. That's all she ever said. I did try to stay away from him. I did. But he'd always find me.

My stomach churns and I cover my ears tighter. The scream is so loud, and I can't make it stop.

I can't make it stop!

Then I feel someone grab me by the shoulders and shake me.

"Kaylee! Kaylee!"

I open my eyes and see Sierra. Her hands are on my shoulders. She shakes me again.

"Kaylee!"

That's when I realize that the scream isn't just in my head. It's coming out of my mouth. I take my hands off my ears and cover my mouth.

"Oh, little one, you scared me to death." Sierra pulls me close and hugs me. She holds me like that for awhile. "Are you okay now? Do you want the headphones?"

I nod and sniff.

"First, can you tell me what happened?"

I open my mouth; but, then I just shake my head.

I can't tell her.

I can't tell anyone.

Not ever.

CHAPTER FIFTY-FOUR

ierra

"RUBE, DID I MAKE A MISTAKE?" Fatigue weighs on me, a heavy cloak of discouragement. "I don't know how to help her."

Ruby leans back in her seat—a wicker chair outside the little coffee shop near Dr. Beth's office. She studies me for a moment and when she speaks her words are measured, thoughtful. "Remember the day Kaylee was rescued from the cabin? What did you tell me you felt as they loaded her into the ambulance?"

I nod. I know where she's going. "I felt certain. Sure God had a plan and that somehow that plan included Kaylee and me together. I knew then that she'd end up with me."

Ruby picks up her coffee cup and takes a sip, her emerald gaze never leaving my face. "Do you trust that God made the right choice?"

I lean my head back and take in the clear blue sky of early fall. How I long for such clarity. I try to process Ruby's question. Did

God make the right choice? I turn back and look at her. "No fair. That's a trick question."

"Just answer it."

"What you're asking is if I trust God. Do I trust that He knows more than I know?"

She is silent.

"I guess I'll choose to trust. I don't feel trusting right now, but this isn't about feelings, is it? Yes, I'll choose to trust that Kaylee's with me for reasons I can't see or understand."

Ruby leans forward again. "What are you feeling right now?"

Her tender tone draws my tears. "Exhausted." I swallow, then take a deep breath. I nod my head as if affirming the feeling to myself. "I feel exhausted."

"I bet. I imagine Kaylee's a little like having a newborn right now. With the nightmares, she's not sleeping through the night and neither are you. On top of that, there's the emotional energy you're expending during the day as you try to anticipate and meet her needs."

Ruby's understanding lifts a bit of the weight from my shoulders. "So you think what I'm feeling is normal?"

"Sure, given the circumstances. Didn't Dr. Beth allude to as much several weeks ago?"

"Yeah, she did. I guess I thought once Kaylee began speaking, we were home free. I was so focused on getting her to talk, but I see now that was just the first step. Now I see it's the words she speaks that are so important. She needs to speak her truth—to tell someone what really happened. It all seems so locked inside of her."

"What does Dr. Beth say?"

"She thinks Kaylee is still protecting her mom. You know, Rube, it's amazing to me how strong the bond between child and mother is. I keep thinking back to Kaylee trying to run away to find her mom so she could take care of her. It's hard to understand her motivation—giving up the tangible—the security of a home and someone taking care of her for the intangible—a mother whose choices cost Kaylee so much. The bond is strong."

"Has Kaylee talked to anyone else yet?"

"No. Van and I are it. And I think she tells most of her secrets to Van. He and Kaylee are the only ones who really know what she's suffered."

"And I bet Van's not talking." Ruby's smile warms me. She glances at her watch. "You better go. She'll be done with her appointment in a few minutes." Ruby reaches for my hand. "You know I'm here for you, whatever you need."

I know. I give Ruby's hand a quick squeeze.

As I drive over to Dr. Beth's office to pick up Kaylee, I ponder my conversation with Ruby. She was wise to take me back to the day Kaylee was rescued and the sense of assurance I felt. The fatigue and discouragement of earlier are replaced by renewed determination. I feel ready to face Kaylee—whatever her mood.

But when I walk across the parking lot and see Kaylee, a dark cloud of swirling emotions, standing outside of Dr. Beth's office and Dr. Beth next to her, my stride slows.

Uh-oh.

"Hi there." I give Kaylee a pat on the back and look at Beth, eyebrows raised.

"Hi, Sierra. Kaylee was ready to leave early today, so we decided to come outside, get some fresh air, and wait for you." Beth turns to Kaylee. "You're good to go, girl. We'll follow you to the car. I need to talk to Sierra for a minute."

Kaylee looks from Dr. Beth to me, then stomps her way to the Jeep.

"Not a good session?" I whisper to Beth.

"Not an easy session. But it was good in the sense that I think we're nearing a breakthrough. Although, if not, I fear Kaylee may break down."

My shoulders droop as we follow several paces behind Kaylee toward the Jeep. "What do you mean?"

"Sierra, Kaylee's emotional state is tornado-like right now. You know, you've seen it. She is a mass of churning, negative energy, and that negativity is leaving a wake of destruction. You've told me she's not sleeping or eating well. She's angry, frustrated, and, from all I can see, depressed." Beth hands me a slip of paper. "This is a prescription for an anti-depressant. Fill it today and have her start taking it."

"Is that really necessary?"

"I think it is. Until she's able to release that negativity—until she's able to speak about what happened to her—I'm afraid the memories and all the emotions whirling inside her will become too much for her to handle." Beth pats me on the back, much the same way I'd patted Kaylee. "Call me if you need me. Or leave a message with my service after office hours."

"Is there anything else I should do? How do I help her?'

"Just keep doing what you're doing. Provide a safe and loving environment for her. And keep her talking."

"Yeah, I'll try. It's easier said than done."

"I know. But if anyone can do it, it's you."

With Beth's encouragement tucked in my heart, I open the door to the Jeep and get in next to Kaylee, who is staring straight ahead. She doesn't acknowledge me—or Beth, when she bends and waves good-bye to Kaylee.

Oh . . . help.

CHAPTER FIFTY-FIVE

ierra

KAYLEE'S SCREAMS break my sleep.

I bolt upright at the sound, leap out of bed, and race to her room.

Waking to her screams is becoming routine, but tonight . . . the sound echoing through the house—through my heart—is worse than ever before.

I reach her side, wrap my arms around her, whisper assurances . . . all to no avail. She's trapped in a house of horrors and can't find her way out

"Jesus . . . please." My tears mingle with hers as I press my cheek against hers. "Please . . ."

Her fingers dig into me, clutching, clawing. Her eyes are open, but what she sees isn't here in this room. Darkness has her in its grip and fights to take her away. From me. From life.

From God.

Anger sparks, then flames. "No!" I cup her face, tender but firm. "No! You won't win! Leave her alone!"

The fury in my words isn't for Kaylee, but it gets through to her all the same. She starts. Her eyes blink. And then I see it. The return from the edge of whatever gaping maw has been tormenting her. I feel her shudder, then sag against me.

"Sierra?"

Oh, how I longed to hear her voice. How I waited and waited. And now, it's torture. Because it's so often filled with such fear.

"I'm here, little one. I'm here. I won't leave you . . ."

Yes, waking this way has become routine, but it's not a routine we can live with. *Jesus, I can't stand seeing her suffer, can't stand not knowing what horrors she's reliving in her dreams, night after night.*

Can you handle knowing?

The quiet question whispers through me, and I close my eyes. Can I? I don't know. But I have to know. For Kaylee's sake.

After getting her settled again, I make my way outside, to the deck . . . and a break. Too little sleep, the anxiety, the inability to help her. It's too much.

"What do I do? Please just tell me what to do!" Standing on my deck, I sob my prayer into the night. *The truth will set her free. The truth will set her free.* Over and over the familiar words play through my mind. "I know! But how do I get her to speak truth?" Finally I walk back into the bungalow and pick up my Bible and sit at the kitchen table. I turn to John 8:32: "Then you will know the truth, and the truth will set you free."

"Then you will know the truth?" What does that mean?

I keep reading—and then I see it.

"So if the Son sets you free, you will be free indeed."

I lean back in my chair. "Jesus is the truth?" I whisper my question, but before it is out of my mouth I know the answer. And there, in the middle of another sleepless night, God shows me the truth. His Son. Jesus.

"When we know the truth—Jesus—then He will set us free."

All this time I thought telling the truth would set Kaylee free. But that's not it. That's not even close. It's more. So much more.

As morning dawns, so does clarity. And with it come the first rays of something I haven't felt for a very long time.

Hope.

CHAPTER FIFTY-SIX

aylee

"Okay, kiddo, we're going to do something different today ..."

Sierra registered me for school, but because I missed a year, she said I have to do school at home for the first semester and she'd help me catch up. So every afternoon now, we do school work. Most of the time I like it, except when we do math. But lately I don't like much of anything.

"I'm going to give you some vocabulary words today. I want you to look them up and write down the definitions for me."

I roll my eyes. "I already know all the words."

"Well, good, then this will be easy for you. Go get your dictionary."

When I come back from my room with the dictionary, Sierra's sitting at the kitchen table writing on a sheet of binder paper. She hands me the paper. "Only three words and, like you said, you already know them. Just look them up and copy the definitions down for me. Then we're going to use those words in a math problem."

I open the dictionary, making sure I bang the cover on the table loud enough to let her know I don't like this. "Are you going to make me do one of those dumb word problems?"

"Just a simple equation." Sierra gets up and leaves me to do the work.

I look at the first word: *Confabulating.*

That's just a big word that means talking or speaking. I turn to the word in the dictionary and write down the definition:

> to talk together, to converse, to chat; to talk together in an informal, familiar way; chat.

I look at the second word on Sierra's list: *Veracity.*

I think for a minute but can't remember what it means. I read the definition, then I copy it:

> 1. habitual truthfulness; honesty. 2. accuracy of statement; accordance with truth. 3. accuracy or precision, as of perception, measurement, etc. 4. that which is true; truth. So basically veracity just means truth.

I write down the definition.

Then number three: *Emancipate.* Everyone knows what that means—it's like the Emancipation Proclamation. We learned about that in the fourth grade. I look up the word and copy the definition:

> 1. to set free (a slave, etc.); release from bondage. 2. to free from restraint or influence, as of convention. 3. in law, to release (a child) from a father's control: used in Roman law.

I hit the paper hard with the tip of my pencil when I put a period on the last definition. "I'm done."

Sierra comes back to the table and takes my paper. "Great." She sits down across from me and writes a few more things on the paper and then hands it back to me. "Okay, I want you to solve this problem. It's simple math—pre-algebra, actually.

Written under the definitions is this problem: $a + b = c$.

"I can't add letters."

"Sure you can. There's a variable for each letter—in other words, each letter stands for something. Write down what they stand for and then you'll have solved the equation." Sierra points at each of the definitions I wrote—she's written a letter next to each one. "Write it out."

I pick up my pencil again and write out the equation.

Confabulating + Veracity = Emancipate.

Then I hand the paper back to Sierra.

"Oh, the last one should be Emancipation. My fault—sorry."

I take the paper back and scratch out Emancipate and change it to Emancipation.

I start to hand it back to Sierra again, but she tells me to keep it.

"Now, I want you to simplify the equation. Write one synonym for each of the words in the equation. Choose a simple word that means what the harder words mean.

"That's easy." I look at the words and think about the simple definitions. Then I know what she wants. I write:

Speaking + Truth = Freedom.

"Perfect. Now, let's go outside. Bring the paper along."

I follow Sierra out to the deck where she scoots the two

Adirondack chairs so they're facing each other. "Have a seat, little one."

My stomach clenches. "Are you . . . are you going to . . . ask me questions again?"

Sierra sits down in the chair and stretches her long legs in front of her. She taps my foot with one of hers. "Questions? No, not today. I've badgered you with enough questions lately. Today I'm going to tell you a story."

I lean back in my chair. A story? Oh good.

CHAPTER FIFTY-SEVEN

ierra

SITTING ACROSS FROM KAYLEE, I pray God will reveal the Truth to her. Her attitude has shifted from sullen boredom to anxiety. Her foot twitches and her question comes out in a stammer—a sure sign of her angst, I've learned.

I take a deep breath, send another silent plea heavenward, and then begin. "When I was five years old, my mother and daddy told me about Jesus. They told me He was the Son of God and that He died on the cross to forgive my sins. And they explained that if I believed in Him and asked Him to live in my heart, that I'd have eternal life. I'd get to live in heaven with Jesus forever."

Kaylee nods for me to continue.

"That evening, when I was five, Mother and Daddy tucked me into bed and I told them I believed in Jesus and wanted Him in my heart. So they both knelt with me by my bed and prayed with me. I asked Jesus to come into my heart and live there forever. But I didn't really understand all that meant."

I turn and look out to the yard. The roses are bursting with the last blooms of fall and the branches of the redwood drape the yard in filtered shade. I'm reminded, through the beauty of creation, that God is with me in this moment. He will lead the way. "Little one, hand me your paper again."

Kaylee reaches for the paper she laid on the deck next to her chair and hands it to me.

"See this equation: Speaking + Truth = Freedom? That's what I've been telling you since you started speaking, right?"

Kaylee's foot starts tapping again. She nods.

I cross out the original equation and write a new one: Jesus = Truth = Freedom. I hand the paper back to Kaylee. "Kiddo, Jesus is the Truth. When we believe in Him, He sets us free. We can't set ourselves free, no matter how often we tell the truth. Only Jesus can set us free. Does that make sense?"

Kaylee shrugs. "Kind of . . ."

"I've told you over the last few weeks that you need to tell the truth about what happened at the cabin with Jack and with your mom. And when you talk about those things, when you tell the truth, you'll be free of the nightmares and memories and all the things hurting you right now. But that's not exactly right."

I pick up my Bible and turn to John 8:32 again. "Jesus said, 'Then you will know the truth, and the truth will set you free.'" Jesus is talking about Himself in that verse. He is the only one who can set you free. When we believe in Jesus, when we invite Him to live in our hearts, it means we'll be in heaven with Him forever, but there's even more. It means we can have a relationship with Him now, here, every day. It means we can depend on Him to help us through the pain we're suffering. We can count on Him to comfort us and guide us. Sweetie, I've been wrong. It isn't talking that can set you free. Only Jesus can do that."

Kaylee's eyes are wide and focused. I have her full attention.

"I still think it's important for you to talk about what happened. I know it will be hard for you, but always remember what I told you, that nothing you've gone through is your fault. You didn't do anything wrong. The thing is, sometimes it's only when we tell the truth that others can help us. I'll give you an example, okay?"

She nods.

"Remember when we talked about Annie?"

Kaylee leans forward in her chair. "Yes."

"I was using drugs when I got pregnant with Annie. Ruby and I were roommates then, and Ruby tried to get me to stop taking drugs, but I wouldn't. I wouldn't listen to her. I just wanted to do what I was doing. The drugs had a hold on me. Finally, when Ruby figured out I was pregnant, she threatened me."

Kaylee's eyes widen at that. "Threatened you?"

I nod. "Not with a gun or knife, but with truth. She told me I'd kill my baby if I didn't stop. She hurled her words across the apartment at me. And told me that someday I'd probably kill myself too."

"That was mean."

I touch Kaylee's hand at the soft words. "No, it was true, sweetie. Ruby didn't want to say those things, in fact, she cried when she said them. But she knew she had to help me. Telling me the truth, even though it hurt both of us, was the only way she could help. She begged me to stop."

"Did you?"

Oh, if only I had. I could still see the scene, how I looked at her and felt nothing. Nothing for the danger I was putting my baby in and nothing for myself. What did it matter?

"No, I didn't. I ignored her and headed for the door, and that's when she hit me with the real threat."

"What did she say?"

"If I wouldn't stop on my own, that she'd call my parents and tell them everything."

Kaylee's eyes widened. "Everything?"

So much fear in that one word. I nodded. "Everything."

I turned and looked at her, to see if she was serious. She just stood there, shoulders squared, arms crossed, face stained with tears. And a few days later . . ."

"What?"

"Mother and Daddy showed up."

"She really told them? Wasn't she afraid you'd be mad at her?"

"Yes, she was. But she loved me so much that she risked losing my friendship to help me. She had to tell the truth."

Kaylee's gaze shifts from me to the ground. "What . . . what happened . . . when they found out?"

"My parents took me to a doctor. They watched me around the clock. They moved me to live here, and they stayed with me. Ruby came too. They wouldn't let me hurt myself anymore. It was too late for Annie . . ." The stab of loss stills my words, and I take a deep breath. "But they helped me."

"Did that make it . . . better?"

The question was so soft, I almost didn't hear it. "Not at first. For a long time, for almost twelve years, I lived in a prison of anger. I was so angry with myself for what I did to Annie. I couldn't accept that God could still love me."

She nodded. "Because you were so bad."

I lean forward and reach for her hand. "Oh, but sweetie, I was wrong. I was so wrong."

Her gaze lifts to meet mine again.

"Little one, it wasn't until I met you, that I discovered the truth! God does love me—no matter what. Kaylee, if Ruby hadn't told the truth, I wouldn't have gotten the help I needed. It was still my choice, but it was a choice I wouldn't have made without the help of others. But even with that help, I was lost. In anger. In shame. In the end, it's Jesus who saved me. The truth of His love and forgiveness. And you know what? Nothing that I'd done, not even causing my baby's death, stopped God from loving me. Not for one second. He loves us, little one, not because of who we are, but because of who He is." I give her hand a squeeze. I've said all I need to say. The rest is up to God.

And Kaylee.

I let go of her hand and stand. "I'm going to go clean up the kitchen, put my easel and things away."

She nods when I leave her there, sitting on the deck, staring out at the yard.

CHAPTER FIFTY-EIGHT

aylee

AT FIRST I try not to think about what Sierra said. I try not to think about Ruby. I try really hard not to think about how Ruby telling Sierra's parents the truth was what finally helped Sierra. I especially try not to think about my mom. Because even though Sierra didn't say it exactly, I get what she was telling me.

My telling the truth might help my mom.

But . . .

I'm trying not to think about that. There are too many what-ifs and the what-ifs make my stomach churn.

I lean back in the chair on the deck and close my eyes. I open the box in my mind and shuffle through my words. But as I visualize my words, I see new words in my box. Words I didn't put there. They're not even hard words.

hon·est—adjective 1. free of deceit and untruthfulness.

frank—adjective 1. open, honest, and direct in speech or writing, esp. when dealing with unpalatable matters.

sin·cere—adjective 1. free from pretense or deceit.

I mentally slam the box shut, open my eyes, and stand up.

I stand up so fast that Van, who's lying at my feet, stands up fast too. His legs are wobbly underneath him. Then he looks at me. His sleepy eyes seem wide with concern.

"Let's go!" I tell him, and he follows me into the kitchen, down the hall, and into my room. I shut the door, plop down on my bed, stare at the ceiling, and think more about not thinking. I get back up before Van even has a chance to settle on the floor.

"C'mon."

He follows me to the living room where I, without even asking, turn on the TV. Sierra says watching TV stunts creativity. Even with the volume up, I can hear Sierra's flip-flops slapping the hardwood in the hallway. She stops at the end of the hall and looks at me. I look back. She just stands there looking at me for a minute and then turns and heads back to her room.

I guess stunting my creativity is okay for today.

I lie on the sofa and watch reruns of old shows that make me laugh. Van sleeps on the floor next to me. I hang my arm over the edge of the sofa and rest my hand in the fur around his neck. We stay like that for the rest of the afternoon. Sierra comes and goes and even brings me dinner on a tray and watches a show with me.

But at bedtime she tells me to turn off the TV.

"But . . ."

"Kaylee, turn it off. It's time." She smiles at me. "Come on, I'll read you a story after you brush your teeth."

Later, long after the lights are out, I remember that the only way to really stop thinking about something is to actually think about it and get it over with.

So . . . I do.

What surprises me is that when I finally let myself think about telling the truth, I don't think about telling the truth at all. Instead I remember what Sierra said about Jesus *being* the truth and the one who will set me free. And I remember the words to the song Grammy taught me: *Jesus loves me this I know . . .*

I pull the covers up over my head and curl into the dark pocket of space between the sheets. My breath warms the trapped air and I feel like a caterpillar in a cocoon. There I talk to Jesus. I tell Him I remember Him from before—from before Grammy died and before my mom left. I tell Him I know He is true and that I want Him to live in my heart just like He lived in Sierra's heart when she was little.

"And Jesus"—I whisper into the dark—"please help me."

After I talk to Jesus, I stay under the covers for a long time and I think. But it isn't as scary anymore. I think about the real things —about how my mom was and how she left me. I think about the drugs and how they changed her. I think about the lie I heard her tell Sierra. And I know, deep in my heart, that even though telling the truth might make her mad at me and make her never want to see me again, it is the only way I might help her get better.

So I make my decision.

I throw the covers back and climb out of bed. I tiptoe into Sierra's room and stand by her bed. She rolls over, lifts her head to look at the clock, then lies back down and closes her eyes again. I put my hand on her shoulder. "Sierra? Are you awake?"

She doesn't move.

"Sierra . . ."

Finally she rolls back over and opens her eyes. "Hey . . ." She looks back at the clock. "It's only . . . 4:46." She pats the other side of the bed. "Climb in."

I shake my head. "No."

"No?" She sits up, leaning back on her elbows, and looks at me like she's trying to focus. Then she reaches over and switches on the lamp on her nightstand. "You okay?"

"I . . . I want to tell you something."

"Now?"

I nod. "Now."

"Okay." She sits up and puts another pillow behind her and leans back. "Here, sit down." She yawns and then scoots her legs out of my way, and I sit down on the side of the bed. "What's up?"

I reach for the comb on her nightstand and hand it to her. "Would you . . . would you comb my hair?"

"Oh, little one, I'd love to. I've missed combing your hair."

She begins running the comb through my hair. "I want to . . . I want to tell you something. I wasn't . . . my mom . . . she said . . . she said I was kidnapped. I . . . heard her. But . . . I wasn't."

Sierra stops combing and rests her hands on my shoulders. She doesn't say anything.

"She . . . she . . . she . . ." I gulp.

"Take a deep breath." Sierra's steady hands are comforting on my shoulders and then she turns me toward her. "Move over here, sweetie, so I can see you."

I turn around and sit in front of her. "She . . . left. And she never . . . came back. She . . . she left me there with . . . with . . ." My eyes burn and my chest gets heavy. Each breath gets harder to take.

Sierra leans forward and reaches for my hand. "You're doing great, Kaylee. You're doing great."

I take another breath and ask the question that's weighed on me for weeks. "Will she get in trouble?"

Sierra doesn't say anything. Finally I ask again. "Will she?"

"Kaylee, she was supposed to take care of you, to protect you. She didn't do that. By not doing that, she broke the law and she'll have to pay the consequences for that. But, little one, she'll also get the help she needs to be healthy."

"Like when . . . like when Ruby told your parents about you?"

She reaches over and puts her palm on the side of my face. "Yes. Just like that."

I stare at the floor thinking about what Sierra said.

"Kaylee, is there anything else you want to tell me?"

I look at her and shrug.

Then I nod.

CHAPTER FIFTY-NINE

ierra

ON A CRISP FALL MORNING, with the leaves outside my bedroom window relinquishing their hold on summer, I sit on my bed with Kaylee and listen to her words as she finally relinquishes the secrets that have held her captive.

Each word is a struggle, pulled from the depths of her soul. At first, when she begins talking about her mom, she sits with her back to me as she talks. But I need to see her face, or perhaps more important, I need her to see mine as she speaks. I place my hands on her shoulders and gently turn her to face me. I reach for her face and hold it between my hands for a moment before leaning in and kissing her on the forehead. "Keep going, little one. You're doing great."

Oh, Lord, help her. Give her strength.

As she unfolds her story, I hold my anger close, not wanting her to misinterpret what I'm feeling, to think my anger is directed at her.

Then this courageous little girl dares to share the unthinkable.

I realize, as I listen, that this child with myriad words in her vocabulary doesn't know the words for what she's suffered. Nor should she.

My anger swells and releases in waves of tears—tears shed for the agony Kaylee suffered at the hands of a very sick man. I cry with her and for her. I cry for all she's lost.

Kaylee cries, too, as she speaks. But as I study her sweet face, I realize hers are tears of shame. At first I'm angry. At him. At what she's feeling because of him. And then I'm determined. She will not feel that one second longer.

Over and over I encourage her and whisper to her. "It wasn't your fault, sweetie. It wasn't your fault."

We pass a box of tissues back and forth.

When Kaylee's words are finally spent, I pull her close and spread the down comforter over us. Holding her tight, I feel her tears subside and her breathing steady.

"Kaylee . . . you are the bravest person I've ever known. I love you, Kaylee Wren, and I always will." I feel the slight nod of her head just before her breathing signals she's fallen asleep. I pray it is a sleep of deep peace.

As I hold her in my arms, my own tears flow again. But this time they are tears of hope and joy. Tears for a lifetime still ahead of Kaylee.

A lifetime of freedom.

CHAPTER SIXTY

aylee

AT FIRST I have to push each word I speak out of my mouth.

I start and stop and start. But I keep pushing. When I finish telling Sierra the truth about my mom, I think I'm done. And I know Jesus helped me say the truth. But then Sierra asks me if there's anything else I want to tell her.

I hesitate.

I can't tell her the rest.

But . . .

But then I tell her the thing I thought I could never tell anyone. I don't decide to tell her exactly, I just start telling. Jesus helps me with this too. I think He makes the decision for me so I don't have to. And when I start talking about . . . about him, I can't stop.

I feel my face burning as I try to explain things . . . things he did to me. I don't even know how to explain it, but I try. I can't look at Sierra when I talk—I can't look at her eyes. But she stops me several times and puts her hands on the sides of my face, like she does, and holds my face until I look at her. Her hands feel cool on my hot skin.

When my eyes finally meet hers, I see she's crying and she says, "It wasn't your fault. It wasn't your fault, sweetie." She says it over and over until I almost believe her. She tells me other things too. She kisses me on the forehead and tells me she loves me. And she says, "Kaylee, you are so lovable. Do you know that?" Then she says again, "It wasn't your fault, sweetie. It wasn't your fault."

We both blow our noses and then I start talking again.

I can't stop telling until I'm done.

I have to be done.

When I am done, I know. I've said all there is to say.

I sit still and wait. I wait for the scream to start in my head, but . . . it never does. It's quiet in my head. And in my heart.

I'm not afraid any more. I can talk. I can tell the truth.

Sierra knows now.

And Jesus always knew.

Sierra pulls the comforter over us and pulls me close to her. With her arm around my shoulders and my head resting on her, I sigh and close my eyes. I feel so . . . different. I've been in a dark and silent place for so long. And now . . .

Now I'm not. Now it's light.

I stretch, yawn, and then snuggle in closer to Sierra.

Maybe . . .

Maybe this is what a butterfly feels like after it comes out of its cocoon. Maybe, I think just before falling asleep, this is what free feels like.

CHAPTER SIXTY-ONE

ierra

KAYLEE'S rhythmic breathing speaks of repeated patterns. Consistency. Something to count on. Those thoughts inform my prayers for this child who's become so much a part of my life—a part of me. As I hold her close, I pray that I can offer her the consistent love she so deserves. But I recognize, again, that I can't do it alone. Only Jesus' love, through me, will offer Kaylee the stability she needs.

The trauma Kaylee suffered—the horrors she dared to share with me tonight—are a chaotic backdrop to my prayers. As I pray for Kaylee, I hold my emotions at bay. But when I finally quiet before God, the images planted in my mind spring forth and anger roils to the surface with hurricane force.

How could this happen? To this child? *Why?*

Just before my emotions pull me under, a voice whispers into the storm: *Peace be with you . . .*

I pull the last tissue from the box and wipe my eyes and nose, trying not to disrupt Kaylee's sleep. My heartbeat begins to slow and a sense of peace that belies the circumstances settles over me. I am reminded, in that moment, that God's love for Kaylee so far exceeds my own. What anger must He feel when one of His children is so horribly abused? My skin prickles with the thought.

The peace He offers comes with the assurance that my anger and grief are the appropriate responses for what Kaylee suffered. I recall Pete's words from Matthew regarding Jesus' anger when one of His little ones is harmed. But what I do with these emotions . . . that's important.

I want revenge. Vindication for Kaylee. Yet God says vindication is His. Instead, I must leave it all in His hands.

In those moments before I, too, succumb to sleep, I surrender my emotions to God. There, under the down comforter, with Kaylee's warmth pressed against me, the fierceness of God's love ignites my soul. And I am finally free to rest in all He's done and will do for me.

And for Kaylee.

My final thought before drifting off is how much I long to share these realizations with Pete.

And?

I smile at the inner question. It sounds like Ruby, but I know it's my own heart asking. And I know the answer, which I let out on a breath as I give in to sleep.

You're right. I long to share something more with Pete.

My heart.

I PICK up the towel lying on the kitchen counter and wipe frosting off my hands, then reach for the phone. "Hello . . ."

"Hi. How are the preparations coming?"

"Good. I just finished frosting the cake for tonight and cupcakes for tomorrow. Oh, Pete, I'm so excited! I don't know if

Kaylee's ever had a real birthday party. Tomorrow five girls who will be in her class this spring are coming for a slumber party! Can you believe it?"

"She's doing great, Sierra. What's that in the background? 'Jingle Bells'?"

"Yeah, we've had Christmas music playing all day. 'Jingle Bells' is one of her favorites. So, what's up?"

"I wanted to check with you and see if you'd have time before the party to meet for a few minutes. I need to talk to you and would like to do it sooner rather than later. Could I come by early —say thirty minutes or so before everyone else arrives?"

My shoulders stiffen. "Is everything okay?"

"Everything's fine. Just some new developments you should know about."

"Can't you tell me now?"

"What? And miss the opportunity to see your reaction—the fire flashing in those beautiful gray eyes of yours?"

"Okay, so I react sometimes . . ." Like now as my pulse races at Pete's reference to my eyes.

I hear his familiar chuckle. "Sometimes?"

"Hey! Can I help it if I have a dozen years worth of emotions stored up? It's about time they came out. Enough said! Come early. I'll be here. You can help . . ."

I hear the smile in his voice. "Great. See you soon."

I finish washing up the dishes and then wander to the living room to check the table one last time. I rented a round table and chairs, and moved the living room furniture against the walls to make room for the table. It's covered in a cherry-red tablecloth— Kaylee's favorite color. So appropriate for the season. The table is set with my china and crystal. I let Kaylee set the table. I smile as I see everything perfectly placed.

Emily Post would be proud.

In the center of the table is Ruby's gift to Kaylee. She brought it over this morning. It's a small sculpture of Kaylee sitting with

her arm around Van, her face nuzzled into the fur on his neck.
I've seen this pose so often in the past months—as has Ruby,
obviously. The sculpture seems to depict both Kaylee's need and
her great capacity for love. I glance down at my sweatshirt
covered in flour and frosting and realize I'd better get myself
ready. Pete will arrive in a few minutes, and the others within
the hour.

I head down the hallway and tap on Kaylee's door and then
open it. "Hey, kiddo, what're you doing?"

"Making place cards for the table."

"Place cards? Oh, of course. When you're finished, you better
change."

"I will."

Though it's been months now since I heard her first spoken
words, I still warm to her voice. "Pete's coming early to talk
through a few things. If you need anything, feel free to interrupt."

"Okay." Engrossed in her project, she never even looks up. She
is content, enjoying this day. Actually I'm not sure which of us is
enjoying it more.

Just as I touch some gloss to my lips, I hear Pete's knock on the
front door. I try to ignore the flutter in my stomach as I steal a last
glance in the mirror. I let my eyes linger on my reflection for just
a moment. Pete knocks again and the flutter moves from my
stomach to my chest. Patience, Dr. Langstrom, I'm coming.

When I reach the front door and open it, Pete thrusts a
bouquet of red roses toward me. Under his arm he holds a box
wrapped in pink paper.

"Flowers for Kaylee?"

"Uh, no . . . they're . . ."

At Pete's uncharacteristic stammer, I look up—and see what I
think is a blush color his features.

He clears his throat and begins again. "They're for you."

"Oh . . . um . . . thank you." I hold the bouquet to my nose and
breathe deep, letting the scent of the roses and pine in the

bouquet wash over me. And taking the moment to hide my own blush.

"Come in." I take the wrapped box from Pete and place it on the coffee table with the other gifts for Kaylee, then head to the kitchen to put the flowers in water. "Have a seat." I motion to a chair at the kitchen table and turn to look for a vase.

"Sierra . . ."

The depth of his voice, his serious tone, cause me to turn back to him. He's still standing. He's followed me into the kitchen rather than sitting at the table where we have our usual meetings.

"Kathryn released Kaylee for adoption today." He pauses, waiting for a response. "Sierra? Did you hear me?"

I heard him, but I can't seem to process his words. They hold too much meaning, too much potential—too much hope. And what about Kaylee? What will this news do to her? How will she feel, in years to come, knowing her mother not only abandoned her, but even gave up her rights to her?

As Pete's news sinks in, emotions swell like a tidal wave—hope, fear, joy, concern, wonder, and then rage.

"Ah . . . right on cue." He smiles.

"What?"

"The fire in your eyes."

"Pete! This isn't funny! You mean to tell me after all she's put her through—the abuse, the lies, the fight to get her back. After we . . . after . . ." My words come through a choke of anger and tears. "After we made her talk about . . . about . . . After we had her testify. After all that, her mother's just giving her up? She's just walking away?! How can she—"

Pete reaches out and puts his hand on my arm. "Sierra, listen. Kathryn was arrested today. Charged with child endangerment, among other things. A direct result of Kaylee's testimony. She knows she has a long road ahead of her. Prison, likely. And her own continued recovery. She's letting Kaylee go for Kaylee's sake. It may be the one positive parenting decision she's made in Kaylee's life. I believe it was a decision made out of Kathryn's love for her daughter. She's requesting an open adoption. She hopes to remain a part of Kaylee's life, if Kaylee wants that."

Pete reaches for the bouquet I'm still holding, takes it from me, and places it on the counter. Then he puts both hands on my arms. "Sierra, the door to adopt Kaylee just swung wide open and I want you to consider walking through it. I want you to think about adopting her."

My breath catches as hope soars. But dare I hope for so much?

"Pete, what will this do to her? It's just one more strike against her—the knowledge that her mother willingly gave her up."

"It may wound her."

His statement is matter of fact, but his tone and expression are laced with compassion. I am taken again by the depth of his care for the kids he works with—his care for Kaylee. This isn't just a job to him.

"But potentially she will be stronger because of it. Adversity, brokenness, suffering—these things strengthen us if we allow them to, and they make our hearts tender toward others who suffer. I can't think of anyone better suited to live that example for Kaylee than you, Sierra. Or to live that example for Kathryn. You're the perfect person to be in both their lives. This is where God's placed you. I hope you will think about—pray about—adopting Kaylee."

"Of course. I just . . . I mean . . . I just can't believe it. Oh Pete, you know how much I love her. I want what's best for her. I don't need to think about it. God's placed me in Kaylee's life. I just never thought . . . I didn't expect so much."

"You're best for her. I believe that, Sierra. She needs you." Pete's hands still hold onto me. Linger there. His eyes hold mine and when he leans toward me for just a moment I think, I hope . . . but then he pulls away and guides me to the table. "Here, have a seat. I need to tell you one more thing."

I sit down and look up at Pete, who is still standing. He shifts from one foot to the other and then clears his throat. "Uh . . . I—"

"If you have something to say, you'll have to sit. I can't see you from down here." I realize how much I want him next to me.

"Oh, right." He turns to pull out a chair and takes the seat next to me. As he looks at me, I notice his jaw clenching and unclenching.

"Pete, what is it? What's wrong?"

"Nothing's wrong. I just need you to know something . . . I . . . uh . . . yesterday, I resigned my position with CWS. I gave six weeks' notice."

"What? Why? How will I . . . I mean . . . how will we . . ." The thought of losing Pete, not having him to walk this journey with me, with Kaylee, pierces my soul.

"Don't worry, another social worker will be assigned to your case."

I shake my head. Why hadn't I simply listened? Pete always listened to me, I should have done the same for him. I wave my hand—trying, really, to wave away the feelings surging within. "No, I know. That's fine. I'm just wondering about you. What led to your decision? Are you okay?"

Pete runs a hand through his hair and leans back in his chair. "It's something I've thought about for a couple of years, actually. I want to begin my own practice, to hang up my shingle, as they say." He hesitates. "And I guess I've finally found a good reason to make the change."

"Really, what would motivate a change like that?" I watch him smile and again I think I see the beginnings of a blush. He shrugs his shoulders.

"A woman, of course." He chuckles. "I think I've finally found the one. But there's a conflict of interest . . . she's someone I work with."

I look down at the floor, unable to meet his eyes lest he see the crushing disappointment I feel. "I see. Well, congratu—"

I stop when I feel his hand cup my chin. He raises my face until our eyes meet. The tenderness I see in his eyes is almost my undoing.

"No, actually, I don't think you do see. It's you, Sierra. You're the one."

"Oh . . ."

He leans in again, and this time, the brush of his lips against mine renders me speechless. When he settles back, his laughter fills my kitchen. "Not exactly the response I was looking for. Should I rescind my resignation?" The ease of his shoulders and the smile on his face let me know he's teasing. He's read my face— the love I can no longer conceal.

Before I have a chance to respond, Kaylee comes around the corner. "Hi, Pete."

Pete reaches for my hand and holds it tight. "Hey, missy. How's the birthday girl?"

Then I hear a knock on the door and soon the bungalow is filled with voices and laughter and music. Kaylee's favorite bell songs ring throughout the bungalow.

Eventually we gather around the table in the living room— Ruby and Michael, Mother and Daddy, who flew in last night, Pete, Kaylee, and myself. The room is lit by the twinkling lights of the Christmas tree in the corner and the crackling fire in the fire-place. Warmth and love circle the table.

"Daddy, will you say grace?"

"You bet." He holds out his hands and we all reach for the hands of the person next to us. I hold Kaylee's little hand in my right hand, and my left hand is enwrapped in the warmth of Pete's grasp. Just before I bow my head, I glance at the picture hanging above the mantle—the abstract of Kaylee's redwood that I finished this fall. I look around the table and see a family circle— my family circle. Our roots are intertwined, supporting one another. Whatever comes in the days, weeks, years ahead, none of us stands alone—we are connected—living and thriving together.

As my daddy prays, I think back to the morning of the day I first met Kaylee—the anniversary of Annie's death. I think of my journal and the snippets of feelings I'd recorded there. I'd so suppressed my emotions—so afraid to feel the pain of loss and my own mistakes. But in so doing I'd also missed the love and grace those who loved me wished to impart. And I'd missed the merciful love of my heavenly Father.

Kaylee, I realize, was God's healing balm for my suffering soul. Through her He showed me the truth of Himself, His unconditional love and forgiveness. Christ is my Savior, but He used Kaylee to save me. To show me the extent of His mercy and grace.

And He's used me to save her. To rescue her from a prison of silence and shame. She will have much to deal with in the years to come, but He's given me the privilege of showing her His love, His protection, and His providence.

Unabashed tears slip down my cheeks as I'm humbled before Him. Just before my daddy says, "Amen," I offer my own silent words of gratitude.

Thank You. Oh, thank You so much . . .

CHAPTER SIXTY-TWO

aylee

I'VE PUT new words in my box this year. Words like *truth* and *sacrifice* and *grace*. They aren't hard words, but they're important words.

Actually, they're imperative.

Grace is something you don't deserve, like a gold star on a math paper that has all the wrong answers. Or like going to see my mom in jail and hearing her say, even after I'd told the truth about her, "I love you, Kaylee. I'm so sorry for everything I put you through. Someday I hope you can forgive me."

Grace is also the love of Jesus, who died for us when we didn't deserve it. That's also the definition of sacrifice. I had to make a sacrifice too. I had to tell the truth about my mom. And about him. The truth was a sacrifice because it meant I had to let go of my mom, at least for now. But I did it because she needed my help and that was the only way I could really help her.

Sometimes keeping a secret seems like the right thing to do

because telling the truth might hurt someone and make it seem like you don't love them. But really, telling the truth is the right thing to do. It's the most loving thing to do. I learned that this year. Just like I learned that when you do that, then you can let the Truth, Jesus, work out the details.

He's really good at that.

The other word I've added to my box this year is *love*. The dictionary defines love like this:

love—1. a profoundly tender, passionate affection for another person.

That's like Pete and Sierra. Or:

2. a feeling of warm personal attachment or deep affection, as for a parent, child, or friend.

That's like me and Sierra.

But really, love is more than that. It's when Van's fur tickles my face and makes me giggle. Or it's when Sierra lets me climb in bed with her in the mornings, even before it's light outside. It's when Pete sits at the kitchen table and helps me with my math homework, even when I don't want to do it. Or when he helps me work through my feelings, which sometimes I don't want to do either. It's when Ruby invites me over to her studio, and lets me play with her clay, and then shows me how to make something out of it. It's when Dr. Beth asks me hard questions and is patient when I can't find the words to answer her. Love is when my new friend, Sarah, let me wear her cute new sweater to Sunday school and didn't even tell anyone it was hers!

Love is just a word until you put actions to it. The actions make the word true. It's John 1:1: "In the beginning was the Word, and the Word was with God, and the Word was God." Pete finally explained that verse to me. Jesus is the Word—the most important word. When God sent Jesus to Earth as a baby, that was God's expression of His love. That was the action that made His love true.

"For God so loved the world, He gave His only begotten Son."

He gave His Word.

I used to collect words because I thought they could protect me. And they did, in a way. They gave me something to focus on so I didn't have to focus on what was happening to me. I see now that my box of words in my mind was a gift from God, wrapped in pretty flowered paper, meant to comfort me when things were hard.

But the words couldn't save me.

The words were superfluous.

Only *the* Word could save me and set me free.

And He did.

AFTERWORD

Dear Reader,

Kaylee's story is my story. It's also the story of one in four women who are sexually abused before they reach the age of eighteen. For just a moment, count off. Think of your friends, coworkers, family members—how many women do you know? One quarter of those women have likely suffered the indignity of sexual abuse. You may not know who they are—survivors are adept secret keepers—but they're in your life and they're in desperate need of the gracious love of Jesus Christ, experienced through you.

Or maybe Kaylee's story is also your story. Like my own story, the setting and circumstances differ, but we're a sisterhood woven together by a thread of shame. Please know that it's you I prayed for as I wrote—though I didn't know your name or your face.

I do, however, know a bit of your pain, and I asked for God's tender embrace as you read. And I continue to pray that, like Kaylee, you'll allow the truth to set you free.

Ultimately *Words* is a story of the redemptive work of *the* Word, Jesus Christ. Sierra represents each of us—she is a sinner in need of salvation. Whether your sin is drug abuse or doubt, promiscuity or pride, you're a sinner in need of a Savior. But not only does Jesus Christ offer us salvation and the hope of eternity spent in His presence, He also offers us redemption here on Earth. In *Words* Christ redeemed Sierra's pain—the loss of her baby and the shame of her drug abuse—by bringing Kaylee into her life.

Christ is also redeeming the pain of my past. I, like Kaylee, found comfort in words as a child. As soon as I could read, I escaped the pain of abuse by losing myself in stories. I had no idea then that God would one day use my written stories for His glory or the pain I suffered to help comfort others.

God promises to "cause all things to work together for good for those who love Him and are called according to His purpose" (Rom. 8:28). God takes our shame—whether suffered through the sins of others upon us or through our own sin—and He uses it for good. Think about that . . . Isn't it awe-inspiring? Not only has God defeated the enemy for all time, but He defeats him moment by moment in each of our lives when we surrender ourselves to His redemptive work.

I hope you'll visit my website: http://ginnyyttrup.com to learn about my other books and work. While you're there, drop me a note. I'd love to hear from you.

Blessings,
Ginny

DISCUSSION QUESTIONS

Discussion Questions

1.As with Kaylee, victims of childhood sexual abuse often lose their "voice." What types of circumstances silence you? How do you gain the courage to speak up when you'd rather remain quiet?

2.Kaylee attempts to be invisible to her abuser by not speaking. Have circumstances in your life ever made you wish you were invisible? How did you deal with that?

3.Kaylee finds comfort in the words she reads in the dictionary. Who or what do you turn to for comfort?

4.Read the following verses. What do they say to us about the source of our comfort? (see Psalm 119:50; Isaiah 5:12; 2 Corinthians 1:3–4)

5.Sierra expresses her emotions through art. How do you express difficult emotions?

6.Sierra struggles to accept God's forgiveness. Many of us share that struggle. How can we, as Christ's followers, truly embrace God's grace in those difficult areas of our lives?
(see Matthew 11:28)

7.Which character impacted you most, Kaylee or Sierra? Why?

8.Kaylee is afraid to speak truth because it may wound her mother. Many of us have had times when we were afraid to reveal truth because it might hurt someone else. What guidelines can we find in Scripture for such situations?

9.John 8:32 says: "Then you will know the truth, and the truth will set you free." Several of the characters in this story lived with untruth in their lives—lies they believed about themselves, about others, or about God. Others kept secrets rather than speak truth. How did living this way affect them? How could we apply John 8:32 to these situations? How can you apply it in your own life?

10.What do you think the redwood trees in *Words* represent?

11.What displays God's power to you?

12.Sierra's dad encourages her to look beyond a person's actions to see that person's heart—to look for what's causing that person to act as he or she does. This was to help Sierra better understand people. How might this advice change the way you look at others?

13.It is easy to judge those who are different than we are. Did Kaylee's, Sierra's, and Kathryn's experiences give you new understanding of what others may suffer? What impact will that insight have on the way you see others?

14.Sierra changes her name in the story to signify a new season of her life. The Bible references God giving each of us a new name (see Isaiah 62:2; Revelation 2:17). What would you like your new name to signify?

15.Pete expressed both anger with and compassion for Kaylee's abuser. How did Pete's reaction impact you? (see Matthew 18:5)

16.John 1:1 refers to Christ as *the Word*. This name for Christ becomes significant to Kaylee because of her love for words. What names for God are significant to you and why?

17.God promises to restore what's been lost in our lives (see Joel 2:25). What would you like God to restore in your life?

18.In the final scene of *Words*, Kaylee lists the ways she's experienced love. In what ways are you experiencing God's love in your life?

ACKNOWLEDGMENTS

Words of gratitude flood my mind as I consider those who've walked alongside me through the years of healing that took place before I was ready to write this book, along with those who encouraged and guided me as I wrote. Words seem insufficient, but they are all I have to offer.

To my Lord, Jesus Christ, You are the truth that set me free. Daily, you invite me to partner with You, and daily, I'm awed by that invitation. I pray my words honor You.

To my mom, Kathy Temple, and my grandparents, Gil and Virginia Foster, you instilled in me a love for books and nurtured me with your love. Grandpa, I wish you were here to read my first book. It's not Louis L'Amour, but you'd have read it anyway.

To Tim Dakin, Toni Horvath, and Dr. Orville Easterly, wise Christian counselors and healers. You each helped me reclaim my voice.

To Rose Lester, you have always seen things in me that I can't see in myself. Your love and friendship remain a constant encouragement.

To Kathy Collard Miller, you were the first writer to critique my work and encourage me. Thank you for cheering me on all these years.

To the faculty of the Mount Hermon Christian Writers Conference, I've grown up as a writer under the canopy of the redwoods and heard God's whispers through so many of you. Gayle Roper, your initial critique of this manuscript and your encouragement to keep writing spurred me on. Thank you.

Steve Laube, I will never forget our first conversation under those redwoods. Your belief in this project and your willingness to mentor me through the completion of the manuscript still fill me with wonder. I appreciate your guidance, candor, patience, and humor. Most important, I appreciate working with an agent who places his relationship with God above all others.

Karen Ball, friend first, editor second. More than a dozen years ago, you agreed to pursue a friendship with a fledgling writer because she thought she'd heard God tell her that someday she'd work with you. Amazing . . . Karen, you are transparent, grace-filled, tender, wise, and hilarious! I am blessed to call you friend. I am blessed to call you editor.

Diana Lawrence, your cover design for the first edition of *Words* took my breath. Your design for the second edition touches something deep in my soul. I believe it will draw the readers who need this story to it. Thank you. You are a delight to work with.

Thank you to my faithful friends who listened to me, offered wise words, prayed for me, and read early drafts of the manuscript: Barbara Wilson, Rachel Johnston, Sharol Josephson, Linda Sommerville, Vicki Newman, Kathy Miller, Renee Baber, Janet Hanson, Laurie Breining, and the dear women from the Invisible Bond Bible study.

Lily Frost, on a summer afternoon overlooking Lake Tahoe, in the mystical way of prayer, I'm certain you prayed this book contract into being. Thank you.

Thank you to artist Eileen Downs, who invited me to tour her studio, shared her collage process with me, and checked the art details included in the manuscript. Eileen's work is as beautiful as her spirit.

Thank you to Lieutenant Commander, California Highway Patrol, David Qualls for checking my law enforcement scenes. Your insight proved invaluable.

Thank you to Linda Kerner, Public Information Officer, Santa Cruz County Human Resources Agency for patiently answering a long list of questions and forwarding information to me as needed.

Special thanks to Laurie Breining. God's given you a gift of tender care for others. During the final stages of writing this book, you helped nurse me back to health following major back surgery and three subsequent surgeries. What a year! On days when I attempted to write through the haze of pain and medication, you sat with me. You gave of yourself in selfless ways. As I worked to bring the second edition to life, your encouragement continued. I am grateful for your friendship.

Ted and Cretia Martinson, you have supported me in so many ways, including providing the means for the second publication of *Words*. I pray God's special blessing on you as He uses this book to offer hope and healing to new readers.

Finally, I offer a heart filled with gratitude to Justin, and Jared. You are incredible young men, in spite of me. I dared to seek emotional health because of you. When the road to health seemed too difficult, I persevered because of you. I fought to break patterns for your sake. I pray you will see God work through *Words* and recognize the role you've played in the birth of this book. I love you . . . always.

ABOUT THE AUTHOR

Ginny L. Yttrup is the Christy, *RT Book Reviews*, and *Foreword Reviews* award winning author of five novels, with her sixth due to release February, 2019. Ginny is a sought after writing coach, speaker, and companion to Bear the Entitled Pomeranian. She loves spending time with her two adult sons and her daughter-in-law. She lives in Northern California.

If you'd like to receive updates on Ginny's work, glimpses behind the scenes, frequent give-aways, and a free novel, subscribe to her newsletter: http://ginnyyttrup.com/contact/

facebook.com/GinnyYttrup

twitter.com/GinnyYttrup

instagram.com/ginnyyttrup

CPSIA information can be obtained
at www.ICGtesting.com
Printed in the USA
LVHW031817140121
676489LV00006B/1117